The McGallister Fiction Series

Book One:

Only A Man

(A Novel)

Lisa Drane

13659-DRAN

To order additional copies of this book, contact:
Xlibris Corporation
1-888-7-XLIBRIS
www.Xlibris.com
Orders@Xlibris.com

CONTENTS

For Roderick:

Thanks for sharing me with Robert. Your endless love and support means the world to me. This one's for you baby!

The McGallister Fiction Series Synopsis

Prior to his twenty-fifth birthday, Robert McGallister, the tall, handsome son of a prominent Detroit minister spent many of his undergraduate, college basketball and fraternity nights in the beds of a scorecard of women that would make the late Wilt Chamberlain in his heyday proud.

Upon pursuing advanced degrees in psychology with an emphasis in marriage and family therapy, and drug and alcohol rehabilitation, Robert could no longer ignore the inevitable calling of his father's pulpit. It takes fewer than two short years, for the fiery, controversial bachelor to more than quadruple the membership at the predominately middle-class African-American congregation, and to raise the eyebrows of the elderly leadership with his questionable Pied-Piper ability to draw drug addicts, former dealers, gang members, welfare recipients and according to his father's contemporaries, the lowliest dregs of society, people from "other faiths removed from the original gospel."

By twenty-nine, Robert has not only spearheaded, two interfaith drug and alcohol rehabilitation programs, but has facilitated the establishment of God's Warriors an originally

13659-DRAN

inspired local movement, of African-American Christian men who have taken oaths of fidelity, fatherhood and fraternity. Not one to evade challenges, Robert manages to maintain a courageous stance on all spirit guided issues, especially, when it comes to marrying the woman who fits the ideal prototype of a "fine young minister's wife," he describes in his first national Christian best-seller.

Ignoring the advice of his most cherished friends and relatives, he is soon confronted with the consequences of his impulsive decision, when his true love, sweeps him off his confident feet from the impetus of his marriage, and embarks him on a long journey of inner soul-searching, turmoil and bliss.

Acknowledgements

All praises, honor and glory to the magnificent Jehovah God and to His Son, the Lord and Savior of my life Christ Jesus. I love the Lord. He heard my cry and pitied every groan, long as I live, when troubles rise, I will hasten to his throne. I'm overwhelmed at the awesome gift that flows almost daily from my mind, through my fingers, onto the keys to produce stories of imagined people with real problems.

Roderick, my first publicist, strongest support, springboard for ideas, financial consultant, business partner and partner in this life, you've watched me blossom from the eighteen year old college student with dreams of having my words touch the lives of many, to the woman I've become today. I've been heaven-blessed to have an up close and personal seat in the life of a hard-working, determined God-fearing soul who has a few wonderful dreams of his own. I love you for life.

To my first readers and fellow writers, Kim and Karla Davis. Thank you. Here's to continued friendship and success in your own publishing endeavors. You both have mad skills! Cheryl Thomas and Nina Hawkins, my third and fourth readers, your persistence in encouraging me to stick with my writing routine is one of the reasons this book is in your hands today. Jackie Cole, thanks for the research and for the listen-

---

ing ear. Denise Mayberry Shackelford, (Nesie), you're my sister girl. Much love to you and yours. Who would have thought that "Robert" would have made us as close as we are today? Anita Pinkerton and Monique White, thanks for waiting on the final proof. Sorry it took so long for me to get it to you, I try to live by Robert's creed, "my word is bond."

To my parents David Goss Jr. and Barbara Branche, the little bookworm on Oakfield who preferred playing records, writing stories and acting them out with my dolls, (and you thought I was talking to myself, smile), turned out pretty decent, I guess. Thanks for not hassling me about going outside to play, ride my bike, or get dirty. (I'm like Elisabeth McGallister on that one, eeew!)

To my nieces Lakya (Boo), Donyale (MelMel) and babies Deja Grace and Airess and to my godson Al, your Pekie loves you.

To my in-laws (Ma and Dad especially) and extended family in all parts St. Louis, West Virginia, Virginia, Louisiana, DC, Texas and the Carolinas. . . . .the Drane's love you.

My forever big sis, (though I've been bigger than you for some twenty years now), you listened to my first novels when we weren't listening to Prince. You had no business plastering that infamous poster from the Controversy album above a ten-year old's head. Speaking of Prince, you're my muse. Your music has "opened my mind to poetry seldom heard." You're a genius, I mean, producer, composer, arranger, performer and over 20 instruments learned by ear only since the age of 12? Please! Talk about gifts. I respect how you've successfully controlled your own career, which is the reason why I'm starting with publishing on my own. Love and peace.

MJ forever, baby! (Both of 'em, Jordan and Jackson.)

Babyface is a genius.

Stevie Wonder, you're phenomenal. Everyone breathing knows that. Period.

To my family at the Wyoming Avenue Church of

Christ . . . we've come this far by faith . . . leaning on the Lord. I miss you Brother Terrell. To the Women of Wyoming, and especially for my sisters . . . you know who you are . . . much love. Lon, I know you were cracking up on the Prince part. Remember there are only six degrees of separation. Who do we know..that knows the man? Brother Davy, thanks for letting me pick your brain. Cynt, you know we're sisters. To the Walkers and the Hollies . . . you already know how I feel . . . I'm getting choked up writing this. Pam (Dog) and Dallas III (Duck), you know you're my number one peops until the end. No doubt. If you need me, call me.

To Eugene Seaborn III, the best principal a teacher could ask for: your encouragement and support is invaluable. You are a gifted artist. Expect to see this cover and all future covers you design for me everywhere. Thanks for being the first man to read my manuscript in its' entirety. Also, you've been a listening ear and a good advisor. I appreciate the attorney reference you gave me. Russell Burns, thanks for your legal advice.

To my very special East Middle school colleagues and friends . . . what a cool working relationship we have. We really like each other! To the '05 Stunnas especially (Amber, Lonnie, Christina, Janae, Yashi, Kristian, Lyrena, Janet, etc) and to all of my students at East past or present, it is a privilege to share in your educational and social development. Douglas Mercier, and Derrick Jefferson, from Henry Ford High, your favorite teacher still remembers you.

Thanks Barb McCune for sharing some of your computer expertise with me. Gary Huepenbecker, you're invaluable.

Thanks Mrs. Bradley, Ms. Spight and Mr. Wells. Your combined efforts are what inspired me to teach in the first place. It was a joy and sort of funny to later become one of your colleagues, a bigger hoot if you thought I would ever call any of you by your first names.

Mr. Sims, where are you? Your adopted daughter wants

to hear your voice. I love you.

Shaunda, MWENDO is going places. Remember our youth and Detroit 300. Hey, Ja-Man.

LaKeisha, Selwyn and the boys, much love always.

Tater-tots, I finally did it!

Elizabeth Adkins Bowman and Travis Hunter, in our brief separate encounters, you both have given me a plethora of information. We'll meet again. I know it.

To the good folks at Xlibris, thanks for the time and effort exerted in the layout and printing of the book. Don't think you guys are going to get rid of me that fast. You're the best!

Valerie, you know I had to come back home, didn't you? Thanks for hooking up my hair and for referring me to Ken Kyle, the makeup artist, for my web photos and cover pic.

If I've forgotten anyone, please don't hold it against me. I'm writing a series remember? Just tell me so I can get it right the next time. Godspeed.

Lisa Drane

Author's Note

This is a work of fiction inspired by the gift the Creator has given me to produce written works from my own imagination. Neither the characters portrayed here nor any of the events that take place in this story should in any way be construed as real.

15

Fast Forward

Year 2007

Reconcilable Differences

"Everyone's got ghosts," Diane Flaggerty shrugged nonchalantly as she and her husband, sat across from the freshly polished solid antique maple L-shaped desk that once belonged to my deceased father during his tenure as minister here at the Rosedale Park congregation. Nestled in a forested, upper-middle class predominantly African-American community located on Detroit's Northwest-side, I've served as the primary evangelist for the past eleven years at the church where I'd grown up.

As I methodically leaned back into the comfort of my sable leather cushioned swivel chair, I paid unscrupulous attention to the body language of the couple I had just married less than two years ago. Both Diane and her husband sat stiffly. Though he, a deliveryman for UPS, would be considered a relatively handsome man by any woman's standards, his profile from the angle in which I was sitting was more than disproportionately transfigured, because of his locked jaw and the frustrated pressing together of his darkened-from-cigarette-smoke lips.

Usually a bright, cheery-eyed attractive woman, Diane, a corporate attorney held a very similar expression. Only she clenched her smooth cocoa complexioned fists onto the center of her lap.

Perfunctorily, I folded my own fingers together and placed

21

them under my chin with the length of my arms causing my elbows to slightly protrude from the armrests. I spaced out momentarily to reflect upon her last truth revealing, piercing statement.

Everyone's got ghosts-something for which to be ashamed-something that remains lurking in the innermost private sanctum of one's own mind, body and soul. Something that one doesn't necessarily want to get rid of; something that one has grown accustomed to, and maybe in the most severe circumstances, something that one cherishes and even loves.

I knew my ghost well. Over the past six and a half years, I've nurtured her and held her hand in critical times of need, and she has ever so softly, willingly and effortlessly, reciprocated my affections ten times over. She is everything I've ever wanted.

She is the only one who could take me to the mountaintop, yet she's the only thing that may cause my name to be erased from God's eternal book of life.

I've even held her in my arms and much, much more, hundreds of times during many stolen moments. In fact, if it weren't for my commitment to the Lord first, his flock and to Elisabeth and the girls, sweet, free-spirited Lorraine, my wife's only sister, would be the center of my world.

" I . . . I mean, M-i-ch-ael isn't perfect." The unpleasant sound of her hissing as if the mere mentioning of his name was repulsive to her own hearing, snapped me back into reality. " He cheated on me with some white woman before we even got married, yet . . . , " she paused dramatically striking the air with her right index finger, a gesture which by the scowl on his face Mike was growing quite irritated with because, she'd employed it often as a dramatic trial tactic.

"There she goes again, Brother McGallister," Mike replied angrily without looking at Diane. In one fell swoop, he slammed his heavy hands against the desk, which caused my glass of ice water to spill onto the most recent 8x10 family photograph of myself, Elisabeth and our three girls. Although the hand carved maple frame protected the picture, I bolted up from the comfort of my chair, to try to salvage the last glass of Aquafina I had left in the church.

"I'm sorry, Brother McGallister," Mike said quietly, averting his eyes from contact with mine. Diane grabbed a handful of Kleenex@ from the box next to the frame and handed some to her husband. She reached for a second handful, and began to lean over to lend him a helping hand, before she snapped herself back into reality.

"It's just water, brother. Don't worry about it." I took the wet tissue from him, faked a basket, then directed him back over to his chair. I waited for him to sit, before I decided to recline again.

"She just pisses me the fu.. I mean," he paused, clearing his throat. I could tell he was trying to find more respectful words to utter in my presence, " She ticks me off, man! Always bringing up the past. She was supposed to have forgiven me for that sh . . . , I mean, mess a long time ago. Well, at least she said she forgave me. Now, she waits until we're *married*, and I stress the word m*arried*, to screw around on me with some bougie phony of a co-worker. I've been very faithful to her. Sure, I've had my chances to screw around, but I chose the Lord's way. I didn't leave her, high and dry. Any woman worth her salt would love a man like me. For the past almost two years, I've worked my ass, I mean, butt, off for her, cookin', cleanin', you know doin' women's work, changin' our son, feeding him, bathing him, taking him to daycare, pickin' him up . . . and this is the thanks I get?'

"Do you see that?" Diane rushed right in, without giving me a second to throw in my two cents. " He makes it seem like I should be worshipping the ground he walks on because he is doing what a husband is supposed to do . . ."

"Wait a minute!" Mike yelled. " Now, I'm a little con-

23

fused. A few minutes ago you were ranting and raving to the preacher here, that I'm all but a no-count blue-collar bum, because I don't make half the money you do, and I ain't been in nobody's college. So, what's it gon' be? I think you better make up your mind, woman!"

"You see how he talks to me, Robert? I get no respect from my own husband."

I was starting to feel the effects of the lack of central air. My sister in-law Sheila, the supervisor of the Agape Christian Academy, our adjoining school was supposed to call the repairman today to have it fixed. I mean, I know I am supposed to maintain professional attire as I counsel clients and meet with various committee members throughout the day, but I'm accustomed to a certain comfort level. And, well, two pieced suits or sports jackets and ties, simply do not mix in with the humid thickness of the June heat in a spacious, yet poorly ventilated office. I loosened my tie, unbuttoned the eyelets of both of my sleeves, and carefully rolled them, as not to cause excessive wrinkles. I still had two more meetings that would stretch onto the late afternoon before conducting the third session of an eight-week marriage enrichment seminar about the joy of marital conjugation entitled, "The Marriage Bed is Still Undefiled". My smoky gray colored blazer hung neatly onto the back of my chair.

I stood up, quickly removed my glasses to wipe the sweat from my brows and nose, and began to pace the floor in long even strides. I inhaled and exhaled deeply, cleared my throat, and made eye contact with Diane.

"Diane, do you still want your marriage?" I asked quietly.

"Huh, I'm not sure, Robert, wh . . . , what do you mean?"

"Come on, Dee. You're an articulate sister. A woman of great eloquence. I'm sure you can find better means to evade the question, then just goin', huh, wh . . . what, what do you mean, Robert." I was quite aware that I had just thrown my smartly dressed, well educated, adulterous sister in Christ a relatively harsh, below-the-belt blow, but my time is precious. I don't like wasting it—especially not on people who refuse to acknowledge the Lord's innumerable blessings in their lives. I'd long since stop conducting marriage and family therapy sessions when my career took off in the first year of the new millennium, choosing to narrow the focus of my psychology practice to drug and alcohol rehabilitation.

My third career as a motivational speaker and nationally recognized spokesperson for the God's Warrior Program my top ace Brother Khalid and I originated back in '96, after I was invited to speak on the theme of atonement to more than a million black men strong at the infamous march, had skyrocketed from a well-received local nondenominational minister and best-selling author within the African-American community to one I'd hardly recognized as my own. But, I loved Diane, and owed her big time for having my back and using her mad skills as a sharp-tongue courtroom goddess to save the lives of many desperate wayward brothers en route via one-way tickets to the state pen. She'd agreed to take on one hundred percent of these cases pro-bono per my request, partially due to the fact she'd been sweatin' me to get with her for a good twenty years, even before I bound myself up with my wife and her sister some seven years ago.

Taken aback, Diane quickly grabbed a tight hold onto her throat as if she were preventing herself from choking on the words she was about to utter in response to my in –your-face question.

Mike, on the other hand, comfortably leaned back into his chair for the first time in our fifty-minute session, wearing the most self-assured, smug cat-ate-the-canary grin I'd ever seen.

"Do you want your marriage, Dee?" I asked in the best scare-the-hell-out-of-them-pulpit voice I could muster.

" Well, when I consider . . ."

" Eeeenk! Wrong answer. You see, the word do, is an action verb that can be placed in front of an interrogative question. All a statement that begins with the words would, could, will, does, and do ever requires is a response in the negative or the affirmative."

"You better preach up in here, brotha!" Mike exclaimed, slapping his knee. He was tickled to death. I was happy for him for that moment, because I knew he would be less than thrilled with the last question I had to ask him.

"Yes, but . . ."

"Naw, naw, now. No buts sister. The but just canceled out the yes." I coaxed. Growing dizzy from the heat, hunger and my mad pacing, I semi-propped myself onto the front of my desk, so I could maintain direct eye contact.

"Yes, Robert," she replied quietly. "Yes, I do want my marriage. I want to honor my original commitment to my husband. I want to please the Lord. I just want, I just want, Michael." Her eyes were full of stubborn wet salt pellets that refused to find their path down her slightly flushed, brown cheeks.

Michael reckoned with his own internal battle. Without looking at her, he allowed his ashy, heavy hand to reach for hers, as his jawbone remained as locked as the security bars we recently had placed on all three of my office windows due to the recent break-ins by some sly jokers who'd probably laughed themselves into a coma at the elaborate, supposedly full-proof alarm system the leadership had coughed up more than five thousand dollars to install.

"Excuse me, Brother McGallister," a familiar perky voice over the office intercom, boomed. It belonged to my mother's best friend, Blanche Calloway, whom my father hired as the church secretary some twenty-five years ago.

"Yes, Sister Calloway?" I replied, after having reached behind myself to press the orange button on my desk-phone. Diane swept her eyes up to the clock, and motioned to

Michael with her right hand that there were only four minutes left in their session. Michael gave me the same look of exasperation I shot my former girlfriend/ personal secretary Kelly Calloway, Blanche's daughter, the night she jumped in front of my big-screen TV during the last second of #23's career with the Bulls. Because of that girl's big mouth and insistence that I'd stopped treating her like some sex object, I missed the play of the century— the one when he left his right arm up there hanging ever so pretty in the air.

"I don't mean to interrupt, but Sister McGallister is on line three. She says it's an emergency."

"Which Sister McGallister?" I asked before making a decision to accept or deny the call. My widowed mother, who oversees my book, audio and video-cassette ministry from my home, would understand my current situation. Conversely, my lovely wife would see things quite differently.

"It's your wife, son," Sister Calloway responded in the knowing voice she inflects whenever she mentions Elisabeth.

"Put her through," I replied avoiding fiery darts aimed my way via a very emotionally charged woman who was due to argue a case in less than thirty minutes. Confident with my decision of avoiding the proverbial doghouse, I cleared my throat and answered the call.

"Is everything all right, Princess?" I asked.

Diane nudged Michael and whispered within my earshot, "I just love how he calls her that, even from the pulpit." Mike shushed her in eager anticipation of eavesdropping on my wife's latest escapade.

I've always been a very observant person. I see and hear things people have no idea I've witnessed.

I heard from Sheila, my sister-in-law, Sister Calloway, and Kelly, the not so far removed from the truth gossip, about everything from Elisabeth's lavish spending habits, to her whiny temper-tantrums when she doesn't get her way, to her obsessions with cleanliness, our three daughters, who were all born within the first four years of our marriage, and staying super-model thin.

Since I moved Elisabeth, the then nineteen year old self-indulgent, spoiled daughter of an orthodontist mother and neurologist father, up here from her suburban hometown of Chesterfield, Missouri, during our whirlwind engagement, she had been singled-out and labeled as "Sista Super Diva," for obvious reasons regarding her ultra svelte figure, long sandy brown locks, the pale color of her skin, and her princess-like attitude. Admittedly, I haven't done much to improve her image, because she keeps a reformed playboy like myself more than satisfied where it really counts, she is one helluva mother and like her father who is the elder of a congregation down in St. Louis, I worship the ground she walks on.

"Bobby!" her high-pitched pedantic voice squealed. "Guess what, honey?" she asked out of breath.

I could tell by the raucous noise in the background, that she was calling me from her cell phone in a very public place. If I knew my wife, one try would leave me to guess that she was in the mall. "Okay, Lisa Marie. Just a minute sweetie . . . Noelle, grab a hold of Lady Bug's hand, before she wanders off. Be good girls, I'm on the phone with Daddy."

"Oooh! Daddy! Daddy," I heard my six year old, oldest daughter Noelle excitedly scream. "I want to talk to Daddy, please Mommy. I want to tell him about the coat, and the contest. Oh, pretty please with sugar on top, Mommy! Please I want to talk to my Daddy!"

Elisabeth laughed softly, before calmly warning Lisa-Marie my female spitting image, who was within a few days of being exactly nine months younger than Noelle to let go of Mommy's dress before she caused it to wrinkle. " And Lisa-Marie, smooth out Lady Bug's hair so that she can get her picture taken.

I don't know what it is with my wife and pictures. Every two to three months, she drags the whole gang to the most expensive portrait studios in town, to have them sit through hours of primping, posing and prodding for the cameras. "Bobby, it's important to have pictures of your children while they're young, during every stage of their precious development, because they are only this adorable once. Besides, you know they have to keep a current portfolio for all of the pageants, contests and auditions."

Initially, I took offense to my mother donning my babies the "Three Little Black Jon Benet Ramseys," but now I just take it in stride.

I'm just glad that Elisabeth is so attentive to enhancing their day to day experiences. Between traveling 10-15 days of each month, counseling, visiting the sick, overseeing an extensive alcohol and drug rehabilitation program, preaching, writing books, conducting seminars, teaching men's and husband's training classes, taping and editing live radio and cable television programs, dedicating my first two waking hours in the early am and my last two every afternoon to my own personal Bible study and half-heartedly praying my way out of the temptation of being a virtual bigamist with my own sister-in-law, whose been a constant fixture in my life since the beginning of my marriage, I barely have time to spend with my wife and girls. I'm sure my guilt over this situation would lend itself to understanding why I would be so tolerant of this unnecessary interruption.

"Princess, sweetheart. I'm in a session. Is everything okay?"

"Yes, Bobby. I guess it could have waited," she snapped. *Just please don't start crying. I don't have time for this. I've got these ticked off people in my face, looking like they want to blow this office up with me in it.*

"No, it couldn't have. Go on," I replied calmly.

"You know that white full-length I described to you last winter . . . you know the one that costs five grand?" her voice taking on the same excited tone with which she had started the conversation.

Her beautifully sculpted high cheekbones were probably emitting that sexy primrose hue they gave the first time she heard me speak at her home congregation, and the first time we'd made love the holiday season of '99.

"Hold on Lisa Marie. . . . I'll let you talk to Daddy too, wait one sec . . . don't cry . . . this girl is so attached to you Bobby, honestly. I've never understood that. She doesn't want anyone else but you . . . but like I was saying, you remember the coat, right?"

Even though I didn't remember one lick, I decided to spare her from the temptation of a you-never-listen-to-one-word-I –say, mini-drama. How many times had I come home for her to describe some coat, collectible porcelain doll, dress, linen or kitchen appliance she desired?

I had issues of a more pressing nature on my mind, like how I plan to conduct my 3:30 counseling session with the fourteen year-old Tanesha Jenkins who was baptized last month, but raped last week by a 25-year old unemployed man on her six block walk to the bus stop on her way to school, or how I plan not to explode like a volcano that had been dormant for half a century, when I become target practice for the older, more conservative brethren at our weekly Friday night leadership council.

"Yes, I remember."

" Good. Guess what?"

"What?"

"I got it half off. Right on the third floor of Marshall Fields! Isn't that incredible?"

"Yes, indeed," I answered tight-lipped, "yes indeed."

Had she lost her mind? Spending almost three grand of my hard earned loot on a coat made from dead animals hair; smack dab in the middle of an unseasonably June, Detroit heat-wave?

"Heee! Heee! It is a blessing. You just can't find a good

deal like that. You just can't. I know you have to go, and I know you want to yell at me because I already have five furs. But, this is it, Bobby. I promise. I will never buy another fur. So you should be happy for me, because it looks good!"

"It looks good, Da—ddy!" Noelle rejoined the conversation, right on cue. She probably was standing close enough to her mother to hear everything I had to say, if I wasn't so utterly speechless. "And, she also got the hat and the gloves too Da—ddy!"

"Boots, too, Daddy! Boots too," Ashley Nicole, aka "Lady Bug", my baby daughter who was fourteen months younger than Lisa Marie screamed with glee.

"Bobby . . . wait, wait Lady Bug, you can't have a frozen yogurt today. You already had a giant pretzel. Your Grandmother McGallister should have never introduced you girls to junk food anyway. Geez! Anyway, Bobby I know you have to go, but, Noelle wants to speak to her Daddy like, really, really badly. Isn't that right sweetie? She wants to tell you about the contest."

"Okay," I said dryly, incredulous that Elisabeth felt this issue was more critical than helping a young couple on the brink of divorce, salvage their union.

"Here, sweetie. Daddy doesn't have long."

" Hello Da—ddy," Noelle sang with supercilious diction. Ever since Elisabeth enrolled her miniature-sized look-alike, diva-in-training in voice lessons and etiquette classes twice a week, Noelle had been speaking with a pseudo-British, soft Princess Diana accent. " Guess what, Daddy?"

"What is it No.., sweetheart?" I thought better against saying her name, because I didn't want my clients to know that my entire family wished to speak to me. Diane had her arms folded across her chest. And, Michael was actually glaring at me. Cussing me out with his harsh reddened eyes. Both of them fidgeted in their seats.

31

"Mother just entered me into a, what do you call that thing, Mother?"

"It's an audition for a Children's World commercial," Elisabeth responded sweetly.

"Yes, that's it, Daddy. It's a tryout for a TV commercial."

"That's wonderful news," I smiled, proudly. "Listen, sweetheart Da . . . I mean, I really have to go now. I will talk to you girls later."

"Wait, Father!" Noelle bossed. "Ashley Nicole and Lisa Marie would like to talk to you."

"Okay, I'll see everyone when I get home tonight. Goodbye, sweetheart."

"He's hanging up now, Mother," Elisabeth's clone announced in a rather snippety voice.

"Fine," Elisabeth whined loud enough for me to hear, " I guess you other two girls will have to make an appointment to talk to Daddy, because it'll be way past your bedtime once he decides to come home from the church, I hope you don't cry yourself to sleep again Lisa Marie. I don't see how you would prefer him over me anyway. Hang up the phone now, Noelle, sweetie."

"I'm going now, Daddy," Noelle apologized.

"Goodbye, sweetheart." I gently placed the receiver of my black cordless phone on the base. *Elisabeth and I have to have a discussion tonight, I don't like when she tries to turn our children against me.*

Even though her last comment was Classic Princess Elisabeth, it was totally unnecessary.

"I apologize for that interruption Brother and Sister Flaggerty. Forgive me, please." I shrugged my shoulders, and shot a quick "you-know-how-it-is" look to Michael, who reciprocated my feelings with a mellow nod of acknowledgement. Diane would be less merciful in overlooking my seemingly bogus waste of her time. She smacked her lips and rolled her eyes heavenward, as if to say, "Anyways!"

"If I recall correctly, Diane, you just reaffirmed your commitment to your life-mate. Are you willing to do what it takes to work at improving the quality of your marriage?"

"I am," she replied flatly.

"Are you willing to stop cheating on your husband, with some fool who could obviously give less than a damn about you, because he was willing to sacrifice your physical safety by showing up on your doorstep while your husband was at home? Are you willing to be released from Satan's pleasurable, yet evil and maniacal grip . . . and to rededicate your life to the Lord of your youth? We grew up together, Dee, right here at this church. I know you love the Lord, but even more impressive than that, He still loves you. Even in your sin. " Diane smiled at the reminiscence of our purely platonic relationship while we were active participants in the youth group and teen outreach programs for senior citizens.

There were times, when we were between sixteen and eighteen that she flirted with me, and offered me her body, but back then, I was too shallow to find any flat-chested, book-wormish girl attractive. However, from my "sowing wild-oats" phases during my junior college stint at Michigan Christian College to my fraternity and basketball playing days at Michigan State to my graduate and doctoral studies in psychology and marriage and family counseling, I was quite the dog, and by definition, dogs can appreciate the beauty in any woman who serves it up to you on a silver platter, airhead, bookworm, choir girl, sleezy, light skinned, dark-skinned, big-boned, flat chested, bloated belly or no.

I'd spent eight years of my life, from the ages of sixteen through twenty-four having commitment-free sex with literally hundreds of black women ranging from high yella to blue black without considering my health or the eternal consequences of fornication.

It wasn't until, my father retired and I took his place, eleven years ago when I was single, 25 and on fire for the

Lord for the first time in my life, that I took a self-imposed vow of celibacy. It lasted for the longest four years of my life, until at age 29, the 19 year-old Princess gave me the sweetest, purest gift she had to offer, her virginity.

Abstaining from sex was quite painful, no one could imagine all the sisters right here in this congregation as well as sisters in the church all across the country, who made me propositions to break the vow I wrote about in *Starting Over and Saving it For My Wife: A Single Brother's Guide To Preparing for Marriage to a Godly Wife in the New Millennium*, my autobiographical best-seller throughout the brotherhood and Christian bookstores nationwide.

These women would blatantly tell me to my face that they considered a 6'4", in shape, well-dressed, highly educated former basketball player, turned minister/psychologists/author/motivator a fine catch. Satan was definitely on the prowl, but I had to live a pure life, if I wanted to hold onto my soul salvation and to my worldly success.

" Are you willing sister, are you willing to lay to rest, to **kill** these feelings of lust towards this other person? That's all it is-lust. Are you willing to lay to rest, the absurd notion that Mike isn't good enough to sweep the floor you walk on because he is not all dignified and educated? Trust me, when it comes to serving the Lord and obeying his will—an education becomes highly overrated in comparison. So what's it gon' be? Are you willing, sis, are you willing?"

The tears that moments ago clung to her lower eyelids now flowed freely in a consistent pattern. They found rest on her upper lip. She didn't bother to wipe them away.

"I'm willing, Robert," she affirmed.

"Don't tell me that sister, tell your man."

Without hesitation, Diane reached for her husband's unshaven face. She held it in the palms of her well-manicured hands. For the first time in our session, Michael smiled. The weeping bug had bitten him too. She kissed him full on the mouth, and began to gently wipe away his tears. Seeing another brother cry always made me feel uncomfortable. I chewed down on my bottom lip, and waited for his punk behind to pull himself together.

"I'm willing, Michael. Please forgive me."

"I already have, baby. I already have. It's just going to take some time to work through all of this." I stood up, quickly brushed the lint off my gray vest, straightened my tie, and reached for Michael's hand. He shook it firmly. I winked at Diane, before I embraced her and kissed her briefly on the cheek. I let out a jubilant chuckle of relief and patted Michael firmly on the back.

"Now, brother, you know this process is far from over. On next Friday, I'll be ready to put you on the hotseat."

"That's cool brother, I ain't perfect," he laughed. "I'm willing too."

"See Kelly on the way out to make sure she has you in the book."

"Cool," he replied. Diane looped her left arm through his, while reaching to embrace me again with her right.

"Are you sure we can't come twice next week?" she asked, as she wiped her lipstick from my cheek.

"If I have any openings, Kelly will let you know. But, I know I'll be away next Friday through Sunday for a three-day gospel meeting in Florida."

"Man, if you think we're in the middle of a heat wave now, yo' a . . . , I mean you gon' fry in Florida."

I laughed and slapped Mike's hand again, before I stood in the threshold of my office and watched them walk away hand in hand.

35

Ready, Aim, Fire

"Are you out of your little private tete-de-tete now?" my wife asked sharply, after the phone had probably rang ten times. I had just seen the Flaggerty's to the end of the corridor where my counseling office was located.

One reason I didn't lose my head, when she used our oldest daughter to pull her senseless hang-up-on Daddy stunt, was I knew she would call back. Elisabeth knows my schedule. She knows my appointments are usually scheduled in the middle of the hour, since it was 4:25 when she first called, she knew to try me back at approximately 4:35. And, she always calls back. She was not one to give up on an impending battle easily.

"My clients just left, if, that's what you're asking," I replied sternly. "You calling to apologize?" I hope she had, because she had deliberately picked a fight with me when she knew I couldn't argue back. She knew I couldn't threaten to take all of her charge cards issued in my name away. She knew I couldn't defend myself against being railed as the "absentee father" when I had fellow church members who look to me as a role model in my presence.

"Apologize? You want me to apologize? Now, that's funny, because it seems that it should be the other way around!" she yelled.

I don't have time for this. Not today. I still have to counsel

Sister LaWanda Jenkins and her recently victimized fourteen year-old daughter who ironically enough was baptized one week before she was brutally attacked.

I needed time for some heavy contemplation-to quietly ponder exactly how I would answer the obvious realistic, embittered straight-to-the-point, questions this mother-daughter duo were bound to throw at me, regarding God's lack of providential interference in circumventing such a devastating crisis from happening to one of his own.

How would I address the particular questions Sister Jenkins, a single-mother of five and former welfare recipient would ask such as,"Why did such a terrible thing happen to my daughter? Is it my fault for being a single-mother of five with no active father figures in their lives? Is it my fault for working the graveyard shift at the Mobile gas station, and not being there to see my children off to school, even though we don't have transportation? And, seeing that God doesn't care about what happened to Tanesha, how can I protect her and my other children from such violence happening again?"

Moreover, how would I provide consolation to the victim herself? How would I address her very relevant inquiries, such as, "Why did this happen to me? Was it the way I walked? Was I dressed too provocatively? Where was my newfound Lord and Savior, when this stranger forced himself upon me, and brutally, took away my most prized possession, without my permission? Will I ever feel normal again? Will I be able to bear children? How am I supposed to face the kids at school, who know all about this, since the gruesome details and a partial description of me have been broadcasted all over the news, along with the three other girls who had been violated by the same monstrous individual?"

During my ministry, I've watched many teenagers make the ultimate confession that Jesus Christ is the son of God, moments before being immersed into the watery grave of baptism. Many of them are downright emotionless and bored, when they as a congregational tradition, after the benediction and closing hymn are escorted with their parents and family members, by the leadership, to the front of the pulpit, to be greeted by their new brothers and sisters in Christ. But, not Tanesha. Tanesha's reaction to her newfound Christian life was altogether different.

Still fresh, yet forever etched into my long-term memory, is the image of her crying delirious tears of Holy Spirit joy, because she was now one of the Lord's chosen.

Her mother, older sister, and three younger brothers flanked her on both sides, trying to calm her down, because she was speaking so fast and excitedly to everyone who greeted her. She had worked herself into such a utopic frenzy, that by the time she greeted Elisabeth, my mother, the girls and I, in the corridor of the auditorium, she erected herself upon her tipped-toes, and reached to hug my neck.

My mother pulled me aside later at Sunday dinner to inform me of Elisabeth's snotty treatment of the Jenkins family. I defended my wife, but it wasn't as if I hadn't noticed Elisabeth's blatant discrimination against the lower-class population of our church. She was also noticeably uncomfortable around former drug addicts and convicts, along with the sick and /or elderly members.

I used to pray daily for the Lord to change my wife, to make her more tolerant of people who were not as fortunate as she was to be born into a three generational family of doctors. But, so far he hasn't, and I don't believe he ever will. He has, however, led me to a better understanding and acceptance of her. I've learned to live with it, even though I don't like it. Elisabeth is who she is from the top of her gorgeous head to the bottom of her well-pedicured, narrow feet.

Elisabeth haughtily examined Tanesha closely from head to toe. She noticed, the ruined pantyhose, the dingy, hanging slip from a too-short grease-stained skirt, and her wild, still damp from the water uncombed kinky hair. She reached for Noelle's and Ashley Nicole's hands, when they didn't respond, she grabbed them firmly, and held them close to her long-skirt covered legs, as if to protect them from impoverishment via osmosis.

While clinging to me tightly, and almost making me drop my middle daughter, Lisa Marie, who still loves for me to pick her up, and carry her everywhere, even though she is five, Tanesha thanked me for preaching my sermon about young biblical figures being on fire for the Lord. She then reached to embrace Elisabeth. Elisabeth's frail body stiffened. Instead of reciprocating the hug, or saluting her with a sisterly kiss on the cheek, as I had seen my own mother do, countless times when she was the minister's wife, Elisabeth forced a superficial closed mouth smile upon her lips, and allowed Tanesha to grip the tip of her french-manicured right hand.

The naive girl didn't seem to notice my wife's snub. Instead she reached for my neck again. To compensate for Elisabeth's lack of sensitivity, I held her tightly with my free arm, and kissed her on the crown of her head. Lisa Marie, who was comfortably situated in the cradle of my right arm pitched in a couple of childlike empathetic pats, for good measure.

Before I felt Tanesha and her little brothers were out of our earshot, Elisabeth nudged me with those pointy little pale elbows of hers, and hissed, " Bobby, you and Lisa Marie are going to like, need to immerse yourselves tonight in a bleach-filled, scathingly hot bath. Omigod, did you see how dirty they all were? And, you guys . . ." she whispered, tipping her head in my mother's direction. "You guys want the girls to go to the Agape Academy with those filthy boys. You must be crazy. The youngest two looked like they had ringworm!"

"Bobby, what are you doing? Are you still there?"

"Yeah, I'm here," I replied dryly, snapping myself back into the hear and now.

" Then, why don't you apologize?"

"What's up with that? You're the one who should be apologizin', baby," I bit the bullet. Though I had already planned to discuss Elisabeth's most recent outlandish purchases, I had prayed that the subject would keep until after tonight's 7:00 brothers' meeting. I figured I may as well get geared up for the inevitable fireworks that would explode between my father's former peers, the older, more conservative elders versus myself and the more liberal deacons who had been installed since I'd become minister.

For at least the past seven years, they had been having big-time problems accepting my so called divided loyalties between my ministry, flourishing psychology practice and the network of black owned businesses, God's Warrior's, a local turned national movement, my right-hand man, Yusef Khalid and I initiated and established on the church's grounds and over the span of one square mile of its' perimeters.

Their most recent complaints included the fact that I as the founder and national spokesperson of God's Warriors had allowed Skylar Daniels, my publicist and right hand woman, to continue to book seminars in cities all across the country filled with eager black men on fire for the Lord, and ready to take the four oaths of fidelity, fraternity, fatherhood and financial empowerment, I'd outlined in my first series of books, audio and vides tapes in '98, the year before I first laid eyes on Elisabeth.

I'm sure they'd had it in for me, and the elders headed by Pops' old cronies Brothers McNichols and Worhy, were more or less about ready to tell me just what I could do with my eleven-year tenure as their number one minister.

"You're always rushing me off the phone. I can't stand when you do that, Bobby. And, besides the girls. . . . they miss you. They want their daddy. They don't understand why you are never home, especially, Lisa Marie, you know how attached she is to you, and it's not my job to explain to them why you can't be bothered."

Over the years, I had grown accustomed to Elisabeth's frequent temper-tantrums. As a matter of fact, I had learned to expect and even accept them to a large extent. I never intended on having a doormat as a wife. On the contrary, during the early single years of my full-time ministry when I penned, *Starting Over and Saving It For My Wife*, I urged Christian brothers to create a Christ-centered bond with their potential mates, one that would nourish a woman's needs to express what's on her heart, without intimidating him or making him feel that she is not a submissive wife.

The only problem I had with Elisabeth consistently testing the theory I concocted before I knew anything about being her husband, is timing. As usual, her timing was foul. *I really don't have time for this crap!*

"Princess, baby . . . look, you just shot a loaded pistol at me. I really have to get myself together. I still have another session. I haven't eaten since breakfast, and I have a very important leadership meeting that is bound to be pretty long and intense. I just need to get my mind together." I searched the room for a comfortable place to rest my aching head. "We can talk later," I added knowing that she would be sleep by 9:30.

Elisabeth was no night owl. As a full-time mother and homemaker, my wife never starts her day later than 6 a.m., when she arises and descends basement stairs to complete one hour of strenuous exercise on her stationary bike, treadmill, weight machine and Stairmaster. Before 10:00, she would have already bathed in any number of lavish bath oils and gels, shampooed, blow dried and styled her almost waist length luxurious sandy-brown, with natural golden highlights mane, bathed, dressed, and styled all three daughters' hair, fed them a super lean breakfast of turkey bacon, fresh fruit oatmeal and toast, and began their grueling four hour home-schooling schedule complete with morning devotion and etiquette lessons.

"You have time for everything and everybody but me, but the girls and me," she whined sounding defeated and hurt, "and, please don't give me that you knew what kind of

41

career I had before you married me. Yes, I knew you were like, 'The Man' and everything," she spat sarcastically, "but I really didn't know it would be like this or else, I would not have . . ."

"You wouldn't have married me? That's the line you wanna run on me again?" I yelled angrily, forgetting that Sister Calloway and Kelly were right in the adjoining office, "Because if you are . . . if you are going to tell me that you regret marrying me, then we have a BIG problem, a huge one!"

"Yes, Bobby," she sniffed. "Yes, I was going to say that I would not have married you. You were already married when I met you . . . to the church, your patients, God's Warriors, and to all the businesses that prejudice, militant organization of yours brought forth! I'm beginning to think that the only reason you took a wife was so that you can indulge yourself in life-long guilt free sex! Now, how about that?"

The veins on either side of my temple throbbed heavily. I flopped down on the leather loveseat that was adjacent to the antique maple bookcase, which had also belonged to my late father. If he were still alive, he would give me that smug, wordless I-told-you-so look. My parents got to know Elisabeth really well during the few weeks prior to our wedding. Because after a couple weeks of depleting all of my American Airlines frequent flier miles to visit her in Missouri, I decided to move her up to Detroit to live with them for the remainder of our make-your-head-spin engagement.

He, not unlike me, was mesmerized by Elisabaeth's stunning beauty, upon first meeting her. But after Ma and my sister-in-law Sheila got through filling Pops head with their own embellishments to my fiancée's daily "episodes", Pops was more than convinced the job of a selfless preacher's wife, was too magnanimous for what Ma calls a "self-absorbed Princess" like Elisabeth to handle.

"You are my wife, Elisabeth. You're the one I come home

to baby. I don't want to take this thing to the next level. I have a headache. I need to eat ..."

"So in other words, you still don't have time to talk to me ... I ... understand. I have to go find the girls anyway. We need to purchase our last minute necessities for our trip to St. Louis in a couple of days. Melissa took them into the bookstore."

I had forgotten momentarily, that Elisabeth and the girls were still out at the mall, which provided me with more justification to ending this dead-end conversation. She was using up all the minutes on her cute little pink cell phone.

Everything she owns is pink. Besides, since the girls were out of her eyesight for the past five minutes, I knew she was getting antsy. Elisabeth doesn't trust anyone, not even my mother with keeping an eye on the girls.

"I know you have to go, baby. But, there's something you need to do for me first," I announced.

"I'm upset right now, Bobby. I don't particularly feel like telling you I love you."

"Then, don't. I'll tell you, instead. I love you, Princess."

She giggled, much like she used to do when we first met.

"Go on," she replied softly.

" I love you, but, I need you to take the coat, and all the matching accessories back to the store, and get a full refund. That purchase exceeded two thousand dollars by about three grand, and two g's was our agreed upon spending limit for you during any given month."

We, or shall I say my reluctant spouse and I had derived that amount a couple of years ago, after another one of her extravagant shopping sprees. Another couple of grand was set aside each month for clothing and providing for extracurricular activities for the girls.

"But earlier, you agreed with me ... that the coat at this price was a blessing ... It was a great buy, Bobby ... and

---

43

now you're telling me that I have to take everything back!" she screamed.

"You either take it back, or you won't receive any more personal spending money for the next couple of months."

"That's cruel!" she cried. I could tell she was pouting, and stomping her feet just as she had vicariously taught Noelle, our oldest and Ashley Nicole, our baby, to do.

"Elisabeth, I shouldn't have to remind you that you had a birthday earlier this month. I just bought you that tennis bracelet you wanted, along with the matching diamond earrings. Also, you're signing the girls up for too many pageants, and activities. I'm sure this two-week trip home will cost us a small fortune, especially since you have to pay out of state fees for some of those pageant related events. We just cannot afford such an unnecessary, frivolous purchase in our budget right now. We're not rich. Things are tight."

Man, that was the understatement of the year. Not only, did I have to contend with the purchases I had enumerated verbally to her, but Ma, who is at my house more than I am, informed me last week, that Elisabeth evaded phone calls from at least ten different retail creditors. Even though I garner a sizeable surplus expendable income from the Christian company that published my last four books, my audio and videotape ministries and from the five or six monthly speaking engagements my publicist and longtime friend Skylar books, I still would like for us to be on the same page financially, by making more investments, giving more away to charity and saving for a rainy day. I mean we had three girls who were all definitely going to pursue college educations, and I suspected that Elisabeth was pregnant again due to her missing her period last month and her extreme moodiness that was even more over the top than usual.

Besides, people were starting to talk. A minister shouldn't obtain great wealth, no matter how effective of a marriage and family counselor, widely published Christian author, or successful national radio and cable TV evangelist he is. He shouldn't dress or live better than his congregants. He should be a man of humble means.

More than that, he has no business driving a silver Jaguar, nor does his wife need to own a brand new white Benz, which she doesn't drive, because all she does is chauffeur their kids around in that eggshell colored Lexus truck.

"But, Bobby. You should see this coat. You'll love it on me. Melissa almost died when she saw me in it," she pleaded, mentioning the name of her best and only friend, as if to convince me to give in. Melissa Hemings, along with her white husband, Rick who was also a minister along with their three children, had a few years ago, relocated from their native state Texas, to labor at a sister congregation, our overcrowded congregation helped to establish.

"I want you to just do as I ask for once without arguing or whining about it. We can't afford it right now. We're ninety-five percent sure we're having another baby. We can't afford much of anything, until you get your spending under control," I stated firmly.

"You weren't complaining yesterday when you strutted up the aisle to the pulpit wearing that four thousand dollar blue suit I purchased for you last week from Jack's Place."

I swallowed hard, and balled up my fist. I sat straight up, and swiftly surveyed the room, to find something to swing at or break.

"You paid four grand for that stupid monkey suit?" I yelled, now sure the Calloway women, along with Sheila and all the Agape kids in the adjoining building heard me as well.

"Don't yell at me like that!" she screamed back, sobbing uncontrollably into the receiver.

"I never asked you to use our money to buy me anything. I'm taking that sucker back. Where is the damn receipt?"

"Now, you're swearing at me too!"

"The receipt, Elisabeth. The receipt!"

" But, you wore it already . . ."

"So, what?" I was so furious, that now I was up pacing the floor, like, to coin a phrase from the apostle Peter's first epistle, like a lion, seeking whom I may devour.

"So, that's just tacky, Bobby. Plain tacky. It's not the proper protocol . . . to not only wear an item, but to sweat in it too. That's just plain tasteless." She lectured, probably projecting her anger at me by nervously twisting a strand of her long hair around her index finger.

"Well, I'm just going to have to be tacky and tasteless then," I growled angrily. " I want you to find the receipt, take that suit to the one hour dry-cleaners and return it to the store today, before it closes."

"What am I supposed to tell the salesman? Do you know how embarrassing that is?" her high-pitched voice cracked between every breathless syllable. *This little tantrum of hers rates right up their within the top five percentile of her noteworthy performances*, I thought.

"I don't care about any of that. Just take the damn suit back, and get a full refund."

She sniffed profusely. " I have to go check on the girls . . . and I'm feeling nauseated, no thanks to you and your temper. I have to go to the ladies room," she snapped. " Are there any other commands my lord and master would like for me to fulfill?"

"No, I don't have anything else to add. However, I do feel it necessary to reiterate everything I've just said, just to maintain clarity and open communication. While you're at the mall, make sure to refund the coat, boots and hat, and any other accessories you may have squandered money on. Then, after doing that, go home, pick up the receipt and the suit, put it in the one-hour Martinizer's around the block, pick it up from the cleaners, and take it back to Jack's Place."

"But, I have a doctor's appointment to confirm this pregnancy. Noelle has a double-session piano lesson, since she's going to miss her next two lessons and I have to drop Lady Bug and Lisa Marie off at the Y out in Farmington Hills for gymnastics all by 6:00, and it's going on five now. There's no way I could possibly do all of that today. I just can't do it."

I plopped back down on the couch, weary from this conversation that should have been over minutes ago. All, I needed was to catch a twenty-minute catnap, then I would be refreshed enough to conduct my session with the Simmons, grab a bite to eat, and attend the brother's meeting.

"Well, then, I'll reach Ma at the house, before she goes home for the day, and I'll have her to drop the suit off at the cleaners. You can pick it up and return it before you start taking the girls to their lessons and practices tomorrow. Just make sure everything else is returned today."

Silence. I waited for my overly verbose wife to either burst into another theatrical performance, or to push the end call button on her cell phone, but she did neither. That's because she needed time to think, think of a way to manipulate this situation to her advantage, as I discovered seconds later.

"Well, since I may never find this coat anywhere else ever on this entire planet in my lifetime at such an affordable price, do you think you can find it in your heart to use the four-thousand dollar refund from the suit to pay for the coat, hat and boots?"

"Elisabeth, you do not need another fur coat. You already have five. You have everything most women dream of having . . ."

" That is like, sooo totally untrue!" she sniped. "Most women would dream of having that coat, but I, like them, can't have it, because, you won't let me get it. Is there any way you would change your mind?"

Why was she asking me this? I hardly deny her anything, but she knew me. Knew that when I put my foot down, that's where it stayed.

"Princes . . . sweetheart, take no for an answer."

"I will, Bobby. But, I am still going to find some way to keep that coat, even if I have to call Daddy and have him wire me the money."

Okay, now it was time to pull out the big guns. She wanted a knock-down, drag-out fight. This wasn't the first time she had used the close bond between she and her rolling-in it rich neurosurgeon father to threaten my spiritual headship as her husband. Not long after marrying Elisabeth, I began to resent her pampered upbringing. True, growing up the younger of two beautiful daughters in a predominantly white neighborhood, and only having attended private academies situated on campuses with weeping willows and lush, green grass, does have its privileges.

I bet Tanesha Jenkins wished she had all the money, clothes, educational and extra-curricular opportunities Elisabeth and her sister Lorraine had. Most of all, I bet she wished, even longed for a father who would spend a small fortune to buy her a BMW for her eighteenth birthday, like my father-in-law had for Elisabeth, his favored daughter, but a father who would take her out for ice cream on an ordinary Sunday afternoon. Elisabeth was spoiled rotten—to the bone, and I had had enough of it.

"If you do that, then you might as well have him wire you enough money to make your visit home a permanent one, because there's no way in hell you gon' dis' me like that and go over my head."

"Fine, that's probably what you want anyway—to be rid of me!"

"No, that's not what I want. What I want, is a sweet, loving wife who trusts my discernment as a husband," I explained.

"I do trust your discernment, Bobby, but you are being unreasonable right now, and I can't deal with it."

"You're going to have to try," I replied gritting my teeth.

I hated giving her ultimatums, but she always somehow managed to provoke me to that point. "If you do call and ask him for that money, be prepared for all hell to break loose!"

"Oh yeah?" she snapped. "Was that a threat? Because, I will have all of our things packed and out of that cheap house in those haunted city woods in no time."

"You're not going anywhere with my children. If you do, I'll fly down there, and ruin everything for your dear ole' daddy. I'll tell the church, which he oversees, the whole story. I'll explain to them, in full detail this argument, and his accepting you, a grown woman, married to a minister of the gospel, pregnant, with three kids and no job, into his house because she didn't want to settle on doing without a sixth fur coat. To top it off, I'll tell my brothers and sisters in Christ how he completely disowned his older daughter, who rejected his dreams for her life and about how he treats her as if she's dead just because she's made some mistakes in his point of view. They'll laugh so hard, and lose all respect for you and your Daddy, you won't be able to go anywhere in that town, without people knowing who you are. Also, they'll boot his ass out of his coveted office as elder, so fast, it will make your head spin."

I had never spoken such hateful, vindictive words to Elisabeth, but she needed to know just how serious I was about her keeping this fight just between the two of us.

Dead silence again.

"You feel me?"

"Completely," she uttered, stressing each syllable perfectly.

"Good, now, you go find our girls, and take the coat back."

"Fine."

"I'm sorry things had to go this way, Princess, you know I love you, but . . ."

"Go to hell, Robert," she replied as calmly as one would say the sky is blue.

———

49

"I beg your pardon?" I asked incredulously.

"You heard me."

"Elisabeth, that ain't even right. You're messed up in the head. You willin' to damn me to hell because yo' spoiled ass can't get yo' way?" I shouted. "**Who are you, woman?** I can't believe I tripped and married someone who would say some messed up shit like that in the first place."

I started to say that Lorraine would never treat me this way. It wasn't in her nature, she was too angelic to even think those thoughts—but I used my better judgment and waited for her response.

"Well, I said it, and I meant it," she coldly replied. "You're too stubborn and unreasonable. You just get a kick out of telling me no. It makes you feel like the Big Man always on top of things, even me!"

I chewed ferociously on my bottom lip to refrain from adding fuel to the fire. Throughout our entire marriage, the only arena in which we'd always maintained exceptional compatibility was the bedroom, with her initiating our creative love-making just as much or even more than I had, even if she'd use it as a bargaining chip to manipulate me into giving into whatever the hell she wanted at that particular time.

After having been married, with children for seven years, we'd been heaven-blessed to still be very much physically attracted to each other, and to still set the sheets afire several times weekly. I felt no need to respond to her misrepresentative remark.

"What you want, " I furiously interjected, "is a punk! A yes-man. Someone who would just let you spend however much you want on whatever you want. We've gone over this, time and time again. You want to be in control and you can't stand the fact that I am the man, that I'm the one holding the reins in this relationship . . ."

"Excuse me!" she snapped, " I take offense to that. You know that I'm all woman . . ."

"You know what I mean." I shrugged, " I mean you wanna take charge, you want me to just punk out every time. Well baby, that just ain't gon' happen."

"And, what's wrong with pleasing your wife, Mr. Super-Husband Marriage Counselor?"

"I try to please you, but you ain't runnin' over me. **WHEN I SAY NO DAMN IT, THAT'S WHAT I MEAN. END OF DISCUSSION!'**

" I hate you!" she retaliated. " I really, really hate you!" Finally, she pressed the end talk feature on her cell phone. I snapped myself out of my momentary stupor, when the annoying dial tone buzzed sharply into my right ear.

I couldn't believe my wife, the one I was bound to for the rest of my life, would ever be so callous. Sweat pellets poured down my temples in a sticky, moist sensation. The hot, humid air in my, now what appeared to be cramped office, tightened in around my throat.

My breathing was short. I directed my hazy vision above my desk, to glare at the 11x20 cameo portrait of Elisabeth and me, taken last year for the program to commemorate my ten years of service here at the Rosedale Park Church of Christ.

In this, one of my favorite pictures of us without the children, the naked eye cannot detect how closely together the photographer had arranged for us to sit in order for him to capture an up close shot that would fit into an oval shaped design. I briefly examined the wide-grin on my face, and remembered how snugly my long arms wrapped themselves around Elisabeth's tiny waste.

Sporting my three quarter length, short lapel, four buttoned charcoal gray pin-striped three-piece suit, white shirt, with a custom-made crimson and charcoal tie, I thought I was pretty dapper that day. But, my self-proclaimed handsomeness paled in comparison to Elisabeth's stunning loveliness.

I concentrated on the slight coy left upward tilt of my

wife's head. An abundance of light brown spiral locks swept over to the right side, cascaded passed her fragile shoulder down the length of her backside. A pearl necklace and matching pair of tear-drop shaped trimmed in sterling silver earrings, which I had purchased for her twenty-first birthday, perfectly accessorized the pastel pink double breasted, neatly trimmed suit jacket with silver buttons, she had tailored specifically for the occasion.

Most of Elisabeth's purchased off the rack clothes are tailored to fit her unique shape. Since she is 5'8 inches, and 120 pounds soaking wet, after having three babies, she has trouble finding clothes to accommodate her lithe frame. Thus, she usually ends up having them taken up by our own elderly Sister Garby, a very talented seamstress who charges Elisabeth an arm and a leg for each alteration.

In this my favorite portrait of the two of us, although Elisabeth is sporting her usual non-teeth bearing, pouting lip, yet demure half-smile, her eyes warm and cheerful, compliment the natural glow of her ivory complexion, coated with a primrose colored blush.

The cantankerous, old photographer who had been biting everyone's heads off for not posing properly or sitting close enough together informed the two of us, that he enjoyed snapping our family photos because we were such a beautiful family.

His mood especially seemed to brighten, when Elisabeth allowed him to take an entire roll of headshots of her to display on the walls and in the windows of his studio located in the downtown Detroit area.

"If you don't mind an ole' geezer like myself sayin' so Rev'ran, yo' wife is the prettiest thang I ever did see. Man, she love the camera, and the camera sho' nuff, love her," he cackled, slapping his right thigh. One late night a few weeks later, Elisabeth stayed up a couple of hours past her bedtime to proudly show me the results of the old man's labor-an array of pictures she had already blown up, hung on our living room and family room walls, and organized into an album. I was most impressed with the black and white shots, along with the one photograph she hates the most.

The one which depicted her in a rare instance, head tilted back, hair blowing in the fan induced wind, laughing with unrelenting abandon-showing her teeth.

He didn't lie. Elisabeth was radiant that day. Almost as radiant as the first time I laid eyes on her.

Beholding her visage pissed me off further. I didn't want to think about her at all. Not after she told me how she really felt about me. "She hates me," I whispered to myself. As I often do when I'm stressed, and would like to feel tranquil, I reached for the snowball collectable on the corner of the desk nearest the couch. It was the first thing Elisabeth ever bought for me. Christmas 1999.

I violently shook it. Artificial flakes of white snow sprinkled out of nowhere-some flakes landed on the church situated in the center of the globe. Others floated about aimlessly searching for a resting place. I chewed on my bottom lip, and recalled how utterly relieved she sounded when she finally told me what she had been harboring in her heart for such a long time. *Hate. She wants to see me roast in hell.* I shook the snowball one final time, before I contorted my body into a professional pitcher's stance, and threw it up against my favorite picture.

Shards of glass broke directly onto our blissful faces. Water dripped down the walls onto the tan carpet. I rushed to pick up the glass and to soak up the water, expecting that at any second, Sister Calloway or Kelly would rush in to see if everything was okay.

I'm sure they had their nosey little ears pierced to the thin wall that separated our offices during my entire phone conversation. I could imagine Kelly, even, with her ear pressed against the base of one of the cheap dollar store glasses she leaves dirty on her desk mostly every night. Knowing them, they were probably cheering me on the whole time, neither one of them, especially Kelly, who Elisabeth suspects of still being in love with me after all these years, is fond of my wife.

I slowly walked back over to the couch, and in one grand defeated gesture flopped the weight of my entire body onto it. I stretched out my long legs, which now felt like rubber, closed my eyes and proceeded to massage my left temple.

This migraine was kicking my butt. I released a long yawn that I'd been repressing for at least twenty minutes, and allowed my thoughts to drift back to the first time I met the Princess, in all of her splendid glory.

Rewind

Part One:

Gotta Have Her

Late

I've always believed that God has been with me every single second of every single day of my existence, because what else could justify why I have been able to accomplish so many goals and escape so many rough situations other than the mercy of a Father in Heaven who loves me deeply? Despite this lifelong personal conviction, the week during my first encounters with Elisabeth Jameson Powell, was straight from hell. Satan and all his legions of demons were in full force to attack me from every angle during the '99 holiday season.

First, Brother Khalid, my right hand man, had agreed to meet my brother Eddie, Doug, the first white member of our congregation since my tenure as minister, and I at the De-troit-Metropolitan Airport, twenty minutes before our flight had been scheduled to depart for Lambert Airport in St. Louis. I was scheduled to run a three-day pre-marital seminar/con-ference that shared the same title of my most recent publica-tion: *Starting Over and Saving It For My Wife: A Christian Man's Guide to Finding a Godly Woman in the New Millennium.*

To culminate the meeting, I was also scheduled to de-liver a Sunday morning message to the Kingshighway Church of Christ, whose minister had been a classmate and close friend of my father's who had relegated all of his pulpit re-sponsibilities to me back in '95.

59

I have a thing about people making me late to airports. I generally have a very low tolerance level for waiting on people. Under normal circumstances, I would have vehemently objected to the agreement Brother Khalid had arranged. However, his wife Fatima, who had not converted to Christianity had delivered their fourth son two-weeks prior to our trip, had a whole list of last minute tie-me over errands for her husband to run before he went off gallivanting across the country with his preacher friend.

Despite my strong sentiments about airport punctuality, Doug, Eddie and I had barely arrived on time ourselves. Doug's beat up old Chevy died in the frigid late November weather on I-94 West en-route to the airport. Eddie and I reluctantly unloaded our luggage from the trunk, as Doug, who has always been in pretty good shape, jogged a mile and a half to the nearest exit to phone a tow truck.

By the time Doug resurfaced, his face crimson, knuckles white, Eddie had repeatedly cursed him and called him every profane combination of every white bastard in the book. About a half hour later, the tow truck appeared. We solemnly bade farewell to Doug's most prized possession.

I thought I caught a glimmer of a tear in his eye, but, before I could rag on him about it, Eddie set in on cussing at him again. This time it was because Doug, in all of the commotion, forgot to call a ride for us to the airport.

"We can try to wave down a taxi," Doug replied apologetically to his long-time friend and work supervisor.

"Doug, man, we're in the middle of the fuckin' freeway!" Eddie hollered. "What kind of cab-driver is gon' stop in the middle of rush-hour traffic on the freeway no less, to pick up a couple of black men with a broke ass lookin' Richie Cunningham to take us to the airport? You don't use your head. That's why I hate taking you anywhere with me! I should have socked your redneck ass for even offering to go with us!"

"Well, screw you too, dude!" Doug retaliated in his usual Caucasian inflection, "don't jump all over my case for offering to help you guys out this weekend. I took off two days of work just to fly down to St. Louis to hear your brother speak. Hell, I'm cold and hungry too pal, but you don't see me crying like a jerk and being a sissy about it."

I laughed, because . . . it was funny. One thing about Doug I could appreciate and admire was his utter whiteness. Being raised in Birmingham, Michigan, he was culturally devoid and inept of diversified experiences, especially the speaking of what some black folks like to call Ebonics. Morever, he didn't get his feathers all ruffled when Brother Khalid and I had to pull him aside after initially coming up with the Warrior's concept, to break him off that although we'd welcome his input in church matters as a deacon, and considered him a close personal friend in the Lord, his being a white male automatically disqualified him from joining the Warrior's program. The flushness in his pale cheeks somewhat dissipated when we'd also shared with him the fact that the sisters were going to be sweatin' us because they couldn't participate either. He'd slapped hands with us and wished us Godspeed on our seemingly insurmountable unenviable task.

"Man, who you callin' a sissy, punk?" Eddie replied, unzipping his jacket, and hurling my cam-corder case unto the sparsely snow-covered grass. "Bob, man, did you hear this white boy call me a sissy, to my face?"

I ignored his inquiry and I angrily pushed my brother, who is shorter and less physically endowed than me out of the way, so that I could retrieve my recorder.

"All I've got to say is . . . my equipment better not be broken E, or you owe me a G spot," I admonished him harshly.

"Your ass is grass," Eddie gritted his teeth at Doug, who standing at 6'1", did not blink or look the least bit intimidated.

61

"Then come on, buddy! Bring it on," Doug yelled, "Bring it to me, brother!"

Eddied lunged full-force at Doug's turtleneck clad throat. I removed myself from the line of fire, so I could obtain a better view of those two fools scuffling. As anxious and tense as I was, about potentially missing our flight, I was ready to haul off into someone's behind myself. But, I chose to remain a spectator. Dressed in a three-piece tan suit, Stacy Adams knobs and a three-quarter length brown coat, with a matching Stetson brim, I couldn't imagine getting myself dirty because those two idiots were behaving like overly testosterone driven teen-aged males participating in a cock fight over some pimply faced girl who couldn't care less which one she wound up with, so long as he was the winner.

"Bobby, man, are you going to actually let him hit me?" Doug asked, his voice resonating the first signs of panic. My brother slammed his left fist into the palm of his right hand, as if he were getting warmed up.

"Well," I paused fully contemplating the repercussions of a fist-fight between my only brother and his right hand man, "yeah." I shrugged. "Ya'll actin' stupid, and well, quite frankly, stupid people deserved to get busted in the mouth."

Before Eddie and Doug could form a temporary alliance for the sake of kicking my butt, I darted over to the edge of the highway's shoulder, turned my back towards them, and stuck out my left thumb. I remember the brutal wind slapping me across the face, and violently attempting to sweep the whole of my 210-pound frame into emerging traffic.

"Bob, man, what the hell you doin'?" Eddie asked me with the most befuddled expression I'd ever seen on his face. I shot a quick devil-may-care glance in his direction, before sweeping my impudent gaze towards Doug. He looked equally surprised.

"I'm hitchin' a ride, man. I ain't tryin' to stand out here and fight with you two fools. I have a plane to catch. I'm scheduled to conduct a seminar and sign books in less than four hours." I strutted over closer to the edge, and began to wave my thumb more vigorously, until Eddie grabbed my arm, and twisted it behind my back, much as he used to when I would get caught red-handed sneaking into his Playboy collection when I'd first reached puberty.

Being five years my senior, Eddie had managed to pin me into yelling the submissive plea of "uncle" until I reached fifteen, and had began to hover over him by a few inches.

"Man, if you don't put that raggedy black ass thumb down, I'm gon' break it off!"

"Such violence, coming from an educated, dignified black man," Doug chided adding fuel to the fire.

Doug was a cool white guy who according to Eddie, resented his success since the day they met. They had both worked at the national headquarters of Ford Motor Company in Dearborn, Michigan for years. Only Doug labored in the sweltering heat of the front line as an engine technician, and Eddie worked in a white dress shirt and tie inside an air-conditioned office as a former mechanical engineer turned supervisor.

However, somehow work relations were amicable enough between the two of them that Eddie began introducing Doug to Christ and breaking the bread of life unto him piecemeal, until eventually, one Sunday morning, Doug, his wife Donna and their five boys arrived to hear Eddie's baby brother light up the pulpit. They'd all been there ever since.

"Doug, man, shut up!" Eddie yelled. "I'm trying to knock some sense into Bobby's head."

"Ed, you wrinkling the getup, man! Let me go!"

"Aw, shucks, Mr. GQ, here don't want to get his expensive suit dirty," he teased, gripping my arm tighter. I flinched.

"Look, man, let me translate my point by breakin' it down in a language a greedy mug, like you would understand. D'argent, loot, dough, bread, etcetera. If you don't help get

63

us to that airport bro, we are going to miss the flight, and if we do, that means, no money, no moola baby. How are you going to rob me blind, you know. . . . skim profits off the top, if you are not there to back me?"

Eddie summarily released his tight grip on my arm, and playfully, yet harshly pushed me forward.

"Man, Doug come on, you lazy bum," he laughed walking over to the spot where I previously stood. He stuck out his left thumb. "Man, get to workin'. We've got a bird to catch!"

Before our hands could grow numb from frostbite, two attractive black women driving an early nineties BMW, with the sorority call letters AKA plastered across the bumper pulled over onto the shoulder. The driver, a mocha-colored, dimpled cheeked girl, sporting a long wavy weave spoke to us first.

"You brothers don't look like rapists. What's the problem?" she first winked at me, smiling at me from cheek to cheek. Eddie nudged me as if instructing me to be the group's charming spokesperson.

Her girlfriend, a darker-skinned version of the driver, elbowed her, and nodded her head desperately towards my direction, as if to say, if you pick anyone up, it better be him.

I stooped down to eye-contact level, and waited for the passenger to at least partially crack her window. To my surprise, she rolled it down completely. I removed my hat, and purposely used my ring free left hand to rest it against my chest.

"Excuse us, sisters," I apologized. "But my partner's car was just towed. I hope you believe me, because, we need a ride to the airport now. . . . our plane is scheduled to depart in approximately thirty minutes." I dashed one of my most flirtatious smiles to the girl in the passenger seat, and shot my make-her –wet-bonafide Robert –McGallister-wink to the driver.

"And, why should we believe you, tall, dark and sexy?" the passenger giggled. Her girlfriend slapped her a fast high-five for thinking of a quick, equally coquettish comeback.

"Maybe, because he's a man of the clothe," Doug announced, extending his right hand to the passenger, whose mouth was so wide open in shock, she could have swallowed an entire army of wasps, had it been the appropriate season.

"Shut up, man," Eddie shoved him. "Let Bobby do this." Throughout my extended bachelorhood, Eddie had lived his never experienced playa days vicariously through me.

Since he'd married Sheila, fresh out of college, and had been quite verbal about being deprived of the experience of sowing his wild oats, he never stifled my innate ability to charm and dazzle the ladies.

"Is it true?" the flamboyant driver asked. "Are you really a reverend?"

"Well, actually, we in the Church of Christ, don't call our preachers reverends. He is our full time minister, though." Doug pointed out in the characteristic condescending tone newly converted Church of Christers use when explaining the minute aspects of the doctrine. " We attend the Rosedale Park Church of Christ on the Northwest side of Detroit. Are you ladies familiar with that church? Robert here, has his own Sunday morning cable broadcast, and he is a successful Christian author."

"Man, shut up, will you?" Eddie snapped becoming more annoyed by the second.

Both ladies continued to stare at me admiringly. Something in their eyes told me they were still not convinced they should offer us our much needed ride.

"I'm Robert." I introduced myself calmly. My gaze never left the passenger's eyes. She looked transfixed. I remember thinking that if I could convince her, we would be home free. I reached for my wallet that was located in its usual spot, the right pocket of my trousers. "This is my brother Eddie and our brother in Christ, Doug. Both serve as deacons of our congregation."

I placed a business card with my picture on it, in the passengers' hand. I allowed my hand to rests in hers for a few seconds. She blushed.

The driver grabbed the card out of her hand, and nodded. "You know what . . . I do believe I've seen one of your books in the Apple Bookstore on Outer Drive. . . . something about saving it for my lady, or something. . . . and, my grandmother, my grandmother who lives in Rosedale Park told me that former crackheads from your church have been on her block, picking up garbage and mowing the lawns. She and her ole biddy girlfriends have even tried to visit your church to thank you personally, but she said your body guards here stopped her from entering."

I chuckled at the thought of slight Eddie and talkative Doug prohibiting a bunch of senior citizens from entering the church premises.

"I beg your pardon, sister," Eddie interrupted. It was the first polite tone he'd taken with anyone all day, "But, had I been there, I would have escorted your grandmother and her friends right back to his office, to meet my brother in person and to receive a few autographed copies of his books. Our church isn't like that. Bobby is accessible to everyone."

" Oh, are you now, Bobby?" the passenger giggled again. This time, it was me who wanted to blush.

"Okay, gentleman," the driver announced. "I'm popping the trunk, grab your bags and get in. You have a plane to catch!"

Moments later, we arrived to the airport with ten minutes to spare. Doug promptly carried our garment bags, which were filled with suits, and my video camera to the check-in luggage counter.

Eddie, once again politely thanked the ladies, and kissed

both of them on their hands, before sprinting into the airport to meet Brother Khalid with the tickets.

"It was a pleasure meeting you ladies," I smiled, nodding at both of them. The driver stepped out of the car. Her sleek black leggings, elongated neck, and four-inch stilettos gave her the appearance of being tall. When she walked over to me, to hand me her phone number, she was standing so close, hairs from the crown of her head tickled my cheek. She placed her hand on my coat covered chest, and rubbed it in a tiny circular motion. She tilted her head upward, and sexily gnarled into my ear, "Call me Reverend, when you get back to town. I want to take your brother up on the offer that you are readily accessible to everyone."

If that weren't enough to make my temperature rise, the passenger, unfastened her seatbelt, and wildly hopped out of the car. She playfully shoved her girlfriend to the side, grabbed onto my arm, and yelled at her something to the effect that she saw me first.

I entered Metro-Airport flattered, but sheepishly looking for a trash can to deposit the numbers. At that point in my life, I had resigned myself to a voluntary vow of celibacy until marriage. I knew that calling either one of those girls or both of them would lead to some wild, frivolous orgy, which I had years since, thank the Lord Almighty, outgrown.

As if we hadn't already experienced enough chaos for the day, my top dog, Yusef Khalid came trekking into the Southwest Airlines department sharply dressed, moments before the woman at the counter announced final boarding pass time. Wearing ultra dark shades as was his custom, and a long black trench coat, with a brim to match, he flashed me one of his best charismatic Louis Farrakhan grins. He briefly shook Doug's hand, exchanged a look of mutual, disgust and contempt with my brother, before sauntering over to me to offer his usual brotherly embrace.

"Let's skip the preliminaries," I snapped looking at my

watch. I'm quite an irritable, perhaps, lethal, brother when I am pressed for time and a bit on the hungry side. "Where are the tickets, Yusef?"

"Hold your horses, Little Brother," he grinned coolly, sticking his leather gloved hand into his coat pocket. "I've got them, right . . . ," he paused before frantically searching his other pocket. Doug's face turned a beet red, while Eddie rolled his eyes heavenward. I sucked my teeth, as I often do when I feel like clobbering someone upside the head.

"Heh, heh . . . , just wait a minute brothers, let me check my briefcase." His speech was erratic and breathy, as if had run the entire extent of the airport. Although he had yet to provide an explanation for his lack of punctuality, I'm sure it had something to do with Fatima, and their newborn son, whom upon her insistence they gave a Muslim name, Jaleel.

"Naw, I don't even believe this," he announced incredulously as he erected himself back onto the full level of his height, which was an inch taller than mine. Standing, at 6'5", and without his trademark shades, some people often mistook Brother Khalid for Pistons basketball great, Grant Hill, especially since there is a rumor running rampant throughout the brotherhood that Hill is a member of the Church of Christ.

He kneeled down on one knee, and furiously began searching the contents of his semi-empty briefcase, in which he always carried an extra pair of reading glasses, a black leather bonded *Dixon's Analytical Study Bible* and a copy of the *Holy Koran*.

Doug had to roughly grab hotheaded Eddie's arm to restrain him from decking Brother Khalid.

"Man, I'm about five seconds off your ass," Eddie threatened, "People keep wantin' to mess with my bread and butter, today." That was good ole' lascivious Eddie, always focusing on how he could earn a quick buck. If looks could kill, Eddie would have dropped dead right before our eyes, from the intense, rapid visual bullets Brother Khalid aimed in his direction.

I was too concerned about our botched flight arrangements to decipher or care about the tension that had been mounting for months between my brother and my best friend. Basically, they tended to avoid each other whenever possible and make pedantic quips behind each other's backs to me, Eddie accusing Brother Khalid of being a freeloading leech, and Brother Khalid threatening to some day obtain proof that Eddie was nothing more than a white collar crook who had committed far more serious infractions than merely robbing me of my inherent birthright of being our Pops' favorite son.

" I don't know what could have happened to the tickets. Maybe if I call home, Fatima will say I left them on the table."

The receptionist's nasal voice announced that there were only five minutes left to final boarding. Doug broke into a cold sweat. I chewed my bottom lip and sucked my teeth several more times.

"I'll go call her," Brother Khalid announced pitifully.

"Here, man, use mine," I replied handing him my cell phone.

"What good is calling her going to do? By time she gets here, the plane gon' be gone," Eddie complained. "What kind of shitty day is this anyway?" he asked to no one in particular. I was beginning to have the exact sentiments.

Fatima, sure enough knew where the tickets were . . . right on their kitchen table. Brother Khalid, who had visited the travel agency a month prior to our departure date, in an effort to curtail his usual absent-minded behavior, had sat the tickets out on the kitchen table the night before. But he had probably not stepped a foot anywhere near his kitchen since he fasts at least two days out of the week.

While Doug and Eddie were both letting him have it, I walked over to the ticket counter to inquire about catching a later flight. After carefully explaining the situation to a middle-aged black woman who looked somewhat bored to be hearing yet another brother making excuses, she informed me that the next flight leaving for St. Louis wasn't scheduled until 7:30 Eastern time, which meant 6:30 Central time. We would arrive in St. Louis exactly thirty minutes before I was scheduled to speak to the brother's of the Kingshighway congregation, provided our plane arrived and landed on time. I thanked God for small favors, before I perused my briefcase to find James Powell's, the church's elder's telephone number.

While dialing the number, I remember praying that I wouldn't convey the impression that I was irresponsible. After all, I was only twenty-nine, and had already earned a somewhat controversial reputation as a left-wing radical in the church.

Powell's phone rang several times before someone answered it.

"Powell residence," the alluring, high-pitched voice sang.

"Yes, this is Robert McGallister. I'm scheduled to speak at Brother Powell's church tonight, is he there?"

"No, he isn't. He's at the hospital. May I take a message?" she asked.

"Uh . . . , is he okay?" I asked a bit taken aback by the inflection of the voice that I assumed belonged to a white person. Pops had failed to mention that Donaldson served over a mixed congregation.

"Why wouldn't he be?"

"Because, you just said he was at the hospital. Is he ill?"

She emitted a tiny giggle before explaining to me that he was a neurosurgeon, who had most recently become chief of staff at St. Paul's Hospital.

Chagrined that my own father, who had resigned himself to the role of substitute minister and elder at our own congregation, had not made me privy to this tidbit, before arranging the meeting, I apologized to the young woman on the other end of the phone.

"With whom am I speaking?" I asked regaining my composure.

"His daughter, Elisabeth."

"How are you doing this afternoon, Elisabeth?" I flirted. I wanted to make a good impression, since a beautiful woman was probably the owner of this tiny sexy voice. I allowed my lustful thoughts to pray she wasn't white, and to wonder how old she was.

"Very well, thank you," she enunciated perfectly. " I could give you Daddy's work number if this is an emergency," *Daddy*, I thought. Why didn't she refer to him as her father, or even her Dad? The word daddy seemed rather cute and juvenile. Maybe she was just fourteen or fifteen. I shrugged it off, thinking I had originally been mistaken.

"Yes, this is an emergency. Brother Powell is scheduled to pick my group up at Lambert in another hour. However, we've encountered some difficulties, and we won't be able to make it until 6:30, instead."

" I see," she replied. "Well, let me give you his number. Daddy's a very busy man. If he can't be reached, maybe it would be in your best interest to call our minister, Cecil Donaldson."

"Will do . . ." I replied. My father and Brother Donaldson went way back. They had attended Southwestern Christian College together, in Terrell, Texas, the place where my parents met. "Will I see you at the meeting tomorrow evening, Elisabeth?" I asked, unsuccessfully able to rid my mind of the impeccable diction of her words nor her mild southern accent. To a native Michigander, anyone who lives south of Ohio is considered southern.

" Oh, definitely," she teased. "I never miss anything at the church."

"That's good to know. How will I know who you are?"

"I won't be difficult to spot. Trust me."

I ended the conversation sporting a big goofy grin from ear to ear. If this young woman, looked half as good as she sounded, I was in for a treat. Moments later, Dr. Powell's secretary had asked me to please hold, while she transferred my call into his office.

"James Powell," a confident, baritone voice announced.

"Brother Powell, this is Robert McGallister," I explained nervously. " I'm supposed to . . ."

"Be here in less than an hour," he interrupted harshly. "Yes, yes, son, I know who you are. I've heard a great deal about your uh . . . *work*." He pronounced the word work, as if it were a euphemism for chaos and confusion. Right away, I knew he wasn't one of my biggest supporters. " Since we do expect you soon, and I know for a fact you're not allowed to use cell phones in the air . . . you must be still in Detroit." After listening to his deep eloquent voice speak for a few seconds, and measuring it up against my short-term memory of how his daughter sounded, I could not assess his racial/ ethnic identity.

"Yes, sir. I am," I responded respectfully, "but I can explain."

"No need to explain, son. I'm sure you have a somewhat creative excuse."

" I beg your pardon, sir?"

"Well, I've seen some of your tapes, and I've watched a couple of your recent debates. No offense intended son, but you tend to have a flair for the dramatic."

If there is one oxymoronic cliché' I detest, it's any statement that is prefaced by "No offense, but . . .", because more often than not, the person who babbles such rhetoric, means to do just that: impose insult and offense.

This man, doctor, elder or what-the-hell-ever, had no business taking on that type of attitude with me. He had no idea how close the volcano within me was from erupting by that time of day.

"Well sir, I've been called a lot of things from stubborn and radical to innovative and liberal, which I do not fully deny. But, what no one can ever accuse me of is being a liar, or a promise breaker. Contrary to what you may believe, I do have a reasonable explanation for not being on a plane right now. The Lord knows I do."

I paused, not because I was out of breath, but because I wanted to give him a moment to digest what I had just said. "and as you stated, I may appear to be a bit dramatic in my approach to winning souls for Christ. No one wants to listen to a boring sermon or lesson about God's Word. To quote the Hebrew writer, sir . . . His Word is sharp and active. It cuts even to the marrow of the soul. Why should it be presented in a nonchalant, lackadaisical manner?"

"Well, Brother McGallister, after listening to that very willful, fiery dissertation, I only have one question for you, son."

"Yes, sir," I asked feeling tense and uneasy.

"Will you be on the next flight down here, or what?"

"Yes, sir. We will arrive at Lambert at 6: 30."

"We," he snickered, "we, meaning you are traveling with an entourage?"

"Well, I don't call my assistant and two of the deacons from our congregation an entourage, sir. They're my support base."

"I see," he replied flatly. " I look forward to seeing you this evening at the church."

"You mean, you won't be at the airport to pick us up?" I asked, crossing my fingers in hope that he would respond in the negative.

"No, son. I wasn't going to be the one to pick you up in the first place. Cecil will be there to greet you. Seeing that he and your father are old college chums, I thought it would be more fitting for him to pick you up and take you on over to the church."

"That'll be fine, sir. If it's the Lord's will, I'll see you shortly."

"Yes, indeed," he replied sternly. " I don't know what your followers up in the Motor City, have come to expect from you son, but down here in the Show Me State, and particularly at the congregation which I oversee, we conduct church business, decently and in order. I strongly suggest to you son, that the next time you conduct official church business of any kind . . . you'd learn from this experience and follow our example."

Several things disturbed me from this unmerited chiding. Foremost was his calling the believers at the Rosedale Park congregation, my followers, as if I were the Messiah himself. Secondly, were the innuendos that I am anything less than professional. Since one of my idiosyncrasies is lack of toleration for lateness, I took great offense to his foreboding comments.

However, to maintain the spirit of peace, and the bond of unity, as the apostle Paul wrote about in his New Testament epistle to the church at Ephesus, I decided to bite my tongue, and to keep the Eddie in me down to an evil keel.

"I'm not into proving myself, Dr. Powell," I replied boldly, my words, sharp and even. "However, I am convinced that the messages the Lord has set upon my heart for me to deliver over the next few days in order to save at least one lost soul from eternal darkness, will more than compensate for any inconvenience our having taken a later flight, may incur."

"Well, son. I was right about one thing prior to ever having spoken with you. You are indeed, full of yourself." Before I could respond, he sarcastically bade me and my entourage a safe flight and promptly ended the call.

I stood there for a few seconds, incredulous to a bishop's,

a pastor's and supposed co-laborer in Christ's treatment, of me, the Lord's manservant and his fellow brother. It deflates my spirit and shocks me to discover Christians who treat each other like enemies. After all, the Lord commands us yet again through the words of the Apostle Paul that we are to do well unto all men, especially unto those belonging to the household of faith.

I decided not to confide in Eddie or Doug about the encounter I'd experienced upon my very first conversation with a man who, unbeknownst to me at the time, was my soon to be father-in-law. After we had buckled ourselves into our seats, and had rifled through two or three bags of Planter's peanuts, I relayed all the sordid details of the call to Brother Khalid.

"Man, this brother sounds out cold. He criticized you worse than your own old man ever could. But, don't sweat it. I got your back Little Brother."

It had been no secret at our congregation that my father had subscribed to the more conservative doctrinal convictions within our non-denominational church.

In fact, I had grown up forcibly sitting at his proverbial feet, on the front pew every Sunday learning all the New Testament scriptures from him that explicitly point to the eternal condemnation of anyone who is not inside the body of Christ. By the time I was fifteen and allowed to enter his esteemed pulpit to deliver my first gospel sermon, I could quote all the scriptures pertaining to the church that one can actually read about in the Bible such as, Colossians 1:18, Ephesians 1:22, 3:10, 5:23-32, Acts 20:28, 1 Corinthians 1:2, Galatians 1:13, I Timothy 3:15, Colossians 1:13, and superlatively-the one scripture that we good and noble, truth-possessing folks employ the most to denigrate all those so-called wretched denominational folks, Romans 16: 16. The King James Version renders it: "Salute one another with an holy kiss. The Churches of Christ salute you."

Of course, to impress my father and his comrades, I face-

75

59-DRAN

tiously maintained my adamant stance against denomination-alism. I was quite successful at this charade until I actually began in my post-Michigan Christian College days, during my early twenties to participate in door-to-door evangelism not only within the affluent Rosedale Park Community, but throughout inner-city Detroit neighborhoods.

When Eddie, Sheila, Sister Calloway, Kelly and I weren't making any headway into converting souls for Christ. I, as the group's most vocal advocate, decided that we should change our approach.

"People aren't interested in being told that if they don't believe the same thing we believe in, they're going to hell. That's played out. We could actually learn a whole lot from them," I first proclaimed on a warm spring day, to my small group of four. "What we need to do is change our focus—speak life affirming words to them, not fire and brimstone. Sure, Jesus Christ is the only name under heaven whereby we must be saved, but who's to say that they're wrong merely because they go by the name of Church of God in Christ, Baptist, Presbyterian or Episcopalian? And, who's to say we're right because we wear a scriptural name? Let's forget about that, and focus on what's true and relevant to our soul salvation, and that is simply stated in Paul's first epistle to the Church at Corinth, Chapter 15, the verses, 1 through 4:

"Moreover, brethren, I declare unto you the gospel which I preached unto you, which also ye have received, and wherein ye stand; By which also ye are saved, if ye keep in memory what I preached unto you, unless we have believed in vain. For I delivered unto you first of all that which I also received, how that Christ died for our sins according to the scriptures; And that he was buried, and that he rose again the third day according to the scriptures . . ." That is my brothers and sisters, plainly spoken the true gospel: *For God so loved the world, that he gave his only begotten Son, that whosoever believeth in him shall not perish* but have *everlasting life.* James states in the first chapter, verse 27 of his

epistle that: *Religion that God our Father accepts as pure and faultless is this: to look after orphans and widows in their distress and to keep oneself from being polluted by the world.*"

"We'd win more souls for Christ if we'd stopped focusing on what separates us doctrinally, but rather what bonds us as fellow human beings. Some of the homes we enter are so completely impoverished, that our main priorities should be fixing them a hot plate, helping them kick a drug habit, pitching in to pay medical bills, or offering them tutorial and educational resources. How could anyone look forward to going to heaven if their lives right here on earth are worse than hell? It is our responsibility then, as Christians to show them Christ living in us as living epistles rather than to beat them over their heads with doctrine."

To concur with Brother Khalid, that typical heartfelt spiel has gotten me into some pretty steep cow manure with not only James Powell, but with my own father, who had often accused me of liberal, bleeding heart sacrilege.

Brother Cecil Donaldson

After a stormy, turbulent flight, our plane was not cleared for landing until a quarter to seven. Twenty minutes later, the four of us trotted furiously with our luggage through the connecting tunnel, until we reached the inside of the airport, As well-dressed as we were, we must have looked like a team of FBI agents, because no one hassled us about moving out of our way.

A short, balding, middle-aged man who I remembered from my childhood as having visited our home on several occasions, emerged from the crowd of family members and friends awaiting the arrival of missed loved ones.

" Eddie Jr.," Cecil Donaldson embraced my brother first. "My Lord, you still look the same after all of these years." Eddie nodded, and told the minister that it was a pleasure seeing him again.

He then introduced, Doug Harrison as one of the deacons of our congregation, along with Brother Yusef Khalid, my personal assistant.

"And last, but certainly not least, Brother Donaldson, you remember my brother Bobby, don't you?"

I chewed my bottom lip, and nervously reached to straighten my tie. Hopefully, Brother Donaldson would receive me more favorably than Brother Powell had. I wondered how much of my "work" as Powell called it, had he heard about or seen for himself.

Maybe, the whole reason he invited me was for he and Powell to rip my ministry apart before a live viewing audience. And, I wondered how much had my own father, his old crony from Southwestern Christian College had revealed to him about my prosperous career as a minister, rehabilitation counselor, author, and radio evangelist.

"Yes, yes. I remember your baby brother, Eddie," he smiled warmly, "I was hoping he'd remember me. After all, he was only knee high to a duck, the last I saw him. Now look at him, towering over both our heads, more handsome than your ole' ugly daddy ever was." He released a loud contagious cackle of a laugh, and slapped me on the back, with one hand, while wildly shaking my right hand.

" You must take after your momma, Bobby."

I released a brief sigh of relief. I liked Cecil Donaldson right off.

"Yes, sir," I laughed, "That's what she never lets me forget." I explained the fiasco of the day we'd experienced, and began to profusely apologize for our lateness, until Brother Donaldson broke into another bout of that hilarious, jubilant laughter.

"Heeee! Heeee! Brothers, brothers, don't sweat it," he flashed us a broad gold-toothed laden grin, while reaching for a dirty handkerchief that was in the pocket of his plaid sports jacket.

"Eddie Jr., your brother here is sho' nuff a humble man, he don't realize how many ladies both single and married have gone out of their way at the church to prepare him a decent meal before speaking to the brothers tonight. He's quite renowned around these parts. We're just honored your daddy talked him into comin' down to our little ole' country church."

"Pops didn't have to say much to convince me to come, Brother Donaldson. I think you're being modest about your church too. Word across the brotherhood is that you all just renovated your building to accommodate your growing membership. You all have a strong male membership as well, thanks in part to your work in the Lord's vineyard. I'm honored and humbled that I will be able to stand in your pulpit. Pops tells me that you've been preaching for over forty years."

"Yes, yes, Bobby, I have," he grinned, reaching for a toothpick out of his vest-pocket. I had the urge to ask him if he had a spare, because me and Pops both had a lifelong affinity for dangling wooden sticks from the corner of our mouths, for no particular reason. Doug looked embarrassed for him.

He was wearing a "I-can't-believe-you're-about-to-pick-the few-yellow-stained-teeth-remaining-in-your-mouth," look.

Eddie laughed aloud at the friendly minister. Donaldson, none the wiser, directed us to follow him out to the parking lot. "You know, I've been calling you Bobby, do you mind that?"

"No sir, I don't mind at all. That's what practically everyone calls me." I lied, not wanting to reveal that the only people who didn't call me Robert were family members and close friends. I didn't want to be rude.

He invited me to take the passenger seat in the church's new white Dodge Caravan. I'd supposed that Powell had informed him that I had an entourage with me. I wondered what else he'd told him about our conversation. I didn't have to wait long to find out.

"We're only about a ten minute drive from the church," he explained. "When we get there, I'm going to take you boys right on downstairs, to taste some of the sister's delicious home-cookin'. There are no cooks like Kingshighway cooks. Believe you me."

"If it's all the same to you, sir," I replied, "we'd rather go right into the auditorium and start the seminar. We're already running a half hour late."

"Speak for yourself, bro," my brother spoke loudly from the van's back seat. "It's been a long, hectic day, I know I for one, can get my grub on ASAP!"

Both Doug and Khalid seconded his opinion.

"But, the brothers are waiting for us. I hate making people wait."

"Now, now, son," Donaldson reached over to slap me on the knee. "Don't you worry 'bout a thang. I know you've got to be hungry. The sisters, especially my two single, still live at home, almost thirty, spinster daughters will never let me hear the end of it, if you don't fix yourself a plate." He cackled once again, congratulating himself on his own sense of humor.

"Oh," Doug laughed, "Bob, you see, Brother Donaldson has a hidden agenda. He has to find someone to marry one of his daughters off."

" No, no, that's only partially it," Donaldson explained. "Listen Bobby, I know Brother Powell spoke with you, about missing your first flight. He told me all about it, but, . . . I know you have a good excuse. Back in my younger days, when I was a traveling preacher, you wouldn't believe some of the emergency situations I faced that caused delayed flights or cancellations."

I nodded in agreement. Then, the four us revealed to him the details of our loopy day sans Eddie's colorful language. The jovial preacher chuckled on a few parts of our story before forewarning me that Brother James Powell could be quite stern and unrelenting. "While, you're visiting us, don't let his tough outer shell get the best of you. Somehow he hasn't realized that he can't treat the flock of God, like his inferiors over at St. Paul's Hospital."

I wanted to inquire about Powell's daughter Elisabeth, but I didn't want to appear to be overtly anxious to meet her just in case she was under-aged.

"So, son, think no more of being late. These brothers

have waited a good long time to finally meet you in person. A man of your stature and success must be used to being fed real good before preaching and teaching the way you do. I've been keeping my eye on you son. You're on your way straight to the top! It's time to start taking advantage of your blessed condition."

I started to reiterate my strong desire to begin the seminar pronto, but judging by the hungry looks on my brothers' faces, and my own growling stomach, I decided to comply with Donaldson's wishes.

Her Mama's White

Once we'd arrived at the medium sized building which situated itself on a canvas of a spacious, neatly trimmed green lawn, Donaldson, dropped us off in the parking lot, at the back door, and told us he would meet us downstairs. Eddie and Doug filed into the nicely decorated fellowship hall, followed by Brother Khalid and I.

Initially, I lost track of all three of them, because within seconds of our arrival, women, both young and old, tall and short, robust and slim-flocked around me as if I were Michael Jordan or Denzel Washington, drowning me in their array of musk and floral fragrances. Many soft, high-pitched, raspy and sexy voices, belonging to black women of all hues, ages and sizes greeted me and aimed questions at me about the enjoyability of my flight and my food preferences. I diplomatically hugged and pecked each sister on the cheek, before a group of them led me over to a long banquet table, located on the opposite end of the kitchen.

As we took our seats, one of the guys stated that he felt like he was at a wedding reception. Another one teased me about all the preferential treatment they were getting because they were a part of my "entourage."

Before long, our plates were filled with a variety of traditional soul foods such as meatloaf, candied yams, collard greens, spaghetti, fried and marinated Buffalo wings, maca-

83

roni and cheese, cornbread, and bread pudding. Since Thanksgiving had just passed, in keeping in the traditional holiday spirit, someone had also purchased a Honeybaked ham and had prepared turkey and dressing. Just when we thought we couldn't eat another bite, more sisters descended from that miraculous kitchen carrying a triple layered chocolate cake, peach cobbler, banana pudding, ice cream, chocolate mousse, and one of my favorites, lemon frosted pound cake, baked from scratch.

In between bites of food, I continued to greet and chat with what must have been half the women in the greater St. Louis metropolitan area. Most of them asked me questions about *Saving It For My Wife*, and what it was like to be a single minister of a flourishing church. The bolder ones inquired about the current status of my availability, and about how long I intended to stay unattached. I responded to all of their inquiries cheerfully and honestly.

" I am prepared for marriage," I said.

"Yes, I'm earnestly seeking a God-fearing Christian woman to be my wife."

"No, I haven't met the woman of my dreams yet."

"Yes, I do earn a good living from all that I'm doing now, and yes, I'm willing to share it with the woman of my dreams."

"Yes, it has been difficult to remain celibate for four years after being very highly sexually active in my younger days."

"Yes, I really meant what I said, as controversial and politically incorrect by today's standards it may seem to our white brothers and sisters in Christ, that I love black women, and a black Christian woman is the only woman on the face of this earth who can identify with struggles I face as an African-American Christian male."

"Yes, the selfless ability to have my children and take care of me and my home is a non-negotiable requirement."

"No, I don't want a wife who wishes to pursue a career outside of the home."

"Yes, I have these strong feelings because my own mother was a preacher's wife, and she supported his career fully, while raising two sons." As interested and amused as the guys were over all the attention I was getting, a half-hour later, when my stomach had been filled beyond capacity, I grew slightly bored and disappointed. I listened to each sister introduce herself. Some even spelled their names for me. Not one of them was this Elisabeth Powell, whom I had spoken with earlier. Then again, I don't know why I was surprised. Even from our three-minute conversation, I could conclude several things about the type of woman she was.

First, given her proper dialect, I could tell she was probably too pretty to get food underneath her imaginably long manicured fingernails. And a pretty woman's modus d'operande is not to participate in a lets-see-who-can-snag-this-young-handsome-single-minister cookout fest.

Third, since her father was a prominent, wealthy physician, she was probably spoiled, a bit snobbish and used to having her way. So, why was I so determined to meet her? Because, I've always embraced challenges, and I probably will remain this way until the day I die.

"Brother McGallister," a small voice called from behind me as Brother Donaldson was leading us up the stairs to the auditorium.

"Yes, yes, Sister Powell," Donaldson responded for me. I froze in my tracks, and chewed on my bottom lip before turning around to finally meet the woman I'd been thinking about, even in the midst of all the other beautiful sisters who did an excellent job communicating their availability to me.

I slowly turned around, and before my eyes, was a petite, attractive, middle-aged white woman with shoulder length, dishwater blonde hair streaked with a few strands of gray, wearing wire rimmed glasses and a white lab jacket. This could not be the owner of the youthful voice that referred to James Powell as Daddy.

"Sister Powell, here is our elder's wife." Brother Donaldson smiled nodding in her direction. I stood there, speechless and processed this new bit of information.

Wait a minute, I thought, *if this is Powell's wife, this must be Elisabeth's mother, which means Elisabeth is biracial. The young woman I spoke with on the phone is half-white?* Meeting her was going to be interesting, to say the least.

Although, back in my basketball, fraternity-active days, I'd had my fair share of sexual exploits with a few women of the fairer race, I'd never even considered taking a serious interest in any of them, knowing that my own light brown skinned, yet proudly black mother would be the first in line to disown me.

"I spoke to your husband earlier on the phone today," I explained. "It's very nice to meet you."

Without removing her calm gaze from me, the corners of her tiny lips curled upwards, into a tight closed mouth smile. After meeting both mother and daughter, I realized Elisabeth inherited this grimace mannerism from her mother.

"The pleasure is all mine, Brother McGallister. I've read your work, and I've seen a couple of your tapes, all because of my youngest daughter, Elisabeth, she is a great, shall, I say   if it doesn't make you too uncomfortable, fan of your work." I dug Sister Powell's gentle, soothing voice. It re-minded me of a female disc jockey of one of the jazz stations in Detroit. "I especially admire your creativity and aware-ness with the need to work with African-American men." She was alluding to God's Warriors, the brainchild Brother Khalid and I created together one Saturday night after watching the Lakers cream the Jazz in the living room of the parsonage I'd called home for four years. The only initiation fee the origi-nal twenty-five Bible toting, scripture quoting, black men from our own congregation between the ages of eighteen and thirty-five had rendered were solemn pledges of fidelity, fatherhood, fraternity and financial empowerment of our community.

Within weeks of beginning the Tuesday night sessions, the membership rapidly grew to include more than three hundred some odd active brothers from Rosedale Park, as well as from the Wyoming Avenue, Northwest, Annapolis Park, Linwood Avenue, Russell Woods, Conant Gardens, Elmwood Park and the Lemay Street congregations.

At the mention of Elisabeth's name, I silently thanked God in heaven for using her own mother as a vehicle to get to know more about her, before I would even lay eyes on her. Even though I assumed nothing serious would materialize from our meeting, judging by the looks of her mother, she had to be at least half-way decent looking enough to perhaps take out for coffee and bagels, or something. Even though I was a bagel lover myself, especially of the salt and cheese varieties, I tended to agree with Brother Khalid's sweeping generalization that white people are responsible for keeping all of the newly erected bagel deli/sandwich shops across the country in business.

"Thank you," I replied coolly. " I spoke to your daughter on the telephone today. She's the one who put me in contact with your husband at the hospital."

"You spoke to Elisabeth on the phone and she didn't mention how much she has been dying to meet you?" her mother laughed incredulously at what seemed like an absurd notion to her.

"No ma'am, your daughter was quite the lady. I couldn't tell if she even knew or cared about who I am," I laughed, appreciating Elisabeth's nonchalance and reserve. "Will she be here tonight?"

"Well, no, because Brother Donaldson informed the congregation at church last Sunday, that this seminar is strictly for men only because he wants you to motivate them to start a similar program . . ."

"Yes, sirree," Brother Donaldson exclaimed. "My wife, daughters and the rest of the fine and decent sisters of this congregation, can have Brother McGallister for the next three nights, but he's here to talk to the menfolk, tonight. As you know, Sister Powell, these brothers here need a little talking to. And, Bobby here, is the man to do it."

Sister Powell smiled that closed mouth smile again. Her soft blue eyes diverted their attention away from me momentarily, as she watched Donaldson escort Eddie, Brother Khalid and Doug into the front of the auditorium.

"I'm not going to keep you, Brother McGallister. I know you have to get started. I've just come to drop off a peach cobbler, Ms. Maggie would have killed me over, if I didn't deliver. The place is packed. I could hardly find a parking spot." She reached inside her worn vinyl bag to retrieve her car keys. I took note of the BMW symbol that served as one of her many key rings. "But, I'll be sure to tell Elisabeth I met you. I may be a little late to tomorrow night's meeting. I've been working pretty long hours at the office."

"Is that right?" I asked taking advantage of the opportunity to learn more about Elisabeth via her mother. "I notice the lab jacket, what do you do?"

" I'm an orthodontist. My practice is only five minutes away from the church. As you can see, I haven't been home yet. We live out in Chesterfield, it's about a twenty minute drive from here," she explained.

"Well, Sister Powell, I'll be glad to see you to the door," I smiled, offering the crook of my right arm to her.

She vehemently shook her head no.

"No, Brother McGallister, you're not going to have all of those men jumping on me . . . they're eager to meet you too. Besides, I think this old lady can manage."

"Call me Robert." I swayed my body over and down a

few inches to kiss her. A few tangled, in dire need of a trim hairs brushed up against my lips, as my awkward aim didn't quite reach her freckled cheek.

"Oh," she snapped her fingers to indicate she had just remembered something important. "Come over here, Robert . . . here is the church directory, I can show you my family's photo now."

I tried not to appear to be overly and outwardly interested, but inwardly, my heart skipped ten beats faster and the proverbial ants in my pants were doing cartwheels. We walked over to the wood podium, which housed the laminated front and back covers of the recently completed, treasured directory. I watched Emily Powell's thin, pale fingers covered with several diamond rings, potentially given to her on various anniversaries; flip alphabetically through the pages until she reached theirs.

"Ah, here we are," she smiled, as her finger landed on their three-person family photo located in the bottom right corner of the page. "My daughter Lorraine, we call her Lori is not pictured," she said sadly. "She's uh, up in Michigan, where you are, in Lansing. She graduated from MSU last December. She has already been accepted at U of M med school, but for some reason, she's decided to extend her stay in Lansing to teach dance, classic ballet, pointe tap, you name it. She also started a program at some Baptist church up there to teach underprivileged youth how to dance, and she teaches the girls pointe ballet, tap, jazz and modern dance. However, we're hoping, my husband James especially, that she'd become a cardiologist or maybe even a neurosurgeon just like her dad." When Emily spoke of her older daughter, her eyes were both wistful and misty. I instinctively wanted to wrap my arm around her loving maternal shoulder and reassure her that whatever the situation was with this Lori, the Lord had a way of working things out.

"That's nice," I nodded, noticing how tired she looked

after discussing such a sensitive subject. "I'm sure you both must be very proud of your daughter."

A few inexplicable tears escaped the grieving mother's eyes, before she used the back of her hand to wipe them away.

"I'm sorry, Brother Mc . . . Robert, I just love Lori so very much. I just worry about her being so far away from us. She left home when she was only sixteen. She graduated form MSU with a perfect 4.0 average in microbiology you know. She also won a fully paid scholarship for med school to U of M for her outstanding grades and contributions to the Peace Corp and Homes for Humanity. She sings like a bird and dances like an angel. She also has a true, love for children, but we're still hoping she'd use those little hands to become a skilled surgeon."

"Lorraine sounds like a remarkable young woman." I smiled, in complete ignorance of the prophetic veracity of the statement, unaware that one day she would own my very heart. The only feeling I could muster for her at the time was empathy, because I knew that if she didn't fulfill her parents dreams for her, one day, they would permanently lose touch.

"Oh, she is," Emily exclaimed. "She's my joy, but, I love Elisabeth too. Here she is, right here," she announced as if she was expecting some sort of dramatic drum roll to resound from the speaker system in the church's audio room.

I concentrated my gaze on Elisabeth's photo. The front section of her hair was pinned up into some sort of alluring French twist, while the back, flowed loosely to an undetermined exaggerated length that could not be ascertained from her position in the picture. Her chestnut eyes appeared flat and unassuming. Hovering closely over her parents, who were seated in the traditional woman between the man's legs pose, her thin, long, perfectly manicured fingers rested on the shoulders of both her mom and praise the Lord Almighty, her almost as chocolaty coated as I am, African-American father.

Even though I expected Elisabeth to have a fair complexion because of her bi-racial parentage, she still looked mostly, if not entirely white. She reminded me of an untanned Barbie doll, without the ample bosom for which the popular toy has both been praised and criticized. Sporting a pale rose-colored long sleeve blouse, a thin silver charm bracelet, and diamond earrings, her cool forced closed lipped smile matched that of her mother's who looked as if she just wanted the photographer to just snap the blasted photo.

My eyes fell lastly on the prominent family patriarch. A broad-shouldered, bearded, distinguished man, wearing a conservative dark navy suit and white shirt glared back at me from the pages of the directory. If the picture would have been taken a second later, the photographer would have caught James Powell, the serious looking doctor and only elder at the Kingshighway congregation with his mouth agape and his large eyes closed.

Although Powell looked professional and dignified, one would have no way of knowing how arrogant, proud and pretentious I'd find him to be after getting to know him. I scrutinized the visages of both her parents a second time, before concluding that Elisabeth did not bare a remote resemblance to either one of them, which was fine by me, because her beauty mesmerized me, right from the start.

"Isn't she lovely?" Sister Powell asked, a question which triggered my memory of the melody with the same title, sung by my favorite recording artist of all time-Stevie Wonder. Before I could respond, I heard my brother's voice from the entrance of the auditorium calmly beckon me to come inside.

"They're all set for you, Bob."

I took one last quick glance at the photo. If pictures are indeed worth a thousand words, this one spoke volumes. Elisabeth's stunning looks captivated me—she looked finer

91

than any supermodel I'd ever seen. Dumbstruck, I stood speechless sporting the most idiotic, schoolboy-crush grin I'd ever had.

"She's, uh, uh, definitely . . ."

"Breathtaking," Emily bragged.

"That, she most certainly is," I smiled, trying to reclaim my lost state of composure. "I look forward to meeting her."

"I'll let her know."

As I walked away, I couldn't deny the disappointment I felt in feasting my eyes on that beautiful photo. As downright pretty as she appeared, she also struck me as being too young for me to get to know, much less marry. I chided myself for lusting over a mere picture of a bi-racial teenager, only moments before entering the pulpit.

Fire 'em up!

Less than five minutes later, an auditorium full of both members and visitors alike applauded when I took my seat upon a left-corner bench of Cecil Donaldson's pulpit.

"Brothers and guests," Donaldson's voice boomed through the microphone attached to the podium. I signaled to Brother Khalid to get rid of both. Eddie tampered with the mini-mike on the lapel of my tan three quarter-length three-piece suit jacket that I had uncharacteristically been sporting all day. Donned as Mr. Clean by my mother, I felt a bit uncomfortable and sweaty. I was in dire need of a warm, no maybe cold shower to eradicate distracting thoughts of meeting Elisabeth the next night from my mind.

" I know you've been waiting months to finally meet our fine brother, Dr. Robert McGallister, who hails from the cold Motor City. As you know, Brother Robert has been the full time minister of the Rosedale Park Church of Christ for how long now, Bobby?" he asked pivoting his stout body towards my direction.

"Almost four years now, sir," I replied in a confident, deep voice. Eddie had situated the mini-mike perfectly.

"That long, heh?" he chuckled. "Brother McGallister here, is the son of Ed McGallister Sr., who as we know, is responsible for the founding of several other sister congregations throughout the Metropolitan Detroit area. He also spearheaded two Christian academies which his son has taken over since his er, um, voluntary retirement, heh, heh."

Polite chuckles from the audience. "Both academies are housed on the church's premises. The Agape Institute, a pre-kindergarden through 5th grade facility boasts a student body of 250. Praise the Lord!" Donaldson exclaimed as he used his index fingers to push his glasses back to a more comfortable position on his nose. He tightly gripped the index cards filled with Brother Khalid's chicken-scratch in his stubby, aging hands.

"The other facility the Christian Men's Leadership Academy, CMLA, boasts a smaller student body of 125, where men are trained to efficiently conduct the worship services, by preaching, praying, singing and serving the Lord's Supper. Over half of the graduates of this school have become full-time gospel preachers, including Robert, himself an undergraduate Michigan State Alumni, who after finishing a Bachelor's Degree in Psychology commuted between Ann Arbor, Michigan and his hometown to obtain a second Bachelor's in Religious Studies while simultaneously completing work towards a three year doctoral program in psychology at the University of Michigan. When his father Ed Sr. started this preacher's training academy," Donaldson confessed, "I was a bit jealous, because I wished I'd had thought of such a wonderful idea. What better way to prepare our men for service in the Lord's church then to start a Friday night and Saturday only school for African-American Christian men who have to go out and work during the week, provide for their families, and who also do not wish to be taught theology from an all W.A.S.P. perspective."

"Amen, brother, Amen," the collective audience exclaimed.

"Perhaps the single-most impressive fact about this young man of 29 years—heh, heh, you don't mind me telling your age, do you brother?'

I laughed and good-naturedly nodded my head yes.

"What impresses me most is his work with former drug abusers and alcoholics." He squinted his tiny eyes once again, straining to read Khalid's cue cards. " With a doctorate's in the duo specialties of substance abuse and marriage and family counseling, he has personally contributed to the sobriety of hundreds of alcoholics, heroine and crack addicts within inner-city Detroit."

A huge ex-con looking brother, wearing a short-sleeved muscle shirt and gold chain, who was seated on the last pew, led the standing ovation.

I looked at Doug and Eddie who were standing in front of their first row pew, bushy-eyed and awestruck over the spiritual icon the minister was describing, as if we weren't one in the same, as if I wasn't the same lanky little cat who used to blow spit bubbles through his older brother's curly A &W straws, or the same handy-man impaired painter who ruined Doug's youngest sons' bedroom, by applying a crooked and circularly designed finishing coat of blue paint over their father's perfect first layer.

The night was definitely looking up. I had completely forgotten about the earlier misfortunes of the day.

"I mean brothers, let me tell you," Donaldson practically shouted. Colossal beads of perspiration dripped down his temples. "I've never seen our sisters soooo excited about cooking for anyone, not for the homeless on Christmas, not for the state youth conference, not even for this old man," he exclaimed thumping his chest. "When Mildred and I celebrated our thirty-five years of service here at Kingshighway."

Still more amens and laughter.

This is going to be a piece of cake, I thought. Feeling quite at home, I leaned back on the pew and allowed my gaze to sweep over the entire audience, then over particular individuals one by one. I failed in trying to match my visual image of the photograph of James Powell to any of the masculine faces in the multitude.

"This young man is a successful author as well. His fourth book entitled, *Starting Over and Saving It For My Wife: A Christian Man's Guide to Preparing For Marriage to a Godly Woman in the New Millennium,* has been a number one best-seller in Christian bookstores across the nation, and has achieved phenomenal success as a top-ten best-seller in secular African-American bookstores."

"Go 'head brother!"

"Yeah, do yo' thang, brother, " anonymous voices lauded from the audience.

"He even has two local Christian radio programs, one an early Sunday morning Bible-based psychology talk show, that is on it's way to becoming nationally syndicated, and the other a Sunday afternoon sermon prepared especially for the sick, shut-in and incarcerated. He recently negotiated a deal with two Detroit cable stations, and the nationally syndicated National Gospel Network to have both Sunday morning worship services and his Wednesday night God's Warriors Bootcamp training televised."

Another incredible ovation.

I searched the crowd to spot Brother Khalid. If there were anyone in the audience that night who deserved a standing ovation and accolades of valor, determination, spirituality and strength, it was Yusef Khalid. Per usual, my right-hand was standing in the back, near the entrance of the auditorium, as if to protect me from any heckler or violent person who may enter the seminar late to cause a commotion. Some Muslim tendencies were just too hard for a brotha to shake.

Trained as a "soldier" in the Nation of Islam's nationally acclaimed throughout the black community Fruit of Islam program, Brother Khalid had served a number of years as one of the bodyguards of their most public leader, Louis Farrakhan.

Whenever I shared his life's story to audiences full of African-American men –without fail, it led to baptism; at least one soul being won over for Christ. I had definitely planned to share it with that fired up crowd—I just hoped he wouldn't mind.

"And, now without further ado, I present to you, Doctor, Brother Robert McGallister, Ph.D, minister of the Rosedale Park Church of Christ, author, therapist and evangelist . . . Brother Robert McGallister. . . . brothers! Robert McGallister!" Cecil Donaldson paternally embraced me, as I approached center stage. Eddie and Doug grabbed the podium, and walked it down three steps to the outskirts of the platform.

"**Testing**," I spoke loud and clearly though the mini microphone. Eddie gave me the thumbs up signal. "**We've co . . . me this fa . . . ar by faith, every . . . day**," I began to sing.

"Lea . . . nin' on the Lo..rd," the deep voices responded.

"**And, don't you know, that we are trustin,'**" I beckoned.

"Trustin' in his holy word."

"**No, no, nooo . . . he ne . . . ver . . .**"

"He's never failed me yet."

"Keep singin', ooooh, oooh, ooooh, ooooh, can't turn around, we've come this fa . . . ar by faith." We all sang together.

"**Now, just the other da . . . ay, I heard a man sa . . . ay, he didn't be . . . lieve in God's Word . . . But, I . . . I can surely say . . . that the Lord will make a wa..ay, be..cause he ne . . . ver failed me yet! And, that's why, we . . . 've . . .**"

"Come this far by faith."

"**Everyday, we're leanin'..**"

"Leanin', on the Lord."

"**And, don't you know that we are trustin'..**"

"Trustin' in his Holy Word."

"**Oh, noooo, nooo, he's never..**"

"Never failed me yet . . ."

I descended the three steps and paced up and down the middle aisle. **"Keep singin' brothers, oooh, oooh, oooh, oooh, oooh, oooh, can't turn a-ro-oun-d we' ve . . ."**

"Come this fa . . . ar by faith."

"Now, don't be dis—cour—a—ged, when troubles, are al—lll a—round. He'll re—lieve all your mis—er—y, all your troubles, all your grief and pain! And, that's why we've . . ."

"Come this fa—ar by faith."

"Everday . . ."

"Leanin' on the Lo—rd." We repeated the chorus and verses to one of my father's favorite hymns several more times, before I walked back onto the stage, and took a few sips of the nasty lukewarm water, Doug handed me.

"And don't you know, that we are. . . . Aaah, sing it like you mean it, church! I can feel the spirit up in here to-night.!"

"Amen!"

"Yes, sir!"

"Praise God!"

" I forgot to tell ya'll, that this brother can sing his heart out!" Donaldson shouted from the first pew.

"Amen! Amen!"

"Praise God!" I exclaimed. "If I have any kind of voice that's pleasing to anyone's ear at all, it's all due to the Al-mighty, Omnipresent, Omnipotent Jehovah God, who's pres-ence is definitely in this house tonight!"

"Amen!"

"Yes sir, brother!"

"We are a blessed people tonight church, I say, we are blessed, because, we are all here, over five-hundred black men strong! Black men who could be anywhere tonight, any-where at all, doing the things our local and national media and Hollywood has portrayed us as doing like drinkin', partyin', shootin', smokin' or snortin' dope, runnin' the numbers, cheatin' on our wives, beatin' our mistresses, jumpin' bail, smokin' weed, playin' street b-ball, robbin' liquor stores, carjackin', dodgin' bullets, eatin' barbecue, watermelon and chitlin's, Lord have mercy . . . and doing only God knows what!"

Wild applause. Some standing.

"Amen!"

" Tell it like it is, brother!"

"But, I thank Jehovah God Almighty . . . Praise Him! We're here! We're alive, we're well, and we're in the house of the Lord! Some of us church folk act all stiff-necked and tight-faced like we too good and holy and dignified to praise him, but David, in the long ago said I will bless the Lord continually; his praise shall ever be on my lips. And wasn't he, the first king of God's great nation Israel, the one who was so ecstatic, overwhelmed and overjoyed that God had delivered him from their enemy, that he stripped himself naked, much to the embarrassment and sheer mortification of his 'holier than thou' wife, and ran up and down the road, all over his village, announcing that God had delivered him!

Oh, I don't know if God's has delivered any of you brothas here tonight from your enemy of working for minimum wage, your enemy of alcohol, your enemy of drugs, your enemy of that other man's wife, your enemy of fornication, your enemy of that tongue so sharp and temper so out of control that no one, not even your wife man, can handle you! I don't know if God has delivered you from your enemies, but I stopped by here to tell you tonight, that he has delivered me from all of my enemies, even my adversary himself, Satan, the Devil. I don't know if he's delivered you tonight, brothers, but if he has, you and pardon the street expression, 'betta act like you know' up in here tonight!

No, I'm not suggesting you get buck wild up in here and

99

run up and down this center aisle in the buff like King David, but when you stand in the presence of God, in the house of God, among his mighty, mighty people, there ought to be a song on your lips! There ought to be a song! That is why you'll never see me step into anyone's pulpit, without leading God's people in a song. Oh, we've come this far by faith, brothers, leaning on the Lord. Hallelujah, and praise Almighty Jehovah!

"Thank you Jesus!"

"Amen!"

"Praise Jesus!"

" It is my only hope that you did not merely come to see me, his humble manservant, but you're here to share with me, what he has so graciously imparted unto me. I hope you're here tonight ready to get fed some spiritual nutrients and get motivated to do what it takes to become better, stronger soldiers on his battlefield. Tonight, I want to talk to you about the subject of my most recent written work. "

Eddie handed me a paperback copy of *Saving It*.

I held it up as if to unveil the final product for the first time. "I want to share with you my own personal struggles of keeping God's commandment to remain celibate until marriage. This is a decision I made four years ago, after I had my fill of pregnancy and STD scares. My celibacy after four years is still something I struggle with today. And, I tell you, my brothas . . . it just ain't been easy. However, it is God's will for us to not have sex outside of marriage—this is why I am so determined to find a godly wife ASAP!

For, I am just about ready to burn, and as the eloquent and dynamic Apostle Paul stated in his first letter to the Corinthians, chapter 7, the verse is 9, it is better to marry than to burn, as the New International Version renders it-burn with passion!"

Many men laughed, some applauded my courage to share my private feelings with a room full of strangers. "I wrote this book with the single Christian black man at the forefront of my mind. I wrote this book to encourage the single man not to settle for less in finding a good, God-fearing, Christian woman. I also wrote this book for the brother who is already married, and needs some direction on how to become a better husband in order to have a better wife, and for fathers who will be bringing up sons into the next sin-filled, wordly, sexually evolved millennium. I'm here to speak to you straight, with no chaser! No apologies! We're all men in here, aren't we? We've all sinned and fallen short of His glory, so I'm not going to insult you by treating these subjects while wearing kid's gloves."

"Go head, brotha!"

"Do yo' thang, brotha!"

"Tell the truth, now!"

"This is why I'm glad Brother Donaldson, here sort of uninvited the women folk. We have to treat them a little differently. We are to give them their proper respect, and well, some of the things I want to talk about in here tonight about my past and about some of your current sexual situations, are just not fitting for the ears of the weaker sex, and I say that from the context of biblical definition of the term, weaker sex."

"Go on, brotha!"

" And, I'm not here to reiterate what I've already confessed to my readers in the book —like my history as a frat dog during my college basketball playing days, when I earned more points in bed scoring with women, than I did on the actual courts—or like the time I woke up with such an incredibly wild hangover I couldn't remember the names of the two naked girls I was sandwiched between, nor where I had met them—or the time when I was too embarrassed to use my father's Blue Cross medical insurance coverage and opted to go to a cheap, second-rate clinic, only to receive bogus, accidentally switched lab tests results that stated I had genital herpes, when all I had was a case of ingrown hair bumps!"

I waited for the laughter to subside before I continued my serious oration.

" No, no, no, brothers. You can read about all my sin-filled faux-pas in the book. It's because of my forthright honesty and the frank nature of communicating, that I have been criticized throughout the Churches of Christ."

My eyes scanned the audience quickly for signs of James Powell's presence. I didn't see him, but I was quite sure he would be there soon, seeing that he was the sole elder of the Kingshighway congregation at the time.

"Leaders at my own congregation have blatantly opposed me, and have tried to tape my mouth shut," I candidly admitted to my newfound confidantes. I couldn't help but think of my own father who spearheaded the small movement of older congregation members to boycott my book because of its secular vernacular. "But, I'm stubborn when it comes to the cause of Christ. If sharing the many skeletons in my closet is going to help some young brother to keep his zipper up, until he's married, or help to keep some tempted man out of those streets, away from loose women and cheating on his wife, or if speaking in real terms about how hot hell is going to be from indulging in sex of any kind outside of marriage, if sharing all of this is going to stir up dissension and controversy amongst our brethren, then so be it!"

A third ovation. Many men were "woo, woo, wooing," like back in the days of Arsenio Hall late night television.

" Let the church be torn up, then!" I shouted. "It's time for us, good church folk to stop being so pretentious and just flat out fake, because everything, and I do mean everything that is out there in the world, is guess what?" I asked, cupping my right hand behind its corresponding ear for emphasis sake.

"Right up in here, brother!"

"That's right. Right in the Lord's church!" I heard Donaldson say.

"A. . . . men! A . . . men!" I exclaimed. "Everything that is out there, is right here. We need to stop pretending like we've never done anything wrong. We need to stop behaving like the Pharisees who criticized Jesus for working on the Sabbath and eating with tax collectors and whoremongers. Shoot, some of us would sleep straight through both worship services every Sunday if we weren't so worried about appearances, evade taxes if Uncle Sam's IRS wasn't so efficient and would sleep with a whore every opportunity we'd get, if we weren't so broke!"

I accepted the glass from Eddie again and gulped down some more water as I directed my attention back to the audience I noticed James Powell, wearing a white lab jacket, very similar to that of his wife's, sitting stiffly, frowning at me, with his left eyebrow raised through thick wire-rimmed glasses. A faint insecure voice from within me beckoned me to cool it, to take it down a notch or two, but the fiery, jubilant energy of the audience buoyed me to be myself and to keep the spirit high.

"If you're here tonight, and you want to read more about how the Lord has turned my life around, I encourage you to, after this seminar is completed here tonight, to see my brother Eddie Jr., here . . . Eddie, raise your hand, " I commanded. He did me one better.

He graciously stood up, nodded seriously and threw a brief wave into the air, before taking his seat. "See my brother Eddie, one of the deacons at our home congregation, or Brother Doug Harrison, a dear friend of ours, and fellow deacon too . . . see these brothers right in the back, out in the corridor, Brother Donaldson . . ." I asked unsure of where he wanted us to conduct our bookselling and signing business.

"Yes, son. It's been set up for you already. You're good to go," Donaldson smiled.

"Thanks. See either one of these two brothers for this book," I announced picking up *Saving It For My Wife* a second time. This book, in Christian bookstores and elsewhere has been selling for $25.95. But here, tonight, praise God, we're willing to bless you with it for a lowered price of $16.95, just because we're family," I laughed.

A few penny-pinching brothers applauded. However, I wasn't expecting an ovation for anything that has to do with a black man going into his wallet.

Eddie motioned to Doug, who held up the newly produced duo cassette audio package of the book.

"And for those of you who don't have time to read this three-hundred page autobiographical account, because of family, work and/or church and community related obligations, I just completed the voice-over for the book on audio-tape."

More applause and amens.

"Yes, yes, so if you're like me, and you enjoy listening to books, songs or sermons on tapes, this deal is for you. I know this is my material, but my brother here keeps track of all the pricing information Eddie, how much are you letting a duo-cassette package go for?"

" Only twenty-nine ninety-five," Eddie replied emphatically, as if the price was a steal. I watched James Powell's saucer-like eyes roll heavenward. He sat with his arms crossed, brooding, probably attempting to calculate what my total gross earnings would total in just that one night.

"Did you hear that, brothers?" I asked, sealing my sales pitch with a sincere smile. " The duo-cassette package of *Saving It* will only costs you twenty-nine ninety-five. We only brought about fifty books, because that's all we could get the publisher to front us for a weekend's journey. Also, if you're interested in any one, two or all of the three other books I've written in recent years, or any of the doctrinal debates I've conducted with leaders of other faiths, we have those available."

"The books are fifteen dollars," Eddie announced. " We only have a few left of each title, as well as the debate tapes. We do have my brother's recent series on committing spiritual adultery, squandering money, and addiction and recovery on tape. Each series of three tapes cost twenty dollars. A single tape is eight dollars," he announced as if he were reading a teleprompter for a promotional advertisement on television. "We accept cash, money orders, and all major credit cards. No personal checks please. And, you know why."

Raucous applause and laughter from the audience. That last ad-libbed comment always generated the same response everywhere we took our little act.

"I guess you all can see why my brother here, makes for a good traveling companion," I deadpanned. "On a more serious note, I would like to take the opportunity right now to thank the leadership of this congregation for inviting us here and allowing me the opportunity to stand where your dearly beloved minister, Brother Cecil Donaldson stands." I bowed in Donaldson's general direction.

A broad gold-toothed bedazzled grin spread across the aging minister's face.

"It's true, Brother Donaldson and his lovely wife Sister Mildred along with my parents Edward Sr. and Ethel go a long ways back. They all attended and met at our very own Southwestern Christian College in Terrell, Texas years and years ago."

"Watch it, son," Donaldson ad-libbed jokingly from the first pew.

"Brother Donaldson doesn't think I remember him from when our families used to visit each other when I was just a small boy. Some of you brothers here tonight, may recall such visitations. However, the most vivid memory I have of this brother, is his voracious, appetite!"

"A-men," many brothers from the audience sang. Some even applauded.

"Yes, sir-ree!" Donaldson yelled.

"I remember sitting around the dinner table with my brother and his two daughters Shirley and Jessica, and both sets of parents—how the women and the children always had to wait for the wives to fix their husband's plate. Well, I remember being about five or six years old, breaking into tears after watching Sister Donaldson clean the macaroni and cheese and fried chicken buckets from KFC out to fix her husband's plate. I remember crying so hard, creating such a fuss because I didn't think there would be enough food for me left, that my father, God bless him, had to drag my little rambunctious behind into the bathroom to give me the whoopin of all whoopins! Brother Donaldson, I just want to take this time out right now, to let you know that my butt is still sore from that beating—and it's because of you, I still eat like a horse to this day. Just ask those sisters cleaning up behind us downstairs right now, as we speak!"

I waited for the audience to finish yet another round of light-hearted laughter.

"I haven't gotten the opportunity to meet Brother James Powell, your elder in person yet. Earlier today, we spoke on the phone, and just before entering the auditorium I was privileged to meet and chat with his wife Emily, out in the corridor. I would like to thank Brother Powell, for extending the invitation for us to come here as well." I met eye contact with my future father-in-law. He grimaced and released a single nod of his head in my general direction. He didn't like me, which suited me just fine.

"To all the deacons at this growing, prosperous congregation, I thank you as well. As I often proclaim from my own pulpit in Detroit, a church just wouldn't be a church without good, supportive, hard-working deacons or servants, as the Bible calls them –to keep things in order. Rosedale Park currently has six deacons, several of whom as I stated earlier, travel with me as often as their busy work and family schedules will allow. My brother Eddie here, is a mechanical engineer and chief foreman of his shift for Ford Motor Company and Doug, seated right next to him is an engine inspector for Ford. Both have been married for years. Between the two of them, they are raising seven sons my nephews Eric and Edward III are 9 and 11, and Doug's children range in age from 2 through 10. Praise the Lord! It takes mighty strong, faithful and determined men to raise our church leaders of tomorrow."

"A-men, brother! A-men!"

107

Ace

"Last, but most certainly not least is my brother in the word, my mentor and best friend in the flesh, Brother Yusef Khalid," I outstretched my long arm toward the back of the auditorium.

The audience riveted its' collective attention to the entrance doors. Brother Khalid maintained his formal military stance, while looking straight ahead through his dark shades. Wearing neither a welcoming smile or a disapproving frown, his regal stance and serious demeanor did not provide a single clue as to the truthful narrative I would strategically and dramatically unfold to my listeners.

"I met this brother just about four years ago, when I first began my full-time work as the minister of the Rosedale Park congregation. It was a normal sunny summer's day in Detroit, with the temperature ranging in the high seventies."

Knowing laughter from the audience, in particularly, from the men who have probably visited our fair city during the summer months.

" I was braking at a traffic light on the corner of Seven Mile Road and Greenfield. Anyone who lives on the Northwest side of Detroit, or who is familiar with this area, knows that you can purchase some delicious, mouth-watering assorted fruits there from the Muslim brothers. Well—brothas, Brother Khalid was one of those brothers out there peddling fruit and selling the Nation of Islam's newspaper, *The Final Call*. One of the first things I noticed about this cat, after shooing him away from my car is the hungry look in his eyes. I'm not talking about a look of physical hunger. I'm talking about the look of spiritual starvation one who is outside of Christ carries around in his eyes, his stature, his demeanor—and his whole outlook on life. While driving away to go on about my day-to-day church business, I vowed to myself to get to know this brother.

I had seen him on that corner, day after day, month after cold, treacherous month, wearing that black trench coat, a white shirt and bow tie and dark glasses, much like he is sporting today still, beckoning drivers and passengers alike to patronize their businesses. But, I never paid any attention to him, until he walked over to my car to talk to me. You see, we often treat homeless people like that. You know, the same ones we drive pass everyday, standing on the corner, wearing tattered, smelly clothes, holding their frostbitten hands out, or wearing a 'will work for food sign.' We stop at a light, we look straight ahead. We're too afraid to rest our gaze upon them, because we don't want to see poverty's, and /or addiction's harsh realities in their eyes.

Their plight doesn't become relevant until someone we know and love becomes one of them.

Well, brothers, gentleman, my man, Khalid wasn't relevant until I looked into his eyes that day back in '95, and realized he was hungry. Hungry for the truth that lies only within Christ's word and his church.

Let me briefly share with you some of the harrowing, horrific and heroic events of this brother's life. His story is one that will encourage and inspire you. One that will send you home tonight, wondering, thinking, contemplating the value of your life as a black man in the approaching new millennium. What is your role in this life with which God has so

109

graciously blessed you? More than that, what are you going to do with those blessings?

Are you willing to reach back to help another brother become a soul winner for Christ, or are you willing to allow another brother go spiritually unfed? This is the story of young Joseph Anderson, known now as Yusef Khalid, model citizen, upright husband, father, friend, my personal business manager, carpenter, and most of all, soul-winner for Christ:

A former cocaine pusher and addict, and convicted murderer, Khalid was introduced to Elijah Muhammad's version of the Muslim religion, in the first year of a fifteen year stint in an Illinois correctional facility. Growing up dirt poor in a ramshackle two-bedroom apartment located in the infamous Cabrini-Green housing projects on the South-side of Chicago, Joseph Anderson was the ninth child born to a family of ten, raised by his single mother Josephine, a heroine addict and prostitute, who had no idea which pimp or john had fathered at least eight of her children.

Three of his older brothers had already been shipped away to prison before Joseph could complete grade school. His sisters had moved into a neighboring apartment with their gaggle of children fathered by several different men to set up their own whore houses by the time Joseph was twelve.

I surveyed the audience to determine if I had garnered their complete, undivided attention. The shocked looks some of them wore on their faces, including the disgusted expression James Powell and the fixated mummified gaze of Cecil Donaldson's countenance told me I had.

"Young Joseph dropped out of school at fifteen, after failing the eighth grade for two consecutive years, and began to run numbers and sell nickle and dime bags of marijuana throughout his subdivision and neighboring projects for a couple of prominent king drug pins. His new 'family' became so proud of his work, that within a year, he was peddling crystallized coke, before it became known as crack to his former junior high school buddies, and supplying his mother with all the heroine she needed to stay high. Initially, Joseph thought he could handle his dealings with the underworld, and even become more successful than his mentors because his nose was clean.

He vowed to himself that he would never become a cracked out junkie or heroine fiend like his family members and growing clientele.

However, the lure of getting high became too great of a temptation for him to deny. By the time he turned twenty-one, Joseph was a self-described, homeless burned-out junkie, whose own addicted, aging mother could no longer stand to have him steal from her. On warmer nights, he slept on the same streets he had eked out a miniscule living begging during the day. In the fall and winter months, he crashed in abandoned, rat-infested, apartments with no heat or windows to serve as barriers for the brutal Chicago winds.

He recalls many nights of praying to an unknown God to be put out of misery via being run over while crossing a busy intersection in a drunken stupor-or by being tracked down by his former employers from whom he had stolen money and dope."

I ignored the "Lord, have mercy's." and the "umph, umph, umphs," that served as the undercurrent backdrop to my explication.

Eddie grinned at me stupidly as if to congratulate me for dramatizing through my choice of words and physical gestures, the life of pain and utter degradation my friend had suffered. I tried to put his misplaced admiration out of mind, so I could concentrate on reaching the ultimate crescendo of this often played melody.

" But the bottom line was no one cared. No one cared that he was strung out. He was just another statistic. Thus, in keeping within the perimeters of being another young, African-American male who was an unemployed, homeless, junkie

– one rainy April afternoon, he broke into his mother's apartment, stole the only handgun she had to protect herself from her johns and drug-addicted children alike, and attempted to rob the liquor store whose Arab owners had even been so kind enough to give him a forty ounce bottle of Budweiser the previous Christmas.

These same people just weeks prior to the robbery found the generosity to give him a new cardboard box to sleep in and allowed him to locate it next to their dumpster which was filled with enough food-scraps to last him for a good portion of the spring. Yumm—mmy!

And, all because he had never stolen from them and his imposing stature kept all the other riffraff from coming into their store. He was their very own free bodyguard slash bum.

In the midst of the euphoric fog of a crack high, Joseph hadn't thought his plan through. He'd forgotten all about the noticeable surveillance cameras strategically placed throughout the store. To scare the customers, and to obtain the mere ninety dollars in the cash register faster, he squeezed the pistols handle and released three piercing shots into the air.

"Oh no!"

"Lord, No!"

"Great God, Almighty," came the startled, intense responses from the audience. I walked slowly down the center aisle, and stopped in the middle, halfway between the pulpit and to where Brother Khalid was standing.

Typically, I could detect him getting a bit squeamish when I reached this part of the account, but on that night, he appeared cool and detached. Through his dark shades I could see his hazel brown eyes staring through me, approvingly. I used my left arm to steady my right forearm, as I drew an imaginary pistol from my coat pocket and directed it to an imaginary cash register.

"The bullet from the last shot ricocheted off the cash register and lodged itself into the owner's wife's heart. Joseph trembled in fear and made a frantic dash toward the door, but not before reaching his sweaty hands into the till to retrieve the ninety dollars. Weak from hunger, and halfway wanting to be rescued from his pathetic life, he'd only reached two blocks away from the store when the police tracked him down and arrested him for armed robbery and murder.

After waiting several months in a holding pin in Cook County Jail, Joseph was shipped to Illinois State Penitentiary to serve a life sentence without the possibility of parole. Within weeks of settling into his newly incarcerated life, Joseph received word via the warden that his mother had died from a drug overdose. He wasn't allowed to attend the funeral, nor to share his grief with his brothers, sisters, nieces and nephews.

Soon afterwards, he started receiving correspondence from the largest mosque in Chicago, which had been successful in converting over half of the inmates on Joseph's floor, including his cellmate Husani Abdul.

Promises of self-employment, sobriety and status within the black Muslim community attracted Brother Khalid to the highly disciplined, respectable, clean-cut group of brothers who visited the prison bi-weekly to uplift the spirits of desperate, suicidal and/or violent inmates. Brother Khalid converted to the religion within weeks of studying with the brothers. By the time he'd reached his fifth anniversary in prison, he'd become a full-fledged minister, proselytizing to the truckloads of young African-American brothers who had entered his ranks.

By the time Joseph Anderson, who was renamed Yusef Khalid, by one of Elijah Muhammad's sons, had been incarcerated for a decade, he'd received his GED, a journeyman's carpentry license, and had successfully completed all the requirements through his Fruit of Islam training to pilot and facilitate a halfway house for formerly incarcerated black men who had converted over to the Muslim faith. Confident that

113

his hard work and credentials would speak for themselves, he petitioned the warden for an early parole hearing. His request was denied. He was told that he'd have to serve at least five additional years on his twenty-year sentence before he could even be considered as a candidate for parole. The longest five years of Brother Khalid's life was spent reading the *Holy Koran* ten times through, converting more prisoners, becoming the chief cafeteria supervisor, and gaining favor in the sight of Louis Farrakhan, who by then occasionally corresponded with him via letters, and collect phone calls.

Upon his release, the Nation actualized his dreams of being in charge of a halfway house for those ex-convicts whose initial sentences had not allowed them to be reintegrated into society. He also supervised Mosque #5's drug and alcohol rehabilitation program. I somehow managed to glean these incredible facts of this brother's life on that same street corner where we'd met.

Man, I remember rapping with this cat for hours, because despite the fact that we'd grown up in completely converse environments, and despite the fact that he was fifteen years my senior, (I know he doesn't look it), despite the fact that I had a father and he didn't, despite the fact that he had spent his early twenties being educated to the gruesome reality of life behind prison bars, while I had spent my early twenties receiving a college education, sleeping around with various women, and taking for granted that I would inherit my father's church-despite all of these differences-this brother and I shared something in common.

We were both new in the ministry. We had both taken vows of celibacy during critical times in our lives. Most of all, we were both committed to helping African-American men and women kick their drug habits.

Within weeks of my initial meeting with Brother Khalid, we both had invited each other to our respective places of worship. I knew that there was no way my congregation of

good ole' sincere Christian folk would understand if their flip-
pant young minister went carting over to a mosque, on a Sunday morning to sit amongst followers of Elijah Muhammad,
instead of preaching to them-no more than Brother Khalid's
brothers and sisters in the faith would understand why he
would be amongst the same good ole sincere Christian folk
who wouldn't lift a finger to help him when he was in prison.
Hello?"

" I know that's right!"

"Tell it like it is, brother!"

"Careful!"

"I had been preaching Jesus gradually, bit by bit to this
brother. He had a lot of questions, which I was more than
prepared to answer. You, as a soldier on the Lord's battlefield, as his elect, as his royal priests, as the Apostle Peter
states in his first epistle, you have to stand ready, be prepared to give an answer to any man about the hope that is in
you, through Christ Jesus our Lord.

You can't shove the good news down people's throat. You
have to spoon-feed it to them. All during these conversa-
tions, I could tell that the emptiness, the hunger in this brother's
eyes was being fed. According to him, it wasn't until I almost
lost my own pulpit, my primary livelihood, that he was fully
persuaded to become a Christian.

Through my visitations and free counseling services at
the Muslim owned and funded rehabilitation centers on the
west side of Detroit, I came to know many of Khalid's Islamic brethren. None of them treated me funny, but all of
them, every single last one of them, welcomed me and encouraged me to continue my efforts in helping heroine and
crack addicts recover. I was surprised when no one kicked
me out for distributing our own literature, or for preaching
Christ to the residents and staff. Now, can you imagine the
reverse ever being true with us Christian folk?

Would we willingly accept someone of another faith into

our midst to help our sick, our widowed, our elderly, our drug and alcohol addicted members-would we accept them, and even go as far as to allow them to introduce their faith to these people, and to treat these people as they deserve, as having mind's of their own, and having the free volition, with which the Lord has blessed us?

You all know the answer to that! A resounding and collective, no! I had been working this program for about six months before it became known to the leadership at my congregation. The program needed more funding to move to a larger facility in order to make more people well. So Brother Harrison here, my brother, Ed and Brother Riley, another good friend, minister and deacon from the church drew up a proposal, outlined and presented all the details to the elders during a typical leadership meeting.

Church, I'm embarrassed and downright outraged to tell you that our request for a measly five thousand dollars was denied. I call it measly, because our weekly offering at that time ranged anywhere from fifteen to twenty grand.

That five thousand dollars could have moved ten more homeless crack addicts off the street and into the comforts of a twelve-step, fully-staffed and professional clinic! But, since my newfound associates were these so-called, "by any means necessary," radical, "blue-eyed devil hating", "anti-Semitic," radical Muslims, our proposal was flat out rejected. But, let me tell you folks, God has the victory. He has the final say, A-men?"

"Yes, sir!"

"Tell the story, now brother. Tell it!"

"Between the three of us," I paused, signaling to Doug and Eddie, "five other generous donors from our congregation who were not diametrically opposed to our proposal, and with the assistance of fifty other churches of various denominations, we raised the five thousand dollars for the Muslim center, and another half million, to create and fund another facility on the Northwest side of Detroit, Interfaith, where myself and other health care professionals of various religious convictions donate our services free of charge several hours a week! Amen, and glory to Jehovah, our God!"

Brothers from the first pew to the last row in the balcony jumped to their feet, and applauded this effort for what seemed like an eternity. I took advantage of the natural break in my oratory to wipe the sweat from my brow with one of the expensive monogrammed handkerchiefs Pops gave me when they installed me as full-time minister. I motioned to Doug to hand me my water glass. I drank down the remainder of lukewarm fluid, and asked for more. I was just getting warmed up.

I hadn't even began to scratch the surface of the topic for the night, but if anything could get these men motivated for the Lord's work, I knew this testimony would.

" Once the plans for building the House That Love Built Interfaith Rehabilitation Center got underway, the elders at my church tried to sit me down. They said I had divided loyalties, that I'd forgotten my upbringing in the church; that I was allowing power, status and wealth to interfere with the true gospel of Christ.

Some lost soul, who will remain nameless, even gathered up a series of names from within the congregation, on some trumped up petition, to get me to tender my resignation. But, I refused. Each time I got up into the pulpit, every Sunday morning, and every Sunday evening, and each time I taught Bible class, or preached for our radio ministry, I prayed. I prayed long and hard, for the church-that we would become more like the one person-whose name is on this building and that one in Detroit. This is Christ's church, and we ought to act like it!"

"That's right!"

"Yes, sir! Speak the truth in love, brother!"

" Well, the final straw came, when one of the ministers

over at the AME church was about to retire. I had the pleasure of knowing this fine, older brother from our counseling work together at the Interfaith center. He was retiring from forty years of service at his congregation. His lovely wife asked me to be a surprise guest on his retirement program.

I readily agreed, because I had a lot of positive things to say on his behalf-he had had phenomenal success as a family and marriage counselor, and as a recovery therapist.

The program was to take place on a Friday night-thus, I had to get someone to substitute teach my open forum Bible class back at the church. Once the elders became privy to the reason behind my absence, they summonsed me to my own office!"

"Uh-oh!"

"Tell us, what happened next!"

"Go ahead, brother!"

"I tell you this part of the story out of love. I love the elders. My father, God bless him, serves as one of the elders-but they are very conservative and traditional. As I stated earlier, if we are to carry out the Lord's Great Commission, then we are to bring the church to the world.

Enough of this stiff-necked, hypocritical dogma that dictates with whom we are to affiliate and not to affiliate! It's time for the church to step into the new millennium.

These brothers, God bless them all, had a serious problem with me speaking on the program for the minister of the AME Church. Never mind the fact that I argued that I would not be preaching. Never mind the fact that I was not going to worship with them! Never mind the fact all the good and positive things this brother has done for the community at large. Never mind all that. They were going to have my job!

Brother Khalid, who had become my closest confidante, encouraged me to comply with the brethren, because they were my elders, one of whom being my own father.

I, however, being the stubborn, willful, person I am re-

118

jected sound counsel, and went and spoke on that "sinner's" program. I even had the nerve to get a standing ovation, much like the ones we've been witnessing tonight. When word got back to Pops and the others about how smoothly things had gone and that Brother Khalid and I had been invited back to speak to their youth about the dangers of drugs, the elders forbade me to preach for a month of Sundays, pending on the number of signatures they were gathering to sit me down for good.

While I was experiencing this turmoil in my life, Brother Khalid was facing his own drama. When he and a couple of the other brothers from the Nation blatantly began to use *The Holy Bible* as their primary text for classes on spiritual instruction, they were accused of committing transgression against the Muslim religion. When they tried to point out their newfound beliefs that the Bible has more merit than the Holy Koran, Khalid the 'so-called' ringleader of this trio was accused of allowing me to bewitch and brainwash him over to the white man's religion.

When the trio was summonsed by the Nation's local leadership, they were asked to recant their beliefs, or else they would have to face the consequences of being reported to the top brass themselves, and being cut-off from the Nation altogether. The other two brethren immediately recanted. Their entire families, moral code and livelihood, for that matter, had been ensconced in the black Muslim tradition.

But, Khalid. Oh . . . Brother Khalid decided to obey the gospel, within that very hour. He politely stood up, confessed the name of Jesus Christ, as being not only the Son of God, but the Messiah, and the savior of the church, turned in his letter of resignation as rehabilitation counselor of their Fruit of Islam operated program, and called me on the phone.

Within minutes, the deacons and I met him over at Rosedale Park, and baptized him. He's been a faithful member ever since, praise the Lord! Oh, praise Jehovah God, Almighty!"

———

Thunderous applause. Stomping ovation.

"Sure, he's made a few enemies along the way. Who hasn't? All godly men, according to the apostle Paul, will at some point in their lives suffer persecution. I suffered persecution for befriending the Muslims. This former Muslim has suffered persecution for befriending me. More hardship, than any one of us is ordinarily willing to bear. You see his wife, right now, God bless her, his dear wife Fatima, has just given birth to his fourth child, a son. This would ordinarily be a joyous time in a father's life. However, since Fatima and all of her family are Muslim, and Brother Khalid is now a Christian, there is inner-turmoil within his own household.

That's what I'm here to talk to you about tonight fellas-seeking and finding a godly woman. It does no one any good to be unequally yoked. But, it comes right down to it—he, this man Yusef Khalid, our brother in Christ wouldn't trade any of the hardship he has suffered in his life, for the world. Who amongst us can say the same? The most amazing aspect of this whole ordeal is that he has made amends with his former Muslim leaders.

They've forgiven him, even Farrakhan himself. No one has come gunning down for him, as some had feared might happen. But, as for me, there are still some supposed Christian leaders within this body, indeed within my very own congregation who can't see beyond my apparent betrayal for affiliating myself with these so called believers of false doctrine, that they can barely speak to me, much more forgive me.

Enough said about my controversial background and the inner-political baggage I carry. It's time for me to really do some teaching up in here tonight, so you can go home and tell all the women folk, that I've earned my keep, and deserve to go to my hotel room to stretch out and relax after my very full and hectic day and delicious meal."

That's Pops For Ya

I didn't hear the phone ringing a few hours later, as I laid my body limp from exhaustion, fast asleep in a queen-sized bed next to my snoring brother. He and Doug pitched another hissy fit when Brother Donaldson dropped us off at the Holiday Inn for the night only to discover that he had only reserved one double room for me to stay for the three-night weekend. At first, everyone remained calm. Penny-grubbing Eddie thought fast on his feet and suggested that we'd use some of the profits from my book and tape ministry to spring for four separate rooms.

I didn't mind, because not only had we sold completely out of the book and audio versions of *Saving It*, we also ran out of each one of my three tape series twenty minutes into the sale.

Although Donaldson apologized profusely and offered to allow two of us to go back to his house to sleep in his spare room, we didn't want to put him out of his way. We all begrudgingly decided to share one double room the first night and to book four separate single rooms for the remaining two nights of the gospel meeting. Doug and Brother Khalid had flipped a coin to determine who would sleep in the other queen. Brother Khalid lost, so he ended up spending a restless night on the hard floor wrapped in the covers from Doug's bed.

121

"Ma, is that you?" I heard Eddie groggily ask the phone after we'd slept through its piercing first rings.

I propped myself up on my elbows and squinted to read the digital alarm clock located on the nightstand just to my right. It read 2:30 am.

"Slow down, Ma. Is everything okay? Wh . . . at? He what . . . Lord have mercy! Is it serious? Where is he?" I elbowed him to tell me what had happened.

"It's Pops. He had a mild stroke," Eddie explained frantically. "He's at Grace. . . . . Ma said he was talking a little when she left . . . he doesn't want you to come home, Bob."

I snatched the phone from Eddie and darted up to pace the floor as I usually do when I'm upset, angry or confused. My father had been the picture of health even after retiring from the ministry a few years earlier at the age of sixty. At almost sixty-five, Pops still arose at 7:00 am every other morning, to walk and jog three miles around the high school track located one mile away from the home in which I had grown up.

Although I knew my parents were aging as evident in Ma' s slower gate, near-sighted vision and intermittent forgetfulness, as well as in Pops' tendency to misplace miniscule items and his increasing cantankerousness, I had not envisioned either one of them becoming ill to the extent that they would have to be hospitalized. Little did I know, this slight decline in Pops' health was a precursor to a condition of a much larger magnitude.

"Ma, tell me what happened." I spoke abruptly, disregarding the usual initial conversational preliminaries.

"Bobby, I didn't want your brother to wake you up. You need to get some rest. You have a long weekend ahead of you . . ."

"Ma, tell me what happened with Pops."

"Bobby, he made me promise to get you to stay down there. Cecil has been trying to get you down to Kingshighway to preach for years. He and your Pops and I go way back. You can't disappoint either one of them."

"Ma, Pops is sitting in the hospital in pain, recovering from the worst scare of his life and you tell me that he doesn't want me on the next thing flying out of here. No disrespect, Ma . . . but I can't listen to you guys on this one. Your judgment is foul. I'm comin' home."

"Bob, maybe Ma is right. I'll fly back first thing in the morning. You should stay here."

"Naw man, I'm not letting my father die this weekend. . . . you must be outta your mind!"

By this time, my raised voice had more than stirred Doug and Brother Khalid. Through my frustration and grief, I managed to overhear them speaking in hushed tones about getting me to calm down.

" He's not going to die, Bobby . . . listen to me. I'm your mother. I wouldn't lie to you."

"Well, Ma, so far you've managed to evade the issue. How bad off is he, really? What really happened?"

"We we're um, lying um, down on the sofa bed in the family room, at around 10:30 tonight," she spoke nervously, trying not to fill me in on too many details of their love life. From the sound of her voice, I could infer that I should not ask too many more questions about what they had been doing prior to the onset of the stroke.

My parents had always been intimate and openly affectionate towards one another. I hoped for the same type of bond in my own marriage. "Then, uh, out of nowhere, Ed started complaining about his arm. He said he didn't have any feeling in it. It had gone limp. I tried massaging it and applying heat to it, but nothing seemed to work. Then he started drooling like a baby out of the left corner of his mouth."

"That must have been scary for you, Ma. Are you alright?"

"I'm a little tired, but I'm fine honey. Honestly. Your Pops will be okay. The first thing he said after they put him on the

EMS, is for me not to call you. He was afraid that you would overreact and come home."

"**OVERREACT!**" I yelled. "**OVERREACT!** Pops had a stroke, Ma. He had to ride on an ambulance for the first time in his life. He is in the hospital. His sons are over five-hundred miles away . . . like I said a few seconds ago, I'll be home on the first flight out. Believe me."

"Let me have the phone, Bob." Eddie stated calmly. I shook my head and tightened my grip on the receiver. I had successfully through lots of prayer and guidance from the Holy Spirit counseled literally hundreds of people about sickness, death and dying amongst treasured loved ones, yet I'd always taken my father's superior health for granted.

Ours had been a tormented, difficult relationship, especially since I had taken over his ministry full-time. Somehow, he couldn't see beyond me being the formerly mischievous, womanizing son who had not appeared to take the gospel and salvation seriously until my mid-twenties. Because of this, he always obligatorily kept his proverbial foot on my neck, which manifested itself in my not being able to make a firm decision on a church matter without contending with his contrary, outspoken verbal opinions and emotional insults.

Though I considered myself completely independent and self-sufficient at twenty-nine, I was still the son of a pulpit legend throughout the brotherhood of the Churches of Christ. As the lowly minister, I still had to consult and defer to the judgment of the more learned, more seasoned elders, my father, being the kingpin of sorts.

Moreover, I resided in the two-bedroom, newly remodeled upon my insistence, parsonage, which was adjacent to the church. My parents had lived there as newlyweds. By the time they had me, they'd become owners of the home, that Ma, as a widow still lives in today.

"Bob, let me have the phone. You thinkin' crazy. There are a lot of people who wanna hear you speak tomorrow, Saturday and Sunday. You can't disappoint all those folk." Eddie spoke calmly as if he was trying to subdue a savage beast.

"Is that your brother asking to speak with me?'

"Yes, ma'am, but I'm not done asking . . ."

"Bobby, I've told you everything. Your Pops will be fine. To prove it to you, I'll have him call you the first thing in the morning. You boys need to get some rest. I'm sure you've had a long day. Now, put Junior on the phone so I can let him holler at Sheila and the boys. They've been with me in the family waiting room all night."

When my mother gets that determined, bossy, maternal tone in her voice, there is absolutely nothing neither Eddie nor I can do to assuage it. I reluctantly handed my brother the receiver, but not before I could tell Ma I loved her.

Even though pangs of guilt consumed me for not having spoken the same words to Pops within the previous several years, it was Eddie, the son he loved, the son whom had nothing to feel remorseful about pertaining to his relationship with Pops, it was Eddie who wiped away free-flowing tears from his eyes.

As he took the receiver, he shot me a how-could-you-not-be-torn-up-about-this-to-the-point-of-tears-look. I read his mind, and shrugged my shoulders as if to say, "I never cry."

When discussing the same subject with Brother Khalid on several occasions, he suggested that too many years of counseling the depressed, abused, drug-addicted and emotionally downtrodden had left me desensitized to tears and crying. Subconsciously, I knew he was right. My eyelids had not produced one solitary tear since I sprang my ankle and tore several ligaments playing street basketball, on the dormitory courts back when I was eighteen, when I was a freshman at Michigan State, striving to perfect my skills enough to garner the attention of the head coach to move me off the bench to the starting lineup, a feat I finally got to accomplish during the second trimester of my sophomore year. Then, I had wanted to wail like a colicky infant, but my pride and recollections of Pops scornfully teasing me when I was eleven years old, and we had to put or nine year old lab, King to sleep, prevented me from noticeably crying aloud for help. Instead, I foolishly exacerbated the jolting throbs by continuing to perform layouts and dunks on every white or black brother alike on the court that night.

Love Offering

I had completely forgotten about James and Emily Powell's breathtakingly attractive daughter, until Brother Donaldson escorted Eddie and me up into the pulpit the following evening. After Ma called the hotel room that morning at 9:30 to report to us that Pops had recovered enough of his strength to offer me some last minute pointers on how to win over the Kingshighway congregation, I knew that he would be back to his old unbearable self in no time.

"Now, son, listen up. I am your father," he annouced as was his custom before going into his whole paternalistic spiel. His speech was slightly slurred. I tried to envision his visage being contorted because of his medical condition, but the thought was just too much for me to bear. I couldn't imagine him appearing so utterly helpless and vulnerable.

"Yes, sir," I replied grinning from ear to ear, while nonetheless trying to conceal the joy in my spirit over his rapid recovery.

"When you get into Cecil's pulpit, I want you to preach to those folks down there like you've never preached before. Those are some Bible-totin', scripture quotin' folks down in that area, son. You get up there, and you preach the true gospel."

Instead of taking that statement as in insult, as I would have normally done, I bit my tongue. Who wanted to ruffle

127

the feathers of a sixty-five year old, ornery man who had just recovered from such a life-threatening scare?

"I mean, all that extra dramatic stuff you throw in may work well up here for these young folk, but what I can remember about that congregation is that it's full of old folk, like your Ma and me."

"Who you callin' old?" I heard Ma who was eight years Pop's junior ask joyfully from the background.

On the contrary, Pops, I wanted to say. Many of the brethren in last night's audience were under fifty, but once again, I held my peace.

"And, another thing . . ."

"Now, now, Ed. Don't wear yourself out . . . you just had a stroke . . ."

"And, I told that ole' devil what he could do with that stroke, baby," Pops laughed. It was amazing how his voice could make the effortless transition from speaking coldly and firmly to me, to speaking all sugar and spice to Ma, "and another thing, you still with me, son?"

"Yes, sir."

" I don't think you should accept the love offering they will probably collect for you on Sunday."

"Beg your pardon?" I asked growing more impatient by the minute.

"Because . . . I'm sure, if I know you and Eddie . . . you probably made a killin' from last night's book and tape sales. Now, you don't have to tell me how much, but you don't want to appear to be overly greedy . . . after filthy lucre."

"That's a messed up thing to say Pops. Real messed up. I know you're doing fine now. I'll give Brother Donaldson your regards. Now, here's Eddie."

"Son, I didn't mean to . . ."

"You did, Pops. You always mean to. I love you anyway." There, I'd said it. Now, my conscience would be clear.

Easy On The Eyes

As Brother Donaldson made several important church announcements and recapitulated the highlights of my seminar from the night before, Eddie and I sat next to each other on a small cushionless bench off to the far right side of the pulpit. I sat upright with one leg crossed atop of the other, straightening my tie, and using the maroon silk handkerchief that matched my three piece, three-quarter length tailored suit jacket to wipe the sweat from my brow.

"Hey, baby bro..looks like you got a full house tonight. Standing room only," Eddie whispered. But, it was too late, he wouldn't have my attention to engage me in our usual pre-oratorical banter tonight. I wasn't listening. *I'd spotted her.*

She was sitting in the second row, rather close to her father. Emily was nowhere to be seen. A twenty-something, dark complexioned short-haired woman sat to her left, looking up at me, as if I was God incarnate, or even lustfully worse, Denzel Washington.

Every few seconds, the young woman nudged Elisabeth, winked at me and giggled. Of course, I'd only noticed this out of my peripheral vision. Within seconds, my eyes were locked into Elisabeth's.

Hers were of a soft hazel/chestnut hue; brighter than I expected, covered with a pinkish eye-shadow. Those eyes.

129

Those soft, sexy, bedroom eyes. They matched that hair-that free-flowing, soft luscious light brown hair, with golden highlights. That picture in the directory, didn't do her justice!

I was in the middle of imagining the two of us rolling around butt naked on the floor of my office her long sandy brown locks securely wrapped behind my back, until Eddie nudged me and began whispering quietly out of the side of his mouth.

"Bob, Bob, where you at, chief? He's about to call me up to do the scripture and the opening prayer . . . I need to know the text."

Elisabeth's angelic eyes surveyed the length of my body, from my size 13, bubble-toed Stacy Adams to my long legs, to my extended torso, to my lips, to my eyes, then back down again. Since I had grown quite accustomed to being the object of other human beings' gazes, her staring didn't thwart me or make me feel uncomfortable in the least bit. As a matter of fact, I became even more conscious of my every movement, just to keep her fixated.

"Bob, man, Bob . . . the scripture?"

She wasn't smiling. I figured she was too deep in thought. She couldn't have been as mesmerized with me as I was of her. That just wasn't humanly possible. She had to have been the finest thing God ever created, and I had been around, I mean *really around* some fine sisters for some thirty years.

Brother Khalid was the one to first get my attention when he approached me to attach the mini-microphone to my lapel. Brother Donaldson was still rambling on, apparently still singing my praises about the bang up job I had done from the night before.

"Where's your mind, Little Brother?" Brother Khalid's deep voice whispered as he wrestled with the tiny electronic device. When I failed to respond, he allowed his eyes to follow mine, right into Elisabeth's.

130

"Who's she?" Eddie asked, somewhat transfixed himself. "Brother Powell's daughter. We were introduced outside," Brother Khalid announced, still trying to situate the microphone. "Why didn't you tell me?" I asked, still looking in her general direction. James Powell sat stiffly, with his arms folded against his chest, glaring at me, as if he read my mind about rolling around with his baby girl on the floor. "When do you suppose I could have done that? Didn't know you were interested." He squatted down in between the two of us, and we huddled together. I'm sure it appeared to the audience, that Brother Khalid was debriefing us on our father's condition, which by then Brother Donaldson had started to explain to his congregation.

"Find out, everything, " I instructed Brother Khalid, slightly slapping him on the back and giving him eye contact so that he could ascertain just how serious I was.

He nodded, before inconspicuously disappearing from our presence.

"Man, she looks young. Sixteen or seventeen," Eddie pointed out, more amused than concerned about me possibly robbing the cradle.

"Yeah, I know," I replied worriedly, trying to regain my composure.

"Man, she is definitely fine. Real fine for a brotha such as myself, if I were still available. Looks mostly white to me. Check out how she's looking down your throat. She wants you man, I can tell. Man, some guys have all the luck. Too bad you're celibate."

My brother's last statement slapped me back into reality. What was I doing? Lusting after some little white-looking rich girl like that, moments before I was scheduled to deliver God's engrafted word? I redirected my attention back to Cecil Donaldson, who was in the middle of introducing Eddie to read the scripture.

131

"Bob, you still need to tell me the scripture for tonight's lesson."

"Read Genesis Chapter 29, verses 13-29." I whispered, with my eyes closed. I just needed a moment to gather my thoughts, and to refocus my concentration on the message I felt compelled to deliver.

"But, I thought you were going to go with a New Testament passage. Pops warned you about how tough they are here on church doctrine."

I turned towards him and looked him directly in the eyes, "Eddie, whose ministry is this, mine's or Pop's?"

He bit down on his bottom lip, rolled his eyes heavenward and nodded reflectively.

"The Lord placed a new message on my heart tonight. I have to deliver it."

"Bet. Then, I know we'll be in for a real treat."

I watched him stroll confidently to the podium to read a portion of the Old Testament love story of Jacob and Rachel. The mixture of the inflection of his voice injected at the appropriate places in the text, along with the excited energy emitted from the anticipatory congregation, provided me with more than enough fervor to do what I had come there to do; preach, and preach well.

"Let us beseech our Heavenly Father to approach his throne of grace for a word of prayer," are always more or less the first words I utter whenever I approach the pulpit. I waited for the audience to collectively bow its head, before proceeding. "All heads are bowed, as we concentrate on our words of thanksgiving, praise, and humility. Our Father, who art in Heaven, Holy and Reverend is your name . . ." Even though the passage of time has erased the lyrical quality of my words verbatim that night, I do recall requesting prayer for my beloved earthly father in Detroit.

By the time I ended my purposely super-eloquent spiel, I felt a bit guilty for trying to impress a mere earthly being whom I had yet to meet, instead of sincerely concentrating on my spiritual Father.

The fleeting remorse I felt did not prevent me however, from pulling out all of the stops to keep Elisabeth's one hundred percent undivided attention. That prayer apparently evoked the most heartfelt and anguishing of human emotions, because after I concluded it through the mighty name of Jesus Christ, our precious Lord and merciful Savior, I stood erectly with my head still dramatically bowed, listening to a few women sniffle and blow their noses into dainty handkerchiefs and tissues.

Even as I waited for Doug and Brother Khalid to remove the cumbersome podium, I still had no clue as to the portion of God's knowledge from his Holy Word I was going to impart. The Spirit Himself would have to guide me, not unlike it had numerous of other times, to give me the right words to speak.

By then, I had long since abandoned the traditional three-point outline, my father, as the founder and director of the Christian Men's Leadership Academy and several other more conservative elders of the church, had shoved down the up and coming younger ministers' throats.

It didn't thrill me to feel Pops' anguishing vibes of disgusts and disappointment, as he used to sit perfectly still, stone-faced in the first pew, to critique everything from my as he called it, "overly-dramatic delivery", to my lack of interjecting enough New Testament scriptures, to my "blatant disrespect of the tradition of extending a hymn of invitation" to the congregation. Though none of this made me feel love and acceptance as his son, I had to be my own man, do things in the manner God led me to do them.

"When my Savior calls, I will an . . . swer. When, he calls for me, I will he . . . ar. When my Savior calls, I will an . . . swer. I'll be some . . . where list..nin' for my name." The congregation joined in as I led them through two more verses and several

rounds of the course to my opening hymn. For me, the prayer, is always followed by the hymn. Donaldson had verbally pegged me as one of "them singin' preachers". I couldn't disappoint.

"Yes sir, yes sir!" I exclaimed, after the song had ended. I descended the four or five step pulpit, so I could be closer to the audience. Usually, I would walk down the center aisle and stop right around the seventh or eighth row. However, since I didn't want Elisabeth out of my eyesight for more than one second, I took my temporary stance at the second row. I was standing so close to James Powell, that if he decided to let out a loud, wet sneeze, my new suit would have suffered the repercussions.

"The Spirit of the Almighty God is definitely in this house tonight!"

"Yes sir, brother, Amen!"

"God is good, I tell you, and he's good all the time!"

I proceeded through the custom of thanking Cecil Donaldson, James Powell and the leadership of the Kingshighway congregation for inviting me to conduct Friday night's seminar. Then, I confided in them the general horrific events of the preceding day. Some people politely laughed when I made light of Doug's car breaking down, Brother Khalid's leaving the tickets, and Brother Powell giving me a firm tongue lashing on the phone.

I placed my hand on his shoulder, as I spoke of him.

"Brother Powell, I must say it's very nice to finally put a face to the man who was as tough on me as my own old man." More polite laughter from the audience. "Just let me shake your hand, sir."

A slow grimace which turned itself into a definite smile, curled his lips. There was no way a man of that much prominence within the church would have rejected me, the young guest minister from out of town. He accepted my hand, looked me squarely in the eye, and nodded as if to say, "You're out of the doghouse for now."

Elisabeth's already pinkish cheeks became more flushed and rosy, the longer I stood within two feet of her. Every time I inhaled, I smelled a soft, seductive strawberry fragrance, which I was sure belonged to her. Her eyes never left me. I chalked up her lack of smiling and participating in the light jovial ice-breaking banter to the fact that she was in a state of complete shock for finally having laid eyes on, according to her mother Emily, the man of her dreams.

Throughout my rendering of the entire 29th chapter of the King James Version of the book of Genesis and throughout my discourse and exegesis of the text, I noticed the woman beside her, nudging her, she only responding with a nod, holding the thin, glossy lips that matched the natural color of her cheeks ajar.

Some sixty minutes later, I brought my message about how hard we have to work sometimes to get what we want to an end. I felt satisfied with the emphasis I placed on the one scripture I highlighted from the entire chapter, verse 20, which reads, *"And Jacob served seven years for Rachel, and they seemed unto him but a few days, for the love he had to her."* I tied this passage into *"The Depths of God's Love,"* the overall theme of the three-day gospel meeting.

"I liken Jacob's love for Rachel, somewhat to the love God feels for us. Notice I used the word somewhat, church, because Rachel, as the Bible tells us in verse17, Rachel, ah, Rachel, was lovely both in form," I paused and used my hands to imaginatively outline the shape of a woman with a nice figure.

When some men in the audience yelled "amen", from the back of the audience, and some women giggled, I knew I had succinctly made my point. " . . . and beautiful. She was easy on the eyes, church! This woman was fine!"

I shot a quick look over to Elisabeth, who was now blushing relentlessly. James Powell glared at me, but I didn't care. I wanted Elisabeth to know that I had every intention on meeting her right after the benediction prayer.

"However . . . her sister Leah, poor Leah, the Bible says in the same verse, that Leah was tender eyed. The NIV renders it 'weak eyed' . . . I think we get the point here church, Leah was ugly!"

Raucous laughter and applause from the audience.

"Wait a minute, church. Hold it! Don't miss my point here . . . Rachel was beautiful. Fine, shapely, of good form. Leah was ugly. Jacob was willing to work for Rachel because she was poetry in motion for him, she was easy on the eyes . . . but church, if we took a long hard look at our lives, and the miry muck of sin which we revert back to from time to time . . . He-llo, now it done got quiet up in here!" I exclaimed.

I strutted up and down the middle aisle, glad that I didn't have to maneuver some long microphone cord out of my way. "I say, my, my, it's gotten awfully quiet. When God looks at us church, do you think he sees Rachel or Leah? A minute ago I said that Jacob's love for Rachel is somewhat likened unto the Almighty God's love for us, right? Right? My, my, where are the amens, now?"

"You go on and preach, bro!" Eddie exclaimed from the front row. Several more people joined in with him to encourage me to finish my point.

"Anybody can love something or someone who is beautiful, of good form, easy on the eyes, but only our Father in Heaven, Jehovah God, Lord of Hosts, can love a Leah. Like Leah, we're weak . . . we may look good outwardly. This audience is a good-looking audience. One of the better-looking audiences I have ever seen . . . just don't let that leak out to the folks at home up at Rosedale Park. We're weak, I say. Weak willed. Weak-minded. Weak –kneed, cowardly, liars, fornicators, adulterers, thrill-seekers, lascivious, covet-ous, pious, religified, all of those things, and much more. We're weak, weak, weak, weak! We're weak, most of all, I say, weak spiritually!

It's no doubt that Jacob loved Rachel, for we read in verses 22 through 28, that Jacob's oily, slick rascal of a father-in-law tricked him. Tricked him into sleeping with Leah. Upon the next morning, Jacob confronted Laban to ask him why he had deceived him in such a manner. After all, he had just put in seven years of hard labor working for his lovely intended, when in exchange all he got was weak-eyed, ole' ugly Leah. It's not our custom, Laban said for the youngest daughter to marry first, you can have Rachel son, but only in exchange for marrying Leah, the oldest, plus seven more years of work-ing for me.

Verse 28, reads, '*And Jacob did so,*' if I may interject, he did so, willingly, because Rachel was beautiful and he loved her. If you don't believe me, watch verse 20. It reads, *Jacob lay with Rachel also, and he loved Rachel more than Leah. And he worked for another seven years.*' Now, you may say, that's some kind of love. But, I'm here to tell you this night, Kingshighway, that God loves us, not because we are beau-tiful.

David, in one of the most beautifully woven psalms, ar-ticulated how we appear to God. He said that all of our righ-teousness, are but filthy rags before the sight of God. There's nothing we can do to appear beautiful before him. He, un-like Jacob, wouldn't choose one over the other.

For in Romans chapter two, the verse is eleven, the Bible tells us that God is no respector of persons. He doesn't care if we are young, old, black, or white, physically beautiful or hard on the eyes, church. He loves us in a capacity that reaches much further beyond Jacob's capacity to love Rachel. He loves us, because He is love. As I come to a close to-night, brothers and sisters, I have a confession to make."

All eyes were on me, as the audience awaited for me to get up close and personal. I handed my leather bonded *Dickson's Analytical Study Bible* to Doug, who was sitting on the front row, holding my burgundy trench-coat, and a glass of water. I reached for the water, and swallowed a few hearty gulps. Brother Khalid was standing at the double entrance doors of the auditorium, arms folded across his chest, wearing his usual dark glasses. He signaled to me that I had preached exactly for one hour. I nodded.

"My confession tonight brothers and sisters is, I too, probably, no not probably, definitely would have chosen Rachel to love over Leah. I mean, I would like to think that I am a little more evolved than going after the fairest woman of them all, but quite frankly . . . I'm not. If you look closely at yourselves, your lives, you will see too that, you are a respector of persons. You too, want to be with someone who looks good to you, feels good to you, smells good to you, makes you happy, etcetera. That's what makes us carnal. We're flesh and blood.

However, as the apostle John said, God is Spirit. He looks beyond our faults and sees our needs. We're not going to sing a traditional congregational hymn of invitation, instead I would like for you to take a few moments quietly, to go inside yourselves and examine your heart, your soul. Is it right with the Almighty God? Are you taking advantage of the depths of His love for you? Are you failing to walk worthy in the vocation in which you were called?

Are you a member of Christ's glorious body, his church, but you have strayed away perhaps by not attending church services, avoiding the fellowship with saints, and failing to study His holy and divine word? Or, perhaps you have sinned in a public fashion, therefore bringing shame upon the collective body and reaping condemnation to your soul?

If you're not a member of this glorious body, the Church of Christ, please allow me to tell you the facts of the magnificent gospel of our Lord and Savior Jesus Christ. The phenomenal facts of the gospel are basically summarized by the Apostle Paul in the fifteenth chapter of the first epistle to the Church at Corinth."

For emphasis sake, I called upon James Powell to utter into our hearing verses three and four of that chapter. As he read, I repeated each set of three or four words after him to reiterate the good news of the New Testament Church. Then, I proceeded to quote the plan of salvation book chapter and verse, using Romans 10:14, Hebrews 11:6, Acts 17:30, Romans 10:10, Acts 2:28, and Ephesians 4:5 for the steps of hearing, believing, repenting, confessing and being baptized, respectively.

I implored wayward congregants and non-members alike to give me their hand and God their hearts, as they proceeded to walk toward the first three pews. Despite the fact, that I specifically requested not to sing an invitational hymn, because I wanted everyone to concentrate and reflect on the moment quietly, a teen-aged young man from the first pew, stood up and walked over to the center of the aisle, right next to me and began a feeble attempt to sing "Just As I Am." I squelched my indignation and walked over to shake Cecil Donaldson's hand.

Instead of accepting my hand, he wrapped his thick arms around me, and gave me a big bear hug, and a hearty pat on the back.

"Brother Powell's nephew up there singing. He got the signal from his uncle," Donaldson informed me discreetly, before Doug rose to help me slide into my coat. I drank the remaining water he offered me and sat down. He slapped me on the back, and Eddie shook my hand. I turned around to catch another glimpse of Elisabeth, since I was now seated on the only row in front of hers. Much to my chagrin, she was gone. That totally blew my mind, and wrecked my concentration for the rest of the night. I elbowed Eddie, but he only shrugged. I looked back again to see if I could read the expression on Brother Khalid's face, but he was gone too. *Good*, I thought. *Maybe, he's out hooking things up for me now.*

Nineteen

The next hour and a half was torture. Not only did Brother Donaldson go on for at least twenty minutes singing my praises but he called me back up to the pulpit, to pitch my books and tapes. I quickly and apologetically explained to the audience that since we had had such success the night before, we were temporarily out of the tape series and the *Saving It* book. However, we still had about twenty copies of the book's audio set, along with several videos for sale. Brother Khalid, my personal assistant, had already contacted our church secretary Sister Calloway to overnight express mail some more merchandise that would be there in time for the next night's meeting, I explained.

Brother Donaldson then beckoned me along with the church's wholehearted encouragement to lead the congregation in at least one other hymn, because I was a true singer with range varying from tenor to baritone. Quite naturally, I obliged. I've never been one to back down from an invitation to sing, preach or teach.

All during the hymn, I kept searching the auditorium for Elisabeth and Brother Khalid. I didn't see either one of them. Halfway through the song, I noticed that Brother Powell had left too. What was going on? Was he out their balling Brother Khalid out for interrogating his precious daughter on my behalf? And, what had happened to the short little dark-skinned

---

141

sister who sat next to Elisabeth? Were they good friends, or was she one of Elisabeth's fans? All pretty girls have other female admirers, who deny being envious. Maybe this girl was only close to Elisabeth because she was fine and loaded.

"Okay, Brother Khalid. Spill it man," I ordered as soon as he opened the door to the hotel room. I couldn't believe how this one tall, slender pale-faced, yet gorgeous woman could truly make me forget about all of the wrinkled up slips of paper and business cards, other attractive, God-fearing, more my age single-women had handed me, while I met and greeted every person in the building out in the corridor.

Doug, out of frustration of not getting his own room, decided to take Brother Donaldson up on the offer he had made to sleep in his extra bedroom, while one of the older deacons and his matronly wife had taken my brother home with them.

"Man, can we get in the door good first?" Brother Khalid laughed, rushing over to his garment bag to cram his belongings inside. Eddie, for some reason, didn't seem to put up a fuss about my suggestion that Brother Khalid was entitled to the only other room available in the entire hotel for the remainder of the weekend. Although there was no love lost between the two of them, I guess he figured that since his career as an engineer and his role as a husband and father of two sons vastly approaching adolescence prohibited him from devoting himself to my business on a full-time basis, I needed someone I could trust who could get the job done in my corner at all times.

I plopped down on one of the queen-sized beds, and removed my Stetson, along with my coat. I then loosened my tie and emptied the contents of my pockets onto the nightstand.

I watched him shove his last few pair of socks into his garment bag.

"Are you done now?"

"Yeah Little Brother, whatcha wanna know?" He removed his dark shades, and his black trench. "Man, I hope the room they gave me isn't this stuffy. Did you hear me coughing all night?"

"Man, skip that. What's the 4-1-1, bro?"

"Well, I ran into her mother, you know the *white* woman you were talking to last night," he always pronounced the word white as if it were some sort of disease.

"Uh-huh."

"Well, man, she's *white*, so that makes Elisabeth bi-racial, man a half-breed."

"Okay?" I asked holding my hands out as if to say, what's your point.

"Well, she was nice. As nice as rich white folks go. She's a dentist with her own practice you know. Came to church late. Said she was too embarrassed to walk all the way up front to where her husband and daughter were. So, she sat in the balcony."

"Yeah, boss. That's all good. But, whatcha scope out about Elisabeth?"

"Man, I think you better hold your horses," he laughed, "lemme take my time with this."

"You love seeing me like this, don't you?" I asked now pacing the floor. I removed my blazer and vest, unfastened my cufflinks and begin to roll my sleeves up.

Brother Khalid jumped off of the other bed and walked over to me to examine my gear.

"Little Brother, those are some fly cuffs. Your name is on them, man."

"No kiddin'?" I asked sarcastically. " I hadn't noticed."

"Man, I see right now, that I'm gon' have to hit a brotha up for a raise. You not paying me enough to dress like that. What's up with that?"

"Yusef . . . Elisabeth?"

"Aw, look at him . . . the big, tall, handsome preacher man has a schoolboy crush on the rich little white girl."

143

"Her father is black. That makes her black," I countered defensively.

"Half black. That makes her half –black, leaning towards the whiter half. Wonder if she's ever tried to pass. She looks pretty white to me," he continued.

"Man, don't get me started. You still believe Mariah Carey is white."

"She is," he laughed.

"Man, she's mixed, just like Elisabeth."

"All I'm sayin' is little sister takes after her mama. Besides, since when have you've been interested in that type, with all those fine Nubian, full-figured single sisters back at Rosedale Park, counting the days until you get back."

"Man, back to your long drawn out story . . . damn!"

"All right, already. Cut a brotha some slack. So anyways, I saw little Miss Prissy get up as soon as you turned your back to let Doug put on your coat. I followed her out into the hall, and called her name. She looked at me as if I was some sort of crackhead or career criminal in a past-life or something."

That was one thing I loved about Brother Khalid. He never took himself or his wretched past too seriously.

"Sorry, man. I wondered who let that cat out of the bag to her."

"You know who. Her stuffy old dude probably couldn't wait to fill her head with nonsense about you providing a living for an ex-con, and former Muslim. Anyway I introduced myself, and
     extended my hand, and Little Brother, man, you're not going to believe how she played me."

"What'd she do?" I laughed.

"She said, *so* . . . and then the heifer looked at my hand like she wanted to spit on it."

After I finished wiping the tears from my eyes from laughing so hard, Brother Khalid continued.

144

"Man, I don't see why you would wanna be bothered with some chick like that."

"Man, she ain't no heifa. No any ole' chick. She's my wife, man. That's the woman, I'm going to marry."

Now, it was his turn to split his guts laughing at me. He threw in a couple of hearty knee-slaps for good measure. When he realized how serious I was by the perturbed expression on my face, he regained his composure and began pacing the floor with me.

"Bob," he said gravely. " I've never heard you say that about any woman. You must have it pretty bad for this girl. When did all this happen?"

"Yesterday, when I spoke with her on the phone."

"You find that annoying, high-pitched, white girl drawl sexy?"

"Yeah man, there is just something about it. Now, spill it, chief. How old is she?"

" She walked away from me, man. Left me standing there, looking stupid. Didn't want to hear a word I had to say. But that totally went against all her mother, you know the *white* woman, had to tell me. She said the girl has been dying to meet you. One of your biggest, quote, unquote..fans, so to speak."

"I know this. Did you follow her?"

"Sister Powell?"

"Yes . . . no, Sherlock! Elisabeth, damn it!"

"I followed her, man, but from a distance, I didn't want her to think I was stalking her. She went into the coatroom, and check this . . . slid into a full-length white minx or fox or something, with the little cute headband, hat thing to match. Man, she has the skinniest little arms I've ever seen. "

"Did you find out how old she is or not?"

"Hold your horses, Doc. One thing at a time. I watched her leave the building, and drive hurriedly off in a pink Beamer, man. Pink," he laughed.

145

"Get out of dodge, man." I laughed, just as tickled as he was.

"Seriously, bro. Pink! A pink, brand, spank new BMW. License plates said, **Princess**, in all capital letters."

"That all you got?"

"Naw, man. I went back into the building and asked about her white mother. Man, she left early too. Found out from the cute little brown chick who sat next to her."

"Who's she?"

"This is where it gets real interesting man. Get this, she's the cook, her mother is the maid. Now, I've never known any black folks to live that high on the hog, let alone white ones."

"I suppose she gave you the story of Elisabeth's life," I interjected, egging him on to get to the point.

"She told me more than that, brother. She told me to give her a call once I got here, so she could hook up with me, if you know what I mean."

"But, you're still legally married to Fatima."

"Man, you know that's dead. By the time I get back home, she would have moved back into her daddy's house with my four kids. Just too spineless to leave me in my face. Besides, you know how long it's been since I've been with her? Try ten months ago, when she got knocked up."

"I know you not about to break, man. If I can do it for four years, I'm sure you'll be okay for another few months, until we can get her to come into the fold."

"Yeah, Little Brother, you keep hoping and praying for that to happen."

"Back to Elisabeth, tell me how old she is."

"Tanya, the cook, says Elisabeth is as spoiled as all get out man. She got the Beamer last year, on her eighteenth birthday."

"So, if she turned eighteen last year, that makes her nineteen," I asked jubilantly, with my fingers crossed.

"It does man, but she is still under-aged. Too young for you, Lil' Bro. You'll be thirty on your next birthday," he pointed out as if I had somehow let it slip my mind. " Besides man . . . he . . . llo, is anyone home? The girl is **white**! **White, man!**"

I shrugged, and motioned for him to continue the story. "She lives at home with her parents. Her father, as you know is some big wig, at some fancy schmancy hospital way out there in the county of Chesterfield, she called it. He comes from a long line of doctors, surgeons, mostly, and so does Sister Powell, who inherited her father's orthodontist practice. Elisabeth apparently treats Tanya and her mother like crap, because she basically didn't have anything good to say about her."

"Go on," I urged, taking a seat in one of the desk chairs next to the bed. I leaned forward, rested my elbows against my thigh, and cradled my interwoven fingers under my chin. Prepared as I was to hear the worse, I was still determined to make Elisabeth my wife. She fit the prototype. Long, luscious locks, tall, thin body, pretty face, and youthful, which meant she had most of her childbearing years ahead of her.

"Uh, let's see, she throws temper-tantrums until her father gives her, her way. She tries to get her mother's respect, but her mom is still so called, in-love with her sister, who is twenty-two, I believe, the same age as Tanya. Lori, I think she called her."

"Yeah, that's her name. Lori. The mother told me about her yesterday. Her eyes did seem to light up somethin' fierce when she mentioned her name. She got real emotional. . . . Tense, started cryin' on me and everything. Felt like chargin' her for the session."

"And I know why she got all tripped out like that," he responded matter-of-factly stabbing his forefinger into the air.

147

"Man, how did you manage to get all of this information? Where was I?"

"You were in the vestibule surrounded by sisters, beautiful **black** sisters your own age, who can do you some good, brother," he laughed.

"Just tell me about the sister, man. The sister."

"Well according to ole' loose-lips Tanya, Lori, who apparently looks like a lighter skinned female version of her daddy, hasn't been back from college to visit the family home in over two-years. When she visits, she stays with the black relatives who still dote on her. She and the old dude had a falling out over church doctrine years ago. The ole dude seems to think that it is his responsibility to cut her off from his household, over her refusal to attend worship services up in Lansing. Apparently, he has used his connections to spy on her way up there. Anyway, he was really through with her, when she openly defied him, by postponing med school. He won't even talk to her. She lives as a border somewhere up in Lansing, and teaches dance. A phenomenal dancer, I hear, which is something the father finds absolutely shameful."

"The bastard," I replied, stroking my chin. I've always maintained a certain disdain for hypocritical church leaders who pretend to shepherd over God's flock, while at the same time reject, judge and pontificate over their own flesh and blood.

"What's Elisabeth's part in all of this?"

"She, according to loose-lips who has grown up right along with these girls, is completely jealous of Lori. Lori was the gifted one with all of the talent-book-smart, warm-hearted, funny, free-spirited, non-judgmental, med-school potential, you know, while Elisabeth has always used her looks to get ahead."

"Oh, really?" I laughed.

"Brother, you're laughing now, but this girl sounds like she would be a bit too much to handle. Elisabeth has refused communication with her sister too because Lori is the one who ratted her out to her parents about an eating disorder, anorexia or bulimia, one of those, I think she has. Her weight has gotten down to under a hundred pounds before, and she is probably, what I'm guessing 5'8" or 9"?"

"Yeah, she is a pretty decent height," I nodded. "I wonder if she's all right now," I queried aloud. Brother Khalid walked over to me, and grabbed my shoulder as if to snap me back into reality.

"Don't do it man."

" Why not. . . . what else you got?"

" Well if the fact that she doesn't eat doesn't scare you away, try this on for size. Tanya told me that Elisabeth is a cosmetology student, just so she can know how to keep her own hair and nails done. She also, just to make her father happy, is taking a few community college courses in interior design, just so she can quote, unquote keep her house wardrobed in the latest fashions. She is a shop-a-holic, a hypochondriac and a neat freak. Panic attacks. Fakes asthmatic symptoms. The whole nine. This girl has problems, Little Brother. I advise you to stay away."

I avoided looking at him, because both on the surface and sub-consciously, I believed him. Yusef Khalid was never one to exaggerate, yet, I had to follow my gut instincts on this one.

How many dreams had I had featuring a woman who fit Elisabeth's description? How many women had I imagined myself with, sharing a life, sharing my children, sharing in both the joys and sorrows that my calling as an evangelist first, counselor, teacher, preacher and author could bring? Many. I had imagined many, but none were as right for me as this one young woman. She simply fit the profile, and those were my exact words to my dearest friend, and brother in Christ.

"What profile?"

"The one I outlined in the book."

After a few seconds of pensive reflection, Brother Khalid decided that I was a hopeless case. He shrugged his shoulders, and walked away from my immediate presence defeated. "I can't argue with you there, LB. You've always talked about wanting a woman who looked like that, but only **black** mind you, and one who wouldn't mind sacrificing her career goals to support yours. Since, it seems like this girl doesn't have any, then, there you go."

I wasn't offended. I extended my hand to him. He accepted.

"Man, I better go call this Tanya chick. To see if we gon' hook up or not. Man, a word of advice though, brotha." He continued, before I could respond, " If I were you, I would check out the eating disorder. Those things can be quite serious."

"I don't think there'll be a need for that. Her parents are loaded. I'm sure they got her the help she needed."

"You sure, you want to run with this?"

"As sure as my name is Bob McGallister."

"I'd figured you would say that. I asked Tanya to ask Elisabeth to hook up with you at the church tomorrow at 6:30, so you can get yo' chit-chat on before service starts."

"And, that's why you're my brother," I grinned roughly grabbing his hand, and shaking the full extent of his lanky arm. "My consigliori," I added in my best Al Pacino, Godfather voice.

I couldn't sleep at all that night. I kept thinking about Elisabeth and how hyped I was to meet her. When my thoughts led me into the dark valley and crevices of sin, I jolted up from the bed, and went into the bathroom. I removed my clothing, and stood under the sharp jolts of cold water from the nozzle in the spacious shower stall. I had to remember to thank Cecil Donaldson profusely for booking me a first class suite. As a matter of fact, I had to thank him

150

for the room service and unlimited access to cable as well. Since I couldn't sleep, I sat up that entire evening watching sports highlights on ESPN. I even managed to catch one of those behind-the-scenes biographies on the greatest basketball player of all time, Julius Erving, better known as The Doctor, Doctor J.

Ever since I was a kid, I'd always admired not only his phenomenal skills on the court, (he could teach Michael Jordan a thing or two about flying), but also his charm and eloquence as an African-American male and public role model.

I was privileged to meet the great Michael Jordan during his '97 season with The Bulls. They were at home, competing against the Indiana Pacers. I was scheduled to run a weeklong gospel meeting at the Chatham-Avalon congregation. Somehow, Brother Khalid used some of his former Chicago Muslim connections to get us, not only front row seats, but also backstage passes to rap with number 23 himself. (And, they say that Muslims aren't interested in sports! I thank God they are!)

The brother was actually pretty cool. He asked if I'd ever played college ball, probably I'm guessing because I only stood two or three inches shorter than him, when I responded in the affirmative, he wasn't surprised. Then Brother Khalid, much to my surprise, invited he and his wife Juanita along with their three children to Sunday morning service. Being my biggest P.R. mouthpiece, Brother Khalid made me sound like some sort of black Billy Graham. I tried to conceal my awe, when he readily accepted the invitation.

I was in the middle of my sermon about the pride and wickedness of women like Queen Jezebel and the complete spinelessness and foolishness of her husband Ahab, when I directed my attention to a family of five, led by their prominent, statuesque patriarch to the third row. I continued preaching as if I hadn't noticed such a fashionably late, yet exquisite entrance. Towards the end of my oratory, I playfully ac-

151

knowledged his presence, as the second greatest basketball player in the history of the game.

He reciprocated light-heartedly with a hand in fist signal, as if to warn me that he was going to beat me down afterwards. Later, Brother Khalid, Eddie, Sheila and the boys along with Doug and the young adult acapella chorus from Rosedale Park were treated by His Airness Himself, to what was then, his restaurant, where we enjoyed a delicious spread and wholesome fellowship with he and his family.

I ordered I can't remember what from the room-service menu. When I tried to tip the busboy, he told me that my money was no good there, that Cecil Donaldson had waylaid all of the costs for me to enjoy three meals for each of the next two days. Yes, if the perks that came along with that room, were an indication that I had "arrived," then I had arrived just in time enough to impress the hell outta my intended.

Bob, The Man

Brother Khalid didn't waste time the next morning having Brother Donaldon drive him to the Avis rental car station located across the street from Lambert Airport. He knew how I hated to be chauffeured around by well-intentioned church folks who felt it their duty to familiarize me with all of the great sights of their fair city. When I am away from home, I like to have independent access to my own transportation. When I am away from counseling church members and rehab patients, as well as from the radio program, teaching institute, Agape Academy, writing, not to mention my own pulpit. I like to chill. Relax. Do the things Bob, the man likes to do, not Robert, God's manservant.

I had plans for us to visit a couple of used record stores so I could search for a couple of Davis' and Coltrane albums to add to my impressive jazz collection. Although at that time in my life I had just acquired a taste for the mature rhythms of jazz and classical music, I had since childhood been a big fan of the Motown Sound, with Stevie Wonder topping my list as the greatest recording artist and lyricist of all time.

"Well, did you get any?" I blatantly asked Brother Khalid as I signaled for him to either scoot over, or walk around to the passenger seat. He'd rented a black Nissan Maxima. Not exactly what I like, seeing that I had grown accustomed to

3659-DRAN

having the legroom cruising around Detroit in my brand new Ford Expedition.

I justified the expenditure by telling myself I could afford it, based upon all the income from various places I was receiving, along with the fact that I still lived next door to the church, rent-free in the two-bedroom parsonage.

"Now, is that any way for a preacha to talk?" he chuckled, gladly walking over to the passenger side. He hated being the driver whenever we'd venture off into unfamiliar terrain.

"Man, I'm not a minister again until tonight at 7:00 when that gospel meeting starts. This is plain ole Bob today."

"Yeah, man, well anyway, Eddie wants you to swing by to pick him up from the Johnstons, but Doug . . . well, Doug got kind of roped in by Donaldson's wife and the ladies Bible class to do some sight seeing."

"Cool, man, now stop buggin'! You know a brotha has to live vicariously through a mug, until I can get Elisabeth up to Detroit."

"Man, have you lost your mind?" reaching over to take my fictitious temperature. "Are you feeling okay? You still trippin' on Little-miss-anorexic-hypochondriac-supermodel-princess-half-breed-brat?"

"Yo, man, ease up on my woman . . . and gimme the 411 on you and loose-lips."

Don't Call Me Liz

"Bobby, hate to disturb you," Donaldson bombarded into his own office without so much as a knock. I began to arise from the kneeling position I was in. I always go into deep prayer and meditation twenty to thirty minutes before preaching. Pops had a big problem with that, because he felt that the minister should fully participate in all aspects of worship, and should not draw attention to himself by entering into the auditorium late. I had managed to stand my ground over the years. No one bothered me during my private time at Rosedale Park anymore, not even his old cronies, because everyone knew that if they'd just leave me at peace for that time-period . . . I would come out on fire.

Apparently, Cecil Donaldson didn't understand this. I wasn't noticeably upset from the interruption. He had no idea of knowing that I was waiting for the Lord to impart unto me exactly what I would preach, and how I would deliver it. He was from the old school. He, like Pops and mostly all of the other preachers within our faith, still read prepared lectures, as I call them from word-processed, or even worse, hand-written sheets of paper.

Before I could fully prostrate myself, in walked James Powell, along with his stunningly pretty daughter Elisabeth.

I shot a quick look at my watch. It read 7:15. She was forty-five minutes late. I could hear the joyful voices from

155

the auditorium ringing out a familiar hymn. I was due to begin preaching within the next fifteen-minutes. Under ordinary circumstances, I would have been pissed that a woman disregarded my respect for time like that, but after taking one look at her, I decided not to even bring the subject up. How was she to know about my pet peeve?

I squared my shoulders and cleared my throat in preparation to speak to the woman of my dreams for the first time. That familiar scent from the night before-that light, alluring fresh strawberry fragrance intoxicated me even though we stood a good ten feet a part. She stood close too her father, those thin closed rose-colored lips smiling demurely at me. Her intense gaze never left mine. On impulse, I wanted to pull her body next to mine, and propose marriage to her right then. But, I decided to keep my cool. I had all the confidence in the world that I would overcome the skeptical, hate-filled glares of her father, whose overpowering physical presence made her appear to be of an even more miniscule weight.

"Brother Robert . . . I'm so very sorry to interrupt your prayer, son. Believe me, I know how it is when you have only a few precious moments to talk to the Father before preaching his mighty and glorious word . . ."

"Yes, I'm sure you do Brother Donaldson," Powell sternly interrupted, still scowling at me, "but this matter is very important concerning the minister here and my daughter, Elisabeth. So, if you don't mind Cecil, if you'd leave us alone to settle this for a few moments . . . I'm sure the minister here will have enough time to re-gather his thoughts."

Donaldson and I exchanged a friendly knowing look. He shrugged his shoulders and nudged my elbow, causing me to stoop down to earshot level. "I'll be in the next office if you need me, Bobby. I'm sure this is all a big misunderstanding. I know you haven't done anything wrong."

I nodded and gave him a consoling pat on the back and a firm handshake. I winked at Elisabeth. She blushed.

"I'm sure everything is okay sir. I've requested this meeting."

"Oh . . . ," Donaldson laughed nervously deciphering my meaning. "Heh, heh, well Bobby, I guess I'll see you out front then."

"Yesss, sirrr, " I sang confidently.

Powell shot me a quick "you-smug-bastard" look before closing the door behind his jovial minister.

"I would like to know Brother McGallister, exactly what your intentions are towards my Elisabeth, here." One thing I appreciated about this man from jump, is that he cut right to the nitty gritty. I hate for people to waste my time, beating around the bush, trying not to hurt my feelings.

"My intention sir," I replied in my deepest of voices, not allowing my eyes to leave Elisabeth's, "is to get to speak with your daughter to see if we can arrange a couple of meetings before I head back to Detroit on Sunday, for the purpose of us deciding if we would like to form a further commitment."

" A further commitment? What is this, young man? Do you know how old this girl is?"

"I'm not a little girl, anymore Daddy," she quipped in that high-pitched sexy drawl. " I'm nineteen years old." Old loose-lips was right.

"Elisabeth, don't start with me tonight, okay Princess? I just brought you in here so you can see this grown man for what he really is."

"And, just what is he, Daddy?" she challenged folding her string-bean arms across her flat chest. She wore a pretty pink, long, snug fitting, but not too tight sweater dress.

At that moment, I wanted to chuckle at the contradictory image of the powerful James Powell, neurosurgeon, hospital administrator, and elder of the Lord's church who had completely ostracized his older daughter for not making sound choices according to his wisdom, while yet standing two-hundred some-odd pounds, docile like next to his buck-o-five baby girl, holding her expensive pink coat. Cashmere, I was quite sure of it. I recognize fine quality clothing when I see it.

"Yes, I would like to know that myself," I chided, throwing in another wink for good measure. I leaned up against Donaldson's desk, unbuttoned my charcoal gray three quarter-length sports coat to expose the matching sable and charcoal vest, stroked my neatly trimmed beard and attempted to strike the most GQ-ish pose I could muster. This girl was classy. I had to pull out all the stops.

"What he is . . . Princess, sweetheart, is a reformed *womanizer*. You've read his books. Didn't even know you had them or knew who he was, for that matter, until your mother asked me this morning if I would formally introduce the two of you. For the life of me, I couldn't figure out why you never told me about this little crush you have on this roaming Romeo of a preacher."'

I couldn't contain myself anymore. I laughed in his face.

Elisabeth cut me a pseudo-serious look of foreboding.

"Daddy, come on . . . you know why I never told you about Doctor McGallister," she whined, cajoling him by grabbing a hold to one of his thick arms, which forced him to release the tight grip he had on the cashmere coat.

I allowed my gaze to follow her perfectly French-manicured hands. She wore a diamond tennis bracelet and a simple gold band on the finger of her left hand, which, I knew would soon belong to me. As much as I strained, I couldn't make out the cursive inscription on it.

"You would have not accepted what I had to say on the matter. You never do, that's because you don't trust me. I'm not like Lori. I will never let you down. I made a promise to you, don't you remember?"

What did she mean that she wasn't like Lori? I guess that was supposed to be a good thing, but in my accurate predictive opinion on Elisabeth's older sibling, I knew her judgment was more than a little skewed. And, what type of promise had she made him? Sounded like it had everything to do with my intentions and nothing to do with them at the same time.

The frown on James Powell's face melted into a half-smile when Elisabeth planted a daughterly kiss on his cheek and patted his back.

"I remember," he said quietly, running his hand over her long sandy-brown locks that appeared to be straighter than I'd remembered from the night before.

"Then, you will leave us alone to chat privately, Daddy, won't you?"

Powell redirected a doubtful gaze in my direction. I gave him a reassuring nod.

"You will leave me to speak with Doctor McGallister, Daddy, won't you?" she repeated more forcibly, cuddling up to him even more. "I'll be out in a few minutes, I promise, okay? Here, take my coat. Here's my purse, take it to Tanya or Ms. Maggie. I'll be out to sit with you guys, okay?" I couldn't decide if I was amused or sickened by the relationship between father and daughter. Maybe I was just a little bit of both.

"Whatever you say, Princess," he mumbled, still seething at me. I extended my hand to his and looked him squarely in the eye, just as Pops had taught me to do when another male challenged me, physically, intellectually or mentally.

"I would appreciate this, sir, " I stated sincerely, without smiling. " She's in good hands."

"Let's hope so, for your sake."

We both held our proverbial breath, until Elisabeth sauntered over to the door to issue one last dismissal peck to her father before closing it.

"Whew," I whistled lightheartedly, gently placing my right hand on her back to lead her into the area where Donaldson's couch was. She sat down beside me, leaving a few inches between us.

As a minister, it was my usual custom to refrain from any physical contact upon meeting a young woman in whom I'd shown interest, at least until after the third or fourth date, but since I knew that Elisabeth was the woman for me, I wrongly misjudged the situation by placing her thin hands in mine. They were ice cold.

"Thank you. . . . Elisabeth, for meeting me here tonight," I spoke quietly, stroking the top of her hands.

"Please, Doctor McGallister . . . I know we both wanted this meeting. I am really looking forward to seeing how far this could go, but you're going to have to . . . uh, release my hands. We just met remember?"

Mortified, I obeyed her wishes without apologizing, I did bother to offer an explanation, however.

"It just feels right, you know. Your hand in mine."

She blushed and batted her lightly made up eyelashes. I couldn't decipher whether they were false or not. Our close physical proximity led me to examine how perfectly made up her face was, probably the work of an expert; hers, no doubt. Through the mask of foundation and blush, I could tell that her skin was still almost flawless. She was definitely a face and hair woman. Impressed with her countenance, I wanted to reach out to stroke her cheek and to run my fingers through those long, magnificent locks, but instead I waited for her to speak again.

When she didn't, I took the lead.

" Like I said, I want to thank you for coming back here. I'm sure you had to pretty much talk your old man into the whole thing." I smiled, still a little bit perturbed that she had the audacity to arrive a few minutes before I was due in the pulpit.

"Yes, I did have to talk Daddy into it. I don't like to go behind his back to do anything," she explained. She held her

---

160

reed-like hands on her lap. When she crossed those long ivory legs, her dress rose several inches to expose the lower part of a meatless thigh.

"*If the fact that she doesn't eat, doesn't scare you away* . . . *Little Miss Anorexic, Bulimia..*," Brother Khalid's words of foreboding danced around in my head. I blocked them out when Elisabeth began to speak again.

"My cook Tanya informed me last night that you wanted to meet me."

"I'm glad she did. But I would have much preferred to have met you almost an hour ago, seeing that we don't have much time to talk right now."

"We don't need much time, Doctor McGallister . . ."

"Robert, call me Robert, or Bobby if you'd like."

"Okay, Bobby," she sang, sweetly batting those long, soft, light-brown eyelashes. "As I was stating, we don't need much time. I came just so I could ask you personally what your intentions are for wanting to meet me. I am," she announced gravely, "only nineteen. I just graduated high school last year."

Her words bolted me back into the harsh reality-that I hadn't been fantasizing about a mature woman at all, but rather a gangly inexperienced adolescent who still lived at home under the watchful eye of her over-protective father.

"You make me sound like some sort or pervert or something," I replied defensively, second-guessing my decision to introduce her into my life.

"Don't be ridiculous," she replied indignantly. "It doesn't really matter about how old I am, you know, because I don't know where this is going to go anyway. That's why I'm here. What do you want from me?" she asked, slowly, whipping her long seductive locks from one shoulder to the other.

Wow, I thought, *this girl cuts right to the chase.* Just like her father. I wasn't used to such straightforwardness from a female, let alone from one who had not yet reached adulthood.

"I want to get to know you, that's all."

"And, how do you plan on doing that?" she asked.

"Well, for starters, how about after service, you send the old man and company packing, and join me for a cup of coffee, and since I'm sure you've already had dinner, maybe we can just have dessert."

I leaned further back into the softness of one of the worn pillows of Donaldson's out-dated tweed couch, to monitor her facial reactions to my having mentioned something fattening. I relaxed when she didn't flinch or look flush.

"No. I won't be going anywhere with you that late," she replied obstinately. She lifted herself from the couch's sunken seat cushions and began smoothing out the invisible wrinkles of her dress. "I don't know what other kinds of loose women you've met and have run around with on these gospel tours, but it is not proper for a lady to go anywhere at such a late hour with a man she barely even knows."

She did the sexy hair whipping thing again as I stood up and walked over to the desk. If she wanted to take on Scarlet O'Hara's flair for the dramatic, then I would oblige her with my best impersonation of Rhet Butler's nonchalance. I walked over to the door and opened it. She wanted theatrics? That's what she was going to get.

"Well then, since you think so poorly of me, maybe it's best to go our separate ways now. We can pretend that we've never laid eyes on each other," I folded my arms, arrogantly, and pointed my head towards the door, hoping, praying that she wouldn't call my bluff.

"Don't be ridiculous, Bobby," she snapped. "I know you're used to having your way with women, but if you want to get to know me, it has to be on my terms."

"Really?" I asked, easing my way back over by the desk where she was standing, pouting, tapping her foot, with her arms folded too. "Well, why don't you tell a brotha what your terms are. I mean, how can this brotha get to know Liz?"

"My name is Elisabeth. Elisabeth Jameson Powell. I hate

being called Liz, Lizzy, Libby, Beth, or anything that is not my full name," she corrected me.

I moved closer to her, examining the tight hunch of her shoulders, the nervous drumming of her fingers against her pointy elbows, the continuous tap, tap, tapping of her narrow foot in designer pumps against the multi-colored dingy rug. Her tense, uptight body language amused me, so I laughed-which only further exacerbated her tiny temper-tantrum.

"Bobby," she whined, her cheeks crimson from embarrassment. "Don't laugh at me. Don't ever laugh at me."

"I'm sorry Elisabeth. I've just never met a woman with such issues with her own name."

"Well, how would you like it if I butcher your name, like Brother Donaldson does and called you Bobby?"

" You're already calling me Bobby, besides, all of my family and good friends do, so, I'd be flattered," I smiled. "So, are you gon' tell me what I can do to live down this Casanova impression you have of me?"

She gave me one final once over from head to toe, as if she was sizing me up to meet her approval and lofty expectations. I leaned up against Donaldson's desk treating it as if it were my own, comfortably accepting her scrutiny; the anticipatory gleam in my eyes challenging her to make the next move.

"You are invited to my house for dinner Sunday afternoon. We usually eat at around two o'clock."

I bit down on my bottom lip and grimaced.

"What's wrong? Are you unable to make it?" she asked me with a twinge of disappointment and challenge in her voice.

I shook my head. "I can arrange for a later flight if at all possible."

"Oh, I'm sorry. I didn't know you would be leaving so soon after morning worship. I didn't mean to assume . . ."

"It's okay, Elisabeth," I consoled, gently stroking her right shoulder disregarding her earlier pretense of setting physical boundaries. As if my touch were magic, she looked as if she could have melted right under my fingertips.

"It seems as if I have a lot of saving face and damage control to run between you and your old man. You two seem to have the wrong impression of me so, I wouldn't mind hanging around these parts a little longer."

Her face lit up and for the first time I saw her smile, completely, with all of her immaculately white teeth showing, exposing the microscopic gap between the two in the front. Smaller than Emily's. It was the only feature, besides their fair skin they shared in common. Once she realized what she had done, she lifted her hand up to cover her mouth. I released the soft hold I had on her upper-arm, to remove her hand.

"Nice," I said, in response to my rare glimpse. " Really nice."

"I hate my teeth. Lori and I, no, well, I wore braces for a few years, but somehow this space between my teeth never went away. I hate it. I really, really do."

"You're very, very pretty." I replied, allowing my hand, to rest on her shoulder again. Who gave a damn about a space in between her teeth you had to be all the way up on her to see in the first place?

"And you have to get out there. I'll be sitting on the second row. Do well, Bobby," she bade softly before leaving me in the office to my thoughts of whisking her back home with me to Detroit on Sunday evening.

No Show

Once again that night as I sat alone in all the comforts of my hotel suite, I prayed to God for my father's speedy recovery. When I called his hospital room that evening Ma told me in a tired, voice, barely above a whisper that Pops had just drifted off to sleep. His doctor had raised her spirits earlier in the day by informing her that he could be released within the next three days if his most recent blood work which was due back from the lab on Monday, came back okay.

She sounded a bit disappointed when I insisted that she didn't wake him to speak to me. I was simply flying too high over the dinner plans I had made with Elisabeth for Pop's untimely lectures and unnecessary words of advice of how to "rope them in" on Sunday morning.

Even though I had decided to keep my mouth shut to Brother Khalid and the fellas about postponing my flight home with them, their continuous prodding on our way to dinner at one of the other deacon's houses before the song service Saturday evening led me to share a little more of my plans of a future with Elisabeth than necessary.

Throughout Doug's and Brother Khalid's game of twenty-one questions, Eddie while smiling like the Cheshire cat, kept patting me on the back and giving me high-fives, as if I had told him she had already accepted a proposal of marriage.

Doug wanted to know more about Elisabeth's eating dis-

3659-DRAN

order, even though he caught wind of the vibes of accusation and betrayal exchange between Brother Khalid and me.

Disappointed that I couldn't detect Elisabeth's presence in the audience that night from my "privileged" first row pew, I was barely enjoying and concentrating on the melodic harmonies of the various acapella groups visiting the Kingshighway congregation from the local congregations of the Churches of Christ when the mistress of ceremony of the song-fest, held on my behalf, called me up to the pulpit to make some closing remarks about the success of the *Saving It* Seminar, along with express my gratitude for the generous fifteen hundred dollar love offering the ushers had just collected and counted for me to take back home with me on Sunday afternoon.

I stood up and eagerly marched up to the pulpit, hugging the nameless woman, and making a sincere effort to thank the Kingshighway congregation and all of the singing groups and visitors who had come out over the past three nights to support my ministries. My outward enthusiasm didn't wane as Brother Donaldson cajoled me into leading the congregation in another song and into offering up the benediction prayer, but I still did not see Elisabeth.

However, as I sang a heartfelt rendition of "I'm a Hard Fighting Soldier on the Battlefield," I noticed seated on the second pew, between Tanya and a plump matronly looking brown-skinned woman, who I assumed to be the maid, Emily Powell's pale face smiling at me, as she wiped away a few tears from her eyes.

Moments later, I greeted them all in the lobby.

"It's good to see you again, Robert. I'm sorry I didn't get to make it to the service last night. I was working late at the office again, but Elisabeth has informed me that you will be joining us for dinner tomorrow after church."

"Yes, ma'am," I smiled, embracing her petite frame. Elisabeth definitely inherited her height from her father, because the crown of Emily's head did not even reach my breast-bone. "Dinner is at two-thirty, right?"

"Yes, but Cecil has informed me that you guys will be taking a five o'clock flight out of Lambert tomorrow, so we'll make it a quick dinner. We don't want you to miss your flight."

"No, it's quite all right. Brother Johnston will be dropping the fellas off at the airport at 4:00. I won't be leaving until Wednesday morning."

"Really?" her face lit up like a Christmas tree on Forty-Second Street. Apparently, Elisabeth hadn't informed her mother of my change of plans. Maybe, she herself was incredulous that I would rearrange my busy schedule just to get to know her better. And rearranging my schedule, did take plenty of contemplation and maneuvering on Brother Khalid's and my part.

I would use the scaled-down in comparison to Rosdeale Park's, radio-room at Kingshighway to tape my mid-week radio broadcast. My boy Mark Riley, another deacon, would substitute-teach for the umpteemth time, my God's Warrior Training Workshop. Kelly Calloway, my part-time therapy appointment secretary and almost former fiancée, would have to postpone at least seven marriage and family and drug rehabilitation sessions. And Eddie, of course who was tickled pink over my impending relationship, readily volunteered to teach my Tuesday night mixed young adult human sexuality seminar, just in case I decided to extend my flight until Thursday morning.

"Well, that's good news, young man," she sang joyfully, tightening her embrace. "My goodness, I'm sure you had to jump through fire to extend your stay. I do realize what a busy, in-high demand minister you are. And to think, you would take the time out to bond with our Princess means the world to me. You just don't know how excited she is over you."

"Yes sirree," the forgotten little gray-haired cute plump

woman standing next to Emily added. "Libby talks about what it would be like to be your wife all the time, Doctor McGallister."

If I were a man given to blushing and embarrassing easily, I would have turned about three shades redder than my intended's rosy cheeks. However, I embraced the woman and introduced myself.

"Oh, I'm so rude, Robert. This is our housekeeper Ms. Maggie. She's been with us for an eternity."

"Yes sir, I used to work for Ms. Emily's parents here. Why I used to change Ms. Emily's diapers, you know."

I thought the woman looked too old to be Tanya's mother, so I used clever means to gather more accurate information.

"Yes, I believe I met Tanya, the other night. She is a very nice young woman. Your daughter, right?"

"You might as well say she is," Maggie Sims replied. "Tanya's my great-niece. I never married and had children of my own, but, well Tanya's mama live out in California. She had seven other kids, by diff'rent daddies by the time Tanya came along as number eight. She couldn't take it no more. So Ms. Emily here, and Dr. James have allowed me to bring up that gal as if she was my own."

"Yes, we've had her since she was a few days old. I flew out with Ms. Maggie to get her. A few weeks later, Jim and I had Lori. We'd thought it would be neat to bring the girls up as sisters. They're still the best of friends to this day."

"Yes sirree," Maggie readily agreed. "My Tanya grew up with the Powell girls. Received the same education as our sweet, sweet Lori and . . . Libby too. Right now, she studying to be a nurse over at UMSL."

I noticed the blinding gleam in both of the women's eyes, whenever they mentioned Lori's name, as well as the cool, detached inflection of Ms. Maggie's voice whenever she mentioned Elisabeth.

"Well, we see you have a long line of people waiting to greet you Robert, so Ms. Maggie and I will be moving on." I hugged both the ladies again, almost forgetting to ask about Elisabeth whereabouts until Ms. Maggie mentioned her name again.

"Oh yeah, Doctor McGallister?"

"Robert. Call me Robert or Bobby, please."

"Bobby," she grinned revealing a perfectly cleaned set of dentures, which I figured was Emily's handiwork. "Libby is a strict vegetarian. Tanya prepares her meals special. But the rest of us fat eating folk will be chowing down on some fried chicken and roast beef. Is that all right by you?"

"Yes ma'am," I chuckled imagining the sight of Elisabeth turning up her nose at the sight of me "chowing down" as Ms. Maggie put it on a plump, greasy breast. "Though I'm not complaining about the hotel room and room service, I'm kinda missing my Mom's and Sister Calloway's cooking right now. Sister Calloway is the church secretary and a mighty fine cook."

"Really?" Ms. Maggie asked, allowing her voice to take on a pseudo-envious resonance.

"Now, I'm sure there's nothing to worry about, ma'am. I'm looking forward to spending tomorrow afternoon with all of you. By the way, where is Elisabeth tonight?"

"Well, you have got to know Elisabeth," Emily laughed nervously.

"Yeah, she makes a big fuss over the smallest thangs, don't she, Ms. Emily?"

"Yes, Ms. Maggie, I suppose she does. I guess you wouldn't believe that the two of us had a major blowout. I take partial responsibility. I shouldn't have provoked her," Emily offered apologetically, speaking more to Ms. Maggie than to me.

" No chile," Ms. Maggie maternally reprimanded. "No Ms. Emily, now, none of that was your fault . . ."

169

"But, you know how Elisabeth gets when you try to get her to do something she doesn't want to do . . ."

"And calling her sister to congratulate her on winnin' that part in that play was not too much to ask of Lil' Ms. Princess."

Brother Khalid, who had been standing two feet away from me meeting and greeting church members and visitors alike, shot me a knowing look from his peripheral vision. I tried my best to ignore it.

"Oh yes, Robert," Emily's face brightened again as she spoke of this super-incredible, highly-revered mystery woman. "Lori, as I told you last night, is in the performing arts. In the evenings and on the weekends, she auditions for parts in these off Broadway musicals. Anyway, she called me earlier today to tell me that she just won the leading role in some up and coming musical sponsored by some big-time African-American theatre and dance-troupe up there. She was really excited about it. "

"Yes, she was. So, you were well within your rights as that gal's Mama to force her on the phone to speak with her sister. Libby throws temper tantrums, you see, Robert. She's at home probably now with her door locked, painting her nails, with her bottom lip all poked out to kingdom come," Ms. Maggie exclaimed with all the sass of Florence, the quick-witted, insubordinate housekeeper on the beloved seventies' sitcom, The Jeffersons.

Brother Khalid conspicuously cleared his throat, and elbowed me. I'm sure Emily caught his indiscreet attempt to warn me to steer clear of Elisabeth. "That gal had the nerve to send her plate back down untouched after Tanya spent at least a couple of hours whippin' up that meatless spaghetti sauce and homemade rolls."

"Now Ms. Maggie, we don't want to scare Robert off here," Emily laughed nervously, reaching up to pat me on the back. "Come now, Robert. Please excuse us . . . boring you with the trite details of a simple mother –daughter dispute. I'm sure Elisabeth has cooled down a bit, since we parted ways. She's probably curling her hair, and primping around in her room, trying to figure out what she'll wear for church and change into for dinner tomorrow. She's beside herself about having you over!"

"Now, that she is," Ms. Maggie readily agreed.

This time, I elbowed Brother Khalid to emphasize the point that at least the pouty Elisabeth did have good taste.

"And, oh yes, how could I forget, she wants you to call her tonight, if you don't get back to the hotel too late. She reminded me to relay this message to you several times before she stopped speaking to me. She hadn't planned on coming tonight for the singing anyway. I think she just wanted to stay home to make sure everything is perfect for tomorrow."

"Yes, yes, I'm sure. That gal is probably re-dusted every piece of furniture in the house, as well as thrown out my artificial plants." Ms. Maggie added waving her hand in my direction. "Only fresh flowers for Miss Princess, honey."

"Yes, please make sure you call her. She is so very much looking forward to this. I just can't express it enough!"

I belted out a hearty chuckle, while Brother Khalid stood there with his tail in-between his legs, glaring at Emily, as if she were the ultimate "blue-eyed" devil incarnate.

Both women kissed me on opposite cheeks before waving goodbye.

Eddie's Habit

Wrapping things up at the church for the night seemed to have taken an eternity. Brother Donaldson wanted to introduce me to several other ministers from sister congregations of the greater St.Louis area. I cordially greeted them, accepted their laudatory comments, and made small talk as I scrutinized my brother from my peripheral vision stuffing wads of cash and personal checks into a huge gold envelope. I couldn't help wondering if he had "borrowed" any loot from the profits I'd earned over the past three nights, but exactly how much he'd managed to steal without thinking I would figure out once I would return home to review my own books with a fine toothcomb, remained an enigma to me for at least another few days.

I'd said good night to a sleepy, irritable Doug, who'd once again been coerced to another day of sightseeing and fixing things around the Donaldson household.

When Brother Khalid noticed my impending restlessness, he interrupted the meaningless conversation I found myself unable to politely escape from, and made some comment about my needing to get back to the hotel to check on my father's status and to review my outline for tomorrow's Sunday morning worship service.

I almost laughed aloud when he'd mention the latter part of his excuse because everyone who really knows me, knows

I freestyle, that I don't use an outline, or read from typed scripts or notes. Impressed with Brother Khalid's ability to always rescue me from these time-consuming formalities, I nodded in approval to his lie. Brother Donaldson and the other brethren bade me good night and shouted out words of encouragement for me to "tear the pulpit up" come tomorrow morning.

We rode in almost complete silence on our way back to the hotel. I could tell that he was slightly perturbed with my decision to extend my stay in St. Louis a few days, but he'd said nothing about it until I pulled into the crowded parking lot close to eleven o'clock, that humid and rainy November evening.

"So, man. I guess you know that I'm about to go make this call, right?"

He nodded without even remotely glancing in my direction. I watched his curious gaze follow a huge annoying gnat fly from one bushel to the next until it situated itself momentarily on the hood of our rental car.

"You may want to ask Eddie for the cash box the first thing in the morning. He was talking about these suits he saw on clearance over at Value City yesterday . . . wants the deacons to run him by there on our way to the airport tomorrow," he announced changing the subject.

"Bet. How many suits did this brotha see, and how much of my money are they gon' cost?"

"None of it, if you grab your dough before he gets the chance to spend it. Man, you can't keep lettin' him do this to you. He's a freeloader. Him and Sheila both man."

"Why would you say some messed up stuff like that about Sheila man, just because she takes a few leftover goodies home from Agape every now and then . . ."

"You call those boxes of cereal, fresh produce, packaged meats, and paper goods I help her take to her car every Friday a few leftover goodies? Man, they are robbing you and the church blind."

Brother Khalid's words were loaded with anger and hostility. This was unlike him. The uncharacteristic, accusatory, judgmental tone his voice had taken on was a bit much for me to handle right then, especially since I had something greater to accomplish that night. We had been out all day. Maybe he was just exhausted or perhaps frustrated over his marital problems and his lack of performing up to Elisabeth's cook's satisfaction the previous night.

I mean, the man was in his mid forties. I'd counseled couples about premature male impotence for a couple years. Some had even as of late asked my opinion about taking ginseng supplements since Viagra, the new wonder drug, had yet to be approved. He snapped me out of my brief amusing quiet speculations and got out of the car.

A fierce slam of the door of the passenger side followed. I mimicked his behavior and hopped out of the car, slamming my respective door behind me.

"Man, wanna tell me what your beef is?" I asked leaning against the car with my arms folded across my chest.

"Little Brother man, this here what you're doing is wrong, man."

"What am I doing, man? What is it?"

"We have been telling you for a few months, even your own mother suspects it . . . Eddie is a thief man, a flat out crook." He looked relieved to finally have articulated the collective concerns he, Doug, Riley and a few of the older men in the leadership had been discussing in hushed tones behind my back.

"Man, is that it? I mean, I have to get up here and call this girl before it gets too late, before I have to go off on old man Powell again."

I reached inside the car, grabbed the key from the ignition, and began to take a few steps toward the hotel. Brother Khalid was right on my heels.

"No, that ain't it man. I wanna know, no we all wanna know what you plan to do about it!"

I shook my head in disgust and impatience, not because I was offended over the railing accusations against Eddie, but because he really thought I was unaware of my brother's flair for making money disappear.

"Look, Brother Khalid. To my knowledge, Eddie has only 'borrowed' from me. I know he and Sheila are struggling right now. Their money is all tied up in that new house they bought out in West Bloomfield. The repairs on it is costing them more than a few bucks. The boys are in private schools and they're trying to save for their college tuition. Besides you know the church pays Sheila next to nothing for supervising the school, man. She could be a teacher or school administrator in the public school system and get paid three times as much as they're offering her."

"I understand your need to make excuses for them. They're your family, man."

"Man, I thought you were too," I said quietly before making my way inside the lobby.

"Aw, Little Brother, you know you wrong for that. I'm just lookin' out for you. Your brother is going to land your ass in a lot of hot water."

"Like I said, he ain't hurtin' nobody. He only steals from me."

"Man, open your eyes Robert, will you please? Get your mind off that little skinny, spoiled, emotionally unbalanced, **white** girl long enough to hear what I'm telling you."

I motioned for him to walk over to the elevator with me, so we wouldn't cause a scene in front of the guests sauntering in and out of the overcrowded billiards, bar and pool areas.

175

"Whatcha telling me, man? Whatcha accusin' my brother of?"

"Man . . . ," he paused, his voice trembling as if he was about to deliver some heart-breaking, life-altering news to me. I thought I detected a glimmer of a tear in his right eye, which made me, for some reason want to sock him right in his jaw. "Brace yourself, Little Brother, man . . ."

"What the hell is it?"

"Over the last month . . . the last five months to be exact, the offering has been two to three grand short, per week . . ."

"Well," I shrugged nonchalantly, "that's because people have been in and out of town. You know how the summer months are, Brother Khalid. Folks take vacation from their jobs, and from their financial obligations to the Lord. We've been over this before."

"The attendance hasn't been down since late August, Bob..late August, and Ed is the only one who counts the money, every single Sunday."

I bit down on my bottom lip and chewed, hard. I pressed the up arrow on the electronic elevator operating panel on the wall.

"Maybe people are giving less. Maybe it's time for Pops to get up there and admonish our brothers and sisters to dig a little deeper in their pockets or maybe I'll speak to them myself, man. Shit happens sometimes. Folks need a little encouragement to remember from whence their blessings come. I even slip sometimes, Brother Khalid. And, if you're honest with yourself, so do you."

"I know this is hard for you to take, but the truth is the truth!"

"You have no idea how hard this is to take! My ace, accusin' my only blood brother in the world of stealing from God's house!" I yelled, this time violently stabbing the second button on the panel. "Where is that damned elevator?" I punched the door, then began to rapidly pace the floor. A few nosey bystanders began to pretend as if they were really waiting on the delayed elevator too. "Just what the hell are you people lookin' at? There's nothing to see here!" I yelled angrily. Instead of walking away embarrassed over having been caught eavesdropping, several more guests gathered around to witness the two tall well dressed black men tear into each other.

"We have it on tape, Little Brother."

"Say what?" I asked balling up my fist. I stepped directly to his face, squared my shoulders and looked him directly in the eye, "Care to restate that in front of all these good folks right here?" I was waiting for him to repeat his last statement, for clarification purposes, I didn't want to waste a good right hook on him for nothing.

"We caught him red-handed . . . we have your brother, the deacon, stealing thousands and thousands of dollars right out of the collection plate over the past six weeks . . . now, you need to do something about it Little Brother..you're the minister . . . you need to take it to the elders or just do something. . . . it's up to you."

I ignored the excited and shocked gasps and murmurings of the strangers surrounding us and released all the resentment I'd felt over the inevitability of Brother Khalid's correct assessment and directed a heavy blow in the direction of his left eye. He staggered backwards for a few seconds. Before he could retaliate, I rushed towards him to polish his other eye, but the strength from the restraints of a few people, men and women stopped me dead in my tracks.

A few hotel employees rushed to Brother Khalid's side to try to restrain him too. It took him a few moments to convince them that he would not strike me back, that we were brothers in Christ and that there was no way he was going to press charges.

I summarily began to explain to the people who had been

holding me back that I didn't normally go around decking people while keeping the fact that I was a minister on the down low. I prayed that they hadn't heard Brother Khalid "out me" a few seconds earlier, or that they hadn't seen me preach on the National Gospel Network cable station.

Some of the bystanders gave me looks of empathy and words of encouragement. Others sided with Brother Khalid and warned me to do something about Eddie before it was too late.

Though I don't recall how the two of us parted ways that night, the memories of my having experienced feelings of resentment towards the messenger or bearer of bad news subsided within minutes and were replaced by intense embarrassment and rage towards Eddie for betraying the trust of the church to such a magnanimous extent.

I hopped in the shower as soon as I managed my way back to my hotel room. As I stood virtually lifeless under the steaming beams of hydration, I imagined the impending conversation I had to conduct with my brother, whom I knew all along to have had a gambling problem.

No matter what excuses I held up to Brother Khalid, the truth was Eddie had gotten himself way in over his head, but up until then, only Sheila and I had been privy to this information. I had been counseling her informally for months in between our review of the budget and curriculum for the Agape Academy or while sharing a jumbo sized bucket of overly buttered popcorn in semi-darkened movie theatres waiting for the fifteen minutes of previews to the feature film to begin.

When she'd first inform me that Eddie was out playing poker at least twice a week, I chalked it up to him trying to compensate for the poor financial decisions he'd been persuaded by her to make, in moving themselves from a nice-sized three-bedroom brick home in northwest Detroit, to a five bedroom home complete with a whirlpool Jacuzzi, and a deck with a picturesque view of the uninhabited wooded area they called a backyard in West Bloomfield.

Then when he'd beat the socks off all his buddies from the plant he became overly-confident and started hitting up all the little old silver haired ladies at denominational church Bingos several times a week. I could imagine him in all his usual McGallister braggadocios bravado, doing the little two-step football victory dance and yelling out, "In yo' face," or worse, "Woop, der' it is," each time he managed to eradicate the denture clad smiles of his counterparts.

After he became bored with Bingo, he took Lady Luck on a whirlwind binge to the casino hotspots made prosperous from the sweat, blood and tears of working class Detroiters over in Windsor and Toronto. Sheila could barely snap herself out of denial that he had a problem, before he became both indifferent and nonchalant about concealing it. The last time my sister-in-law, with sheer exhaustion and through anguished tears, reminded me of my vow of counselor-client confidentiality is when she'd informed me a week prior to the trip that Eddie had been squandering his entire two-week, twenty-five hundred dollar paycheck in our two relatively new local casinos.

I stepped out of the shower in a haze of confusion and disgrace. Who should I call first, Elisabeth, the vision of loveliness from both my day and nighttime dreams, my thieving, liar of a brother, or Yusef Khalid, who was probably standing in the bathroom mirror of his suite, holding an icepack over his eye, regretting he'd ever said anything to me?

"Yo bro, what is it, man? Is it Pops?" Eddie's deep, groggy voice asked via his new cell phone. I knew my anger towards my brother superceded any lustful thoughts of Elisabeth, or remorseful feelings for decking my best friend, when I found myself furiously searching for his number, tearing through my brand new Italian leather wallet, my secretary and former

179

love interest Kelly Callaway purchased for me on my twenty-ninth birthday.

"No, Ed, man. It's you," I replied harshly, not attempting to mask the accusatory inflection of my voice. "Be here, at my suite at 7am tomorrow morning, before early worship service. And, don't be late. Donaldson asked me to preach for both a.m. services. What we need to talk about is urgent."

Long pause. I figured he had already surmised by the sharp diction of my words, that I had unraveled the mystery of his double life as a hardworking, educated, church family man by day, and two-bit conniving drinking gambler by night.

"O . . . kkkayy, mmann," he stuttered. "Wanna tell me what this is about Bob . . . or are you ggggo-ing to leave a brro—tha in sssus-pense all nnight?"

" I'm afraid you already know what this is about Ed," I replied in a more sympathetic tone. "I have a couple more calls to make, so make sure you roll through here tomorrow, no matter what. I ain't bullshittin' around with you."

"Wwhat-evver yyou say man. I'll get someone to bring me by. You okay, Bob? I mean you sound sort of . . ."

Click. I hung up on him mid-sentence, and dialed Brother Khalid's room. He picked it up on the first ring.

"Apology accepted, Little Brother," he said jovially before I could utter one word of remorse.

I chuckled, "Man, did I shine you up or what?'

"Oh yeah man, it looks like I've just gone ten rounds with Ali."

"The father or the daughter?" I laughed. "My bad."

"Man, you do know that if this would have been as recent as five years ago, when I was just a baby Muslim in training, I would have kicked your black.."

"Ay, ay, now. Remember who you talkin' to bro, I'm a man of the cloth."

"Talk to Ed yet, man?"

"He'll be here at 7 am."

"You need backup?"

"He's my brother, Yusef, I doubt it would come to that."

"Yeah, whatever man. When I was out there real bad like that, whenever one of my no account brothers tried to step to me with my faults, I tried to take them out. I'm not saying that Eddie is violent or anything. But, just give me a buzz, if things begin to blow up in that luxury suite you've got over there."

"No prob, gotta go."

"You 'bout to call that *white* girl, ain't ya?'

"Yes sir. Yes sir, indeed," I laughed without reprimanding him for calling Elisabeth white.

"I wanna tell you Little Brother, only me and Riley know anything about it. Your moms has been trying to sniff things out, but we're trying to protect her, you know, keep her and Sheila out of this."

"Doug doesn't know?"

"Naw, man just me, you and Riley. That's how things should stay. We don't want this thing to escalate or turn around to slap you in your face. We showed the tape to Ed last week."

I felt myself getting angry again. I bit down so hard on my bottom lip that I could taste blood. I was beginning to think that I would have to replace the suite's plush off-white carpet from all my rapid pacing back and forth. I looked for something to smash against the wall, but all the vases looked too expensive for me to replace.

"What'd he have to say?"

"What could his ass say? He's guilty as hell."

"I'll take care of things on my end," I replied dabbing my bottom lip with a tissue.

"Little Brother, man. You don't sound too cool."

"I'm straight man. I'm straight. In the mornin' man, in the mornin'."

"Yeah well, As-Salaam-Alaikum, my brother."

I nodded my response.

———

181

"Man, I said go in peace, brother."

"Wa Alaikum Salaam," I replied dryly.

Eleven-thirty was just too late for me to even think about disrespecting the Powell residence to speak to Elisabeth, however, I did promise Sister Powell that I would give her eager daughter a ring that same night. Since I was too much of a germaphobe to sleep in the buff under any covers but the ones on my king-sized bed at the parsonage, once I'd slipped on a pair of brand new boxer shorts and a white t-shirt, which still smelled of the spring-fresh fabric softener I used at home, I pulled the ugly, paisley printed comforter back on the bed and hopped in, clutching my cell phone and praying that the Princess hadn't transformed herself into Sleeping Beauty.

"Hello," a familiar high-pitched voice sang on the other end of the receiver.

"Elisabeth. It's Robert."

"Oh, hi Bobby. Mother told me you might be calling me tonight," she replied rather nonchalantly.

I apologized for calling her at such a late hour, offering a vaguely true explanation of church business and family problems as an excuse. She asked about my father's status. I felt a tinge of guilt for only being able to inform her of what my mother had told me the night before.

"That's good news. He should be home then, about the same time you'll get there. Mother told me that you definitely plan to stay here until Wednesday now. I can't believe you would do that just for me."

"Well, I think you are a very special young woman, and I just didn't want to waste an opportunity to get to know you better. Would you like that?" I flirted.

"I'd like that very much," I could tell she was smiling broadly, since she probably was the only one in her bedroom, on what I knew to be her own personal line. "I have to ask you this Bobby, right away, and I need an honest answer."

"Shoot," I replied nervously assuming she would ask me something about my sordid days as a womanizing undergraduate and graduate student.

"Are you currently involved with anyone?"

"No, I'm not. I haven't been involved sexually with anyone in four years."

"What happened with your last sexual relationship?"

I was slightly taken aback yet flattered by her straightforwardness because it indicated that we were mutually interested in surpassing the rigid perimeters of a platonic friendship.

" She works for me as my appointment secretary, and well, you can say that I've learned my lesson never to mix business with pleasure again."

"You're being vague," she said coyly.

I chuckled, "That was my intention."

"Well Bobby, how do you expect us to build a foundation of trust in this relationship, no matter how new it is if we don't talk to each other? I've read all of your books, especially the new one several times. You wrote that you are tired of dating and ready to get married and have a family. You wrote that you weren't going to beat around the bush with the next woman you dated and that from the impetus of the relationship the two of you were going to ask each other some critical questions."

"Quoting my work is going to earn you a marriage proposal right now, if you're not careful." I answered half-in earnest. "I guess I should paint a bigger picture for you then. Kelly and I were just not compatible."

"Kelly," she snickered, "what a juvenile name."

"Yeah, well, I dare you to say that to her face." I laughed conjuring a mental image of 105 pound Elizabeth entangled in a cat-fight over me with a 200 pound Kelly.

"I will, if I ever get the privilege of visiting you at your church."

"The door is always open. Why don't we arrange to make that happen?"

"Yes, why don't we?"

The remainder of our conversation flowed more smoothly than I'd initially expected. Before bidding her sweet dreams, she expressed to me how excited she was about the next day's events.

" While you're up there preaching, look for me on the second row."

"You have any idea how distracting your presence is while I'm up there doing my thing?"

Knucklehead

Eddie, who had never bothered to show up on time anywhere in his entire life, including his own nuptials, interrupted my shaving and grooming ritual ten minutes before seven the next morning. Brother Khalid had already phoned to "check on things", as he called it.

"Man, want me to come down there just in case things get out of hand between the two of you?"

"No thanks, brother. I can handle Eddie, besides having you here may take things to a whole 'nother level. He may try to blow the joint up once he figures out you're the one who told me."

"Well, shit, he can bring it on, man. I've got a lil' somethin' for him if he gets in my grill. But, man I'm more concerned about his safety. I've seen you provoked before man, and I know you ain't wrapped too tight when you mad, so I was offering my support to protect that fool."

"I'll be fine," I reassured him, only after I belted out a long overdue, hearty laugh.

He'd appeared to have aged by at least a few years, as he crossed the threshold into my suite. Although my brother didn't have a proclivity, comparable to mine, for selecting, coordinating and adding his own stylish taste to his attire, at least to the common observer, he didn't look like a total idiot.

Thanks to my many lectures on such vital issues as the

——

185

proper process to shine and buff the only two pairs of decent shoes he had in his drab wardrobe, his appearance had recently begun not to embarrass me.

The physical attributes he shared in common with our mother from his broad, ready smile, to his fair complexion, hazel colored eyes, and fine, slightly wavy, "good hair" that he kept neatly trimmed and faded on the sides, garnered the admiration and flirtatious attention from his fair share of women. Pretty boy, I called him, much to his wrath and vindictiveness, when I was your basic pre-teen, run-of-the-mill, tattle-tale nuisance of a little brother.

Despite his looks, and the constant propositions and temptations he claimed he received everyday, he reminded anyone who'd listened often to his boastful testimony of never having cheated once on his high-school sweetheart and love of his life Sheila, who at 5'7" stood just a little shorter, though chunkier, than her husband. No one, including myself had any cause to disbelief his proclamations of fidelity, unless you count the ongoing, dead-end simultaneous affairs he was having with lady luck and the bottle.

Although I wasn't expecting his usual bear hug of a greeting, he didn't so much as murmur a dry hello as he moped pass the bed to plop down into the recliner next to it.

Dark circles outlined his sleep deprived, reddened eyes. The burgundy and green eyesore that he tried to pass off as a tie hung loosely knotted under a dingy button down off-white shirt. Blackened scuffmarks danced their way across the front of the unpolished tan colored Stacy Adams I had given him two years before.

As I approached him, I caught a hearty whiff of the residual night-before consummation of alcohol and marijuana, mixed in with a dose of bonafide, I-haven't –showered –in-over 24-hours, underarm funk that permeated through his pores. He swatted at an invisible gnat on his scraggly goatee and began massaging both his temples with his thick, massive hands.

Wearing a white cotton, tank and the smoky gray pants to match the three quarter length jacket, which along with a recently purchased super-fly accommodating tie, hung on a hanger of the opened closet door, I plopped down on the bed, picked up the left shoe of my twice-worn pair of black Johnston and Murphy's with one hand, loosened the lid of my most reliable, bright to the bone, Kiwi shoe polish, and began my ritualistic, tedious labor of love.

Eddie admired my work quietly for a few moments, before he allowed a look of smug contempt to make its way across his yellow face. He sucked his teeth as was his custom, whenever he was about to make a mockery of one of my physical appearance maintenance rituals.

"Oh . . . so, I guess you been pumpin' iron behind a brotha's back?" he hissed at me roughly, arrogantly waving one of his hands in the general vicinity of my uncovered biceps. Once the repugnance of his breath hit my nostrils, I got pissed— indignant at his unremorseful demeanor and began to exert more elbow grease than necessary on my poor shoe. "How much you pressin' now, man? One, one fifty?"

When I ignored his inquiries regarding my daily workout regiment, he got the message, and leaned himself further back into the comfort of the recliner.

"Man, what's so important for you to have me drag myself out of my hangover, way over here in a triflin' taxi cab? By the way Bob, you owe me thirty dollars man. That idiot of a driver decided to take the scenic route over here from the Motel 6."

Somewhat relieved that he had not embarrassed himself, nor our family by shacking up with church members after having festered in the possible ramifications of his actions, he had probably taken some of the loot he had stolen from my book and tape ministry to afford himself a few losing hands of blackjack at one of the casinos in downtown St. Louis and stumbled upon a tawdry $29.95 per night room at the cheapest place to sleep in town. No wonder he looked like hell.

"Man, let's not bullshit each other here. You know why the hell you're here as well as I do."

"No the fuck I don't man! So, why don't you enlighten me baby boy?" he grimaced evenly, challenging me with those tired eyes. I shot him a more intimidating, I'm-bigger –than-you-so—don't-let –me-have-to-break –my-foot –off-into-your-ass-before-I have-to-go-break the-bread-of-life-into-God's-flock look.

"You need help Eddie. The first step is admitting that you have a problem. You need to acknowledge the fact that you're a gambler, and that your addiction has led you into a life of stealing not only from me, but from your brothers and sisters in Christ as well."

Forgetting about the migraine he'd been nursing, he jumped out of his seat and boldly stuck his finger in my face.

"Man, yyyou nnot talkin' to one, one of tthose muthafuckin' ccrack-heads or heroine addicts you counsel down in that cult like, Moos-lim ran reh-hhab ccenter you hang out at in your spare time. I'm yo' big brotha boy, I don't care how big and tall you are . . . you betta recognize."

Momentary insanity, I thought. Didn't he know I could beat his ass for breakfast, lunch, and dinner? I am well versed in the gospels . . . I know when confronted with a threat to one's physical self Christ taught we were supposed to turn the other cheek. But, I've never thought of myself nor pretended to be perfect. As a matter of fact, I realized that I was a severely flawed human being because as infuriated as I was, my dear hung-over brother had two seconds to remove his index finger from my comfort zone, before I decked him a twin version of the shiner I put on Brother Khalid's eye just the night before.

"Man, I think you better back up off me," I warned, not budging an inch myself.

He took my words into consideration and eased away slowly without relinquishing the sting of his hateful glare.

"If you don't ever see that bastard Yusef Khalid again or Mark Riley for that matter, you tell the fuzz to come lookin' for me."

I looked at my troubled brother and remembered who he was and what he meant to my life. My eyes filled with bitter tears from the anguish and pain he had not only brought upon me, but upon himself, Sheila, his boys and unbeknownst to them, the members of Rosedale Park congregation, our church, the place where we'd both had grown up on the front pew listening to our father preach. I refuse to let a solitary tear trickle an unfamiliar path down my face. I couldn't allow myself cry. I just didn't know how.

Brother Khalid had been right all along. I realized at that moment that my trepidation of crying maybe had more to do with my life of listening to the hardships of people day after day that had hardened or desensitized me beyond the point of becoming weak or vulnerable in the sight of those who I had been blessed to help and encourage, rather than my father balking at me for weeping when we had to put King to sleep.

"Have you seen the tape?"

"What tape?"

"Man, don't play with me, the tape . . . the tape that your ass kissin' wannabe disciples have of me upstairs in the deacon's office."

I turned my back on him and slowly walked to the glass door of the balcony to squint at the newly risen sun, which carried a promise of love and hope for the lost and downtrodden in this unfriendly world.

"Tell me how much you stole altogether," I spoke quietly, my voice trembling in a low staccato. I could feel him standing approximately six feet behind me.

As I peered through the transparent door, I watched his head-hung-low, shoulder-sunken reflection drag itself back to the recliner.

"Man, what difference does it make? I'm busted. I did it. I'm sorry. I'm ashamed as hell. I've sinned before God," he in one fell swoop, dramatically dropped to his knees in a very successful, callous effort to piss me off further, clutched his hands tightly together as he was begging for mercy and scooted himself over to my comfortable position at the window.

He jerked his head upward, poked out his bottom lip and batted his long girlish eyelashes in puppy dog face fashion, "But most of all my most honorable, chaste and white as snow baby brother, I've sinned against you. What must I do to atone myself of the wrath I so admittedly deserve?"

Having lost every ounce of respect I had for him at that point, I reached down with both hands and with very little effort, thanks indeed to my weight training, jerked him up by his dingy little collar. In order to bring him within an inch or two of eye contact level, I took advantage of the full force of my lift to elevate him to stand on his toes.

"I'm glad you asked. First, you gon' enroll yourself in Gamblers Anonymous, which is on the second floor of my little cult-like Moos-lim rehab center. Then you gon' take your ass up to the third floor to AA. Then, you have to pay me back the G-spots you owe within the next year, not in cash, but by completing, let's say twelve hours a week, along-side yours truly, in community service working with those so-called crack heads and heroine addicts you think ain't wor-thy of cleanin' up your shit . . ."

"Man, who the fuck do you think you are?" he yelled, showering my face with a few specks of tart spittle. He was now sobbing big, wet, sloppy tears like some little timid girl. "You can't make me do none of that bullshit!"

I released my tight grip on him and punked him by placing my large right hand on his sweaty forehead and pushing it roughly away from me. And just because I could, I walked behind him, grabbed his arm effortlessly, and twisted it behind his back much in the same manner he used to bully me before I outgrew him mentally and physically.

"Oh yeah, big bro . . . ," I whispered fiercely in his ear, "well, how does a nice long prison term sound for stiffing the church of tens of thousands of dollars? With Bubba, the three-hundred pound former bouncer as your cellie, I bet you won't be able to brag about how faithful you've been as a married man then, pretty boy. Just gimme a reason to blow the whistle on yo' raggedy ass."

He emitted a few loud whimpers as he tried to break away from my firm grip. I loosed him because I felt myself getting sweaty and I didn't feel like taking another shower.

While massaging his sore arm, he shook his head at me as if I had been the one who had invoked open shame upon the church.

"As far as atoning for stealing from God's people. . . . I've thought about it all night and I hate to drag Sheila into this, but . . ."

"Then don't!" he yelled. "Please leave Sheila out of this Bob, man. The two of you are tight, man. I don't want that to change. She counts on you. She doesn't know. It would kill her, and Ma and Pops."

"Yeah, well, you should have thought about that before you started sticking your hand in that plate. Folks work hard for their money, man. You messed up, so your ass is just gon' have to suffer the consequences. Sheila earns twenty-five grand a year for running the school man. Unfortunately she's going to have to sacrifice her earnings for at least a year to make up for what you've done."

He plopped himself down on the bed and with outstretched arms, continued to weep uncontrollably.

"Mr. Fuckin' Perfect!" he yelled, as he watched me walk over to the closet to finish getting dressed for the 8:30 service. I wanted to provide myself enough traveling time to get there at by 8:00 so I could meditate and receive a word from the Lord as to what he felt I needed to say to the congregation.

"Yep, Bobby the Preacher man, Mr. Q-Dog . . . ," he laughed deliriously at his own reference to my overly-sexed hazed collegiate days of participating in the most notoriously raunchiest, womanizing African-American male fraternity. "Bobby, the infallible. . . . doobie smokin', sneakin' a quickie with the ho-ish Shelton twins in the church supply closet before preachin' one of your first gospel sermons in Pops' pulpit . . ."

" I was attending Michigan State then. ..man, not even twenty years old.. . . . way before I fully converted. Years before my ordination," I replied calmly, while inserting my silver cufflinks into the sleeves of my monogrammed starched white shirt.

"Oh yeah, that was years before your so-called celibacy, although when you were seeing Kelly's fat ass, her little hooptie Escort stayed parked in the driveway of the parsonage way past her working hours . . ."

"Man, you don't know what the hell you talkin' 'bout, so I suggest you shut it up, before I shut it up for you, understand? And, another thing, I never . . . had sex with Kelly."

"That all depends on what you call sex . . . but, I better shut the hell up before you try to rough a nigga up again, huh? I bet your newest pretty young white tenderoni would be surprised to know that you've got such a fucked up temper."

Before I showed him the door, I warned him not to show

Book One: Only a Man

up at church that day and not to speak one word to Brother Khalid on the flight home, unless he wanted the church, including our parents to find out about his little problem.

My Cherie Amour

I saw to it that I didn't overly linger in Brother Donaldson's pulpit for the 10:30 message on unity in the church I'd preached a few weeks prior at my own congregation. Though I prayed for the Lord to send me two original sermons that Sunday morning, Satan, with his weaponry of fiery darts, slung thoughts of hurt, confusion, and anger towards my brother to render my half-hearted, semi-earnest requests useless.

During the latter service, five people, a record number from the Kingshighway congregation, accepted the Lord's invitation and put him on in baptism. Another ten or twelve made confessions of having brought open shame upon the church. After the benediction, I stood in the cramped vestibule flanked by Brother Khalid of course, Brother and Sister Donaldson and several of the deacons. As I greeted the congregants whose faces had become familiar to me, Donaldson couldn't stop patting me firmly on the back and flashing those yellow-stained, out-dated gold-capped teeth at me.

"Son, you sho' turned this house out this mornin'! Yessirreee! Heee! Heee! We've never had so many folk get saved on the same day. Why, your message cleared the entire first rows on both sides."

I nodded respectfully and told him that all praise and honor for so many lost souls being added or returning back to the fold, was due to the Almighty Jehovah, and that I refuse to take credit for simply being the vessel he used to get them to the altar.

Besides, I thought to myself, if he thought that was an impressive feat, then he would crap bricks, if he'd ever visited the Rosedale Park congregation. In the four years since I had taken over the ministry we'd baptized at least twenty souls per month and on an average Sunday, at least the first three pews on both sides were filled from penitent Christians making confessions. Kickin' much butt for Christ's sake. Brother Khalid had begun a new custom of roping off those designated rows each Lord's Day, so no one would occupy them before hand.

"Magnificent message, Robert," a familiar, sultry smooth voice congratulated me before a few people cleared the path before me. "Wow, I've heard your father preach several times before, but I must say your sermons are so down to earth and practical, with just enough dramatic effect to even keep the attention of our young people. The Church of Christ has needed that for a long time." Emily Powell flashed a brilliant white smile, with that tiniest of baby gaps separating her two-front teeth. I couldn't help being drawn into it, not only because a person's smile revealed an awfully lot about their true natures, but because from my past observations, few white women had gaps. Lauren What's-her-name. That old white model from back in the day. Used to grace the covers of Vogue and Elle magazines. That's who she reminded me of. Lauren Hutton.

She reached upward to hug my neck. Ms. Maggie's maternal almost smothering embrace followed, along with a rather seductive caress from Tanya and a gripping, challenging handshake from James Powell. The lovely Elisabeth boldly stepped up to me, lifted her head full of soft, light brown curls and gently kissed me on the cheek without uttering a word. Brother Khalid, who was standing to my right gave me a rather conspicuous nudge, as Emily reached for her husband's arm to tell him to come along.

"I know you won't be through here until about 2:30, so let's push dinner a little further back, let's say, 3:00," Emily suggested.

"That'll do just fine Sister Powell," I grinned not taking my eyes off of Elisabeth who was ogling me twice as hard as she had been two nights before.

"I like to have my food good and digested before evening service, son. So, you make sure you're there on time," James Powell ordered, raising his right eyebrow, as if to intimidate me. Before I could respond, Emily playfully yanked him away and winked her eye at me.

"Well, Ms. Libby, you comin', little gal?" Ms. Maggie asked sassily as she placed her hands on her hips.

Elisabeth sighed heavily and rolled her eyes heavenward at the sound of her abbreviated name, defiantly drew nearer to me and clutched my hand.

She looked coyly up at me and batted those long beautiful eyelashes that silhouetted chestnut colored, perfectly oval-shaped eyes. "No, Ms. Maggie," she snapped. " I'm going to wait here for Bobby, if that's alright with you, Bobby," the words directed towards me were demure and syrupy sweet. Brother Khalid shot her a mean "give-me-a-break " glare that she didn't seem to notice, before he sulked away, probably to tend to the shiner he'd successfully concealed underneath his trademark dark shades.

"No . . . I don't mind at all," I assured her, although I'd planned to return to my suite to shower and change into a new suit, because once Donaldson heard it through the grapevine that I had extended my stint in the Gateway City, he, without asking me, made the announcement to the congregation that I would be delivering another powerful message that evening. I would then be presented with the love offering that the ushers had collected after the second service that day.

I had also intended to stop by a local floral shop to pick up flowers for the women in the household, and perhaps stop by the market to purchase a bottle of white wine for dinner. Ma had taught me well; there was no way I was going to accept an invitation to dinner from anyone, especially rich folks, without bringing a few tokens of gratitude.

"See, Ms. Maggie. I'm going to wait right here with Bobby, run along."

I couldn't believe that I actually witnessed her shooing someone away like some pesky fly with those finely manicured, bony hands.

Ms. Maggie wasn't one to be easily dismissed. She walked up closer to Elisabeth scowling, and through clenched teeth, told her that she would not put up with her disrespect any longer. Elisabeth's naturally rosy cheeks turned crimson red from embarrassment. She looked at me to rescue her, so I did.

"Ms. Maggie, we'll be fine here. I think we're both a little excited about us finally having some time alone together, that's all." By then, Elisabeth had threaded her skinny arm through mine and as if a predator were about to attack what belonged to her, tightened her grip, while glaring hatefully at Ms. Maggie who was at least six or seven inches shorter than her.

I bent down to plant a kiss on her plump, dark-brown cheek. She smiled up at me, but it quickly faded when she directed her attention back to Elisabeth.

"You didn't even ask the man if he had something to do before he comes over, gal." One thing was clear, in all her haughtiness the Princess' tirades were no match for the abominable Ms. Maggie.

"It doesn't matter Ms. Maggie," Elisabeth yelled, capturing the attention of the congregants who had been waiting patiently in line to greet me, "so why don't you just go away, and leave us alone!"

Not one to embarrass easily, I stood there mortified, like some hen-pecked fool, not knowing what to say next.

"Fine," Ms. Maggie responded gritting her teeth, "but, you best believe your mama is gonna find out about this episode, lil' gal." She stormed off, with several of her elderly cohorts trailing her heels to console her. Brother Khalid, who had returned from the bathroom, stood there, tsk, tsk, tsking away and shaking his head. If I weren't in the middle of this ludicrous situation, I would have been on the floor laughing.

" Like, for goodness sake, everyone! What are you guys staring at? Aren't you going to greet the minister?" she snapped at the people who had been clucking their tongues and discussing her diva-like behavior within our earshot. "I hate some of these old hags here, Bobby. They always try to keep stuff going." She clutched my arm even tighter and stood silently, her head held high, gloating before the other women, as if she had won some prizefight.

Not one of them bothered to speak to her. Instead they all gravitated towards me. She smugly watched them hug and kiss me without releasing the grip she had on my arm until the last one was out of sight.

"Little Brother, we need to talk, in private," Brother Khalid announced a few seconds later.

Her daze didn't leave me as Brother Khalid escorted me out the of the glass doors, and unto the porch.

"Man, you sure you wanna stay here with that bitch?"

Annoyed, I nodded my head and began to walk away. He grabbed my arm,

"Man, what's with all the pullin' and yankin' on me today?" I laughed.

"Little Brother, I don't think you should pursue this potna," he said seriously.

"Why not, man? What's wrong with her? So what she has

a flair for the dramatic, and she's a bit spoiled and Erica Kane-ish man, but man, look at her," I chuckled boastfully full of pride and bliss. I fanned my hand out toward her direction and playfully bowed. She smiled that closed-mouth smile again and waved demurely to me from the opposite side of the window.

"Isn't . . . she . . . lovely? Isn't she . . . won..der . . . ful?" I sang, loud enough for her to hear me.

Brother Khalid, for the first time looked at her, as if he were appraising an expensive piece of art. The pupils behind his darkened lenses softened. His lips turned up to a semi-smile of appreciation.

"Man, look at me!" he ordered, snapping himself out of my world of lust of the eye and the flesh. "Bob, she's no good for you man. She's poison. Haven't you heard and seen enough, Little Brother?" His tone was frantic and fast paced, much liked the one we'd both used when we were trying to get an addict to not take another hit from the crack pipe.

"Man, do you see her over there? She's the one," I practically yelled my gratitude to God for finally answering my prayers. "You know she's the one I wrote about in my book."

"Yeah man. Been there, done that."

"She fits all the right criteria. She's tall, but not too tall, lean . . ."

"Bones man, skin and bones. Anorexic."

I chose to ignore his jabs and continued reciting the list of wonderful qualities my future wife embodied. " She's very young, which means she's impressionable. I could teach her a lot of things . . ."

"Like how to respect her elders and how to be decent to people in general," he quipped.

"Man, she's refined. She's polished."

"She's bratty and snobbish. Do you want a woman like that. . . . who doesn't know our struggle . . . the black experience in America you're always preaching at the Warriors about?"

"Give it a rest Brother Khalid, man. She's still half-black you know. Besides," I added enthusiastically, "have you checked out those little sexy lips, and those soft brown eyes, and that hair, man she has hair for days. And that complexion, it's so smooth and . . ."

"White!"

"Man, she ain't white," I chuckled, shrugging my shoulders. "I'm done trying to talk some sense into your head. I'm sold. I'm going to marry that girl within the next couple months."

He looked at me incredulous. Shocked. Speechless. Defeated.

"Just you mark my words man . . . ," I continued.

"That's what I'm afraid of Bob. That's what I'm afraid of. I'll touch base with you once I get back to Detroit and after I check in with Riley."

"Be safe, Brother Khalid." We did our standard, brother to brother touching of the fists. "And stay away from Eddie on the plane." As he walked away, I called out to him, "Start saving up for your tux, potna. Start savin'!"

Cruisin' The Beamer

Elisabeth, clad in sexy three-inch sling-backs, stepped out onto the porch, folded her arms across her chest and patted her foot impatiently. "Are you ready to go, Doctor Minister?"

"Sure thing, sweetheart." I extended my elbow to her, so that she could re-clutch it. When she willingly obliged, we began to make our way over to the parking lot.

"How are we going to do this with two cars?" she wondered aloud.

"No worry. I'll just ride with you back here after dinner and pick up my rental. Donaldson is dropping Brother Khalid, Doug and Eddie off at the airport for me."

"Speaking of your brother, a very attractive man, I might add. I missed him somehow today. Was he here?"

I bit down on my bottom lip hard, scratched my right temple with my free hand and shook my head. "He, uh, well, he wasn't feeling up to par this morning. So, I left him back at the hotel." Although I felt quite comfortable with the familiarity Elisabeth and I had already established between us, I still wanted to avoid the subject of my brother like the plaque. She nodded her acceptance of my answer as truth and released my arm to reach inside a tiny pink purse to retrieve a single key contained on a BMW key ring.

As we approached the luxury car, I noticed that Brother

201

Khalid had been wrong about one thing. The car wasn't pink, it was off-white, but the pillows and miniature stuff animals displayed in the window were pink, along with the white Missouri plates trimmed in pink letters that read PRINCESS.

If he had been in error about something as innocuous as the color of the woman's car, chances were he had been wrong about some of the other less than flattering things he'd said about her too.

"So, now is my chance to be chauffeur driven," I announced rubbing the fuzz on my chin. I couldn't remember the last time, a woman, besides my mother before I got my license, had driven me around anywhere.

"You're not comfortable with that are you, Bobby?" she flirted, batting those sexy lashes at me again.

"Well, actually I'm not. But, I can deal just this once."

She pressed the alarm button on the car, threw me the key and slid herself gracefully into the passenger seat. I stood there smiling at the metal object in my hand, trying to decide if I was more thrilled about my first test run in a Beamer or that she didn't feel it necessary to challenge one of my many antiquated male-chauvinistic tendencies. "I think I'm in-love," I said to myself, not caring if she heard me. She patted the driver's seat and asked me if I were going to get in some time today.

"I meant to tell you that I have to stop back by the hotel to shower and change suits, if that's cool with you. Donaldson asked me to preach tonight."

Her eyes shifted nervously to her feet. She reached not too-far up to twirl a long strand of hair around her forefinger. After I started the engine, I placed her trembling hand in mine.

"Or, if you prefer . . . I could drop you by your house first . . ."

"No, no. Don't be ridiculous, Bobby," she sighed as if my suggestion was way out in left field. "I'll just wait in the lobby. Just don't leave me down there all day. I need to get changed for dinner too, you know."

"You look fine," I replied evaluating her immaculate appearance from head to toe. She was wearing a darker fuchsia version of the same designer tailored suit from two nights before, with matching fuchsia heels. Her neatly one-inch above the knee trimmed skirt, clung to her small hips and buttocks without being too tight, while she was standing.

But I could tell she was slightly uncomfortable with the shortened length of the skirt her seated position in the car was causing, because she kept using her pink leather cover Bible case to conceal most of her thigh and a part of those sharp knobs she called knees.

Once again, her makeup mostly of a faint pinkish-red hue absolutely complimented her smooth, blemish free, alabaster complexion.

She used the lever on the passenger seat to recline her back and rested her eyes in a closed meditative state. I assumed she had accurately surmised that I knew how to find my way back to the hotel, because she didn't bother to offer any directions.

"Yes, you are *very* fine," I repeated replaying the fantasy of us getting it on, on the floor of my office.

Without opening her eyes, she blushed instead of saying thank you.

"Welll . . . ," I sang waiting for some acknowledgement of my compliment.

"Welllll . . . ," she repeated. " I know."

I laughed aloud at her self-absorbed conceit, which would have repulsed an ordinary cat, but not me. I respected her honesty.

"You know this, huh," I teased. "Well, what about me, can a brotha get some love? I mean here you were just a hot second ago talkin' about how attractive you think Ed is . . . and I'm sittin' here dressed to the nines, with a fresh fade, clean shaven, with buffed knobs, I might add and a sista' can't recognize?"

"Recognize what?" she shrugged nonchalantly, failing to understand the Ebonic interpretation of the latter phrase.

"Recognize, what?" I mimicked, trying to feed her a dose of her own vainness, "All of this," I thumped myself manly on the chest. "The-glory-that-is-me," I replied in my best impersonation of James Earl Jones' melodic baritone.

"You're, like, not half bad," she mumbled, somehow managing to refrain her pupils from fluttering underneath her closed lids.

She'd also failed to catch the biting three-point, slamdunker sarcasm I threw her way. She couldn't think I was serious. Enough women had been clamoring for my attention since my high school days, that if no female ever jocked me again, I could ride high enough on past compliments for five lifetimes.

"Well, that puts me in my place," I replied quietly, a bit offended that she couldn't muster up a simple compliment for me or to admit that she was mutually attracted.

She shrugged, sighed loudly and opened her eyes. "What's the matter, now?"

"Nothing, I was just trying to figure out the fastest way to the hotel."

"You're lying," she laughed. " I think you wanted to hear me tell you how good you look."

Not ever one to stay upset at a pretty woman, for long. I joined in her laughter. " Okay, okay, I'm busted."

"I suppose I could tell you that, but given the way you carry yourself and all, I figured you already knew. Besides, Bobby, you should know just as well as I do, that the last thing gorgeous people like us need to be told is how fine we are or how good we look. There are enough ego-maniacs in the world anyway."

I nodded in agreement. "Now, that, baby, is the smartest thing I've heard you say yet."

"Just keep living," she flirted, batting her eyes and twirling her hair.

By the time we made our way to the hotel for me to change suits and to Schnuck's supermarket to pick up a bottle of wine and flowers, I was starving. Due to my feud with that idiot Eddie, the only thing I'd eaten that morning were a few stale crackers Donaldson had in the top drawer of his desk in his office.

Afraid that Elisabeth could hear my stomach growling, from the passenger seat, I pumped up the volume of one of the CD's contained in Stevie Wonder's, *Musicquariam* collection.

She rolled her eyes and folded her hands across her chest, as we made our way down Interstate 270 to the Olive Exit to get to the hotel.

"What's up with you? The music too loud?" I practically yelled through the chorus of "Do I Do".

"Yes, it is," she whined. I leaned forward to adjust the volume.

"Better?"

"I guess, considering the circumstances," she frowned.

"Wha . . . , please don't tell me, you don't dig Stevie, the Master Blaster, Wonder. Please, don't . . . or I'ma have to make you exercise those long pretty legs to walk home."

"Okay, I won't tell you I don't," she huffed. "I'm just sick and tired of him, that's all."

"What do you mean by that? It's not like he has some new stuff out, or anything."

"Yeah, but after having grown up on this, listening to it day in and day out, I wouldn't care if I ever heard another stupid harmonica playing in my life."

"Hold up, baby . . . hold up," I feigned disgust. " I really

205

am gon' have to put you up out of your own ride . . . who's the big fan anyway?"

"My *sister*. Who else?" she pronounced the word sister, venomously, as if she had been sucking on a lemon. "Her bedroom was right next to mine and when we became teenagers, my parents, especially Mother, for some inexplicable reason allowed Lori to do, like, whatever she wanted, especially blast Stevie Wonder until the wee hours of the morning."

"So, what you're trying to tell me, is that you're dissin' the eighth wonder of the world because your sister is a sistah after my own heart?"

Her cheeks turned a crimson red. Avoiding eye contact, she directed her gaze straight ahead and closed her eyes again. "Basically."

"What's up between the two of you anyway?"

"I have no idea what you're talking about."

I decided not to enlighten her about the conversation her mother and Ms. Maggie had in front of me about the jealous rage she had over Lori winning a leading part in some off-broadway produced and directed African-American musical. Neither was I willing to confide that I had Brother Khalid check her out via her cook Tanya, so I pretty much had to let her own words hang her out to dry.

"You act like you hate to bring her name up. I guess I just sensed a tad bit of animosity there, that's all."

She squinted suspiciously at me before pensively looking upward, as if she were trying to find the adequate words to describe the most profound, complex, human relationship that ever existed. I appreciated how open and honest she was being with me, even though in my line of work, it was par for the course.

" Lori, well, how should I describe her . . . Lori, is . . . what you call a free spirit. We have virtually nothing in common and for that reason, no one seems to think we should be able to get along as well as we do. Mother has done a fine job at trying to botch our relationship over the years. We're totally different. . . . I love her, but I just don't get her. People like to be around her because she has all of this talent . . . and she is sooo annoyingly modest about it, and I must say very beautiful, even though she won't do anything to train that wild, super wavy fro of hers, or wear the slightest hint of makeup. I must admit though, she is the only person in this entire world, except Daddy who really gets me, and puts up with me in spite of myself. She's basically, your run of the mill, all-American, girl next door, gone bad."

"Girl next door, gone bad?" I intentionally echoed her, in an effort to get her to keep going.

"Yeah, a few weeks after she moved into the dorms up at Michigan State when she was still sixteen, she got pregnant, by some guy darker than you," she replied disgusted with her sister's poor judgment in committing fornication in the first place. For the first time, I wondered if Elisabeth considered herself black. She didn't look black at all. Why, if we had lived back in the times of slavery, she would have probably been one of the sisters who tried to pass, like Queen, Alex Haley's great-grandmother. Had she realized that her own father, Ms. Maggie, Tanya and all the members of her church were black, and she and her mother weren't? Moreover, she was hatin' somethin' fierce on Stevie. All black folks love them some Stevie, even if they weren't as fanatical about it as me. Made a brotha wonder. I didn't want to discuss such a sensitive, explosive issue at that moment because I was learning a lot about her just by listening to her analyze and dissect her sister's life.

"No one knew about the pregnancy except for me and my parents of course."

"What happened to the baby?"

"She miscarried. Thank God. Could you imagine the shame and embarrassment that would have brought down

---

207

upon my father's head, as the only elder of our church, at the mention of his oldest daughter having a child out of wedlock, at sixteen, as soon as she went away to college? They would have practically kicked him out of the church for even thinking about letting her graduate two years earlier."

"Kids screw up when they go off to college. I know I did. How upset could your old man have been?"

"Are you kidding me? Daddy like, practically disowned her. Mother begged and pleaded Lori's case, and talked him into allowing her to stay up there, which in my opinion is a big mistake. Maybe if she would have like, come home, she would not have let those people brainwash her."

"What people?" I asked, growing more intrigued by the minute.

"This group of people who studies and embraces some aspects of all the major religions of the world. They call themselves free spirited liberals or something or the other. They talk all that mumbo jumbo about God being neither male nor female and all that stuff about the journey of a thousand miles beginning with yourself. They believe in letting your conscience be your guide. . . . that there is no Satan, hell, nor day of final judgment. They don't endorse any orthodox or corporate worship services. Lori, later in her first year, pretty much rejected our church's teachings, and fell in with them. She and Daddy have not had more than two words to say to each other since she was home that Easter and refused to attend church because she said that she didn't have to believe the same doctrine to be saved. She claimed that the Spirit lived within her and that no amount of attending worship services would affect her chances of being saved. She even, like, oversees some group of teenaged girls who use street dancing and rhythms to so call praise the Lord."

"That's deep," I whispered, as I approached Elisabeth's cul-de-sac slowly. I shifted the gear selection stick into park at the corner. I wanted her to finish the story before I could step foot outside the car. "Then, Emily told me how upset they were that she ditched her plans for med school. That must have really ruffled the old man's feathers."

"Yes, it did. But, he pretty much wrote her off during her freshmen year. Mother was still holding out for her to redeem herself in his eyes by becoming a surgeon. But, instead she's some kind of dance teacher, slash wannabe actress-singing sensation for right now. Besides, she would have probably gone into veterinarian medicine as opposed to neurology. She loves animals, especially dogs."

I smiled in thinking about my own affinity towards the furrier species. For the first time since I'd arrived, I wondered who had been taking care of Cherie and Deuce my two, one hundred pound plus rotweilers since my mother had been holed up taking care of Pops in the hospital all week.

I could tell Elisabeth was growing tired of recounting the life of the person she both admired and envied most in the world. If there really were a tangible fine line between love and hate, this little doll was walking with the grace of a skilled circus acrobat. She folder her arms across her chest and directed me to turn left.

"Our house is one of three in the alcove, just on the other side of this wooded area we're about to pass," she enunciated perfectly as if she were a sophisticated English tour guide pointing out such historical monuments as Big Ben and Buckingham Palace. As I approached what appeared to me as three mega-mansions, I had no problem determining which one belonged to the Powell family.

Right in front of the light Maplewood double-doors, parked at the apex of the semi-circular cove, was the sporty silver '96 Jaguar, shined to perfection, that I'd seen Drs. James and Emily Powell, along with their cook Ms. Maggie drive away in from the church almost two hours prior to our arrival.

Now, I'd spoken to audiences of more than a few thou-

209

sand Christians and non-Christians alike, I'd dribbled dozens of Wilson's basketballs up and down the courts of college stadiums throughout this land and country as a Spartan for Michigan State University. I'd also shared the gospel with the meanest bunch of bench-pressing, solitary-confined inmates that one could imagine, and I've never felt one iota of insecurity or stage fright. Ma tells me that I was born without a single trace of reserve or self-doubt in my entire body.

"*Why, my Bobby came out cooing, not crying, but singing at the top of his little precious lungs. He charmed the socks off of every doctor, nurse and resident in that delivery room,*" she would brag often to any woman at the church, in the supermarket or at the beauty salon, who had been blessed to be expecting a newborn baby.

"*Yes, indeed. He was born to teach and help others. Just like little Jesus, when he was twelve, and his parents lost track of him, where was he? In the midst of the temple teaching some of the most learned men of his day and age. Well, when my Bobby was twelve, his Pops and I lost track of him too! We were downtown, doing some last minute Christmas shopping at the Hudson's building before it closed down, when we also lost track of Bob, well, do you know where he was, girl?*" Ma would pause at this part of her little story not to catch her breath, or to ascertain if she had a captive audience, but for dramatic effect.

"*I say, do you know where we found him? We searched all up and down the block, in every neighboring store within a half mile radius, we found that boy, that lil' handful, in the pool hall, chalking up one of those cue sticks and telling all of those drunken, no-account gambling, dead-beat dads, that Jesus was coming back soon for his church and that every man, woman, or child had better be ready when the bridegroom comes for his first love, the church! Now, isn't that ironic? Isn't that just wonderful?*" Ma would conclude gleefully with that proud maternal gleam in her eye as the poor woman who had been subjected to such a lengthy recollection was left wondering whether to congratulate her on raising such a fine young man or to start praying to God that very hour to be as equally blessed with her impending offspring.

The Princess' Palace

Ma wouldn't have believed her eyes if she would have witnessed the buckets of sweat pouring down my forehead and back, as Elisabeth took my hand and led me up the seemingly mile long walkway nestled between the most meticulously trimmed shrubbery I'd ever noticed. The picturesque multi-colored perennials enclosed by miniature garden night-lights created a never-ending border around the house.

She released the light grip she had on my left hand to rap on the door with the wooden knocker, which produced a hallow echo, that caused my gaze to be directed upward to the cathedral ceiling with the elegant crystal chandelier made transparent via the colossal window located just above the entrance. I prayed that my intended wouldn't notice me shifting my weight from one leg to the next and tightly gripping the bottle of wine and the bouquet of flowers I held in my free hand. Somehow my attempts of common chivalry and courtesy seemed quite meager to the luxury and splendor to which this family, especially Elisabeth had grown accustomed.

"My goodness gracious, children," Ms. Maggie pronounced flashing that perfectly straight smile of false teeth through fat dimpled cheeks. "Come on in. Come right in. Libby, girl, you have the key. Why are you knockin' on this door like some stranger, chile? Bobby, come on in dear, and let me take these things from you."

Elisabeth rolled her eyes at Ms. Maggie and slid her thin fingers in between mine.

She pulled me into the house filled with scents of fried chicken and apple pie and attempted to dart right past Ms. Maggie, for the sole purpose of ignoring her completely.

Before she could walk me clean out of sight, I managed to turn around, throw Ms. Maggie a conspiratorial wink, mouthed my gratitude, and offered a brief explanation as to the recipients of the flowers.

"For you, Ms. Maggie, as well as Emily."

"Thank you, Preacha," she practically yelled down the front corridor as Elisabeth tugged on my arm more forcibly to avoid her altogether. "I'll put these in some water . . . why don't you let Ms. Libby take you on in the formal dining room? Me and Tanya will be serving dinner right away while it's hot."

"Yes, ma'am."

"Don't 'yes ma'am' her, Bobby. Maggie Sims is the type of woman who lets common courtesy go to her head. She thinks she's more to this family than the 'help' anyway, thanks to mother," Elisabeth complained.

Instead of using speech to come to Ms. Maggie's defense, the reflexes in my lower jawbone betrayed me, as my mouth popped open at the sight of the ostentatious formal dining room. Elisabeth released the grip on my arm to open the double door entrance with a dramatic flair.

A long polished to perfection dark maple antique table surrounded by ten matching colonial style chairs with hand-carved high backs, and plush embroidered seat cushions greeted me as I stepped into the room which reminded me of a scene from Lifestyles of the Rich and Famous.

In the center of the table sat a one hundred percent re-flection-bearing heirloom tea-set, which I'm quite sure was solely used for decorative purposes. Each place setting contained a multitude of silverware before each part of the meal was to be served.

I thanked God for all the years coming up when Ma, who'd never failed to serve dinner at 6:30 sharp, forced me and my hungry brother to shower the b-ball funk off of us before even approaching and perfectly aligning the silverware on her eight-piece fully decorated dining room table, that would make Martha Stewart proud.

To the right of the entrance, I noticed a huge china/porcelain dish collection displayed within an attractive curio. A crystal chandelier more luxurious than the one hanging in the foyer area, hung over the flat ceiling with its own built in lighting system. Monet watercolor paintings framed three of the four walls.

The success of my ministry had taken me into homes of other black men who could afford equally exquisite works of art, but the piece that captivated my attention the most was the giant-sized family oil painting located right behind the head of the table. From where I stood, I could decipher that the four-member family had decided to wear elaborate colonial costumes to compliment the décor of what was probably the most distinguished room in the house.

The family patriarch sporting some sort of ridiculous navy military uniform, complete with gold ropes which hung loosely over both of his husky shoulders, sat stiffly next to his Caucasian saintly-looking handkerchief bearing wife, who, wearing a matching navy blue dress with a tightly-buttoned white stiff collar, had her dainty arm looped through his. Wearing a dour, "I'd-really-rather-be-out-on-the-golf-course-instead-of-indulging-the-little-women", grimace, I was tempted to laugh out loud at the thought of him donning one of those poofy white wigs men wore back then. I thank God in heaven, that the only hair remaining on his practically shiny bald-in-the-middle head was neatly faded on both sides.

The two pubescent girls flanked either side of their parents. Elisabeth standing tall and pretentiously regal with her narrow chin pointed upward and her long straight brown locks draped seductively over one of her slight shoulders that peaked through a rose-colored, ultra-frilly shawl, looked every bit of an eleven year-old, overly made-up wanna-be model.

I pointed, playfully nudged her and laughed aloud at her image. She, still standing snugly close to me, used her right hand to cover an embarrassed grin.

"Back then, I was, like, totally enamored with Scarlet O'Hara. What can I say?" She smiled coyly, through crimson cheeks, twisting a long loose tendril around her fingers. She drove my raging, dormant-for four years hormones completely crazy when she did that. After all, out of all the women I've dated and/or fooled around with, none of them had a naturally grown crown full of beautiful hair like hers.

"Daddy had this painting commissioned for my thirteenth birthday . . ."

I nodded politely to inform her that I was still passively listening, while I walked over to the north wall and folded my arms across my chest pensively, as if I had been called upon to appraise the value of the original Mona Lisa.

A set of perfectly beautiful, white teeth, accompanied by a rare pair of dark, yet clear, equally alluring large onyx eyes drew me in, and invoked in me a sense of supernatural je ne sais quoi. Impulsively, my right hand did its own thing by reaching up to the smooth dimpled cheek of the girl with the soft sensuous lips and the jet black naturally wavy hair. I noticed the ample-bosomed, slim angelic creature was the only family member sporting a happy, contagious smile, that made the dark pupils in the wide eyes she'd inherited from the old dude, gleam. A vision of honey-brown loveliness, plain and simple, unmade up, with the exception of a light coating of lip-gloss on her full inviting lips. A familiar voice distracted me from my awestruck stupor.

"Robert, I see Elisabeth has shown you her most prized

possession," the proud mother observed, standing a few inches behind me. I nodded my appreciation for such an exquisite work.

"And you see, here, here is our oldest daughter Lori. I told you about her the other night," Emily added maternally reaching out to touch the waistline of Lorraine's tightly corseted dress, as if to smooth out any visible wrinkles. "She's naturally radiant, isn't she?"

I had never heard a more accurate description of anyone.

"Emily, you have two very beautiful, intelligent daughters. I know you and Dr. Powell are very proud."

"Yes, we are," she replied wistfully mournful. "I just wish I didn't miss her as much as I do . . ."

"Oh Mother, please. Please don't worry Bobby with your obsession of Lori," Elisabeth whined defensively threading her arm through mine once again, as if threatening to bolt me out the door, if Emily failed to comply with her demands to snap herself back into a cheerful, hospitable mood.

"She's not worrying me," I replied without hesitation. "She's just being a concerned mother . . ."

"Yes, but this dinner is for you, Bobby. You are our honored guest, so Mother, if you don't mind, I would like to take Bobby on a tour of the house while you all are putting the last touches on dinner."

"Yes, yes, dear," Emily conceded, wiping a tear away from the corner of her eyes, forcing a smile. "That sounds perfect. Thanks for the wine, Bobby. It's one of my favorite kinds."

"Just hurry it up, Princess," James Powell's forceful voice urged, as he entered the room to take his seat at the head of the table. He nodded a dry greeting in my direction. I reciprocated his half-hearted gesture. "Daddy's hungry, and Ms. Maggie wants to serve the food while it's nice and hot."

"Yes, Daddy."

I successfully masked my sheer fascination of the pretentious manner in which the Powell's had chosen to live. If I would have seen the elegant décor of their mini-mansion in one of the elaborate photo layouts of one of those Better Homes and Gardens type magazines, to which Ma and Sister Calloway subscribes, I would have bet my last dime that the owners of this home were blue-blooded "old-money" millionaires.

Elisabeth took pride in pointing out that she had dusted every room to perfection and that she had ordered Ms. Maggie and her assistant Dorothy to rearrange the furniture to give the house a face-lift.

"Ms. Maggie, has an assistant?" I asked finding the very notion absurd. *A maid's assistant. Dig that.*

"Of course. Ms. Maggie has gotten very old and forgetful. Since Mother works such ridiculous hours and doesn't care about domestic things, I have always supervised the help and delegated their responsibilities. A couple of years ago, after I found a series of dust bunnies in every corner of every room and some of my most expensive clothes smelled like moth balls, I convinced Daddy to hire someone, who was actually willing to do as told, and to not sit back on her laurels and take advantage of her past history with the family. She and that Tanya have been mooching off this family for years . . . but I know this is probably boring you, so we'll just tour the second floor before washing up for dinner, okay?"

"Sure," I chuckled, tickled over her incessant chatter and the complaints of the over-privileged. One thing about this woman, I realized right away, is that she would never bore me.

She led me hurriedly up the winding staircase into a long hallway of closed doors to the right and left of us. She nonchalantly pointed out an old playroom of hers, along with her mother's barely used sewing room, which had its own connecting sun-porch. The northeast corner of the second floor hosted her parent's master suite, which included a king-sized four posted water-bed, matching black bureaus and armoires accompanying the manly black and gold drapes that were dramatically drawn to expose the scenic pasture view over the veranda.

I caught a glimpse of the sable Jacuzzi trimmed in gold, private shower room, with his and her countertops and wash basins within the luxurious gold painted walls held together by black marble tile. Just when I thought I could have died and gone on to meet my Lord in heaven, my intended tugged my arm to follow her quickly to the grand finale, her room. But, to get there we had to pass, Lorraine's old boudoir.

She stopped at the double doors that led into her sister's room, pondering if entering without her permission would be considered an intrusion. Deciding to follow her first instinct, she maneuvered the levers of one of the doors and afforded me a peek into the mystery woman's former habitat.

Upon first notice, the room looked dull, almost bare compared to the others, I'd seen including the ultra-finished basement, complete with a pool-table, another whirlpool and tanning room, for Emily and Elisabeth, I suppose, and an impressive ten-seater movie screening room.

A fresh coat of plain white paint, coupled with plush, untrampled upon white carpet, comforter set, canopy, and mega-sized fluffy pillows gave the room a calming and ethereal quality. A tattered homemade poster of cardboard and dingy yellow yarn containing a child's first feeble attempts at cursive hung off one of the southern posts of the bed. A pair of pink ballet shoes were strapped around the opposite post.

I strained to decipher what the sign said, so Elisabeth removed her three-inch heels, sauntered over to the bed and flipped it over. It read: *"This room is a private dwelling place for me, and me only, Lorraine Jameson Powell. Keep out!!! This means you, Libby!!!"*

I laughed at Elizabeth's dramatic interpretation of a sign that was at least a decade old. She pointed to the shelves over in the far right hand corner, filled with at least thirty trophies both small and large of all of Lorraine's accomplishments in cheerleading, gymnastics, vocal performances, dance competitions, thespian endeavors, and academic achievements such as National Honor Society and Phi Beta Kappan. Both her high school diploma from some exclusive all girl's academy in Chesterfield and her bachelor's degree from Michigan State were mounted on the walls in white frames.

I also noticed many photos of Lorraine from her youthful to late adolescent years on top of her vanity table, dresser and armoire. As tempted as I was to remove my shoes and run my feet across the inviting carpet, to capture Lorraine's essence through the photo montage, I opted against it, once Elisabeth stretched her arms in one grandiose outward gesture, and declared her sister's room as, "Mother's Shrine to her beloved ungrateful daughter, who had not stepped foot inside her old bedroom in three years."

As tour guide Elisabeth carted me off to the door to the left of Lorraine's room, my mind was still reeling from the sheer dedication and maybe even obsession Emily had of the prodigal daughter, when the Princess flung yet another pair of double doors open to expose a rather large bathroom, complete with a full soft-pink colored Jacuzzi, matching throw rugs and towels monogrammed with the initials EJP.

Elisabeth rambled on about the many fights she had with Lorraine about the adjoining facility that connected their two bedrooms. Since Lorraine had been gone for six years, I could imagine that it didn't take the Princess long to convince her folks to spring for the lofty costs of renovating her very own private bathing area.

An assortment of makeup brushes, sponges and expensive perfume bottles filled the space along one side of the rose colored marble countertop, while at least a ton of body powders, oils, shower and bath gels occupied the remaining half of the space she once shared with her sister.

A full length antique mirror encased in sterling mounted on the backside of the door, complimented the dainty vanity set, which also boasted the initials EJP within the intricate artistry of the silver backside of the chair made comfortable by the pink oval shaped seat-cushion.

Elisabeth ran the fingertips of her free hand along the shined to perfection old-fashioned faucet knobs and glanced up to me to ascertain the level of my appreciation for the finer things in life, before she explained one of the fashion/style/etiquette tips she'd collected in her lexicon of mores among the chic bourgeoisie.

"I just don't understand why people have been so attracted to gold for centuries and centuries, the world over," she piously commented, twitching her nose as if she'd detected a flagrant odor.

"What's wrong with gold?" I challenged, before pointing out that her parents room contained more than its' fair share.

"Why it's garish and gaudy looking. The only reason Daddy likes it so much, is because he's an Alpha man, and black and gold are their colors. As you've probably noticed by the jewelry I'm wearing," she expounded, showing off a silver necklace and heart shaped locket, also monogrammed with her initials, along with tear-shaped sterling diamond studded earrings and the intriguing single band around her left finger that caught my eye the night of our official meeting in Donaldson's office.

" I much prefer silver because gold is just plain tacky . . . in fact, the only way you would like, ever catch me wearing anything gold is a wedding ring," she blushed, realizing that one of her favorite topics of conversation was leading to the inevitability of us having to discuss our future together before I was scheduled to fly back five hundred plus miles to Detroit within the same week.

"You know what? Traditionally Omegas and Alphas don't

get along too well. Maybe that's your old man's beef with me."

"Oh yes, you're an Omega," she retorted amazed that an upright man of the cloth, would ever have a past of fraternizing with a rough and tough, womanizing organization of African-American male collegiates. "I remember reading about your partying days in your last book."

"I was a Q, back in another life," I promptly reminded her. "Now the only brotherhood to which I belong is the brotherhood of the body of Christ." I then reminded her that her father would probably be hunting us down within a matter of seconds if we didn't hustle down to the dinner table.

"Would you like to use my restroom or the one at the bottom of the stairs?" she asked, as she headed towards the steps.

"It doesn't matter. I'm *your* guest, remember?" Man, I wanted to kiss her. I guess I'd sent out all the right messages through my body language, because within a few seconds, I got my wish.

"Use mine," she replied softly, batting her long eyelashes just to tease me all the more. " I'll be waiting for you at the bottom of the stairs."

Even though she was wearing heels, she still had to stretch her neck to the fullest extent upward to place a slow, lingering peck on my cheek. I felt the quick swish of her soft eyelashes open and close against my neatly trimmed goatee. I wanted to tell her to back up off of me before she'd start something she knew she couldn't finish, but once again, I refrained from coming on too strong. After all, given the impossible standards she'd placed on herself as being the ultra-untouchable, virginal godsend to all of mankind, I didn't want to frighten her away by shoving my hormonally driven, wildly experienced tongue down her throat in the middle of the grand hallway on the second floor of her parents' palatial home.

———

221

Call me a true romantic, but it just wasn't the right time or place.

"Oh, and Bobby?"

"Yes, Princess?" I replied, allowing the sound of her appropriate nickname to flow from my lips effortlessly for the very first time.

"No peeking inside my bedroom. I didn't show it to you because I didn't think it would be appropriate. And, never mind what I said about the wedding ring thing. I didn't mean anything by it."

"That's disappointing, baby," I grinned. "I was hoping you did."

She wrapped her arms around my neck and buried her head into my chest, perhaps to safeguard the rare and captivating smile she so often elected to hide from mere mortals, myself included, all because of a slight dental imperfection.

I stroked her chin with my right hand before gently tilting it upward, so her lips could meet mine. She pulled back from me slightly to look at me with baffled eyes.

"Bobby, this isn't how I wanted my first . . . I mean . . . our first, real kiss to go . . . I hope you understand."

"I've waited for you to walk into my life for this long, what's a few more days?" I shrugged, all geeked up over her accidental admission of never having had another unworthy cat tongue her down before. I expected some trite, coquettish response from the arsenal of an inexperienced adolescent, instead, and much to my delight, she planted a few more quiet kisses on my neck with lips that emitted the familiar sensuous smoldering sensation that I'd long since forgotten. This time, it was I who led her by the hand to the feast that awaited us.

Lyin' For My Baby

As expected, Ms. Maggie's culinary skills measured up to all the bragging she'd done at the church. As ensconced into Powell family life I thought she and her niece Tanya were, I expected them to join us in our dining and polite banter. Instead, Ms. Maggie circled the table several times to ensure that the four of us had all the condiments and beverages we needed. James Powell, Elisabeth and I sipped on Perrier water and iced tea, while I overheard the woman of the house, seated at the foot of the table, request Tanya to bring up from the cellar an elegant white wine, definitely more aged than the one I'd bought, that would be more complimentary to an early Sunday dinner.

As if to cajole her father into accepting me, Elisabeth, full of nervous energy, seemed to never exhaust me and my accomplishments as a topic of conversation. Emily sat pouring over her wine wearing a small smile of amusement over my apparent discomfort and lack of input.

"Daddy, don't you think Bobby's sermon today was really thought provoking?" she mused, while massaging the bicep of the arm, with which I was eating.

"And, what exactly did you find so thought provoking, Princess?" he asked with a mouth full of Ms. Maggie's succulent oven roasted ham.

"Eeeew. Don't talk with your mouth full of swine, Daddy.

223

That's like, sooo disgusting!" she spoke harshly at him. "Besides, if I have to tell you what was thought provoking about a sermon about the indwelling spirit, then you weren't really paying attention at all."

I waited for James Powell to lash out and reprimand his little Princess with strong words, coupled with an invitation to show me to the door, but much to my surprise he didn't so much as raise a brow, nor give her the evil eye.

"Our Elisabeth is a vegetarian," he explained calmly to me, as if I hadn't noticed that my intended was still struggling to complete her first bites of a rather appetizing looking Caesar salad with croutons and parmesan cheese Tanya had whipped up just for her. "She doesn't eat much. But, you can just dig in. I know a big, strapping former college basketball player, almost turned professional, such as yourself would like an extra helping of fried chicken and ham."

"No sir," I replied, growing a bit irritable and tired of the sarcasm. "I've had quite enough." I placed my napkin on the tabletop, and arose when Ms. Maggie and Tanya entered the room for the umpteenth time, carrying a tray complete with a vast array of dessert choices and a pitcher of water to replenish our glasses. "Ms. Maggie, and Tanya, everything has been so delicious. You ladies have really gone above and beyond my furthest expectations."

"God bless this young man, Ms. Emily," Ms. Maggie grinned, with a gleam in her eye that looked as if she wanted to squeeze my cheeks. "Now, have a seat, Doctor Preacha. You don't have to go interrupting your meal every time, this gal here and I come prancin' into the room to wait on you. Sit on down and enjoy your dessert."

"Yes, please," Tanya replied shyly, her guilty eyes averting everywhere else, except into mine, which provided me with a satisfactory response to my inquisition of the exchange between she and Brother Khalid over the past three nights. "Libby baked this apple pie just for you."

Elisabeth hastily motioned for Tanya to remove my empty dinner plate and silverware, before practically snatching the crystal family heirloom away from her servant and proudly placing the still warm, hearty heaping of apple pie a-la-mode before my eyes.

I didn't have the heart to express to her that I wasn't much of a dessert man, even though I was sure by the looks of her, she rarely treated herself to any non-green food. So, ignoring her parent's curious glances in my direction, I picked up my dessert fork and thanked Elisabeth for her effort.

"Well, go on taste it. Let me know what you think, Bobby," she nodded her head earnestly, eager for me to experience my first taste.

"Yes, please let us know," Emily chuckled crossing her fingers. "This is Libby's first attempt to bake anything. I don't think she's ever opened the stove other than to check to see if it's been thoroughly cleaned."

"Mother!"

"Em's right. . . . I tell you Doctor Robert McGallister, Minister Extraordinaire, this girl is really impressed with you. You had better act like you like it," James Powell, in a feeble attempt to ease the tension between the two of us, urged in a pseudo authoritative voice.

"Oh Daddy, will you guys just hush up long enough for him to try it!"

All five pairs of eyes watched me as I dramatically slid my fork right down the middle of a hard scoop of french vanilla ice cream, into the flat, flakeless crust of Elisabeth's labor of love. If I'd deciphered my peripheral view correctly and if I were a betting man, I would have sworn that I saw both Ms. Maggie and Tanya clutch hands and gulp silently as they awaited the big moment.

I decided before letting the first morsel melt away in my salivating mouth, that even if it tasted terrible, I still would love it, because she cared enough about me to try to impress

225

my palate. I cast an appreciative glance at Elisabeth as my teeth worked overtime to grind up the tough, under-baked apple filling.

"Well, young man, how is it?" Powell smirked as he unbuttoned his sports jacket to expose a rotund, not quite a beer belly yet, stomach.

"Delicious," I lied, without feeling one ounce of guilt. Elisabeth momentarily, looked dejected, because in lieu of taking another bite, I opted to refill my water glass and take a few gulps of it before uttering another word.

"It's awful, isn't it, Bobby? I knew it," she giggled, that familiar high-pitched sound unashamedly at herself, covering her smile with her usual right hand. "I knew I should have left the cooking to the help. Here, let me spare you from any further pain and agony." She reached for my saucer. I quickly swatted her hand away.

"Hey, keep your hands to yourself," I chided. "I'd like to finish my dessert."

She rested her head on my shoulder and released a loud sigh of relief.

"Isn't he just incredible, Mother and Daddy?"

"Chile, he must be, to lie to you somethin' awful like that just to please you," Ms. Maggie sang joyfully as she and Tanya chartered back off into the most unfamiliar territory in the Princess's palace.

On The Shadow of The Cross

On Monday morning, when I called from my hotel to ask her out to a movie for later that afternoon, she told me that she didn't like attending public viewings of movies, but if I didn't mind we could watch whatever film of my choosing I'd wanted to see in their very own private cinema.

" Um, I don't know baby. Somehow, watching an action flick with such awesome graphics and sound effects in a room smaller than my office at the church pales in comparison to sitting among a bunch of rude hecklers, reeking of alcohol or worse, munchin' popcorn in your ear or throwing it at the screen."

"Why, Robert McGallister," she sighed heavily into the receiver. "I don't believe a man of your prominence and position in the church would want to be caught dead watching an R rated movie anywhere, let alone in a theatre full of unsaved people."

Here, we go again, I thought to myself. Here comes my ole-I'm-just-a-regular-brother-who-just-so-happens-to-evangilize-lost-souls-for-a-living-spiel. I allowed a slight pause in our discourse in an attempt to search for words to convey my position on the issue at hand, without sounding as if I had to defend myself.

227

"One, I consider myself no better or worse than anyone else. Two, according to the review I read in Entertainment Weekly this particular film does not contain any gratuitous sex scenes that would make us uncomfortable, and . . ."

"But, it contains violence?"

"Uh, violence . . ."

"Yes, does the film contain violence Bobby?"

"Well, hell yeah, it contains violence."

She gasped, as if I was threatening to siphon the oxygen from within her very lungs. "This is an action film; a film about war. Folks get killed in it. Just like they did back in biblical days," I chuckled. "But . . ." I conceded, not wanting to completely destroy her beloved image of me as a revered saint, "if this type of movie offends you, then we don't have to watch it."

"Thank you, very much, Bobby," she squealed delightfully. "Why don't I come pick you up at the hotel, since I have to come downtown anyway to audition for a fashion show at one of our major department stores. Then later, we can do some shopping over in University City. There are some awesome bookstores there, some of which have very extensive Christian literature sections, seeing that I know you're pretty well read and all."

"You model?" I asked fantasizing her strutting her stuff, along the narrow European runways, hair blowing in the artificial winds of hidden fans, sporting a few lovely pink negligees.

"I do a little," she replied modestly. " Anyway, are we on?"

"Of course," I agreed reluctantly. "So long as we do what I want to do tomorrow night."

"Uh-oh, should I be afraid?"

"I don't know. I'll let you decide that once you strap on a pair of skates."

"Cool," she sang, sounding more and more like your typical white girl by the nanosecond. "We're going ice-skating. I haven't gone in years, but I think I'll do just fine, hopefully. I know, we can go to the arena located on . . ."

"Yeah, that'll be the day, you catch this brotha in a pair of ice-skates," I balked at the thought. "No, we're going roller skating."

Silence on the other hand.

For effect, I blew several short breaths into the phone, much as I would into the microphone, whenever I was speaking and wanted the audience to realize that I was aware of their lack of positive response.

"You still there?"

"Bobby, you've got to be kidding! I cannot roller skate! Do they even still call it that? Isn't it roller blading?"

"No ma'am, baby, I'm from the old school, where cats still skate with rhythm and soul, where we still call it skatin'."

"But, I'll fall," she whined.

"I won't let you," I replied seriously, walking into the bathroom to start the cold shower. I prayed that I could hold out a little longer, just until the honeymoon.

"But, what if I do?"

"I'll catch you."

"But, I don't dance, I have no coordination. Don't you need coordination to skate?"

"I have all the coordination you'll need, and then some."

"Oh, Bobby," I could tell by the tone of her voice that she was blushing at the innuendo of my last statement. "Okay, already. I'll be on my way in a few minutes."

"I'll meet you in the lobby, because Lord knows what would happen if you were to come up."

.....

Elisabeth was more than a little disappointed when she was told upon arrival at Dillard's department store that they

229

were scouting for more ethnic looking models for their impending Christmas television advertisement campaign.

She marched out of the talent agent's office of the executive suite, clutching her purse so tightly that I could see blood rush through her pale hands to her fingertips. Angry tears flooded her perfectly made up face. I picked up my black leather jacket and beebop, stood up and reached to embrace her, but she was in no mood to be coddled.

"What's wrong with these idiot scouts, anyway?" she practically yelled. "They wouldn't know a good model if one were to slap them in the face. I mean, like, how ethnic do I have to be? My father's black and my mother is part Sicilian and part Irish," she sniffed, reaching into her purse to retrieve a pink tissue.

Before I could respond, two small-framed, petite, relatively young looking white women approached us, as I was helping Elisabeth into a chic blue cashmere coat.

"Excuse us, Miss Powell," the pretty one with the green eyes smiled. " You left before we had the chance to thank you for entering our contest, and giving you our card for future opportunities."

"Yes, yes, Meagan, but, she also left this," the younger brunette one added, shoving a leather photo portfolio in Elisabeth's direction. Elisabeth mumbled a dry thank you, without making direct eye contact. Both women were totally oblivious as to how they had insulted her self-esteem by further perpetuating the severe envy she felt towards her darker older sister.

Neither paid attention to her determination to vacate the premises as soon as possible, because they were both gaping at me, as if I were some lab specimen under a technician's microscope.

"Perfect bone structure."

"Yes, Beth, and very well groomed."

"Intense, sexy eyes . . ."

"Even complexion, seductive aura."

"He'd be perfect for this show and to do some shoots for our spring campaign."

Elisabeth folded her arms, tapped her foot impatiently and cleared her throat to indicate that we were actually two non-hearing impaired individuals.

"Uh, oh, we're sorry, Miss Powell, we get excited about our work sometimes, but your, uh, companion here, is absolutely . . ."

"Gorgeous!" Meagan exclaimed, motioning for the two receptionists behind the appointment counter to walk around the platform to witness their latest discovery.

"Damn!" the black girl sang, as she high-fived her Middle-Eastern counterpart. "Where has this one been hiding?" she continued circling around me to evaluate me from head to toe.

When Elisabeth noticed that I was more flattered than insulted, more nonchalant than modest, all of the blood drained from her face. Her eyes became narrow and full of venom.

"He's been hiding in Detroit behind the pulpit and the shadow of the cross. This is Doctor Robert McGallister, psychologist, author, but most importantly, minister. You ladies just ought to be ashamed of yourselves!"

Conspicuously mortified, all four women dropped their heads in shame. The black girl extended her apologies first.

"Oh, Reverend, I am soooo, very sorry. I don't normally behave this way. Could you please excuse me, I think I hear the phone ringing."

"Yeah, right," Elisabeth mumbled smugly, reclaiming my arm as her territory under no uncertain terms.

"We're so sorry Pastor. We had no idea," Gertrude, smiling demurely, averted her eyes in my direction and clutched her hands in the praying position as if she were addressing the Almighty himself.

The Middle-Eastern woman cowered away from me as if

she'd been caught with her hand in the cookie jar, while the brunette called Beth, remained mummified.

"It's no problem ladies, none at all," I reassured them. "Thanks for the compliments. Miss Powell and I will be on our way . . ."

"Yes, yes, we understand," Gertrude nodded, shaking my right hand, looking as if she wanted to kiss it, like I was the Pope.

"Personally, I don't know why I'm wasting a good drool on that mixed up brotha anyway," the boisterous black woman allowed me to overhear her remarks to her Middle-Eastern co-worker. "The Reverend must thinks he really done hit the jackpot, with that white chick on his arm."

Elisabeth sulked in the car for a few minutes, before I threatened her with pulling out one of my Stevie Wonder CD's, if she wouldn't talk to me.

"It's just that I went to get that job and they offered it to you, and you didn't even apply for it. I mean you don't impress me as the modeling type. You seem kind of, like, rough . . . real manly, rough around the edges to me, but I do mean that in the best possible way."

"I know, trust me, I've never considered myself to be the pretty boy type either."

"So, now that I've made, like, a complete idiot of myself, I guess that we can just cheer me up by going shopping, but you owe me one. I don't let anyone steal my thunder and get away with it."

"Alright, already, Your Highness. How may your humble servant make it up to you?" I laughed.

She rubbed her hands together and licked her lips to indicate that she was thinking of a devilish penance for me to pay.

"I want amnesty."

"From what?"

"From going roller skating with you tomorrow night. I

mean I don't have a single thing to wear. Not one pair of pants."

"Wait a minute," I laughed, taking my eyes off the road momentarily to look her in the face. "You don't own any pants, not even a pair of khaki's or dress pants?"

"Pants are for men, Bobby," she cried rolling her eyes as if I was the one from another galaxy. " I'm sure you're quite familiar with Paul's epistles . . . especially the ones where he admonishes women not to wear men's apparel."

Not wanting to offend her in her time of grave conviction, I tried to stifle the boisterous guffaws emanating from within my throat, while wiping away the tears trying to break free from the corner of my eyes.

"Don't ever make fun of me," she moaned, reaching her right hand across her seatbelt to playfully slap me upside the head.

"Whoa-ho, I'm so . . . rrry, Lisa . . . beth. It's just such a . . ." I chuckled, now holding my aching sides.

"Such, a what, huh?"

"It's just such a misinterpretation of that particular passage as found in the New Testament. You . . . have to look at the historical context . . . of those times. Of course men are not to dress effeminately today, but . . ."

"But, you're saying there's a double standard. That women are supposed to wear pants, now that times have changed? Well, would you ever be caught dead in this skirt, I'm wearing, would you?"

"Now, I think you know the answer to that one."

"Well, then. So there."

"Well, then," I mocked her, just to irritate her all the more, "So there? You mean to tell me, that you wouldn't even wear a pair of Capri pants in your favorite color, pink?"

"Don't be ridiculous, Bobby. Capri pants are for . . ." she tossed her hands up as if she were searching for a term that she wouldn't find unladylike.

233

"For . . . ," I teased, rotating my hand in the universal circular motion as if to say, 'out with it already.'

"For tramps. I mean what kind of self-respecting woman would want to wear a thong with a pair of too tight high-water slacks? I mean, like, either you wear a thong, or worse, expose your panty line, by wearing some gripping bikini or granny bloomers. Either way you decide to sport them really, is quite trashy, and unchristianlike to me."

"Man, I tell you, there's never a dull moment. Now, I know that you're the one for me." I found the words just rolling from my mouth, without even thinking. I watched her recline the passenger seat and close and open her eyes quickly as if she were praying that she'd heard me correctly.

"You mind clarifying your last statement, Brother McGallister?" she flirted as I halted at a red traffic light in the middle of a busy intersection located within the University City shopping district.

"I mean you are a very impressionable woman Elisabeth Powell. A rare and passionate soul, and a blessing in my life," I gently lifted her left hand out of her lap, and brought it to my lips. Her closed eyelids fluttered as she welcomed the tingling sensation my slight, chivalrous gesture brought to her body.

Just Like That

Instead of roller-skating on Tuesday evening, we'd both grown restless and a bit lustful, after we'd sat on the couch for a couple of hours discussing everything from my father's recent health scare to my insistence on her acceptance of me as an ordinary man who wanted to get to know her better and see her on a regular basis.

"But, you're no ordinary man, Bobby," she sighed, from her cuddled up position beside me. Her head rested on my chest, so that if she were quiet enough she could hear my heart thumping. "You have God's anointing on you. You have been called to do his work. Look at what all you've done for people. Look at how many people you've led to Christ and the programs you've started."

"Elisabeth," I retorted quietly, caressing her thigh through her long tailored gray skirt. "I don't need a fan. I haven't played college basketball in eight years. I need a wife, a wife who loves me for me, a wife who sees all of me. That's who I want you to be."

She slowly pulled back from me to look at me as if she were meeting me for the first time and rubbed her soft manicured hands alongside my whiskers.

"Oh Bobby," she sighed not holding back the tears, "how soon do you want to set the date?"

I blinked myself out of my euphoric daze to realize that

235

I'd not even offered the woman a ring. It was the least she deserved.

"Oh Bobby, Bobby," she squealed jumping up, clasping her hands together. I watched her through smiling eyes pace the floor back and forth, babbling on and on about her prayers being answered and about sleeping with the picture from an autographed copy of *Saving It* under her pillow for the entire six weeks prior to my arrival.

Delirious from the sheer blissfulness of the moment, I hopped up from my comfortable position and scooped her up in my arms. Leading her back to the couch, I gently laid her down and began to controllably release a miniscule amount of over stored sexual tension, by placing soft kisses along her neck. Just as I'd seen white girls with long bouncy hair in the movies do countless numbers of times, she seductively piled her sandy brown locks on top of her head, and held them there so I could have better access to work my magic.

Moans of pleasure escaped her lips as she gripped my back snugly and begin to tug on my shirt.

Not like this. Not right now. Hold on Bob, man. Hold on. Just a little bit longer. You've been successful at this for four years. Be a man about yours, and wait until you marry her.

"Damn," I muttered, reluctantly resuming my upright position on the couch. I pulled her onto my lap by her waist. All of her lipstick had been smeared off and had probably stained the collar of the beige shirt I wore underneath a matching sports coat.

"What's wrong, Bobby?" Her lips, from right on top of my earlobes whispered.

"You know we can't do this, this way, don't you?"

She nodded guiltily, before practically bolting from the security of my lap.

"Well, then. When can we do it?" she asked in a much more level-headed tone. "Because it's apparent that we won't be able to hold out this way this much longer."

"How about in a few weeks?" I suggested, standing up trying to shake off my apparent arousal. I walked across the Great Room to the bay window seat to put some distance between us. She didn't try to follow me. When my eyes met hers again, she was looking at me reflectively, trancelike.

" Uh-oh, no one has sat over there in years," she explained in a semi-frightened voice as if she were expecting one of her parents to appear from nowhere to scold me for violating some unspoken family rule.

"Why not?"

"Because, that's how Mother wants it. That spot where you are right now . . . belongs to her beloved . . ."

"Let me guess, Lorraine," I replied shaking my head, incredulous that in Emily's eyes, Lorraine's spirit still dwelled in their home even though it had been six years since she'd physically vacated the premises. "Well, let me just remove my butt from the monarch's throne." I chuckled, out of respect for my future mother-in-law's wishes. Since everyone around there considered the second daughter as the Princess, I thought, than the first daughter, must be the Queen.

"Mother can be quite ridiculous sometimes," Elisabeth replied, making a mad dash in my direction. She feigned dizziness in order to collapse right into my arms. I wrapped my arms around her tiny waist as she stood above me, planting kisses on my forehead. Just as things were about to heat up again, the headlights from Emily's BMW almost blinded us as she slowed into the alcove driveway just in front of the window.

My new fiancée leapt out of my arms and sprinted to greet her tired mother who was carrying two grocery bags as she entered into the foyer. I rushed to help her.

"Hello Robert," Emily smiled, reaching up to hug my neck and peck me on my cheek, "and thank you. These old arms are tired."

"Mother, Mother, you wouldn't believe . . . I have . . . well,

237

we have some amazing news," she blurted out, clasping her hands with joy again. Bobby has proposed marriage and . . . I said yes!"

"Oh Elisabeth and Robert. My goodness gracious! I. . . . don't know what to say."

"We would like your blessing of course, Emily," I smiled.

"My blessing . . . isn't he priceless? Ms, Maggie, Tanya, James . . . come here at once," Emily beckoned in the loudest voice she could muster through elated tears.

"No one is here, but us Mother," Elisabeth cried. "I'm getting married mother. I'm not only getting married, but I'm marrying . . ."

"Robert McGallister," they both exclaimed simultaneously. "Can you believe it, my dear? Oh Princess, Princess!"

In all the jubilant commotion between mother and daughter I felt a bit like the fifth wheel. Like I wasn't one in the same with this magnanimous persona to whom they were referring. I cannot rationally express how I wanted to deck an upper-left to this paragon of sheer perfection.

My oxymoronic emotions sent me staggering over to the staircase so that I could remotely observe the women rant and rave over the source of my envy. I couldn't possibly live up to their image of me, nor could I ever have imagined it being humanly possible to be jealous of one's own self. A stranger in my own life.

"So, Robert," Emily beckoned for me to rejoin the conversation. "What'd I tell you, huh? I knew you would love my Libby. Have you guys set a date?"

"Uh, no ma'am, not yet. But, it needs to be soon," I replied casting a knowing wink in Elisabeth's direction. Both women blushed profusely.

"Well, how soon is soon, Lib?" Emily gushed. "I have to get a dress and all, and Robert's dad is still recovering."

"Pops is going to be just fine," I smiled. " I spoke to him just last night."

"And does he or your mother know anything about our daughter and your plans to make her your wife?"

I shook my head, "No ma'am, but they will, just as soon as I arrive home tomorrow."

"Okay . . . that's fine by me," she cackled. "Oh, wait until I phone Lori. She is going to make a beautiful maid of honor of course and I'm sure you'll fall in love with her voice when she sings the Lord's Prayer at your nuptials. . . ." Emily started making her way up the stairs before bidding me a good night. "Where is that phone, now? I want to call her before she goes out to that homeless mission for the evening. She's been spending so much time at that old house lately, I . . ."

"Mother, Mother! Come back here, right this instant," Elisabeth hissed knitting her fashionably arched eyebrows together and folding her arms across her chest in fury. "This is like sooo totally unfair. . . . this is my moment, for heaven's sake. Do you see that, Bobby? Do you see that?"

I too, stood next to Elisabeth wearing a stupefied expression, frozen into a state of shock that a mother would prefer one child over the other in such a blatant manner. At that point, it was no wonder Elisabeth had very few kind words to utter on Emily's behalf. I decided then, that I would never allow the sore spot that existed between mother and daughter and sister and sister negatively effect how deep my feelings ran for Elisabeth. I would be her champion and help her fight for her natural birthright of receiving her mother's love.

"What are you going on about, Princess?" Emily replied turning on her heel as if she hadn't heard a word Elisabeth screamed. "You shouldn't frown so much. Practice smiling more, dear. You have to relax your facial muscles more or you're going to ruin your beautiful bridal pictures. Good night, Robert."

She waved from the top staircase. "She's not yours yet, so bring her home at a respectable hour."

"Yes, ma'am," I answered, reaching for Elisabeth's hand, to pull her back into my comforting arms. " I hope to see you before my plane leaves tomorrow."

As I reached to open the front door for Elisabeth, who had grabbed both of our coats and hats, we both heard the sound of her mother dialing Lorraine in Lansing on speakerphone. I helped her with her coat. Elisabeth, crying, opted to rush to the car, before I could fasten the first button on mine.

Going to the Chapel

Wednesday evening at her favorite pricey Mediterranean restaurant, she watched my Adam's apple bob up and down as I gulped down the last swallow of some weird green herbal tea and lemon concoction she'd insisted I order with my disgusting meal. I reached into my wallet to retrieve the Citibank Visa, which I had proudly paid down to a balance of zero prior to our five thousand dollar visit the night before to the most expensive jeweler in the greater St. Louis area.

It goes without saying that all the bitter sobbing and sulking over living in her sister's shadow ceased, when I gave her, her choice of rings.

Brother Khalid was going to have a field day on my whole whirlwind romance once I got back home. I could hear his voice now asking me, *"Little Brother, man, are you sure you wanna marry that little pale half-breed high and mighty diva, who got you to propose to her and drop five G's on her within a week of you knowing her? Man, I know you're as horny as all get out, but come on, bro. Be real with yours!"*

We sat in a cozy-dimly-lit booth for two in the all white joint. The only thing darker than me in the entire eclectic restaurant was the little useless leather folder the snooty waiter placed the forty-five dollar bill we'd managed to wrack up on various bland assortments of tofu, pita bread and humus.

As was her custom, Elisabeth sat twirling her fork into

241

some unrecognizable pasta dish, sporting a rather glum pouting expression, which made her even sexier to me.

She'd been unusually quiet throughout the full-course meal for one apparent reason; we didn't want our precious time together to come to an end.

Soft music sung in an unrecognizable language served as the backdrop of the intense conversation about our future we were about to conduct.

"Princess . . . you alright?" I broke our silence after the waiter walked away to retrieve for me a large black coffee with sugar, no cream.

"No, I'm not," she replied weakly as her bottom lip trembled. Given all my dealings with previous relationships and in all my experience in counseling women who have deeply entrenched emotional issues, I'd never known a woman to cry at the drop of the dime, quicker than the Princess. "You're leaving in the morning and I'm not going with you."

"But, you'll be joining me soon. We have to plan this out . . . logically. . . . Pops just got out of the hospital. I will be away from Rosedale Park the next Sunday due to a gospel meeting I'm conducting in Florida . . . and to be quite truthful, I won't have a free weekend at least until February," I replied dejectedly, as I wished for February to be just another day away.

"February," her eyes brightened, "my birthday is Valentine's Day. And next February fourteenth falls on a Saturday, I believe." She reached inside her pink Liz Claiborne bag to retrieve her palm-held personal planner. She owned the same one Brother Khalid used to keep my life organized.

"Wait, no . . . it's on a Monday," her words shot out from her lips fast and full of disappointment. "I guess we could still do a Valentine's Day theme the Saturday before, huh?"

"That's fine with me, baby."

"The only thing is, I don't won't our bridal party dressed in anything red."

"Well, you won't be catching this brother in pink, in this lifetime, baby. Forget that."

"Oh Bobby," she smiled. " I wouldn't do such a thing. We'll have plenty of time to discuss colors . . . but, eeew," she paused tapping her nails on the tabletop as if she had some major life and death decisions to contemplate. She punched some more buttons on her palm held, "It's the end of November. This means we only really have December and January to throw this thing together."

"That shouldn't pose a problem . . . why don't we just elope that weekend?" I suggested in jest. When she didn't find the statement humorous, I placed my coffee back on its saucer and scooped her fragile hands into mine. "Look at me, Princess. You're going to turn into a crazy woman over this wedding deal, aren't you?"

"No . . . no, I'm not. I promise," she twitched her nose playfully and leaned over to kiss me, full on the mouth. " But, we haven't discussed any of the important issues yet, Bobby. Like if you're getting married, who marries you?"

"Pops, of course. That one is a no brainer."

"Well, I was thinking that since I'm making the greater sacrifice and all, that Brother Donaldson could marry us, here . . ."

"Okay A, " I chuckled, "how are you making the greater sacrifice, and two,"

"Don't you mean, B?"

"No, I do really mean two. Fat chance. There is no way Ed McGallister Sr. is not going to marry us."

"Well," she pleaded to deaf ears. "I'm going to be totally uprooting my life here and I'd figured since we're going to be living in your city and attending your church, that at least, my minister could marry us."

Since I didn't want to have our first squabble before I

could even get her down the aisle good, I conceded slightly. "Okay, baby, that is negotiable. Maybe we'll have Pops perform one half, and Donaldson the other. Works for you?"

"Sure," she grinned temporarily appeased, that we'd worked that one out before I could finish my coffee. She seemed oblivious of the snide and blatant glares from all the white men hurled over in my direction for having the audacity to show my black face around their parts with a woman of the same fair complexion as their overweight, dowdy wives.

I continued to listen to her recall to memory anyone she deemed worthy to participate as a bridesmaid, but for some reason everyone she mentioned was either related to her or employed by the family.

" I'll have that Tanya, and my twin cousins Tracey and Stacey on Mother's side, and then, there's Lori, of course. Mother would just die if she's not my maid of honor, and has a solo to boot. But Lori can just eat her heart out, once she sees this ring," she bragged admiring her own reflection through the 24-karat flawless marquis diamond band of gold that circled her finger, "and your great church, and you, of course."

"Yes, of course," I chided. " In all the weddings I performed, the bridegroom has always been a very essential element to the entire festive occasion."

Once again, she failed to grasp the humor in my sarcasm. She rolled her eyes heavenward, before asking me if she had forgotten anything.

"Yes, as a matter of fact, you have," I said seriously, stroking my chin. "You've forgotten to tell me you love me. "

"Oh Bobby, don't be ridiculous, of course I do."

"Okay then, that's all good for now, but I do have something else to discuss with you of a more serious nature."

Her back stiffened and lips tightened as she braced herself for me to reveal some horrific secret I'd successfully hidden from the rest of the living world until that moment.

"I'm listening."

"I'm a minister, Elisabeth."

She giggled over my understatement of the conspicuous.

"I'm serious."

"Yes, I know you're a minister, Bobby. I've known that all along . . . that's part of your appeal."

"I'm also a sinner, Elisabeth."

"Aren't we all?" she shrugged nonchalantly.

"Let me put it all together there for you baby . . . I'm a minister . . . I'm also a sinner. . . . I make mistakes. I sin everyday the Lord blesses to send my way. I need for you to understand where I'm coming from."

"Yes, of course."

"I'm away from home a lot, baby. I need you to understand that."

"I do."

"No, you don't. You haven't dealt with it yet."

"Bobby, both my parents and my mothers' parents, and Daddy's sisters and brothers are all medical doctors. They keep crazy hours. That's why Lori and me, and all of my cousins have been raised by the Ms. Maggie's of the world."

"I leave town frequently. You'll be home alone many nights."

"No . . . Tanya will be there, or the new girl we hired, plus we're going to have children right away right? At least that's how you stated you wanted things to go in *Saving It* . . ."

"Elisabeth, you can't bring Tanya with you, or any other hired help. I'm a servant myself, baby."

She sighed heavily before reaching for her glass of herbal green tea. She closed her eyes and took a few sips. I could tell she knew that I wasn't going to give in to her every desire and that there was no way I would ever consent to paying someone to cook and clean for me.

"That's an honorable thing to say, Bobby . . . but, I'm going to need some help in all of the new responsibilities

245

that I'm going to incur. I will have just turned twenty on our wedding day. I don't know the first thing about being a minister's wife, let alone slaving in anyone's kitchen, not even my own."

"I haven't asked you to do any of those things. I'm just asking you to be my spiritual partner for life. Is that okay?"

"Yes, it's very okay."

" I counsel patients around the clock..."

"Yes, yes, I know this, Bobby. You're a caring individual. You didn't earn a doctorate's in psychology to sit around twiddling your thumbs, when there are like some really mentally screwed up people out there."

"How familiar are you with God's Warriors?'

"You've got to be kidding me." Conspicuously insulted, she rolled her eyes and shook her head. " I know all your tapes backwards and forwards."

"Have you paid attention to the two tapes on financial empowerment?"

"Of course," she smiled smugly, before sighing slowly, as if the very redundant act of exhaling oxygen would channel a complete regurgitation of my presentations to Rosedale's first group of two-hundred newly inducted soldiers. "You've laid out plans for the church's premises. You expect to pool all the Warrior's financial and educational resources together to create a self-sufficient African-American community that will no longer have to predominantly rely on Arabs, Koreans and white Americans for goods and services. You're modeling your concept after some of the success stories of several black denominational organizations within the Detroit area."

"Now you're talkin'," I smiled proudly at my number one supporter.

"So, I've passed the test," she batted those long, soft eyelashes coquettishly.

"You do realize how much time I have to spend in business meetings about this whole process. We're looking at erecting a separate facility for Agape and CMLA, as well as a community center by the end of spring. Recently, we've received the green light for Paul Williams, my boy I grew up with, to open up his law firm, as well as my former frat brother Darius to run a clinic once he completes his residency at . . ."

"Must we talk business now, Bobby?" she frowned her disinterest.

Though I was a bit peeved that she cut me off mid-flow about the subject, only second to the Word, I held most dear to my heart, she more than pacified me when from underneath the table, she ordered her cold narrow foot to slither up and nuzzle against my right pant leg to tease me a tadbit, before awakening the aroused landmine of my manhood.

I almost spat out the disgusting green-tea concoction Elisabeth insisted I'd ordered from the overpriced menus of scant options.

"Uh . . . heh. . . . well. . . . what else do we need to discuss?" the slow broad grin that inched it's way across my lips informed her that the ball was in her hands.

"Let's talk living arrangements."

"I've lived in the parsonage, adjoined to the building for four years now, is that acceptable for now?"

Her dead silence was an in yo' face slam-dunk dribbled superbly the length of the stadium of our newly staked romance. That blinding boulder on her tiny left-ring finger informed me she definitely had the home court advantage.

"Is it?"

"The church is in Detroit . . . *Detroit?*" she asked apparently reconciling herself to the fact that she would no longer be living the suburban life.

"Yes, it is. You've seen videotapes of the inside of the building . . ."

"Of course, of course. It's a lovely building Bobby," she acknowledged as if I had designed the original blueprint and laid the foundation brick by brick myself.

———

247

"And, but . . ."

"Well . . . when do you think we can have our own house built?"

"Built?" I asked calmly massaging the impending ache in my left temple.

She exhaled deeply again and began tapping her fingers nervously on the table, wearing an expression that her life's dreams were being ripped apart bit by bit.

"Well, Princess, I don't know about having a house built anytime soon, but I'm sure within a year or so we can find a palace within the same neighborhood suitable enough for your superb tastes and high standards."

I broke her resolve. She giggled. She did a whole lot of that. Made me feel like I was back in the fifth grade, ditching recess behind the ramshackle school portable trying to convince Mary Wilkes that I had to see what color her panties were and to feel her down in order to be promoted a year in advanced to the neighborhood gang of middle school, reefer smoking hoodlums, who all sported Converses and swore like marines.

"How spacious is it . . . the *parsonage*, that is?" The word parsonage spat off her tongue like crumbs from a burnt slice of toast.

"Big enough for the two of us, and Cherie and Deuce of course."

"Cherie and Deuce?"

"My two rotweilers."

She frantically reached inside her purse to retrieve a stiffly ironed white handkerchief with pink lace and her usual monogram. She patted at a few invisible beads of perspiration on her forehead before doing the sexy-hair-pile-on-top-of-the-head thing to wipe her neck.

"Dogs make you nervous?"

"I'm, like, very afraid of anything with fur, except for if it's dead and I'm wearing it. I hate pets."

"But Deuce and Cherie ain't just pets. They're family. I've had Deuce for three years and Cherie for four. Deuce weighs about one hundred and forty pounds and Cherie, his woman weighs about ninety five to a hundred . . . which is right about in your weight division, huh?"

"Ha, ha, very funny," she sang. "Now, when are you going to get rid of them?"

"Get rid of Deuce and Cherie?" I repeated pensively, biting down on my bottom lip.

"Yes, Bobby, you're going to have to, like, lose the dogs if you want me to live with you. I'm very much afraid. I am not exaggerating," her voice trembled as she made her pronouncement.

"I believe you."

"So, the dogs will go?"

"If you're afraid after you've met them, then I'll pack their bags and send them over to Eddie's. He and my sister-in-law Sheila have two boys."

"Whew," she held the back of her hand to her forehead in relief. "I thought we were going to have to call the whole thing off, before it even got started."

I placed her hands in mine once again and kissed them.

"Marriage is about compromise, my dear," I reminded her. "So, are we gon' do this thing right?"

"Yes, we are."

"I am really, really involved in my work as a psychologist, baby . . ."

"I know," she nodded wildly. "You didn't earn a doctorate's to waste it.."

"Yes, but I'm trying to tell you that I work very long hours."

"I can deal with that."

"That's what all the ministers' wives say at first. Then they end up miserable."

"Well, how did your own mother handle it?"

"Like a champ."

"Well then, Bobby, so will I."

"But then again Pops never did have to deal with drug and alcohol rehab, or juggle two cable broadcasts with two radio programs. People have my tapes. I'm on TV, now. . . ."

"I'll adjust, Bobby, I promise."

"So, I guess that means you're down with my whole program, huh?"

"Where do you get all of these urban macho bravado sayings from anyway?" she mused, before excusing herself to the bathroom.

Twenty Questions

Later that night, after I had winded Elisabeth's plush Beamer into the alcove in front of the Powell's colossal bay window, the stern-faced old man quickly ushered us in from the cold. And, in so many words ordered his surprisingly compliant daughter, to find something else to do until he had a little chat with me in his own personal den/study.

I sat on hard wooden stool next to a wet bar complete with non-alcoholic beverages, as I watched him reach into an antique curio to retrieve a box of vintage cigars. He calmly searched the top drawer of his maple wood desk for a lighter. After several flicks, the reluctant flame decided to ignite so he could have the privilege to inhale his first puff.

He blew four perfectly circular clouds into my face before he bothered to speak.

"Here, have one. I hear congratulations are in order."

As badly as I yearned to accept his offer and kick back on the lazy boy to join him in watching the highlights of the Bull's previous championship season, that had been conveniently muted on his 36" inch television, I resisted, figuring that we were embarking upon a test of two equally stubborn wills.

There was no way I was going to allow the big-shot doctor and elder of the flock to lord it over me to his wife and daughter, that I, within the privacy of my own company, ap-

———

251

preciated a sweet savory drag of the occasional celebratory, "It's a Girl or Boy," variety myself.

I nodded a quick no thank you before offering a semi-sincere apology for not asking his permission to marry his daughter prior to proposing to her.

"It just sort of happened," I attempted to explain.

"Oh, really?" he raised his voice and squirmed his large body around in his beige lazy-boy.

"Yes sir . . . I was planning to ask Elisabeth for her hand eventually, but I didn't think it would come together for us this soon."

"Brother McGallister, you fly down here from Detroit for a four-day gospel meeting, sweep my daughter off her juvenile feet within the same four days, and propose to her three nights later . . . I mean, work with me here. Wouldn't you have a problem with it, if you had a nineteen-year old virgin as a daughter?"

I marveled at his confidence in asserting and broadcasting his daughter's lack of sexual experience. Maybe my years of listening to and observing everyday people jaded my perception of there actually being pure and innocent souls remaining on earth.

"Sir, with all due respect, my intentions are good."

"I'm not concerned about your intentions son, I'm concerned about my daughter leaving everything she knows and loves behind just to be another trophy among the collection of all your magnificent feats. I mean from what I've noticed, everyone worships the ground you walk on. You're supposedly the biggest thing to hit the Church of Christ throughout the country since the reformation movement. I mean two thousand members after your first two years. Another two years later, more than double that. Why, my Princess would disappear standing in your shadow."

I chuckled at the absurdity of notion.

"I beg to differ, sir. I don't think Elisabeth is the type of woman who would go unnoticed."

"She has never been away from home more than a couple of nights without me, Emily, Ms. Maggie or one of our other family members."

The flat expression on my face coupled with my raised eyebrow indicated that Elisabeth's lack of having a travel companion to become my wife was the least of my worries.

I folded my arms across my chest and awaited the remaining cliche "father-to-future-son-in-law" scare-tactic lecture. He'd earned his right as her dad to scrutinize my every response, so long as it didn't take too much longer; my butt was starting to ache from sitting on that hard stool.

"Are you aware of how she got her nickname?" he asked wearing a grimace of paternalistic pride. I drooled over the savory fragrance of his stogie, admired his ability to drag and puff on it so effortlessly and prayed that he wouldn't bother to offer me another opportunity to smoke with him.

"Yes sir," I smiled. "I believe that's quite obvious."

"T'was a nice little ring you bought her. Probably set you back about five or six grand."

He didn't flinch at my raised eyebrow that asked him how he'd hit the hammer on the nail.

He shrugged, "Em told me everything last night."

"I see."

"I guess you know by now that the Princess has a fetish for the finer things in life."

"Yes sir."

"Yep, bought her that BMW last year when she graduated from high school."

"Sir."

"A cheap man can't afford her," he added, reaching for the lever to recline himself further back. He gave me the quick once over from head to toe, "but then again, son, you don't look like much of a penny pincher yourself."

"You'd be surprised."

"She gets awful moody and throws these out-of-this-world tantrums, man . . ."

"Sir, let me just spare you from further trying to intimidate me from not marrying . . ."

"When she was fifteen, she was hospitalized for anorexia. She still struggles with self-image today. I think it was due to Em's overt convincing. . . . that she wasn't as good as her sister. Lorraine was my other daughter."

"Was?"

"Yes sir," he replied in his usual self-assured bold manner. "Been gone away from here and the gospel since she was a teenager. . . . but, she's not the point. Elisabeth is. She's all I've got left. You understand?"

"Has Elisabeth had any more bouts of her disorder in recent years?" I wondered aloud, half-not expecting an honest answer, seeing that he was adamantly campaigning to dissuade me from becoming her husband.

"Would it change your mind about wanting to marry her?"

"No sir," I answered without hesitation.

"Good," he replied with a brisk nod of his head as if to conclude that portion of our conversation. " I met Emily Jameson at the University of Missouri. It was the early seventies. You know back during the Black Power Movement. Ever heard of Huey Newton, son?"

"Yes sir. He was the most prominent spokesperson for the Panthers out of Oakland. The Warriors . . . God's Warriors, the group of brothers Brother Khalid and I formed, have watched several documentaries on the time period."

"Well, he was my first cousin."

"Get outta here," I chuckled, trying hard to imagine the conservative, most-likely Republican James Powell, as an Afro wearing, gun-toting, black renegade.

"I'm not kidding. Our mothers, God rest their souls, were sisters, but I digress . . . I used to be one of those angry, uptight militant brothers. I mean, man, we used to protest everything, from the traditional, so called, white bred, American staple meals of roast beef and potatoes they served in the cafeteria, to forming demonstrations outside the student government building to demand more black representation in the various student caucuses. Man, the girl I was engaged to prior to meeting Em, was about your complexion, you know." He paused, took another enviable drag on his stogie and glanced up at me to see if I was paying more attention to the crowd's muted reaction to another one of Jordan's pretty jump shots, than his ramblings down memory lane.

He had my undivided attention. I folded my arms across my chest and nodded my appreciation of this candid glimpse into the life of such an accomplished man.

"Vanessa was her name. Vanessa Collins. She's a teacher down in Atlanta, now, probably near retirement. Never married, I hear. . . . .because she never got over the fact that I not only left her standing at the altar, but that I'd chosen Em, who'd happen to be white to spend the rest of my life with. We eloped a few hours before I was due to say 'I do' to Vanessa, you see."

"Yes, sir," I egged him on to reach the predictable climax of his belabored point.

"My parents, my brothers and sisters, along with all my former fraternity brothers, cousins, neighbors you name it, disowned me; thought I had betrayed my race for marrying a white woman. Thought I was trying to runaway from my roots. My mother, who passed on earlier this year, God rest her soul. . . . I thought would never forgive me, until Lorraine was born and came out just about a shade or two dark enough to be considered light-skinned. Even opened up more to Em once she rejected the teachings of her Catholic upbringing and was baptized and became a member of the Church of Christ."

"How did Emily's family react to that decision?"

"They at first thought I'd brainwashed her, but later on down the line, don't you know her mother and father both became members and served faithfully in their congregation down in Tampa until death?"

"What a blessing."

"Yes, son, it was. But, Em and I have overcome so many trials and tribulations because of our mixed marriage. I've been harassed by the white police in this area countless times. You know when we first had this house constructed, back twenty three years ago, I was walking on the nature trail right through the woods that connects our subdivision with the one behind it . . . I was walking along with Em, minding my own business, carrying a nightstick for our own protection when one of the neighbors who hadn't gotten word that a biracial couple had moved into their oh so pure neighborhood, called the police on me. Accused me of forcing an attractive, petite white blonde woman, into the woods with me, with my nightstick, so I could rape her, and ruin her from ever being with another white man again. You know what happened next son?"

He didn't wait for my befuddled response. He took my dropped jaw and gaping eyes as a signal to continue his story without much interruption from his captivated audience.

"I'm not proud of this son. Never shared this with anyone, but you. After the police approached us. Asked to see me over at their patrol car to chat with them in private. I clarified that we were man and wife simply going on a stroll behind our new home. They put us in the back seat of their car and escorted us up our own walkway so I could go retrieve our driver licenses, to verify my unlikely story. All the while, mind you, they kept Em out with them as if to protect her from me. Well son, I came back outside, not only carrying our licenses, but my medical degree and credentials to rub their smug red noses in the fact that I had defied all stereotypes and preconceived notions they'd undoubtedly had of me. Felt like I had to prove myself all the time.

Every day of my life, even now, after twenty-five years of marriage, you wouldn't believe some of the condescending sneers and snide remarks ignorant people make. I get it the worse, son, I'm sad to say from our own people. You wouldn't believe how many waitresses and customer service folks, black women in particular, who hesitate or refuse me service when they find out my wife is white. Do you understand what I'm trying to tell you son?"

"Yes sir, I believe so."

"The Princess, well, she uh, as you know takes after Em's side of the family."

"Yes sir, but, you're her father. Half the blood running through her veins comes from you."

"The Princess could easily be mistaken for white. She always has been."

"But, she isn't *white*," I replied dejectedly.

"I must admit, Emily almost divorced me back when the girls were real little. You see I kinda like ordered her to have a blood test to see if I was the Princess' real daddy."

"I'm sure she must have been pretty hurt about that."

"Irate, is more like the word, but you see I waited around four or five years for my second baby to turn as dark as the first, but she never did, and once again, I'm embarrassed by my past behavior. I let my mama's naysaying get to me and my sisters, brothers, colleagues, etcetera. Couldn't take it anymore. Dragged my wife kicking and screaming, threatening to file divorce before the ink could dry on the test results which of course proved without a doubt that I am the Princess' biological father."

"How did Emily manage to get over that?"

"She never has. She never will. I've tried to make it up to her in every possible way, but something died in our marriage back then. A lot of what was left of us went out the door with Lori. Em is definitely obsessed with that girl. Certifiable. It's ironic how I ended up after my black child left being closest to my white child, the one I couldn't claim as my own until I had definite proof."

"But, Elisabeth isn't white," I insisted again, pissed off that her own father had resigned himself into denying one half of his youngest daughter's identity.

" We know this. But you have to admit, if you didn't know I was her father, you probably would have never given my baby a second thought."

"Yes sir, you're probably whi . . . I mean, right about that."

"Son, there are a lot worse things to be than white. You make it sound like a crime. I'm just trying to say that you have your work cut out for you in convincing your *followers* that your wife is fifty percent black."

"No offense to you or Emily, sir," I asserted, "but Elisabeth and I are not you. Times have changed. People are more educated about the various hues of our beautiful race, ranging from lily white to jet black."

"I've asked Elisabeth to show me a few of the tapes she has of yours. I've seen the one where you tell all those Muslim looking men to love and cherish the black woman because she's God's greatest creation."

"Yes sir, she is."

"Well, son, how do you think those men are going to react when you introduce them to the Princess?"

"Hopefully, they'll be very happy for me. Honestly, sir. I know Elisabeth and I will be fine with this color issue thing. The children the Lord blesses us with will be seventy-five percent black anyway, so there is really no big deal."

"If you say so, son," he replied with a patronizing smirk that insinuated I had a lot to learn about the hardships of interracial love.

"Tell me more about this God's Warrior program of yours,"

he ordered, determined to pinpoint some sore subject to knock me off of my apparent high horse.

"I don't claim the program as mine, sir. All the glory, honor and praise for the accomplishments and successes of God's Warriors belong to our Heavenly Father."

I relaxed a little more comfortably on the butt aching stool as I began to discuss one of my favorite subjects. I shared with my future father-in-law Brother Khalid's initial concept of brothers within our faith coming together on a weekly basis to admonish, teach and uplift one another in order to glorify God's kingdom and to draw more souls to Christ. I explained how before our first Tuesday night session, Mark Riley, one of the deacons, along with Brother Khalid and I sat down to examine the spiritual, emotional, mental, intellectual, financial and physical needs of black Christian men living in today's times and to discuss the purpose of our group.

I remember that late Sunday night in my office after evening service. We'd just devoured one of Ma's weekly, prized home-cooked meals. The two of them dictated to me as fast as my fingers could peck across the keyboard of my computer, the collective voice of the weaknesses of the men throughout the brotherhood. A few hours later, we'd formulated the first rough draft of our mission statement to include oaths of fidelity, fraternity, fatherhood and financial empowerment based upon the feedback we'd received and tallied from a survey Brother Khalid created and distributed.

"The core group at our congregation alone now includes over a couple hundred brothers strong, some of whom are former drug and alcohol abusers. Most are working class to professional brothers. Besides holding down full time jobs, attending college, taking care of families and attending regular worship services, there are always at least twelve of them on hand to serve as ushers, scripture readers and pallbearers at funerals. They have formed their own sick visitation committees, music ministries, community outreach programs and most importantly, they have evangelized door-to-door, at least thirty percent of the population of our congregation today. "

"Yes, that's fine and dandy, son," Powell concurred, before I could finish my spiel, "but, on the tape I heard you criticize your own father and the elders of your congregation for their sound advice in asking you not to use the word ministry so loosely. Many of the men in your little exclusive group have titles, man-made titles that you and Brother Khalid have taken among yourselves to give them, just so they could feel important. Minister of Music. Minister of Personal Evangelism. Minister of Community Outreach. Although it's a fine concept, I think you all have pushed the envelope a little too far on this one."

"And I think that you and my Pops are going to get along just fine."

"You know your father and I didn't get to be elders over the flock solely on our good looks and charm. We happen to know a thing or two about the saving of souls. Back in our day, we didn't need those puffed up superfluous titles to carry out the mission of the cross."

"I believe that those names are mere distinction of roles, like deacons and elders, not titles, sir," I countered defensively. "These brothers are very humble men who don't seek any type of reward or recognition for themselves. They have been instructed and trained not by the two of us, but by the word of God."

"Well, what about the pledges they have to sign? Upon what scriptural basis do you base these obligations? To me, and forgive me if this offends you, it just sounds like you've allowed the influence and former practices of that ex-convict, ex-Muslim, personal assistant of yours to push your own agenda and to elevate you within the ranks of those souped up TV evangelists who gross more per year than I, as a neurosurgeon and chief administrator of a prominent research based, hospital would ever hope to earn."

I hesitated in answering his questions, partly out of exhaustion over having yet another elder call me to task on that particular aspect of my ministry, but mostly over my impatience with having to forgive another narrow-minded dinosaur for not watching the complete God's Warrior video-taped series, in which I enumerated and provided scriptural references for all twenty-two tenets of the program that every participant had committed to memory:

- I, as a soldier on the battlefield for Christ, will first and foremost serve no other god, (put nothing else above) before Jehovah God. (Exodus 20:3).
- I, as a soldier on the battlefield for Christ, will not forsake the assembly of the gathering of the saints. (Hebrews 10:25)
- I, as a soldier on the battlefield for Christ, will abstain from fornication. (Romans 1:29)
- I, as a soldier on the battlefield for Christ, will abstain from adultery. (Exodus 20:14, Matthew 19:8)
- I, as a soldier on the battlefield for Christ, will love, honor and dwell with my wife, according to knowledge, as the weaker vessel. (Ephesians 5:25, I Peter 3:7)
- I, as a soldier on the battlefield for Christ, will abstain from gambling, smoking, drinking or any social behavior that may offend another brother or sister in Christ. (Romans 14:21)
- I, as a soldier on the battlefield for Christ, will give cheerfully to the Lord's church, as I have prospered. (II Corinthians 9: 6,7)
- I, as a soldier on the battlefield for Christ, will train up my children in the way they should go,

so when they are old, they will not depart from it. (Proverbs 22:6)

- I, as a soldier on the battlefield for Christ, will not provoke my children to wrath, but bring them up in the nurture and admonition of the Lord. (Ephesians 6:4)
- I, as a soldier on the battlefield for Christ, will admonish/encourage my fellow soldiers. (Romans 15:14, II Thessalonians 3:15)
- I, as a soldier on the battlefield for Christ, will bear my brother's burdens. (Galatians 6:2)
- I, as a soldier on the battlefield for Christ, will study the word to show myself approved unto God, a workman who needs not to be ashamed, rightly dividing the word of truth. (II Timothy 2:15)
- I, as a soldier on the battlefield for Christ, will wear the full armor of God, (having my loins girted with truth, wearing the breastplate of righteousness, having my feet shod with the preparation of the gospel of peace, wearing the shield of faith and the helmet of salvation, and carrying the sword of the Spirit, which is the word of God), so that I may be able to withstand the wiles of the devil. (Ephesians 6:13-17)
- I, as a soldier on the battlefield for Christ, will do the work of an evangelist and make full proof of my ministries. (II Timothy 4:5)
- I, as a soldier on the battlefield for Christ, will visit the fatherless and the widows. (James 1:27)
- I, as a soldier on the battlefield for Christ, will honor my father and mother, which is the first commandment with promise. (Exodus 20:12)
- I, as a soldier on the battlefield for Christ, will follow the example of Phillip in his conversion

of the Ethiopian eunuch and will not hesitate to share the full gospel with anyone who seeks the truth from me. (Acts 8:26-40)

- I, as a soldier on the battlefield for Christ, will not be ashamed of the gospel of Jesus, for it is the power unto salvation to everyone who believes. (Romans 1:16)

- I, as a soldier on the battlefield for Christ, will present my body as a living sacrifice before God, by eating healthy and getting the proper exercise. (Romans 12:1)

- I, as a soldier on the battlefield for Christ, will serve the Lord faithfully in order to receive the crown of life that will never perish. (II Timothy 2:8)

- I, as a soldier on the battlefield for Christ, will follow the examples of financial interdependence set by and among first-century Christians who shared all things as a community. (Acts 4:32)

- I, as a soldier on the battlefield for Christ will reside over and/or invest in and contribute to the cause of financial empowerment and independence among and between fellow Warriors first, other Christians and African-Americans in general.

"Brother Powell, I can assure you that I'm by no means, a wealthy man. Self-promotion is not what I'm all about, sir. Perhaps, before you can come to some definitive conclusion about the God's Warriors ministry, I would suggest and encourage you to watch the second and third tapes in the series to get the full explanation and scriptural basis of the program."

Satisfied that he hadn't managed to break my resolve to walk away with my self-confidence in tact, he straightway pushed himself forward to extinguish his cigar into the ceramic ashtray on the end table next to him. As he stood up, he let his eyes wander around the room, to search for some lost, treasured object. A few seconds later, he walked over to the wet bar and felt around on the counter-top until he located his remote control.

He adjusted the volume of the game to a level, which would have been satisfactory to me and all of my sport fanatic boys, including Eddie, Doug, Brother Khalid, Riley, Darius and Paul. The nerdy, bowtie sporting, commentator had just announced that Jordan had scored thirty-six points and it was only the middle of the third quarter.

"That brother is amazing," I thought aloud.

"That indeed," James Powell concurred, walking around the counter to search for an appropriate beverage to serve himself, an elder of the Lord's church, and I, an evangelist who was about to rob him of the joy of his life.

"You still play?"

"Aw, no sir . . . every now and then, just to be foolin' around with my potnas out in the back of the parsonage or in the gym of the church."

"Oh yeah," he responded, holding up a bottle of seltzer water and two champagne glasses. "How much you pressin'?"

"About my body weight."

"Do you know what I'd do to you, if you ever used your physical strength against my Princess in any way?"

"I can imagine. I've never hit a woman in my life, unless you count the a couple of times, I've beaten down my smart –mouthed tattle-tale female cousins who used to break into my room to steal my stash of candy, back when I was a kid."

He didn't find my witty comeback funny. Maybe Elisabeth inherited her sense of humor or lack thereof from the old man.

She Ain't White

The following morning, Elisabeth insisted on driving me to Lambert Airport to see me off even though I had made previous arrangements with Cecil Donaldson.

"Bobby," she insisted from the passenger seat of her car on our late drive back to the hotel that evening. "I'm going to be your wife in less than three months. I'm sure you're going to need me to do things for you sometimes."

Reluctantly, I accepted her invitation. As highly emotional and weepy as she'd been over the previous twenty-four hour period, I just didn't feel like participating in a dramatic, tear-stained goodbye.

As predicted, Brother Khalid didn't take too kindly to my subtle announcement of my pending nuptials. To compensate for his faux pas of causing us to miss our originally scheduled departure, he made a big deal about his arrival an hour early to the airport, just to pick me up and offer me a lift over to my folks' house. Pops had been released that same morning. Immediately, after we'd picked up my three bags from the Southwest baggage claim department, he started filling me in on the goings on at the Rosedale Park congregation I'd missed.

"Sister Pearl tripped over her grandson's shoe that he left untied on her stairwell. She tore ligaments in her ankle, and pulled some type of tendons in her leg." His words were

---

265

filled with animation, until he'd noticed I didn't grasp what he found so humorous. "Well, man, the doctor said she was going to be all right. You know she doesn't have good transportation. Was on your voice mail Monday, wanting you to take her to her follow up appointment."

We crammed my bags in the trunk of Fatima's black Honda Civic and climbed in. I searched for the seat adjuster in order to free up some leg space on the passenger side. As his elaborate reports continued, I found myself staring out the window, allowing my thoughts to drift back to the enticing, full-tongued kiss Elisabeth gave me, seconds before she waved goodbye, with one hand, while wiping away the stream of tears flowing from her eyes with the other.

Tanya, who upon James Powell's insistence, tagged along so Elisabeth wouldn't get lost on the expressway en route back to Chesterfield, had stood enviously eyeing us from five feet away. As I walked away, she ran up behind me to hand me a folded up sheet of perfumed stationery she asked me to give to Brother Khalid. I promised I would.

"Bobby, call me as soon as your plane lands. I want to know you made it all right," Elisabeth called out to me in between sobs. Tanya rolled her eyes and pulled her playfully by the arm.

"Come on here, Ms. Thang," she teased. "You'll be moving up there before you know it . . . so stop all the crying and embarrassing us in public."

"And Sister Angel Williams' husband has been jumping on her again. Threatened their oldest boy with a gun..held it right up to his head and dared him to take up for his mother again." He looked over at me, noticed my trance-like stupor, mumbled under his breath about the outrageous parking lot fees at Metro and sped off, headed towards I-94 Eastbound, Detroit. "She is a fine woman, with a pretty stable job . . . I don't understand why I couldn't luck out with a gorgeous sistah like that. Man, some brothas don't know what they've got till it's gone."

"Mmm-hmm."

"Little Brother, man," he laughed. "Where you at?"

" Huh," I replied snapping myself back into the hear and now. "Did Angel leave a number for me to contact her at that shelter again?"

"Yeah, it's in the palm-held. You can check it out and all your other messages once I get you to your folks' house." He gave me a "I-don't –know-what-kind-of-spell-that-little-white-girl-has-cast-on-you-but-you're-sure-as-hell-home-to-your-life-full-of ministerial-responsibilities-now-look. "What's up with you bro? What you trippin' on?"

"I got engaged Tuesday night," the words sounded foreign coming from my own mouth. I had to repeat them with more enthusiasm, and with my hand held organizer closed for him to slam down a congratulatory slap.

He released his right foot from the accelerator, which automatically caused the redneck driver of an eighteen wheeler Roadway truck to flip him the bird, yell out some obscenities and zoom past, leaving us in a cloud of dust.

"Mind the road, Yusef. Mind the road," I chided lightheartedly.

He reached to reduce the volume of a sermon I'd done entitled, *"Hell's Ghetto: There's a Project and Slumlord Waiting for us All, if We're Not Careful,"* a few months back, on Fatima's cheap non-CD player, AM/FM radio, cassette deck.

"Man, you must be out of your black ass mind," he cursed in his best Eddie impersonation. "I knew better than to leave your sexually frustrated ass with the Jungle Fever Princess."

"Man, I keep telling you Elisabeth's half-black," I retorted sharply growing weary of his continuous condescending references to the lack of sufficient pigmentation in her complexion.

"Oh yeah," he shot back swiftly. " Like I asked you before, has anyone ever told her that? I bet she would beg the friggin' differ."

I chewed on my bottom lip and glanced over at him out of the corner of my eye.

"Besides Little Bro, how do you think the church is going to handle you marrying a white woman? Huh? Do you know the backlash you're going to get from the sisters who are sistah's man? They're the ones buying all your books and tapes and stuff . . ."

"Elisabeth's not white. She is bi- . . ."

"Yeah, right man . . . whatever."

Furious that my best friend on the planet couldn't muster up enough compassion in his heart to even offer a semi-sincere congratulatory response pissed me off. I reached back to retrieve his organizer out of his briefcase. He didn't offer to help when he noticed me fumbling with the combination.

We rode in silence a few minutes, until we both could calm down enough to treat each other with some manner of civility.

"You really gon' do this, huh?" I detected a slight glimmer of hope in his tone. Hating to crush it, I manipulated some buttons on his organizer to look at my calendar for the week to see if the appointments he had recorded were consistent with the ones in my own.

"She's moving up in here in two weeks so we can spend more time together and go through pre-marital counseling with Brother Forbes."

"Yeah, now I know you buggin', man . . . out of your damn mind."

I reached into the coat pocket of jacket, searching for a stick of Wrigley's Spearmint Chewing gum. Once I found it, I began unwrapping it and offered him a stick. Frustrated and convinced that my mind was pretty much made up, he pushed my hand away and asked me for the date.

"Her birthday is Valentine's Day, so we're going to do it the Saturday before."

"Oh how sweet," he replied batting his eyelashes facetiously in an impressive sissified manner. " The preacher man is marrying his little Prima Dona near the day of her birth."

"Man, stop. You know you wrong for that," I snapped, annoyed as hell.

"And, just where do you suppose she's going to stay for the next couple of months, until she hooks on her ball and chain?"

"This would be the reason why I want you to stop me by the folks crib."

"Aw, naw," he laughed into his balled up fist. "Out of your damn mind, Little Brother, for real now. Your moms will eat little Miss Attitude for breakfast, lunch and dinner, especially when she finds out she's white . . . or excuse me, white-looking. I have got to come in to get a front row seat for the main event."

269

Deuce and His Woman

A few minutes later, I changed my mind about Brother Khalid going with me to share my wonderful news with my parents and decided to go home shower and change into one of my more casual fall slacks and sports jacket ensembles before calling Sister Pearl to see if she needed me to stop by the pharmacy to pick up one of her monthly loads of prescription refills. A hypochondriac to the death, the elderly living on a fixed income, retired school teacher, not only wanted me to pick up and pay for her one hundred dollar meds, but she also asked me if I could find it in my heart to buy her a heating pad for her swollen ankle.

"But, Sister Pearl, I thought you were supposed to keep that ankle elevated and apply ice." I shook my head smiling as I studied the note on the refrigerator Ma had left. It read:

Cherie and Deuce are fine. Your nephews have been coming over to feed them and walk them every day. Deuce ran your poor elderly neighbor's cat up the tree for the zillioneth time. I think you'd better take some of my infamous banana bread over there as a peace offering. Cherie refused to let Eric bathe her and kept trying to bite Tre' on the behind. I think she needs some type of dog therapy, because you're gone so much. Love, Ma.

-P.S. Come by to see your Pops, and get a hot meal after you've come home to check on your babies, shaved and cleaned yourself up. Don't I know my son? (Smile)

"That so?" Sister Pearl, who was partially deaf in one ear yelled through the receiver. "Well, Brother Preacher, could you bring the heating pad anyway for my achin' back . . . ole' Arthur is creepin' up on it again. And oh, if it's not too much trouble, could you bring me a pack of Bubblicious Bubble Gum and the icepack, too . . . for my . . . er . . ."

"Your ankle, Sister Pearl. You have a sprained ankle," I replied trying to refrain from laughing at her forgetfulness. A clicking noise on her line indicated she had another call waiting. She put me on hold, for a lifetime. "Here Cherie, come here girl," I quietly called down the basement steps to my deviant furry offspring, who was going to work on a huge beef rib, probably offered to her by Tre in their temporary truce.

When she heard my voice, she looked up at me with lazy, sad puppy dog eyes, as if to say, *"Oh, it's you, so you've gone away and have come back for the fifteen hundreth time, and I'm supposed to be all geeked up to see you? Yeah, right. Get over yourself!"*

To signal my return, she barked over to Deuce, who'd been resting in his jumbo-laundry basket/makeshift bed that I'd put together to keep him warm on chilly days.

As expected, good old Deuce appeared from behind the dryer where he would normally drag his basket, ran up the stairs and waited for me to unlock the bottom half of the safety door I'd attached for the protection of those houseguests who were terrified of them.

"Hey boy! Hey boy," I grinned, rubbing the fur underneath his double-chin. "Look who's back, kid. Daddy's back."

When Sister Pearl returned to our conversation, I concluded it by telling her that under no uncertain terms would I be purchasing any type of chewing or bubble gum for her because it would ruin the work she'd just had on her dentures just two weeks ago.

That Thursday afternoon, I spent most my time in the near-vacant dentist office waiting room, writing job recommendation letters on my laptop for "graduates" of the drug and alcohol rehabilitation program and trying to, on my cell-phone in the most inconspicuous manner possible, talk one of my long-time patients down from the pangs of crack withdrawals.

Marcus, a six-month resident of the Interfaith center had started his love affair with the crystallized chemical substance, not unlike a lot of other brothers I treated by happenstance. After pushing it a few months, to neighborhood prostitutes and even to some cops who were on the take, to resell and make profits, he'd started experimenting with his own wares, and wound up losing his wife, children and even a permanent address.

" Marcus, you need to hear me and hear me good," I threatened, tired of his foolishness and ready to go full force in my bad cop/worse cop routine. " If you take your good-for-a-quick-fix, sell-your –soul-to-Satan-narrow-hundred pound behind to score, then you'd better get so high that you won't ever come down. But if you do . . . and you try to come prancing your way back into the program and your little comfortable room in the woe-is-me hotel, guess what, my man? You gon' find your key won't turn in the door. And, when you want to throw a tantrum and cry like a punk in the hallway, you know those mean Muslim cats who stand guard for us, to protect our patients who truly are trying to get well from druggies like you . . . well, I've seen what they do to dropouts like you, besides beating yo' ass behind the building, say it involves a straight jacket and two needle toting paramedics who will be ready to take you on an all expense paid trip sponsored by God's Warriors to a medical facility far, far away."

As expected, he cursed me out through the barely there rotten teeth remaining in his mouth and called me every "punk, nigga, fake, bougie, hustlin' preachin' pimp wannabe, theivin', black gorilla" in the book.

272

"Yeah, I've got your hustlin' preachin' pimp wannabe, fool," I replied. " But understand this, you 'd just better be sure that you're on lockdown in the joint when I roll by there at any time I damn well please. Comprende'?"

Short Fuse

Changing into a casual pair of gray slacks, white button down shirt and gray sports coat, offered professional, yet comfortable relief to the stuffy feeling of having worn complete suits with three quarter length jackets for at least four of the seven days I spent in St. Louis. It took me several attempts to finally get an answer on one of the phone numbers I had for Angel Williams, the twenty-eight year-old, butterscotch complexioned, shoulder-length brown haired, school secretary and battered mother of three on the phone.

Grabbing the keys to my Ford Explorer and cramming my planner into the pocket of my stylish gray wool coat, I was just about to push the "End" button on my cordless phone and try her work number at the same elementary school her two older kids attended, when on the fifth ring, her hot-tempered high-school dropout, unemployed, husband Derrick answered the phone out of breath, sounding as gruff as ever.

"What the hell you want here, calling my house, Rev?" he shouted through the receiver. I silently cursed the inventors of Caller ID, as I mulled over a calm response in my head. "Man, don't tell me you're trying to get my hoe to fuck you again. She wrote about that shit in her journal, which was the reason I knocked that bitch out a few days ago, after I picked up the phone on her ass and heard her askin' your little flunky Farrakhan reject when you were gon be back in town. And don't try to deny that ya'll got a thang goin' on. That little shiny fo'head muthafuckin' two year old crawlin' around here, too tall for his age, got your big ass feet and hands . . ."

"Whoa . . . wait a minute brother, slow yo' ro' for a minute or two, and let's try to talk calmly and rationally."

"Fool, fuck that! Who you tryin' to talk that psycho babble bullshit to? I shoulda never let that ho' prance up in that church with my two babies in the first place! And the one, she got in her belly now . . . I know ain't mine . . . you wanna know how, because I ain't fucked her in the time she talkin' she conceived. Muthafucka, I oughta reach through the phone and whup yo' ass right now!"

Stunned speechless at the revelation that Angel had the unmitigated gall to have sex and get pregnant by someone other than her lunatic husband, from my standing position in the front door, I removed my gray, black banded Stetson and flopped down into the black leather recliner that was perched right in front of my 53' inch big screen television in the living room. I activated the truck alarm button on my key ring and began to massage my temples.

"Listen brother . . ."

"Man, I ain't yo' damn brother, you understand," he yelled ferociously. "I wanna kill yo' ass. I'm watchin' you . . . I know where you live . . ."

"Mr. Williams, you threatenin' me?" I asked, not intimidated, knowing that the legal arsenal I'd acquired myself as being a drug rehab therapist and a reputed in-yo-face no-nonsense, minister of a congregation growing in former convicts and addicts, would more than impress the common hardcore thug, Derrick Williams, notwithstanding.

"Hell yeah, I'm threatenin', yo' black monkey ass," he muttered. I made a mental note to have Brother Khalid's wife to round up some of her brothers and cousins to come stand guard at the parsonage and at my folks house, before the

275

Lord's omnipotent spirit allowed me to conjure up the visages of two high-ranking Detroit police officers stationed at the William's west-side neighborhood precinct, one of whom, a lieutenant, newly converted to the Church of Christ after having listened to my weekly radio broadcast, had even asked me to be his firstborn's godfather, before learning that the church does not subscribe to the doctrine of original sin and christening babies.

"Okay, then. I guess this head to head is pretty much over . . ."

"Aw, hole' up Mr. Playa, wannabe shotcalla! This shit ain't over until I say its over. You betta recognize . . ."

Tired of tolerating his imitation of the street lingo used by gangsta rap's brightest and best, I stood up, walked over to and glanced out of the window. Paranoid already that he had sent one of his henchmen to take me out, I nervously paced the floor back and forth.

"You better not try to fuck with Angel . . . ya understand,,, like try to take her to one them shelters for battered women an' shit . . . ya understand . . . because I made her leave yo lil' rugrat here and I'm gon' break every bone in his muthafuckin' body if she don't come home with my two muthafuckin' kids."

An attempt to rightfully deny my paternity of little Parnell would prove to be useless, given the volatile nature of the conversation. Instead, I urged him calmly not to hurt Angel's son and reassured him that knowing Angel's loyalty to him and to their family, she would come directly home from work with his children.

"Well, she just betta', or I'mo kill this lil' bastard chile' of yours," he hollered, just before hanging up on me.

"*Man, why do you always get yourself in these situations?*" I thought as I stormed up and down the familiar worn path of the hardwood floor I hadn't had time to rebuff for a couple of years. "*Always trying to be Superman and save the world, you stupid idiot . . . you're going to fool around one day and get your-self hurt, coming in between husband and wives, roughing up crack heads, pouncing on your big brother, telling folks if they don't straighten up their acts, the devil with his welcoming committee of demons in his fiery pit awaits them in the after-life. I mean . . . who do you think you are . . . stupid egomaniac, arrogant, self-righ-teous, son-of-a-bitch."* The more I tried to quiet the negative voice resonating from my own self-doubt, the louder it be-came. *"You deserve what you've got comin' to you, accepting money for doing the Lord's work, self-promoting memoirs of your own, trashy, lascivious exploits with all types of, as Derrick calls them, hoes and sluts, like that damned Angel, who got your black ass into this mess in the first place.*

Damned fool . . . if you're going to be accused over and over for doing these women, you've never even touched inappropriately, you might as well be guilty. You might as well have screwed them all..instead of senselessly immersing your whole existence into your work, while depriving yourself of releasing your own, natural, God-given sexual energy for the past four years. What a complete fool, you are brotha, a complete idiot."

I vehemently shook my head, waved my fist and shouted the word, "no" into the air, to a listening God who'd prob-ably was quite indignant with me for even entertaining such harrowing, abhorrent thoughts and to a smug Satan who'd was probably doing the hustle on the prickly, coal covered floors of hell.

I removed my sports coat and perfectly starched white shirt to expose the white tank top I was wearing and ran down-stairs with one determined mission. Cherie, now in the mood for bonding with her long-lost master, ran up to me and leapt onto my chest with the assistance of her robust hind legs, I angrily pushed her off of me and ordered her to sit. She sheep-ishly obeyed.

After having appraised the brief interaction between us, Deuce, who had been lapping up the last drops of water in

his name engraved water bowl, scowled at me for assaulting
his life partner's self-esteem, jumped up from his relaxed
position, then yelped out several angry barks.

When I through squinted malevolent eyes didn't flinch,
he pensively studied my frustrated demeanor and wisely decided to join his sweetheart in a sulking match behind the
dryer.

I walked over to the punching bag that hung from a hook
on the ceiling, which was within two inches of grazing the
crown of my head, balled up my left fist the tightest I could
get it and delivered a quick one-two-one-two, then another,
then another, then a hearty right uppercut, followed by a left
hook and another quick one-two-one-two. A few minutes into
my literal exercise in futility, I realized that I was beginning
to sweat and didn't want to take another shower. I glanced
over at the Rots, who were defensively glaring at me, as if I
were a stranger before darting back up the stairs to gather
my thoughts.

Out of breath, I pulled out the first chair of the two-seater
dinette in my kitchen and more out of habit then desire, began to pray in hopes that an ounce of contriteness and sincer-
ity would seep through my feeble words.

"My Lord and My God," I mouthed the first initial words,
without worrying about dressing them up eloquently for an
audience. *"Thank you Father. I thank you Lord for all the many
blessings you've showered upon me from my earliest existence, to
this very present time. You've delivered me safely home from yet
another gospel meeting, in which twenty some odd souls were saved.
Glory halleluiah!"* I began to speak the words quietly, as I
grew more comfortable with approaching his throne of grace.

*"You've blessed me from a very young age, with the ability to
help people, comfort them and soothe their broken spirits, Father.
Sometimes I begrudge such an awesome responsibility . . . and question why I've been cursed with such a talent, that I know I must
use, Father. I ask forgiveness of that sin, Father. I ask forgiveness*

of all sins I've committed within the last few hours, from wishing a very lost soul, in the person of Derrick Williams dead, to wanting to impose further bodily harm on his wife Angel for insinuating that we've had sexual relations and have conceived, not one, but two children together. I'm angry, Father. I'm angry, I'm torn and I'm hurt, Lord.

Other people seek me out for spirit-led counseling, Father. But, where does the counselor go to be counseled? To whom do I turn for advice here on this earth?" I smiled, knowing the answer to such a rhetorical question, and began quoting the 121st division of Psalms, one of my favorite passages in the entire Bible.

"Father, as King David said in the long ago, My help cometh from the Lord, which made heaven and earth. You will not suffer my foot to be moved . . . you will preserve me from all evil: and you shall preserve my soul. Lord, protect me from the vindictiveness of Derrick Williams. Help me to make the right decision, in this regard, by involving the police and not taking matters in my own hands.

Lord, you know I want to empty a spray of shotgun bullets into his cold, unremorseful heart for all of the years of abuse Angel has suffered and for threatening me in the first place. Cleanse my heart oh Lord. Take away this spirit, which is not of you, Oh Lord. Preserve my goings and my comings in from this time forth and even for-evermore. This is my feeble plea, Oh Lord, and my prayer—in the name of your darling Son, the Precious Lamb of God and my Savior, Amen. Amen."

———

Angel

Feeling burdened-free almost immediately after ending my conversation with the Lord, I freshened myself up, picked up the keys to my Explorer and headed for the drug store, to pick up Sister Pearl's long list of personal requests.

Chagrined that I opted not to come in to keep her company for an hour or so and to have our standard coffee-two-day-old-stale-donut –discussion-of-the-news session, she reached up in house-shoed feet and hugged my neck tightly, before thanking me and planted a sloppy kiss on my cheek, close to my collar, which I'm sure left its' usual pink stain.

From there, I headed straight to Angel's school to persuade her as calmly as I could to have Derrick arrested and brought up on charges for domestic abuse.

I stood at the counter of the main office being ignored for several seconds, until one of the young secretaries got bored with word-processing and decided to look away from her computer monitor. Our eyes met. Once she'd recognized me, her whole sour, restless, can't-wait-to-4:00-attitude shifted to one of coquettishness and sexual availability. She unbuttoned the first two snaps of her blouse, stood up, smoothed out her short black wool skirt and sashayed over to the countertop, resting her ample bosom right beneath my interested gaze.

"You're that preacher . . . the one I watch every Sunday

on cable. The one who wrote that raunchy book that made the bestseller's list," she said excitedly, through seductive eyes. "You probably don't remember. But, you autographed it for me right up there at Apple Book Center. My cousin owns the place!"

"Is that right?" I grinned still having a difficult time distracting myself from her at minimum, double D cups.

To make matters worse, she recognizing my lack of eye contact, backed away a few inches, took on better posture and stood up straight, so that my thirsty eyes could survey the rest of her body.

I grunted underneath my breath, before thanking her for supporting my ministries and asking for Angel Williams. Angel, who had been employed at Lincoln Elementary School for the past eight years, had been recently promoted to head secretary. She had miraculously not missed any work due to her complicated home situation.

"She's on an errand, but she'll be back shortly," the sex kitten purred. "I'm sure she'll be most happy to see you here waiting for her. She talks about you all the time. I can see why."

I stood there gripping my hat in my right hand, smiling sheepishly at Ms. Playboy Bunny of the Week until I felt a delicate tap on the shoulder. Upon turning around to respond, I was horrified at the sight before my eyes. Wearing dark glasses and a ton of pancake makeup that failed to mask the blue, green and black bruises on both her cheeks, Angel looked up at me and smiled, before covering the side of her swollen mouth.

Ms. Hot Stuff resumed her lean across the counter so she could eavesdrop into our conversation. I nodded in the direction of the door, before taking Angel's hand and leading her into the hallway. It was 3:45. The students had been dismissed a half-hour prior to our rendezvous.

Before saying anything to her, I gently placed my hand

on her chin, and lifted it upward to me. Then, I removed her shades that revealed not one, but two black eyes. A flood of tears released themselves from their sore, puffy, sleep deprived eyelids. I embraced her. She clung to me tightly and began a terrible bout of sniffing and trembling. I wanted to kick myself for worrying about her blowing and/or wiping her nose unto my coat.

"Sssshhh, now," I whispered, my lips resting in the crown of her naturally light brown hair, which reminded me of Elisabeth's. *Elisabeth, I thought, what kind of husband am I going to make you, seeing that my preoccupation with the lives of church members filled the hectic days of my existence?* I'd been home for three hours and had failed to call her.

Normally, bruises aside and scars withstanding, the woman I held in my arms was any man's petite vision of loveliness.

Standing at about 5'2", a bit too short for my taste, Angel's other physical assets compensated for her lack of stature. Her greenish bedroom eyes, two or three inch beyond shoulder-length wrapped hair would have been enough to pass her off as a Vanessa Williams look-a-like. But through previous locker-roomish b-ball game watching discussions, I discovered that what most of my partners Doug, Ed, Riley and especially Brother Khalid found most attractive about Angel Williams was how she still managed to maintain the body of a goddess, complete with a plush bosom, rounded bottom and curvaceous hips after giving birth three times.

Though all of the boys were married and many other men of our congregation were also, the lot of them, along with all of the available bachelors, stood regularly on the side-lines, waiting to comfort her, each and every time she darkened the church's doorposts wearing the badges of her endurance as a battered wife.

How they would hate on me if they could see her in my arms at that moment.

"I. . . . I'm just soooo tired Robert. I'm tired," she sniffed onto the breast of my three hundred dollar black cashmere coat.

"I know. I know," I whispered, caressing the back of her wool blazer. She stepped back from me, reached in her pocket and retrieved a tissue. I turned my head as she delivered several hearty blows into the tissue before tossing it into the nearby trash receptacle.

She walked back over to me standing so close a common observer would have thought we were slow dancing.

"I spoke with him today. He thinks I'm Parnell's father," I grimaced, trying not to allow my anger to surface. A startled and bewildered expression etched its' way unto her weary face.

"You . . . you . . . spoke with Dderr-ick. . . . how . . . why?"

"Brother Khalid told me you called me the other day and that he'd spoken with you. I just got back this morning, so I'd figured you were at home . . . considering the circumstances." I explained touching the bruises on her right cheek. I couldn't resist the temptation of trying to feel what she felt, nor trying to offer a gentle counterpart to the blow responsible for the marks.

"I . . . I never . . . miss . . . work, you know . . . so, what else did he say?"

"What else," my voice rose at the unmitigated gall for her to shrug off the potency of my first statement. " He thinks I'm the father of your two-year old son, and the baby you're carrying now."

"He told you I was pregnant?" her eyebrows knitted themselves into an embarrassed question mark.

"Yeah. He also threatened to take me out."

"He wouldn't do that . . . that's just talk . . . you know . . . he's a hoodlum . . . he doesn't know any better."

"Is that what you told yourself during the last beating?" I asked, losing patience as I watched her hug herself with trembling hands. "You have to report him. This is why I'm here-

---

283

to escort you and the children to the twelfth precinct, where Brother Jacobs and Brother Daniels have a clerk waiting for you to complete the paperwork. They will make an arrest tonight."

She chewed on her bottom lip, looked me directly in the eye for the first time during the conversation and ascertained my matter-of-fact expression that she basically had no choice since my very own life was at stake to no fault of my own.

"Why did you write in your journal, something you know wasn't the truth?"

She shifted her weight from one leg to another and averted her eyes heavenward, as if Christ himself was going to descend from heaven with an acceptable response.

"I didn't write any lies in my journal Robert."

"Don't insult me," I threatened, shaking my head in disapproval.

A lonely tear that she refused to wipe trekked down her face. Her pleading eyes met mine. She swallowed an invisible lump in her throat and released a loud sigh,

"I . . . don't mean to in . . . sult, you . . ."

"Then don't lie to me . . . don't ever lie to me. You insult me when you lie to me . . . and you know good and well, we've never . . ."

"Don't you think I know that?" her voice snapped, revealing her disappointment in the veracity of her words. "Out of all things that I've ever wanted and dreamed for . . . don't you think I know that it will never come true?"

Under ordinary circumstances I would have been flattered, ordinary, being a highly relative term. The fact that she was bound to a loser, was expecting her fourth child, coupled with the realities that I was not only her minister, but her psychologist as well and was about to marry the woman of my dreams, dampened any remote possibility of egocentric pride within me.

"Well then, what did you write?"

She placed her left hand up against the corresponding eyebrow, as if providing a shield to protect her conspicuous embarrassment.

She shook her head vigorously before quickly saying that she didn't believe what she was about to confess to me.

"What is it?" I asked, half-not wanting her to pour out her heart about anything involving me.

"You know I . . . I . . . love you, right?" she smiled nervously, wringing her hands together. Her soft emerald eyes widened as they rested on my intense gaze.

I swallowed the lump in my throat and inwardly demanded my heart rate to slow down.

"I've been in-love with you from the moment I sat and listened to you preach for the first time, when I came carting into your church with one of my infamous black eyes, carrying Jessica in one arm and holding DJ's hand with the other. That Sunday you spoke of God's grace and mercy and how he'd delivered you from your wild days as a college ball-player, frat brother, drinkin' womanizer. I listened to that sermon, Robert. And, I watched you . . . from that day onward. I watched you, to see if you were sincere. I was there when your father ordained you as minister of that church and I cried tears of joy when you humbly accepted your new position," she paused, more so for dramatic effect, than to take a breath.

"At home, I had this horrible . . . nightmare of a person to deal with . . . and two demanding children . . . I've always enjoyed writing . . . as you know, all while I was growing up with various sets of foster parents who abused me in one way or the other until I reached eighteen and ran off with Derrick. . . . and later found out he was selling drugs . . . I wrote . . . I wrote in journals . . . all of my life..to get away from my problems . . . in those journals, on many pages . . . are fantasies of you. . . . I'm sorry for springing this on you all at once, Robert. I really am."

I didn't blame her for seeking refuge via journal writing.

———

285

In fact, I'd suggested to many clients over the years, herself notwithstanding, to keep an ongoing written dialogue with their own conscience in order to relieve inner tension and turmoil. But how could she be so implicitly naive and downright stupid enough to record these very private thoughts and leave them in the same house with her brutal tormentor?

"Derrick says he knows with assurance that he isn't Parnell's father."

She dropped her eyes from mine and hung her head in shame.

"Tell me how he could say that so confidently."

Silence.

"He said you got pregnant during a time when he didn't have anything sexually to do with you."

She hid her face in her small in need of a manicure, hands.

"My head is throbbing. . . . I can't talk about this now. It's almost four o'clock. . . . I need to go upstairs to pick the kids up from latchkey . . . and I'm beginning to worry about Par . . ."

"Who is Parnell's father, Angel? Sweetheart, you've got to tell me . . . and what did you write on those pages that points the finger back at me?"

"Robert . . . I can't tell you that. I swore to *him* . . . that I would never tell anyone about what *we* did . . . especially you."

"I can't help you if you're not one hundred percent up front. We need to work together to straighten this mess out. As your therapist, I have taken an oath of confidentially to never reveal anything you've shared in secret with me to anyone else."

The suspense was killing me. I felt like shoving the fragile damsel against the drab gray tinted wall and socking her myself for involving me in the first place. When she'd noticed the throbbing veins in my neck and my mad pace up and down the corner of the hall where we'd been speaking in hushed tones up until that point, she reached inside her purse again to retrieve a mangled, crumpled up, torn apart, but taped back together piece of yellow notebook paper and handed it to me.

"Tell me yourself," I grunted, chewing on my bottom lip, not wanting to invade the sanctity of her written words. "It's okay . . . read it . . . please. . . . this is what led to the explosion Tuesday night."

When I failed to reach for the evidence of her infidelity, she grabbed my wrist, unfolded my fingers, which had been curled tightly into a fist, and forced it into my hands.

She watched me intently, as I struggled to make out the words of the one paragraph entry dated approximately six months prior to Parnell's birth.

It read:

*I can't believe one night of sweltering, forbidden passion in the king-sized adjustable bed of the church's parsonage, led to the conception of the love growing inside of me. A McGallister, full and true. Although I feel ashamed for holding a secret that could rip his family apart and although he stands a lot to lose for that night of unbridled lust, if ever the truth stumbles upon any of my fellow brothers and sisters in Christ . . . they'd put me out the church and force him to step down from his position. I'm still very elated and satisfied that he wore **his** robe and his cologne, and I bathed in **his** tub, and he kissed me in places beyond my imagination. I ate from **his** silverware, and drank from **his** goblet, and used **his** soap, and the same bath towel **he'd** probably used the morning before . . . I will never forget one moment of it. Never."*

I balled the entry up and stuffed it into my pocket. I turned my back to her so I could privately collect my thoughts.

"You see why he thinks you're Parnell's father?" she reasoned weakly, from behind. She placed one hand on my shoulder and nudged it for me to turn around. "Please . . . say something, Robert. I've never seen you like this before."

I spun around, my piercing eyes darting accusatory bullets at her.

287

"Why would you make something like that up. . . . and how in the hell do you know I sleep in an adjustable bed?"

"Because it happened in your home . . . Robert. It was the only way *he* could get me to make love to *him* all those times, knowing that my heart was with you."

Dizzy and overheated, I practically ripped my coat from yanking it off . . . and exhaustedly, pressed my back up against one of the munchkin-sized lockers to keep my knees from buckling under. I closed my eyes and massaged my aching temples before managing to blurt out the words to an inquiry to which I did not want the answer.

"Who is *he*?" still with my eyes closed, in silent prayer that she wouldn't accuse my father, the retired minister and elder of our congregation as fathering her youngest offspring.

"He can't know that you know . . . I promised him . . . I don't want to mess things up for Sheila and the boys . . ."

"Eddie!" I opened my eyes to look into hers. "Eddie has never cheated on Sheila. He's very proud of the fact that he's been faithful to her for twenty years."

"Eddie is Parnell's father, Robert. I've slept with two men, in all of my twenty nine years, and your brother is one of them," she cried, rubbing her blossoming stomach. " This baby in me right now is his too. Remember when I thought I was rid of Derrick for good a few months ago, when he went off with some scraggly white chick from Grosse Pointe, who was slummin' with him at one of the crack houses on our street. . . ."

I nodded my recollection and signaled for her to go on.

"Well, Eddie kept sweatin' me, asking me if I wanted to do it again, like how we'd done it a few times before at your house while you were away. He told me that he knew I was still hung up on you . . . but if I did it this last time with him . . . he'd convince you to be with me. I was desperate . . . and very devastated to have my husband of ten years leave me for some slut. I wanted to pay him back. . . . I wanted to be with Eddie too, though . . . be . . . because, he, he was the next best thing to having you."

"No!" I yelled, ramming my balled up fist into the locker, causing a dent in the cheap metal substance.

Angel cowered away from me, her eyes filled with fear, unsure of what to do or say next.

How dare that two-bit gambling bastard risk his happy home to take advantage of an abused woman's twisted affection for me? From that moment on, I vowed to distance myself from my only sibling. I had to cut him off, even though it would cause me much pain, and many sleepless nights, Eddie's presence in my life had to be reduced to a bare minimum.

"I'm sorry I scared you," I replied quietly, extending my opened arms to her. She looked at me pensively. "Come here." She fell into my arms and kept whispering the words, "I'm sorry," over and over again.

"I hate that this is hurting you so much . . . I'll do whatever it takes, Robert . . . to get out of this situation. I'm very, very sorry, for even insinuating in those journal entries that I'd been with you. I know a God-fearing, decent, man of your caliber, wouldn't be caught dead loving someone like me back."

"I do love you," I corrected her, rubbing her back, "just not the way you want me to love you. You are my sister in Christ. I'm here for you . . . you have to do the right thing. . . . you have to report Derrick . . . today, before someone else, myself included, gets hurt."

Damn that Eddie, I cursed under my breath.

"I don't want Jessica and D.J. in any police station, Robert," she replied softly, casting her eyes downward. " I don't want them to see their father being carted off to jail either . . . and besides . . . he has Parnell with him. He . . . may get it in his head . . . to . . . to hold him hostage or something when they come to make the arrest."

Not willing to be talked out of my resolve, I placed her

fragile hand inside of mine and held it against my chest. This gesture caused her unrecognizable cheeks to turn a crimson red underneath all the batter smeared on them. Remembering that she was an attractive woman didn't take any time. She batted her eyelashes at me and inched in even closer, so I could get a whiff of her expensive perfume, probably a consolation prize from allowing hubby to pounce on her the other night.

"Look at you, sweetheart," I replied, in earnest placing my other hand on top of hers. " You're a good-looking, vibrant, Christian woman, with three beautiful children and one on the way. DJ is ten years old now and Jessica is seven. You've been at the mercy of Derrick's brutal attacks and verbal insults for eleven years . . . isn't enough, enough? Don't you want to be free of him? Don't you want your kids to be healthy . . . and unafraid? I mean, Brother Khalid told me how he almost broke every bone in DJ's body for defending you. This has to happen today."

"But I'm scared, Robert."

"A man isn't dangerous if he's behind bars."

She nodded and reached up to stroke the stubs on my face with the back of her hand. "You don't understand, Robert. I'm not afraid of him being behind bars . . . I'm afraid that he'll beg and plead with me like he did three years ago, when I first fell for Eddie's lies. You remember . . . he kept calling me collect two or three times a day for almost a month, telling me how sorry he was and how much he missed and loved me and the children, until I went down, paid his bail and dropped the charges."

"That was before he broke your arm, busted your nose twice. . . . and pistol whipped you in front of the neighbors. Angel..sweetheart . . . you need to do this . . . you need to do this, if not for yourself then for those kids."

She wrapped her arms around me again and wept over the important, life-altering, decision she was about to make.

"You think I'm a stupid tramp don't you?"

"Not at all," I replied quietly. " I'm not here to judge you. I'm here to help."

"I'll do it," managing a feeble smile, she looked up at me. "The kids and I will be just fine . . . without him. . . . I guess I've depended on him for so long because I have no family to speak of . . . a few cousins here and there . . . who are all on welfare and can't take care of themselves . . . maybe, that's why I've stayed with him . . . he's the only family I've got."

"Family doesn't do this to you," I snapped, placing my index finger on the bluish ring underneath her bottom eyelash. " I'll follow you to the station, to file the report. The kids can sit out in the truck with me. Then I'm going to my folks house for dinner . . . call me there . . . after you've gotten home and after they've come by to arrest him."

"Can I really do this again?" she asked, still holding on to me for dear life, relishing our physical closeness.

"Absolutely. This time for good. Go get your coat and the kids from latchkey. I'll, on second thought, in case we're being watched, will just meet you at the station."

Slap On The Face

Ma was asking me to remove my shoes before I went dirtying up the new plush ivory carpet she had recently laid on the first floor of the newly modernized four bedroom, two bathroom ranch home in which I had grown up.

Though sometimes over cluttered with all the brick-a-brack she collected from one particular craft hobby to the next and with sections of the *Detroit News/Free Press* Pops read daily, and was afraid to discard, as a professional homemaker for, almost forty years, Ma kept a pretty clean house.

A pot of homemade something or the other was always simmering on top of the stove along with a pan of Pops favorite banana bread or triple layered German Chocolate cake baking in the oven. She made regular use of all the cooking gadgets they'd acquired over the years, such as several Crock Pots, indoor barbecue and fish grills, vegetable steamers, waffle irons, juicers and blenders. You name the culinary device and Ma had it. Many of her cronies from the sisters' group at our congregation and from the United Sisters Bible Class, would suggest for Ma to host any number of their luncheons, candle and Mary Kay parties and teas.

She took great pride in her antique china collection she'd inherited partly from my paternal grandmother and had on display in a huge lighted curio in the dining room.

Even though they always expressed great interest in one

another's past times, Eddie and I had as of late, been teasing Pops about him being "whipped" by sometimes driving Ma as far north on I-75 as Frankenmuth and as far south as Monroe to some of the antique china shows.

Family portraits taken of the four of us for the church directory every other year until Eddie went off to college sat on the mantle above the fireplace in the living room. Other photos mounted on the walls and the built in bookshelves featured Eddie, Sheila and the boys, along with individual portraits of me in my All-American letterman's jacket from high-school, Michigan State basketball jersey and shorts, sporting my fraternity jacket and paddle, from when I'd first crossed the line.

Mounted on the wall, just above the ivory sectional, an 18x30" picture framed in gold, of my first official photograph as minister of the Rosedale Park congregation was undoubtedly the most embarrassing manifestation of Ma's sense of maternal pride.

I complained when I first perused the negatives of the extensive photo shoot because my eyes seemed too intense and serious. Also, I disliked the cloudy ethereal sky-blue background and the fact that my right hand was placed on the Bible, as if I had just taken an oath as an elected official.

"What in the devil took you so long to get here, Bobby?" she scowled at me, as she opened the door to their bedroom, where an unfazed, fully recuperated-looking Pops was propped up, with six or seven fluffy pillows against the head-board of their king-sized bed, channel-surfing with the remote control. Wearing a new pair of khaki colored pajamas with blue trimming around the collar and his stylish wire-rimmed eyeglasses, Pops barely acknowledged me once he looked up from catching the latest news developments on CNN.

I sat on the foot of the bed and waited for him to finish chewing and swallow a mouthful of Ma's tender roast beef with gravy and made from scratch, buttery whipped mashed potatoes. My stomach churned as I realized that I hadn't eaten anything since Ms. Maggie's homemade buttermilk pancake and egg breakfast at least thirteen hours ago. Pops, always proud that he still had at least twenty-six of his original teeth left, didn't make those annoying sucking and slurping sounds folks his age and older usually made with their denture clad mouths as he cleared his plate.

My parents still made a handsome pair after all those years. Often told he resembled basketball legend Julius Irving, for his distinguished salt and pepper hair, alluring smile, and even brown skin tone and playfully referred to as Dr. J by family members, Pops, at 6'3", in his mid sixties, was only an inch shorter than me. Ma, beautiful in her own right, often boasted of his good looks by telling anyone who would listen that he could charm the socks off a snake-oil's salesman.

Eddie inherited his yellowish complexion, pretty hazy eyes and easy to manage, naturally curly hair from Ma. Although Ma was a fierce cook, she'd maintained her weight of about one-hundred and twenty five pounds since they'd tied the knot back in the early sixties. In recent years, Ma had grown tired of trying to maintain her dyed, dark brown shoulder-length locks and had been sporting a chic close crop fro, in which she allowed just a few gray highlights to show. Their almost identical eyeglasses made them look a lot alike.

"Pops," I smiled, placing my right hand on his slender leg and shaking it. "Man, how ya doin'? Don't ever scare us like that again."

"Sorry I scared you, son. Ethel, could you get me a refill on this delicious ice-tea, sweetheart?" he held his empty glass up to Ma.

Usually pretty submissive to Pops' every beck and call, Ma folded her arms and tapped her foot, angry about God knew what.

"Not until this boy, tell us where he's been. We were

trying to wait for you to eat, son. You know your father is a diabetic. He has to eat on schedule."

"My apologies, Ma," I facetiously bowed and waved my arms up and down as I was worshipping an idol. "I had some very important, confidential business to take care of."

Ma and Pops exchanged knowing looks. She, a minister's wife by profession, had grown accustomed to hearing this excuse and even accepted it without so much as a second thought.

"Well, you could have called. At least if you would have called, we could have relayed several messages to you from. . . ."

"Not yet, Ethel. Don't start in on the boy. Are you going to get me that tea or what?" he flirtatiously winked at Ma. Ma took the hint and ordered me not to let Pops go anywhere near the little bell, on the nightstand her only sister Aunt Bev, had given him as a prank gift.

"I'll fix your plate, Bobby. I know you must be starving," I could still detect hostility in Ma's voice, whenever she spoke to me. She refused to allow me to gaze into the hurt expression of her eyes.

"What's up with Ma, Pops?" I asked him, taking the remote control out of his hands to switch to ESPN. He didn't object.

"We'll get into that in a minute. So I take it that things went well for you on Sunday morning and evening. Cecil told me you tore the roof off the place."

I smiled almost embarrassed to receive the closest semblance of a compliment my father had given me since my ball playing days at State.

"Said over twenty souls were saved," Pops added, stroking his neatly trimmed goatee. "I still can't figure out what kind of spell you cast on these folk, boy. I wish I would have had some of your magic, back when I was your age and Rosedale Park, only had about a hundred, really active members. Remember that, boy?" I nodded my recollection, barely comfortable that Pops was pouring it on so thick.

"Ed and the kids been by to see you since you've been home?" I asked shifting the subject away from me.

"Sheila and the grandkids. Your mama and I haven't talked to Junior since he got back from St. Louis. It's almost like he's hiding something."

Try being caught on tape, embezzling thousands of dollars and fathering two offspring, behind his devoted wife's back, I thought.

We sat in silence, watching football highlights for a few minutes until Ma re-entered the room carrying a tray of food with two tall glasses of ice-tea with lemon slices. I stood up to help her. She didn't thank me.

I watched her nudge Pops to scoot over. He conceded only a little so that he could still be close to her. He wrapped his long arm around her waist and squeezed it, as if to tell her to calm down. A tear trickled down her face; she reached for the tissue.

"Ma, Pops, are you guys going to tell me what's wrong? Ma, what's with the tears?" Men never like to see their mother's cry.

She looked at Pops to get his approval before completely going postal on me.

"You're wrong, Bobby! It's you . . . you're what's wrong!" she yelled.

"But Ma . . ."

"Let her finish, boy . . . and eat your food your mama slaved over to make just for you."

That was low Pops, even for you, I thought, knowing good and well Pops had three hots waiting for him every day of their married life, come rain, or shine.

I got up and sat the tray on a doily on top of her chest of drawers and walked over to her. Taking one of her hands, I inhaled deeply and prepared to face yet another drama of the day.

"Aw, boy . . . look at him Ethel . . . thinkin' he can charm, skin and grin his own mama . . ."

"Pops, please," I stated firmly.

"Aw . . . right. Aw..right, I'm just sayin'," he laughed.

I wondered what in the world could have Ma's breeches tied in a knot to the point she couldn't stop crying. Pops, however, couldn't be tickled enough. He reached to hand Ma a box of tissue as he looked at me, wearing a you-sly-dog grimace.

"Ma, please . . . stop crying . . . tell me what I did wrong. I'll fix it."

She blew her nose into a tissue and laid her tiny head on Pops broad chest. This was too much for me. Too much. I jumped off the bed and started pacing the floor like a rabid dog.

"Boy still has that temper on 'im, huh?" Pops chuckled. "He got that from your folks, Ethel." He squeezed her shoulders.

"You went off and got engaged while your Pops was in the hospital! I talked to you every night Bobby . . . every night while you were away . . . and you never once mentioned you'd met someone! Never once!" her embittered words, were like fiery darts thrown at my soul. I plopped back down on the bed, ignored the smirk on Pops' face that indicated he was impressed with my actions, and reached for Ma's hand again. She looked at it as if it were poison, before picking up another tissue.

"How'd you guys find out?" I asked sharply before making a mental note to kill Brother Khalid, "Brother Khalid tell you?"

"You mean to tell me Yusef knew before we did?" she shrieked, wearing an expression that looked as if she wanted to jerk me up by the arm, much as she did when she'd caught me stealing a couple of times from Farmer Jack's supermarket when I was six or seven.

297

"Yes, he did," I admitted quietly. " But . . . I'm just curious, how . . . did you guys find out? That's all I wanna know."

"Your future mother-in-law called three times looking for you on behalf of her distraught daughter, Elisabeth. Said you were supposed to call her as soon as you stepped foot off the plane. The first time she called she'd just identified herself as Sister Powell, the elder's wife . . . I told her that I had heard from you . . . and was expecting you over for dinner in another hour. She didn't seem satisfied. . . ."

"So she called back a couple hours later, asking if you'd made it in," Pops continued the story, as we watched Ma blow her nose again. "Your mama told her you hadn't, and you know how feisty your mama is, son."

"What did you say to her? Ma . . . were you mean to Emily?"

"Of course not," Ma snapped. " I asked her very civilized like, what her business was with you . . ."

"Then your mama started screaming like a banshee because that white woman told her that her daughter was upstairs, locked in her room, balling her eyes out, because you hadn't called her . . ."

"You forgot to tell him that part, that she called her daughter, his fiancee'," Ma added, disapprovingly. "I'm soooo . . . very . . . disappointed in you, Bobby . . . I don't know what to do!"

"But, Ma . . . you know that I've been looking to settle down for the past four years."

"That's right, Ethel . . . you know how hard the boy's been lookin' . . . he's turned down all those fine young sisters at the church and all the ones who visit from other churches too . . ."

"Pops, please . . ."

"Yeah, I wonder why," Ma replied suspiciously.

"Ma, you know why . . . I just wasn't feelin' it . . ."

"Hmmph . . . said he wasn't feelin' it," Ma reported to

Pops, as if I wasn't in the room. I forced her hand into mine and kissed it.

Pops could have died laughing. "Easy, Casanova . . . easy . . . that's my woman, you know."

"Ma, tell me what your problem is . . . is it that I'm getting married?" I paused, waiting for her to reveal her true apprehension.

"No, of course not. Tell him Ed . . . I've been looking for a wife for him, all these years . . ."

"Your mama says . . ."

"Pops!" I yelled. " Ma, look at me. . . . is it because I did it so suddenly? You know I don't believe in long courtships. You know the scriptures . . . it's better to marry than to burn with passion. . . ."

"You talkin' the talk now boy," Pops instigated.

"Or is it because you think Elisabeth is white?"

"**BINGO! BINGO!** You've gone and hit the jack pot!"

"Ed, this is serious!" Ma vented her fury in his direction for the first time in the conversation.

"Because if that's what it is, I can clear that up for you right now. . . ."

"You're trying to tell us the voice on the other end of the receiver, did not belong to a white woman? Be for real," Ma shook her head incredulously.

"No, Ma. I'm trying to tell you that Emily is white. Her husband, James Powell, Dr. Powell, is African-American."

"She must be very pretty son," Pops smiled his approval.

"Oh please, Ed, now how are you just gon' up and assume she looks good just because she's mixed," Ma raged.

"Aw . . . she is definitely the best looking woman I've ever seen, Pops. Gorgeous. Here . . ." I paused to reach for the leather wallet in my pocket. Elisabeth had given me all eight of the poses she'd taken, the previous year, when she'd graduated from high school.

Pops whistled his consent and handed the pictures to Ma. Ma barely looked at them, before tossing them back at me. "Bobby, those are yearbook pictures.. just how old is this girl, anyway?"

"She'll be twenty on Valentine's Day. A couple of days after we plan to get married."

"Congratul . . ."

Ma smacked Pops on the chest to stop him from shaking my hand. We watched her get up to start pacing the floor, making dramatic motions with her hands, as if she was trying to sort through the mess she'd figured my life had become.

"Bobby, it is almost December . . . you couldn't possibly be serious enough about this girl. She is so white looking. . . . I bet she is on cloud nine right now . . . ," she ranted, spitting out the pronouns in reference to Elisabeth as if they were poisonous venom. "I know I would be . . . if I was going to marry someone as handsome, and God-fearing as you . . . with a successful career to boot. I bet this girl just wants you for what you represent, your status, you know and.. . . . and what you can give her . . ."

"But Ethel, Emily told us that she and her husband are both doctors," Pops interceded on my behalf, before winking his eye at me and saying. " I think she purposely told us that so we wouldn't think her daughter was a gold digger."

Nothing in me would allow me to retaliate against my mother's wrath. She had every right to be concerned, and I should have told them everything, right after we'd announced our decision to her parents. But knowing my mother wouldn't take things lightly, I thought twice about dropping something so heavy on her over the phone while she was trying to bring Pops home from his ordeal at the hospital.

As Ma was still venting her frustrations, the telephone rang again. We all froze like mummies, anticipating the caller to be Emily Powell again.

"Well, don't just sit there staring at the thing, son . . . pick it up," Pops ordered. Ma, pouting, picked up my tray and took it back to the kitchen without me ever having touched it.

"McGallister residence," I answered, calmly.

"Bobby," Elisabeth's high-pitched, child-like voice called. "Is that you . . . Bobby?" I chewed on my bottom lip and stood up, because she was crying. I could detect her sniffing through the phone.

"Yeah baby, it's me," Pops shook his head and grinned at my efforts of playing mac-daddy.

"Good. . . . I'm glad we finally got hold of you . . ."

"So am I . . . I was just about to call . . ."

"Save it, Robert McGallister. Save it. I'll be mailing your ring back to you overnight express, the first thing in the morning."

This can't be happening, I thought. I turned my back toward Pops, so he couldn't pick up my facial expression. I didn't have enough energy left within my tired body for any more drama today.

"Pops, do you need anything? I'm going to take this call into the other room," I offered, trying to cover the receiver with one hand.

"She's mad at you already, boy . . . way to go."

"You don't have to take the phone to the other room," she shrieked, loud enough for Pops to detect the outrage in her voice. "This is going to be, like, really short."

"Elisabeth, baby . . . listen. Some very important church business came up. I had to handle it . . ."

"I don't care!" she yelled. "You promised me you would call. Here I've been waiting by the phone all afternoon and evening waiting and waiting . . . praying nothing had happened to you . . . I can't deal with faulty promises. . . . and your notion of out of sight, out of mind . . ."

"Elisabeth, calm down . . . don't say anything else, you're going to regret. I have no reason to lie to you. I just made it

301

to my folks' less than a half hour ago. They bombarded me with questions about us . . . before I could even explain to them." Pops was all ears by the time Ma got back to the room. I heard him filling her in on my attempts at begging and making a complete idiot of myself.

I walked out into the hallway and turned the knob on the door of my former bedroom, turned guest quarters. As I entered, a wave of lemon-fresh furniture polish and apple-cinnamon potpourri engulfed me. I plopped down on the new queen-sized mattress my own body never got the satisfaction of knowing. I listened to Elisabeth's dainty sniffs that were growing further and further apart.

"I love you, Elisabeth. I want to marry you . . . make you my wife. I will never do anything to intentionally hurt you."

"So, you didn't forget about me?" she asked sweetly.

"How could I forget your lovely face?"

She giggled.

"Just a minute ago, I was showing Ma and Pops your pictures. Pops thinks you're fine too."

"Well, I've heard your father speak on several occasions down here for gospel meetings. You look just like him," she replied. "I bet your mother had to fight the women off of him with a baseball bat."

"Ma's been pretty cool about all of that," I replied without hesitation. A click on the other line interrupted our conversation. I asked Elisabeth to hold on.

It was Angel.

"Robert?" she asked without waiting for an answer. "The police just left five minutes ago . . ."

"They took him?"

"Yes . . . he's gone. Found some weed on him too. Stupid fool. The only way he can get out now is if he makes bail, before his trial. "

"Thank God," I sighed a loud relief.

"And thank you, Robert. Now the children and I can go

on about our lives . . . that is, if you don't blow it for Eddie. I don't want anything from him. I'm even disgusted that I had anything to do with him."

"My word is bond sister. Good night."

"Good night."

Elisabeth didn't like to be kept waiting, but I buttered her up again once I told her I couldn't wait to see her pretty face in another two weeks.

"Who says you have to wait two weeks?" she flirted, fully knowing the physical effect that voice had on me. "My parents are announcing our nuptials at church this Sunday. They're hosting some type of engagement dinner for us next Saturday at the Hyatt. They, like, rented the entire banquet hall for us."

Suddenly, the pages of my mental Rolodex flipped through my mind. I knew I had a wedding to perform on the same Saturday, in question.

Also, Saturdays are the only days the Christian Men's Leadership Academy is open at Rosedale Park, and I definitely didn't want to be absent from all three Sunday worship services two consecutive Sundays in a row. There was something else I had planned, but I just couldn't put my finger on it.

"Bobby. . . . I know you probably have other obligations on those dates, but, I'm moving up there the same weekend of the banquet . . . so you won't have to keep flying down here. I couldn't get a moving company on a Sunday and I don't want to wait any longer than I have to for us to be together, so if it's okay, maybe like a couple of your friends could fly down with you, to help. By the way, do your parents know that I'll be staying with them?"

"Not exactly. They were just informed of the engagement, remember?"

"Well, when do you plan to tell them?" she asked, letting a slight tone of panic resonate through her tiny voice.

———

"As soon as we're off the phone. Can I call you back in the morning once I speak with Ma, Kelly, Sister Calloway and Brother Khalid? They know more about what I have going on then I do. We may have to rearrange some dates."

"Oh no," she whined. " I just hope we don't have to change the banquet date because that's the only opening the Hyatt has until March."

"Do we have to have an engagement banquet at all, baby?"

"What?" she asked sharply, "I am *sooo*, like, going to pretend you never said that."

"Well, do we have to have it at the Hyatt? Why not have it at Kingshighway a couple weeks after we're back from our honeymoon. You guys have a pretty decent sized fellowship hall."

She laughed at the apparent absurdity of my statement.

"Number one, you don't give an engagement party after the wedding ceremony. Number two, according to like, proper pre-nuptial protocol you have the engagement party six to eight weeks prior to the ceremony. And, number three, having a basement bash at the church, eeew?"

"Okay . . . okay," I conceded, relishing the fact that she had put forth so much time and effort into the planning of our celebration.

" I'll check back with you first thing in the a.m. Love you, Princess."

"Me too," she replied surreptitiously. " Oh . . . and Bobby . . . don't forget to clear off some-time to help move my things up Sunday. Daddy says you're going to have to rent a full U-Haul. I'm only bringing my clothes and personal items, no furniture . . . and I called The St. Louis American and the Michigan Chronicle today. They are on standby waiting for me to set a date for our engagement photo to be printed with the announcement. Mother suggested *Jet* magazine, since you are, like, a celebrity and all. A photographer and journalist from Johnson's Publishing Company is willing to fly down here to do a story and spread on us taken here at our home. Mother has a beautiful winter garden and gazebo, to provide scenery."

"Whoa . . . you're going all out for this aren't you?" I replied, sitting straight up on the bed, a bit overwhelmed at the lengths even she would go through to seek attention. Though I didn't consider myself a celebrity by any stretch of the imagination, I envisioned myself sporting a three-quarter length, black tux, gray vest, and matching bow-tie, with shined to perfection knobs, standing on the platform of the gazebo, my arms wrapped tightly around Elisabeth's diminutive waist, who was dressed stunningly in a sleek-fitting wedding gown Elizabeth Taylor, the queen of wedding gowns, would envy.

"I only want the best for us, Bobby. We're only getting married once. Might as well go all the way. Don't forget to call me first thing in the morning to confirm these dates and get some rest. You're going to need it."

Cronies

Since I would be away so much over the next two weeks, I deemed it necessary to call a meeting Saturday morning with the church leadership and my own personal staff. While my small 8:00 class of second-year psychology students sat in with Brother Forbes, a fellow laborer and psychologist, who'd substituted for me from time to time, Ma and Sheila were the first to arrive to the conference room located on the balcony deck of our three level building.

Ma, who had pretty much accepted the fact that I was going through with the marriage, assisted Sheila and Aunt Bev, who was there just to be nosy, in setting up coffee, donuts, bagels and cream cheese.

As was the Rosedale Park tradition, the elders occupied the five chairs to the right of the foot of the table where Pops usually sat. While the deacons occupied the five chairs to the right of my seat at the head of the table, Sister Calloway, Brother Khalid, Kelly, Sheila, Aunt Bev and Ma sat together at an additional table connected to the outskirts of ours.

Immediately, upon walking in fifteen minutes late, I offered my apologies for calling a meeting with only a one-day notice and for being tardy to our roundtable due to the fact I wanted to greet each of the fifty male students of the Christian Men's Leadership Academy personally.

Several of the deacons who had been appointed since my

ordination, nodded their acceptance. My father and his cronies, on the other hand, all wore similar scowls of disapproval
as they allowed my mother to refill their coffee mugs. I noticed the seat to my immediate right was empty. Eddie, mortified for having been caught on tape by Brother Khalid and
Mark Riley the deacon, usually sat in between him and Doug,
was probably at home, still licking his wounds that he would
have to resign most of his responsibilities toward the church.

"Brothers and sisters," I beamed in a clear and boisterous voice, almost loud enough to be heard in the basement
where classes were being conducted simultaneously. "I've
gathered you all here, bright and early this morning . . ."

"He's got the early part, right," Aunt Bev nudged a curious Sheila and rolled her eyes heavenward. Three years, my
mother's junior, my recently widowed Aunt, who had relocated from Atlanta to the Detroit area to be closer to Ma,
could always be counted on for delivering an uncanny punch-
line.

"Not to discuss official church business, per se, but to
make a grand, yet somewhat anticipated upon announcement." My eyes quickly surveyed my captive audience.

Pops, wearing the same silly congratulatory grin he wore
the night I, a Spartan, scored eighteen points against the in-
domitable Wolverines back in my sophomore year, leaned
back comfortably in his seat opposite me.

Our newest installed dedicated deacon, and one of my
hanging buddies, Mark Riley, wore a grim expression of be-
wilderment as he braced himself for either the most earth-
shattering, heartbreaking or the most exciting, captivating
news of his life. Riley, a lifetime friend who had grown up at
Rosedale Park, close to a generation before me, had at that
time been retired from a twenty-five year career in the United
States Marines. At forty-three, Riley and his wife Nicole, the
proud parents of two teen-aged daughters, owned and oper-

ated their own catering business. Next to Brother Khalid, and my potna from childhood, Attorney Paul Wilson, Riley and I could have not been tighter, had we been born biological brothers.

Doug's cheeks emanated a flush crimson glow, as he remembered the past weekend, and was fortunate enough to witness Elisabeth's stealing my heart.

Kelly held her mahogany hand complete with gaudy, costume rings, bracelets and fake three-inch fingernails, up to her mouth and twisted uncomfortably in her chair, ready to bolt towards the door as soon as I'd confirmed the fruition of her worst nightmare.

"This past week, I proposed marriage to a young Christian woman from St. Louis. I'm getting married on February, twelfth, right here at the church."

Kelly let out a loud gasp, stood up, used the same overly decorated hand to cover her mouth and bolted frantically for the door, holding her stomach with the other hand as if she were trying to contain herself from puking all over the office table.

Riley and Doug nudged each other and snickered like two school boys while Ma and Sister Calloway ran after little Ms. Drama Queen. Pops' cronies sucked their teeth and shook their heads in shock as Aunt Bev mumbled that I'd always found the most creative ways to gain everyone's attention.

"My goodness, nephew," she laughed, wiggling her hippopotamus hips out of the seat. "You've gone and broken that girl's heart. You know she's been hung up on you her whole lil' life. Couldn't you have found a more discreet way to announce this news?" Her next action contradicted her words. She walked over to where I was sitting and pressed my head into her cushiony bosom, before planting her soft lips to my forehead. "Congratulations, Bobby. Ed tells me this girl looks like she's straight off the pages of *Vogue* magazine."

"That she does. I just wanted to inform everyone here today that I will be announcing the engagement during our worship services on Christmas Day. I've asked Brother Forbes from the Oak Park congregation to take on our pre-marital counseling. I didn't want the leadership to be caught off guard by this."

"Well, it's about time you've found yourself a wife young man," Brother Scott, the oldest elder of the bunch beamed from his chair right next to Pops'. A still vibrant, physically fit octogenarian, Brother Scott had been a deacon at the time Pops had been hired as the full-time minister, five years before I'd been born.

"That's for sure," echoed Brother Worthy, the youngest elder, who'd had since his youth, done all he could to impress Pops and the other elders, including casting his vote with them each and every time an important leadership decision had to be made.

"I'm happy for you, son, " Brother Hudson, Sister Calloway's twin brother smiled, through stained yellow dentures. "But couldn't you have taken my niece for a bride instead? You know how she feels about you."

Brother Worthy nodded his agreement.

I looked at Pops to bail me out from the sticky situation, but per usual, he didn't. Instead he glared back at me, as if I had all of a sudden stabbed him in the back.

" I mean, weren't you two pretty serious..back here, a few years ago?" Brother Hudson challenged.

"Almost got married," Brother Worthy threw in his no count two cents.

"Worthy, man stay out of it." That was Riley, who always had my back when the heat was on. "I think we should all be mighty proud of this brother here. Our preacher is finally getting married. That's reason enough to celebrate."

"Well, who is this woman, Robert? What does she do and

is her family in the church?" Brother Scott, the drill sergeant fired away at me.

"Does she know anything about being a preacher's wife, son?" Brother McNichols, the one who usually spoke last but had the most self-serving ulterior motives, shot at me.

He and Pops had come up as boys together, serving the Lord in a little storefront church in Mississippi before they'd both as newly-wed impoverished black men, relocated themselves and their brides, to Michigan in the late fifties to work for Great Lakes Steel.

Brother McNichols often credited himself to landing Pops his pastoral role at Rosedale Park, seeing that his uncle Lester had been the first minister and he had put in a good word for him. "Like how much you do for the congregation and all of your er, rrr, extra—uh-curricular activities with your patients . . . and those other folk over at the rehab center."

I looked first at Pops who was by then, nodding his head to affirm his consent to his cohort's line of questioning. Then my eyes fell upon Worthy, who had gotten up to pour Brother Scott and himself another cup of coffee. Damn flunkie.

"Yes sir, Brother McNichols. Elisabeth is quite aware of my responsibilities. I can guarantee that our marriage will not interfere with them."

"That's not our concern, Robert," Brother McNichols replied firmly. "Our concern is that all your extra responsibilities will interfere with the quality of your marriage. You know I've told this story many, many times. My aunt Buela, God rest her soul, almost divorced my uncle Lester after they'd been married a good fifteen years because for every one of those years, he'd spend more time being the preacher, than he did being a father and a husband. He'd put everyone ahead of them . . . and he lived to regret it. One Sunday she went up front and told the whole church about how trifling a daddy he was. Remember that as good as yesterday even though I was only knee high to a duck. Yessirree."

"Yes son, you are a little over extended. We've been concerned about that for quite some time," Pops pointed out. "And as elders of the flock, we anticipate problems before they even occur," Brother Scott piped in.

"Yes, Doc," the flunkie added. "You've been lookin' quite exhausted these days. You're on cable every time I flip my TV on. You've always had too much on your plate...."

" So, maybe it would be in your best interest to drop some of your other ... err ... rrr..pro..jects, if you will ... before taking the plunge into matrimony. We don't want the scandal of a divorced minister before you're even married off good. No woman, no matter how beautiful she is on the outside, would ever be able to err..rr, understand the self-imposed complex nature of your schedule," Brother McNichols placed the closing exclamation point at the end of their own conspicuous, classic choral rendition of "Let's-gang-up-on-Robert-to-see-when-his-fuse-is-going-to-blow."

Much to my delight, I didn't feel the least bit discouraged or frustrated at any of their remarks because I'm the type of man who does not intimidate easily, nor give in to popular opinion when it doesn't sit well within my own spirit.

I leaned back in the comfort of the cushioned swivel chair, my arms folded across my chest, wearing a smug grin, waiting for my attack dogs to bite the bullet. It didn't take long for them to stir up the pot.

"With all due respect, gentlemen," Riley, my pseudo defense attorney grunted angrily. "To me, what it seems like you all are doing, is trying to push your own agenda."

"What are you talking about now, Brother Riley?" Brother Scott sighed grievously, his tone insinuating that he felt Riley was a trouble-maker.

"You know good and well what he's talking about," Brother Khalid's monotone voice emanated from somewhere behind me. I'd almost forgotten he was there.

———

"No, we don't, Yusef," Brother Worthy snapped. "But, I'm sure you're going to enlighten us."

"You brothers have been trying to get Little Brother here to sell the people down at the rehab center out because they are Baptist, Methodist and Muslim. You've also wanted him not to run his private therapy practice in the church building, nor use his radio and cable programs to promote his books. You've tried to run every aspect of his life, since he took his father's job four years ago . . ."

"Yusef, that's enough," Pops ordered across the table to Brother Khalid, as if he were a mere child. "We've heard your unfortunate opinions of this leadership once too many times . . . and we've warned you once too many times, that you would not be invited back to our meetings if you can't adjust your negative attitude."

"Amen to that, Brother McGallister," Worthy huffed ignoring the fiery, visual darts the deacons threw in his direction.

"Brother Khalid is my chief staff person, Pops. He works for me. I invite him to all the meetings concerning me. No one can uninvite him. Not even the elders."

Our eyes locked into one another's, each pair daring the other to speak disrespectfully, each pair beseeching the other to be the bigger man and back down for what could have been an explosive confrontation.

For a few seconds, no one bothered to so much as sneeze as we all sat sulking over the fact that what should have been a joyous celebration, was turning into another battle of wills between Pops contemporaries and mine. I thank God that Ma re-entered the room when she did, to lighten the mood.

"My goodness, what's everyone so quiet about? This isn't a funeral. Bobby just announced his wedding plans and you gentlemen, look as if someone died," she laughed.

"You're absolutely right about that, Ma," Sheila smiled standing up, and rushing over to be the first in the recessional. "Bobby, congratulations. I love you, kiddo. I know you're going to make a wonderful husband, just like Pops, and even Eddie. I love you."

Even though Sheila, my brother's wife, was the object of one of my first adolescent crushes and was still by far, my best female confidante, I found it difficult to accept her embrace, not because she compared me to my unfaithful brother, but because she appeared to be still so in love with him and so utterly clueless about his dealings with Angel Williams.

"Yeah, Bob. Congratulations, dude. It's wonderful news," Doug smiled. "I think we all should get together, to throw the minister here a good, clean bachelor's celebration. . . . the weekend before, guys. Whaddayathink?"

"Sounds cool to me," Paul Wilson, my best sidekick from childhood and deacon agreed, as he approached me and gave me some dap, a familial greeting, exchanged by two black men, formed, by taking the bottom of one's upright fist and gently pounding it on top of the other man's fist, before he reciprocates the gesture. "Man, what's this Doug tells me about this girl being of the Caucasian persuasion?"

"Man, don't worry about it brotha, she's only half white."

Within minutes, every brother, even the reluctant Brothers McNichols and Scott had greeted me warmly and bade me Godspeed for our upcoming nuptials.

"Brother Caleb"

The next two weeks flew by without me being consciously aware of the implications taking a wife would have on all of my ministries. Between flying back and forth to St. Louis for two separate photo shoots for *Jet* magazine and the St. Louis American, the elite Missouri African American newspaper, performing a marriage ceremony at Rosedale Park for Darius Smith, the only formal fraternity brother of mine, with whom I'd remained close, conducting two funerals, one of which for a non-member who lived directly across the street from the church, counseling sessions around the clock, taping two cable shows and a radio broadcast—any ordinary person would have been fit to be tied.

I, on the other hand, could not have been happier. My super workhorse ethic kicked itself into purely adrenaline inspired overdrive. The elders, like my parents, had reluctantly thrown in their half-hearted support. Pops, much to Ma's foreboding of a subsequent relapse in health, even agreed to cover all three worship services for me the Sunday following the Saturday pre-engagement bash held for us at the Hyatt in Missouri.

Using my frequent flier discounts and some of the profits from *Saving It*, which had in its second printing, miraculously returned in hard-back for the holiday season to the best-seller's list of both national Christian and Afrocentric bookstores, I purchased plane tickets for Ma, Aunt Bev, Sheila, my nephews, Sister Calloway, a reluctant Kelly, Brother Khalid, Doug, his wife Donna and their two youngest boys, Mark and Nikki Riley, Paul and Jasmine Wilson and newlyweds Darius and Corrine Smith.

Within a meager seventeen-day period, I had seen enough of Lambert Airport to purchase stock in American Airlines.

Cecil Donaldson offered his services to pick us up from the airport and to drop us off at the Hyatt, via one of the Kingshighway church vans. All of the women, my own mother included, lamented over having to doll themselves up for the black tie affair in the impersonal women's restroom facilities, for which they headed as soon as the men escorted them off the van with their garment bags in tow.

Aunt Bev swore litigious threats at one of the bellhops after Brother Khalid, Riley and I all had to help lift her two hundred and fifty pound buxom frame off a pool of December black ice that greeted her as soon as one her raggedy tennis shoe clad feet danced a jig for us inches away from the entrance of the revolving doors.

My nephews, eleven year-old Edward III, better known as Tre' and eight year old Eric followed Riley and the other brothers into the men's room to change into their rented tuxes.

Brother Khalid hovered over me as I explained to the other men that I was going to check out the ballroom and to see if Elisabeth and her mother had made it there although the party wasn't due to start for another hour or so.

He was right on my heels, shaking his head and clucking his tongue, like an old mother hen, as I marched with determined speed to find my fiancée.

"Brother Khalid, waz up . . . have somethin' to say to me, G?"

"Nope."

"Ah . . . ight, then, bet," I replied shrugging my shoulders nonchalantly as I pushed the number three on the floor selection panel next to the elevators.

He waited until we squeezed into the miniscule almost filled to capacity cabinet, before he started pontificating from the lofty position he had created in the Vatican of his own imagination.

"Man, I think you shouldn't have brought Kelly along. She's been moping for a couple weeks now, ever since you put a monkey wrench in her program. I just know that she and Little Ms. Princess won't get along. . . . , not to mention the antics Aunt Bev is sure to pull," he murmured.

I waited for four of the five passengers to spill out onto the second floor before responding.

"Man, I'm not going to concern myself with K nor Aunt Bev. Not tonight. Once they see Elisabeth and the two of us together, they will know that we were meant to be. So, stop sweatin' me man, all right?" I chided lightheartedly.

He released a loud sigh before storming off ahead of me a few yards or so, once the elevator reached our destination.

As we entered the exquisitely decorated ballroom, the two-dozen or more glittering chandeliers that dangled from the high ceiling immediately directed our attention upward. At least twenty tables complete with eight formal dining ware place settings each, along with three specially marked reserved tables and a head table occupied about three quarters of the floor space, while a sixteen piece predominantly Caucasian ensemble, occupied the other fourth. We watched the frantic musicians scatter to and fro to arrange their instruments and sheet music to provide for our big band and classical, jazz and easy listening pleasure.

A handful of servants, also dressed in black and white, stopped hustling and bustling long enough to notice my almost six and a half foot, casually dressed in trendy FUBU denim slacks, jacket and sweater along with the latest to date Jordan's. Having sized me up from my neatly trimmed facial hair to my size thirteens, one of the female attendants abruptly stopped working and rushed up to me as if to ask me for an autograph.

She looked through the tiny squared-shaped yellow tinted frames of my spectacles to lock her green-colored contacts into my dark brown eyes.

"Excuse me . . . sir. . . . but, are you anyone famous? Like a basketball player or somethin'? You look kinda familiar," her coquettish voice drawled in the same gateway to the Midwest accent with which my intended spoke.

Brother Khalid and I exchanged knowing looks, but before I could respond to the young lady's inquiry, in sauntered my future mother-in-law, dressed in a smart two-piece, light grayish suit with silver sequins surrounding the hem of her lapels and matching shoes. Brother Khalid's usual watchful, stoic stance was broken once he had to crack a smile to witness her practically leaping into my arms and planting her thin lips onto mine to greet me.

He shot me one of his infamous, "I-don't-understand-your-mouth-salivating-momentary-insanity-effect-on-women" looks.

"Bobby, darling, you're here," Emily sang in that throaty, raspy voice, "and don't you look more handsome every time I see you?"

"Yes, he does, Mother. Even sporting that awful baggy urban-wear, he is still a sight for sore eyes," a familiar voice resounded from behind us.

All eyes were on the resplendent Elisabeth as she sashayed her way over to the enclosed circle we'd formed. Wearing a full-length sable mink coat with her usual straight brown but curled at the ends locks, that were fanned out past her shoulders reaching extreme lengths down her back, the Princess carried in a box of party favors, along with the cold air that brightened her cheeks to a sexy pinkish glow. Brother Khalid reached down to lighten her load as the eavesdrop-

317

ping waitress enviously rolled her eyes at Elisabeth and disappeared into oblivion.

"Thanks, Brother Caleb," Elisabeth smiled. Her soft pink lips curled into its familiar tight smile.

"That's Khalid, sister," he corrected, letting the slightest hint of annoyance slip through his voice.

"Oh, so sorry," she giggled, wrapping her hands around my neck and pressing her layers of fur into my chest and pelvic area. Right from the beginning, she knew how to make my temperature rise.

Disgusted at the toothpick dangling from the corner of my lips, she signaled for me to remove it. We kissed fully in the mouth, for what seemed like longer than I would have been able to tolerate without experiencing any type of masculine physical repercussions during my heyday of tawdry, pornographic film watching.

"Hmmm, mmmm," Emily cleared her throat conspicuously. "Sorry to interrupt this little love-fest . . ."

"Please do," Brother Khalid said dryly. " This is a tad bit much for me to handle."

"Libby, honey, you promised Daddy that you would go back to the car to help he and Ms. Maggie unload the rest of the trunk."

"Mother, you ruin our fun," Elisabeth cried as she gently pulled herself away from the tight grip I had around her waist. "I'll be back shortly, Bobby. Oh yes, you better get changed. . . . you don't want to like, look thuggish at your own engagement celebration, do you?"

"No ma'am," Brother Khalid chided in a pseudo-pretentious voice, ignoring my evil eye. " Far be it from this distinguished clergyman, esteemed psychologist and published author to even remotely resemble Joe Schmoe, your average brotha from the D."

I could tell by the grim expression and the raised eyebrows on my mother-in-law's pale face, that Brother Khalid's sarcasm had not fallen on deaf ears. Elisabeth, on the other hand, elected not to respond angrily to the remark or allowed it to fly over her pretty little head altogether, because she just flitted her long mascara-laden eyelashes daintily and shrugged her shoulders.

" Oh, Brother Kareem, you're such a funny man," she laughed. "I can see why Bobby always wants you around."

Brother Khalid mumbled under his breath that he'd see me shortly after I announced that I had intentions on helping the others unload the car.

A Mother's Pride

All of the men, including myself had shaved, dressed and made it up to the ballroom before any of the women emerged.

"Bobby, the guests are filing in," Elisabeth whispered nervously from the seat to my right at the head table. " You think I'll get the chance to meet your mother before everyone else does?"

"Don't worry, Princess," I winked at her, and squeezed her hand. " You'll know Ma the moment you see her."

"Brother Donaldson tells me she is quite the looker."

I smiled and held up my hand, so that Ma, Aunt Bev and all the other women I held dear to my heart appeared at the entrance all sporting equally awestruck expressions. When I'd noticed Aunt Bev pointing to the chandeliers, and everyone shifting their head in the same upward direction, I stood up so they could see me. Aunt Bev nodded, grinned and hurried the others along to be introduced to the Princess.

"Well, that you can determine for yourself," I replied proudly. Earlier that day, after my barber Sam had robbed me blind for a fade I could have done myself, I stopped by the house to pick up Ma, Aunt Bev, Sheila and the boys. I'd run my clippers, over Ma's close crop and trimmed the remaining loose hairs, with a pair of trimmers.

A few speckles of gray gave her short curly hair a refined salt and pepper look. With a slightly made-up face and not a

facial wrinkle in sight, Ma opted to sport a pair of disposable
contact lenses instead of her usual stylish wired rimmed
glasses. Based upon her petite, girlish figure to accompany
her brilliant youthful smile, anyone guessing her age would
have assumed she was at least fifteen years her junior, which
is why my poor wife-to-be did not make a good first impression.

A look of sheer amusement sprinted across Elisabeth's
eyes as she hastily stood up to walk around to the other side
of the table without me. Sister Calloway, my boy's wives,
Sheila and Aunt Bev gawked at the Princess, who was wearing a simple, yet elegant, formal, straight, soft pink gown
with a chiffon shawl draped around her shoulders.

I noticed Kelly glaring lasciviously at the sparkling diamond necklace and earrings I'd purchased for her on my last
visit to accessorize her ensemble, not to mention the mon-
ster rock that weighed her skinny ring finger down. Elisabeth
giggled softly as she outstretched her arms to Aunt Bev. Aunt
Bev, all smiles and eager to fall into the Princess' loveliness,
reciprocated the gesture and reached to embrace her.

Instead of hugging her, Elisabeth decided to gather two
scoops of Aunt Bev's fleshly cheeks into the tiny grips of her
perfectly manicured hands and squeezed, as if Aunt Bev was
some chubby little baby.

"Mother McGallister," Elisabeth squealed, sounding
more white by the syllable. "Oh, how good it is to meet you.
You are soooo . . . cute and cuddly. I'm Elisabeth, your future daughter-in-law and I look forward to getting to know
you better next week when I move in with you and the minister."

Kelly, Jasmine, Corrine, Donna, Sheila and Nikki all covered their mouths with one of their hands to refrain from
laughing at Elisabeth's gesture of friendliness.

Aunt Bev swatted the Princess' hand away as if it were an
annoying mosquito.

"Chile, get your cold, little boney fingers off my cheeks. Can't you see how much foundation and rouge I'm wearing?" Aunt Bev replied coarsely as she yanked on Ma's arm to come forward.

Elisabeth looked up at me worriedly and took hold of the cradle of my arm as if she would never see me again. Emily and James Powell, along with Ms. Maggie strolled over to make their introductions, but no one paid them any attention, because they were all glaring at Elisabeth.

"I don't get it, Bobby," she whispered. "What did I do wrong?"

"Is there a problem over here?" Powell's voice boomed as he released his wife's fragile hand.

"No, sir. There isn't. I would like you to meet my family, at least most of it anyway. Everyone this is Dr. James Powell and his wife Dr. Emily Powell, Elisabeth's parents. You've already met my nephews over there. My brother, unfortunately couldn't be with us at this time . . . but this is his lovely wife and my close friend, Sheila McGallister. She runs the school at the church and these are my buddies wives, Nicole Riley, Jasmine Wilson, Donna Harrison and Corrine Smith. This is Sister Calloway, the church secretary, and this is Kelly, her daughter, my personal secretary." Kelly's body stiffened as I placed my hand on the small of her back, a gesture that I had not realized Elisabeth noticing until later on in the evening.

Everyone nodded their respective how-do-you-do's.

I shook my head and chuckled before I reached for Aunt Bev's hand and nudged her closer to Elisabeth and me.

"This, Princess," I smiled, "is not my mother. This is my Aunt Beverly. As you get to know her she will put you in the mind of Ms. Maggie."

"Well, your auntie looks like a fine woman, Bobby," Ms. Maggie replied enthusiastically. " So I will take that as a compliment."

"Well, I thank you, Ms. Maggie. You look like a fine woman too," Aunt Bev grinned.

"And last, but surely not least is my mother, Ethel McGallister."

Emily and Ms. Maggie inhaled deeply as they took a second look at the impeccable middle-aged woman before them. Ma smiled brightly as James Powell reached for her hand and kissed it. Emily stepped forward to embrace Ma first. Ma hugged and kissed her and welcomed her into our family. Speechless, a mortified pinkish flush rushed over the Princess' naturally pale countenance.

"Well, Elisabeth, aren't you going to greet your new mother?" Ma smiled sweetly. I uttered a quick prayer of relief as I watched my mother hug and kiss Elisabeth.

"Mother McGallister, I would . . . have . . . never . . . thought . . . you would be so . . . so . . ."

"Hot," Sheila laughed, reaching to hug her. "I'm the only big sister Bobby's ever known so I want you to take good care of him, hear, or I'm gonna come after you with a pair of scissors to chop off all that long pretty hair. Isn't it gorgeous?" Sheila asked the other ladies. They all nodded their affirmation.

"Yeah, she's a regular Rapunzel," Kelly mumbled from beside me in a voice loud enough for all of us to detect.

Clearly uncomfortable with Kelly's jesting, Elisabeth stared into her face blankly not knowing how to respond until Ma saved her.

"Baby, I'm simply Ma or Mama Ethel to all these young ladies here, including my first daughter-in-law here, so just feel free to call me either one of those."

Elisabeth maintained her blank stance as the others responded by staring at her, like she was some mannequin on display.

"When you feel comfortable enough to do so of course."

323

She looked up at me for a quick save. I placed my arm around her waist and nudged her closer to me.

"It's okay, girl, Mama Ethel don't bite," Kelly snapped.

"It's just . . . just . . . that I can't see your name being Ethel. . . . you seem much too young for such an . . . an . . . archaic name. I'm just going to have to get used to it that's all."

It was Ma, this time who froze. Mortified, she cleared her throat and batted her eyes as if to say, "Excuse me?"

"No, she didn't," I heard either an incredulous Jasmine or Nikki say to the other.

"Well, baby," Ma replied in an extra-syrupy voice. "I guess everything takes a little gettin' used to. Like this whole marriage thing in the first place."

"I'll say, amen to that," James Powell winked conspiratorially at Ma. " We've seen more of this young man in the last three weeks or so than we care to admit."

Polite laughter from all around.

"Yes, but not for long, sir. I'll be out your hair for a little while after tomorrow, once we get Elisabeth all moved up to Detroit."

"I must admit," Ms. Maggie added in her usual jovial manner, "we gon' miss this lil' ole' gal, Ms. Libby."

Elisabeth blushed, " Everyone, this is Ms. Maggie, our housekeeper."

"Housekeeper, dig that," Aunt Bev thought aloud. Everyone except Ma and Kelly looked impressed.

"Princess, dear," Powell reprimanded softly as if speaking to a toddler. "Ms. Maggie is more to us than a housekeeper. She practically raised you and Lor.. . . . well, while your mother and I were off being doctors."

"Yes, Ms. Maggie raised me as well," Emily boasted. "I guess she's trying to say she's going to miss sparring with the Princess here and I'm sure you'll miss your dear Ms. Maggie too Elisabeth, huh?"

Elisabeth sighed softly before conceding, " I suppose."
Ms, Maggie rushed over to take her into a bear hug. She
kissed her several times on the cheek, leaving several stains
of brownish-red lip coloring of which I knew Elisabeth would
not approve.

"Oh, Ms. Maggie, please now, geesh, you're wrinkling
my gown," she complained.

As if on cue, Aunt Bev and all her cohorts rolled their
eyes heavenward and shook their heads.

"Stop your bellyaching,' gal," Ms. Maggie laughed,
smacking her heartily on the back leaving a red handprint on
her spine. I tried unsuccessfully, to not notice the protrusion
of her pointy-shoulder blades. "Come on ladies, let me take
you over here to your tables, where your husbands and the
kids are waiting. Sister McGallister, since you are the mother
of the groom, we have a special seat for you up there at the
head table with Libby, Bobby and with Dr. James and Ms.
Emily," Ms. Maggie announced as she walked away.

"I apologize for my husband's absence," I heard Ma explain to the Powell's as Old Man Powell pulled out the seat
on my left for her. " Whereas he should be at home still recu-
perating from his minor scare, he's probably at the computer,
writing out the sermons he's going to preach on our son's
behalf tomorrow."

Emily smiling knowingly, picked up her glass of white
wine and tasted it, "We do understand, don't we James?"

"But of course," her husband conceded. Not one to miss
taking a shot at me, he added, " at least my contemporaries
still have the skill and love of the Lord's word to preach it,
the good old fashion way, hard-hitting, yet, plain and simple,
without personal theatrics. You know, I remember hearing
your husband preach about six or seven years ago. His delivery and ability to preach the one true church was straight-
forward, short and to the point, yet so very compelling. Some

325

of our younger upstarts could learn a thing or two from men like Ed McGallister Sr., including his own son."

I cringed, as I reached for my glass of wine. Before I could wrap my fingers around the stem, Elisabeth quickly removed it from my hand, and replaced it with a glass of water.

"That's wine, Bobby," she explained in a low whisper. " I have this water here for us. Can you imagine Mother, the nerve of her, ordering wine for the minister? Some people have no sense of what's right or wrong so long as their insatiable palette is appeased."

As much as I could have used a few sips of the spirits to mellow me out from having to sit with Mr. Pompus Self-Righteous Jackass, I didn't protest my lady's grandiose gesture of concern. Instead, I placed my left arm around Ma's chair as I listened to her let him have it ever so graciously.

"My son," Ma replied in her haughty Diahann Caroll voice, " is the most nationally renowned preacher in the Church of Christ right now. He has increased the membership of five hundred, we had just four years ago, to almost five thousand plus. We are in the process of broadening our facility a second time within a two year period, or maybe even beginning a sister congregation with similar goals because people from all walks of life of other religious beliefs, notwithstanding, have come to sit at his feet."

"But, Sister McGallister . . . those are fine attributes for a person who wants to show himself off as opposed to Christ. . . ."

"Daddy, please don't. Not tonight. I'm not up for this. This is our night, right Bobby?"

My eyes quickly scanned the banquet table for an object sharp enough with which to stab through the layer of fat surrounding Powell's seemingly embittered, cold heart.

Ma ignored him and continued her tribute to a person, I barely recognized as myself. " He's a learned biblical scholar as well, Dr. Powell. He studies his Bible four hours daily, which is more than I've ever seen anyone study . . . including Ed Sr., but most of all, he helps people. He helps make them well . . . and he leads them to Christ, which after all, is the whole point . . . isn't it, I mean, wouldn't you be able to say from an elder's standpoint, as overseer of the flock?"

"I'm going to need more wine," Emily squirmed a bit flustered and restless from her husband's standoff with my mother. " Bobby, dear, would you mind passing yours down to me, seeing that you haven't touched it . . . and Princess, sweetie, why don't you follow suit?"

"Oh, Mother. You're such a lush. Must you embarrass me everywhere we go?"

The gleam of respect in James Powell's eyes for my mother brightened when Ma went in for the kill.

"Of course, your Princess here will make a lovely life partner and suitable helpmeet for my son. Robert tells me she was baptized at age nine."

"Yes, ma'am," Powell boasted. "She's my baby; the apple of my eye. You see that ring she moved to her index finger after your son, placed that boulder on her ring finger? Well, wanna know what that is?"

"Oh, Daddy . . . do we have to get into this now, right here at the dinner table?" Elisabeth chided as she twirled the salad fork I'd yet seen her bring to her lips around in a bed of crisp romaine lettuce. *Baby, please eat, baby, please eat,* I prayed to myself.

Ma and I braced ourselves for the answer to the riddle that had invoked my curiosity since the day we'd first met.

"Well, I'm just so proud of you, Princess," he explained looking past the two of us to his favorite offspring. " I just want this man to know that he's getting a chaste woman. Someone who promised her parents back when she was twelve years old that she wouldn't remove the symbol that represents her virginity until her wedding night. My Elisabeth is a precious, precious jewel."

A tear glimmered in the corner of Ma's eye as she watched me take Elisabeth into my arms. For the first time that evening, I noticed the soft jazz music in the backdrop provided by the ensemble on the bandstand. I wondered how much of my money this whole ordeal cost, seeing that as Ma reminded me, the groom's family is traditionally responsible for the engagement party and the honeymoon. It seemed ridiculous to me at twenty-nine years old, after not ever having taken a thin dime of my folks' money, since I'd left undergraduate school, to ask them to spend such an exorbitant amount of Pops' retirement fund to spring for two costly ventures.

Thus, I'd, upon the visit to St. Louis, prior to the bash, left Elisabeth with a brand new credit card attached with a warning for her not to exceed five thousand dollars.

"You have every reason to be proud," Ma smiled at the Powell's, concentrating her gaze on Emily, who was finishing up her third glass of wine.

Powell stuck out his chest a little further and winked at Elisabeth, who in turn, blew him a kiss. Ma had done well to assuage the potentially disastrous turn of events at the dinner table, until she innocently asked the question that almost ruined the rest of the night for us.

"Is Elisabeth an only child?"

"No, she isn't," Emily replied all too happy to expound upon her favorite topic of conversation, reaching under the table into a Famous Barr shopping bag, for some undisclosed object." Our older daughter Lorraine, Lori, who's twenty-two lives in Lansing. She graduated from Michigan State at the age of twenty, because she'd been double promoted back here at the academy for the gifted and the performance arts."

The next thing I knew, Ma had scooted her chair closer to the enthusiastic mother's to be taken on a pictorial tour of

Lorraine's latest astounding feats, which she housed in a scrapbook that appeared to have taken hours to design.

"After she graduated from Michigan State, she served in the Peace Corps over in Rwanda for two years. Those were the hardest two years of my life. . . . only having her back in the states for Christmas."

"I understand. Every mother hates to be separated from her children for long periods of time. No matter how old they get," Ma empathized, as she flipped the page to notice the shapely Lorraine, in several stage shots wearing an ivory colored tutu, spinning around and leaping on her tipped toes.

Elisabeth huffed impatiently as, both out of courtesy and curiosity, I stretched my neck over to the left, after Emily had shoved the album right in front of Ma so it could be in the middle. In most of the shots, the honey-brown complexioned Lorraine was smiling angelically as she floated around, in between and in front of the men dressed as toy soldiers on stage. Her naturally wavy locks were subdued and had been brushed into a neat, dancer's bun, which forced the common observer to pay more attention to the artistic structure of her high cheek bones, and crystal-clear, large illuminating eyes.

Ma commented on Lorraine's apparent limberness and beauty as she remained focused on a traditional warm-up pose of Lorraine stretching her finely sculpted body along a bar using both hands to wrap the long slipper straps around her shapely leg.

The V-neck line of her leotard led my eyes to wander lustfully over the rest of her body. They involuntarily fixated themselves upon the hardened rounded nipples pressed against spandex material. To cool off, I turned my head away from the album and poured myself another glass of ice water.

As I was pouring a second glass for a pouting Elisabeth who had covered her partially eaten entree of specially ordered grilled salmon and steamed vegetables, Ma uttered the conspicuous.

329

"What an incredible young woman Emily and James. Just beautiful." James Powell pretended not to hear my mother's laudatory remarks. He, unlike Elisabeth seemed to be enjoying his meal, chewing on the bland prime rib as if he'd never devoured a hunk of meat in his life.

"Yes, yes. . . . maybe I'm a bit biased, but she gets more utterly breathtaking every time I see her. She's a ballerina you know, and a gifted vocalist. . . ."

"Come on, Mother. Give me a break! One leading role in an off-broadway African American production of *The Nutcracker* does not a ballerina make!" Elisabeth finally snapped, the hand on her glass shaking nervously as she brought it to her lips. I placed a supporting hand on her knee underneath the table.

"Oh, I beg the differ Libby," Emily retorted mildly, without giving Elisabeth eye contact as she continued to flip through the scrapbrook. "Lori has been classically trained in pointe and ballet, as well as tap . . ."

"Yes, yes, yes!" Elisabeth exploded. A few of the brothers and sisters from the Kingshighway congregation looked up at her from their table right below us to determine who was making an outburst.

Once they saw it was the Princess behaving in typical fashion all red-faced, arms flailing about, standing up and throwing her napkin on the table, they exchanged looks of knowing before resuming their meal and quite possibly making her antics the center of discussion. "We all know the whole spiel, don't we, Daddy? Mother McGallister, let me also inform you that Lori feeds the homeless and even sold the brand new Jacquar Mother bought for her graduation to donate to the shelter for battered women she volunteers at regularly. She also sings like a bird, raises the dead, and walks on water too! Did you know that? I mean, isn't that right on target, Mother? I mean, since we have to bring the subject of Her Royal Highness up on the most wonderful night of my life, up until now, then we might as well shout it out and get it over with! I really hate you, Mother for doing this to me, once again!"

Now, the table of my own invited guests was gaping up at us. Brother Khalid looked embarrassed for me, whereas Kelly looked quite smug, shaking her head in tsk, tsk, tsk fashion. Then suddenly, Elisabeth stood stock still at the realization that everyone within an eight table radius had overheard every truthful, unabashed word she yelled at her mother, who aggravatingly enough wore a look of stunned innocence on her face. Elisabeth glanced down at me apologetically before making a dramatic beeline towards the door.

Someone motioned for the band to stop playing. The conductor looked a bit ticked off that a crescendo of a familiar Harry Connick Jr. tune had been interrupted by something as trivial as the bride to be having an emotional meltdown.

Ma nudged my elbow and whispered the words, "Do something, quick." But I sat dumbfounded, without a clue. The impulsive action to stand up and run after her would have only brought more attention to the scene, yet if I remained seated, doing nothing Elisabeth would feel dejected that I didn't come to her rescue immediately.

The old man grimaced at his wife and by the stoic expression of his face, I could tell he was sticking it to her pretty harshly. She deserved it. Even if this Lorraine person was everything her mother made her out to be, it still gave her no right to dangle her in front of Elisabeth's every effort and accomplishment.

The prominent physician arose from his chair and standing regally, held up his wine glass. All eyes were upon him as he cleared his throat. A tight grin spread across his lips.

"Ladies and gentlemen, what you have just witnessed is our dinner theater performance of the anxious bride-to-be, overreacting to a few unintentional discriminatory remarks made by her Academy Award nominated mother, Emily. Emily, dear, stand up and take a bow!" He smiled jovially and put his thick hands together to lead the round of applause by the confused audience.

Emily obeyed her husband, stood up, waved as if she were Ms. America, taking her famous walk and curtseyed to both the right and the left of her. "Now, band, what are you waiting for? Play something I want to hear, do you know any Nat King Cole?"

A group of stuffy doctors sitting at another table within earshot all cheered and nodded their affirmation of one of their supervisor's favorite requests at formal functions.

A middle-aged white couple seated at the table registered a non-verbal cue to begin the dancing. They graciously sauntered over to the floor and began to slow dance as far apart as physically possible to an instrumental rendition of *Unforgettable*.

Powell snubbed his wife and decided to further take advantage of his jones for Ma. He extended his arm to her.

"May I have this dance, radiant mother-of-the-groom?" he smiled, at her, the perfect gentlemen.

Ma looked to me for my permission. I shrugged. "Suit yourself, Ma."

She hopped up instantaneously and didn't even look back to see if Emily minded. She didn't. She slid over to Ma's vacant seat next to me and motioned for me to hand her Elisabeth's wine glass. I obliged. We sat there quietly, listening to the music and admiring Ma's light-footed glides across the floor. Brother and Sister Donaldson joined the other dozen or so couples, including the Riley's and the Smith's on the dance floor.

Thankfully, everyone had seemed to have forgotten all about Elisabeth's tantrum, except for the two of us left at the table.

"Thank God for James, huh?" she sighed with her eyes

closed. They did a lot of that; Elisabeth and her mother, speaking, dreamingly through shut lids. I wondered if Lorraine's thoughts resided in the clouds as well. " I don't know why Libby hates me so much."

"Your daughter doesn't hate you, Emily," I replied, loosening the bowtie's tight grip from around my neck. "She feels invisible to you. She wants you to see her."

"I do see her, Bobby," Emily replied quietly, as if doubting her own statement. Her pupils darted nervously back and forth under her lids.

"How can you see her when you have resigned her to a life of being in Lorraine's shadow?" I stared at her directly, and waited for her to open her eyes. She opened them, took the first sips of Elisabeth's wine and massaged her temples as if her head was hurting. "Somehow, since I've known you over the past few weeks, you've seen to work Lorraine's name into every conversation you've had with me or around me. I would take issue with that if I were Elisabeth too."

"I just miss her . . . miss her so much until it hurts," a few tears trickled down Emily's face. I reached for an extra dinner napkin, held her tiny chin in the palm of my hand and wiped them away without staining her makeup.

"How often do you see her?"

"Every chance I get, even though she's not the type who wants to be smothered. Never was. Always so independent and carefree. I've visited her only three times this past year since she's been back from Rwanda. James doesn't approve of course. She'll be performing on Christmas Eve in *The Nutcracker* at the Music Hall in Detroit. I was planning to ask your mom if we could stay with them. That way we can spend Christmas as a family." She tilted the glass and gulped down the beverage. " Libby got very depressed too when Lori left. She acts like she has it in for her, but she loves her to death. Lori was always so good to her."

"She hates when you call her Libby."

———

Emily looking up at me and as if the thought had never crossed her mind, appeared to be making a mental note of my pronouncement. "You're so good for her, Robert."

"Did Elisabeth stop eating when Lorraine left?"

Emily reached for her throat as if gasping for breath and closed her eyes again, allowing a tiny moan of displeasure to escape from her lips.

"I have to know. She's going to be my wife," I stated firmly. I needed to know how I could try to fill the void in Elisabeth's life, since from the age of twelve or thirteen, she'd lost the only true friend she'd ever had, while simultaneously growing up without the unconditional love of a grieving mother who had rated her second best.

"She was hospitalized shortly after. Missed most of her tenth grade year. She made it up in summer school though. Now that she has you, I think she'll be fine."

"Emily, I need her to be fine with or without me. I'll be back shortly."

Ma was still hamming it up with James Powell. A concerned Brother Khalid stood under the threshold of the entrance, anticipating that I would soon begin the search for Elisabeth.

"She's in the bathroom, Little Brother. I saw Sheila follow her out."

I nodded my thanks and patted his shoulder before walking around the corner to the ladies facilities. Two of the servers who had been attending to the head table, were now on their abbreviated breaks, smoking cigarettes on the benches across from the bathroom. I asked one of them if they didn't mind peeking inside to see if my fiancée was in there. One quickly obliged. The other, through squinted watery eyes and a cloud of smoke, appraised me in my monkey suit, from head to toe.

"You make a mighty handsome groom, sir," she smiled.

"Thank you very much," I replied not really in the mood for polite conversation.

A few seconds later, the first server reappeared. "She's not in the big bathroom, but there is a private family restroom at the far end of the hall, on the right."

"Thanks," I strolled quickly down the hall, in a panic stricken state, not looking back when I overheard the second one say to the first that if I couldn't find my fiancée she'd sure be glad to take her place.

"Elisabeth," I pounded on the door of the closed restroom. I heard the toilet flush followed by running water, and a familiar voice, speaking soothing words to someone inside with her. "Sheila . . . it's me. Open the door."

"No . . . Bobby . . . I'm fine. I'll be out in a minute," Elisabeth sniffed faintly, sounding a bit hoarse. Then, I heard several gut wrenching coughs.

"Princess, open the door. Is Sheila in there with you?"

"Bobby, we'll be out in a minute, now, everything's fine," Sheila added. More piercing coughs from the other side of the door.

"Sheila, open the door!" I ordered impatiently.

"No . . . Bo . . . bby," Elisabeth barely managed to say, before she began choking and gasping for breath again. Then, one of them turned the water off and flushed the toilet again.

"Damn it, Sheila!" I pounded on the door several more times. "I'm not goin' away. Now stop playin' with me and open the door!"

Elisabeth's cries became hysterical between all the wailing and the coughing, I couldn't make any sense of the muffled words emerging from the other side of the door.

Suddenly, the lock switch and the doorknob turned, Sheila grabbed my arm and pulled me into the private restroom complete with a vanity and powder table. She led me into the stall where a weeping Elisabeth was curled into a semi-fetal position next to the toilet. Various yellowish remnants of vomit formed streaks down the top portion of her dress. Thankfully, either she or Sheila had the sense enough to remove her shawl before the regurgitation started. Sheila stooped down and apparently resumed her stance of holding Elisabeth maternally in her arms and smoothing her hair back.

"Elisabeth," I said quietly, hovering over the two of them. She struggled to calm her own breathing pattern as she buried her head further into Sheila's plush bosom. Sheila, motioned for me to help Elisabeth up and over to the recliner next to the vanity in the powder room. From a couple of failed efforts, we could not get her to walk. I then stooped down and scooped her thin frame into my arms, and led her over to the settee, placing her on my lap and holding her in my arms, much as I had done over the last three weeks.

Sheila rushed over to the water basin and ran some lukewarm water over a towel she'd found in the linen cabinet underneath. She kneeled down beside us and placed the towel on Elisabeth's forehead before wiping the dried spittle away from the corners of her mouth.

Smoothing her hair back, Sheila spoke touching words of encouragement to Elisabeth and promised her it would be all right.

"Just take this burden to the Lord and leave it there, sweetie. It'll be all right. You can do all things through Christ who gives you strength."

Elisabeth trembled in my embrace. Assuming she was cold, I sat up and with my free hand finagled my way out of my tuxedo jacket, lifted her up and wrapped it around her shoulders, covering up her goose-bumped arms. My sister-in-law gazed up at me, through tear-filled, sympathetic eyes of concern. For a moment, I felt her pity. I refused to accept it and politely dismissed her after thanking her for staying with Elisabeth.

"You want me to leave, Elisabeth?" Sheila asked. Elisabeth shrugged. Then she leaned her head onto my shoulder, wrapped her arms around my waist and nuzzled her face into my neck.

"Just please, don't tell anyone about this, Sheila. Please, don't. Not anyone. Not Mother or Daddy, especially, not them . . ."

"Don't worry. I won't," Sheila guaranteed, her eyes locking into mine. Working in the same facility day after day, with a minister and psychologist, Sheila had been witness to myriad emotional meltdowns and had nonverbally vowed confidentiality to me from the first day of her employment.

Elisabeth stood up in her weakened condition to walk over to the door to lock it. Then she plopped down next to me, her hands covering her mortified face.

"I'm so so . . . rrry, Bobby . . ." she began crying all over again. " I hope this doesn't change anything between us. Please say it doesn't. I need you. I really need you."

I reached for her and drew her onto my lap again, kissing the crown of her head.

"Elisabeth."

Cover it Up

Fifteen minutes later we re-entered the ballroom, arm in arm, accepting the round of applause from the dancers and purse watchers alike. Elisabeth, obviously accustomed to putting up a good front, had reapplied her makeup immaculately and tied the shawl around her upper arms to shield our guests from possibly figuring out what she'd jetted out to accomplish.

"Here comes the future Dr. and Mrs. Robert McGallister," the band conductor announced, through his pinned on microphone. "Let's see if we could get them to grace us with a solo dance, just for the two of them."

Elisabeth held onto my arm firmly and through a stiff smile, mumbled that she did not want to dance in front of over three-hundred people.

"Dance, dance, dance!" most of them chanted loudly.

"Come on Princess, just follow my lead."

"You dance, Bobby?" she asked unexpectedly.

"Put it like this, I can keep the beat on slow grooves," I bragged. " And I've choreographed a mean step routine back in my frat days."

"Oh brother," she laughed nervously.

I ushered her out into the middle of the floor. Both strange and familiar bodies cleared the area, by backing away to gawk at us from the periphery of the dance floor. I wrapped my arms around Elisabeth's waist and slowly pulled her to me. The corny band broke into a melodic instrumental version of the classic, *"My Funny Valentine"*. To avoid looking at anyone directly, Elisabeth pressed her right cheek up against my chest. I could hear her heart beating twice as fast as normal.

"You okay?" I asked breaking the silence of a suspended eternity.

"I will be, as soon as we're done dancing."

"You're not so bad. You only stepped on a brotha's toes three or four times," I kidded.

"I've made a total fool of myself. I feel that everyone's watching me," she confessed, caressing the back of my neck with one hand as the other rested on my shoulder.

I felt a slight tap on my shoulder. When I looked over my shoulder, old man Powell was standing there with his massive hand outstretched to Elisabeth.

"Do you mind if I cut in to get my last dance with the Princess as a single woman?"

"I do mind," I smiled. "But, it's up to her."

"I think it's okay Bobby. Why don't you go ask that Kelly girl who's been staring me down, green with envy all night to dance with you, seeing this will be your last time dancing with anyone else besides me, in our lifetime."

Kelly Calloway was the last person I wanted to put my arms around, especially after the ill-mannered way she'd been treating me during the work week up at the church. Over the past two weeks, at the office, my usually efficient receptionist, had tried everything to get under my skin, from double-booking several counseling appointments to forgetting to relay phone messages from Elisabeth to me.

If it weren't for good ole' reliable Sister Calloway, I would have fired Kelly a few weeks into my vow of celibacy, right after I'd broken off our so-called "engagement" for which I had never even popped the question, announced to anyone, or purchased a ring. Her attitude shifted for the worse towards me once I broke the news that my conscience would not allow me to continue to use her to gratify my own carnal nature before my ordination ceremony.

Somehow, she couldn't manage to get it through her airhead skull that I could not very well get up teach, preach and write against fornication if I kept allowing her to make excuses to spend the night with me at my old apartment, when after treating her to dinner and a movie, she would treat me to her quick, mesmerizing, one-act –done-in-five-minute routine before she would "accidentally" let the time slip away from her and make up the excuse, at twenty-some odd years of age, of not wanting to disturb her parents by creeping into her bedroom window late.

On my way over to my friends and family table, several impeccably dressed strangers stopped me to congratulate me on our engagement. Most of the women stated that, after discovering the fact that little Elisabeth Powell was marrying "the Robert McGallister" they'd gone out to special order my book in droves, to ship it to all of their single girlfriends for the upcoming Christmas holiday season. Though the book had been on the shelves for almost a year prior to that date, it still humbled me that God had allowed it to reach the hands of so many men and women, both Christian and non-Christian alike.

Aunt Bev, Eric, Tre, Sister Calloway, Kelly and Sheila were finishing up their desserts of some chocolate mousse variety, when I walked over to tease the boys about not liking girls enough then, to actually ask them to dance. I playfully mussed Eric's curly-top fade, as Sheila arose and asked to speak with me for a minute, in private.

"Elisabeth is a very beautiful young woman, Bobby. I am so happy for you both," Sister Calloway smiled at me warmly.

I stooped down to thank her for coming, and to kiss her on her cheek.

"What's wrong, a sista' can't get no love from you no more, now that you have a little white Barbie doll to call your own?" Kelly butted in with much attitude.

"You know it ain't even like that, K," I replied. Trying to lighten her mood, I placed my right hand on her shoulder and squeezed it. Reaching down, with the intention of giving her a quick consolation peck, she suddenly, conveniently swished her head around, so that my lips would land on hers.

In response, I quickly stood up straight, looked over my shoulders to ascertain if Elisabeth had witnessed Kelly' latest stunt. As my luck would have it, she'd seen the whole thing, from glancing over her father's shoulder, who was holding her in his arms awkwardly, as if she were some porcelain doll about to break. The boys gave each other high fives, and made obnoxious kissy faces and noises as I used the back of my hand to inconspicuously remove the bright red lipstick from my own lips.

Moments later, Sheila and I stomped it up on the dance-floor. Claiming that she was the greatest ballroom dancer in the world, I followed her lead in dipping and spinning her around to the beat of the more modern, hipper music the band had begun playing as the night wore on.

"You jammin', baby brother," she laughed. "I didn't know you still had it in you . . . but then again, you had rhythm when you were my boys' age."

"Well, you know," I bragged. "What can I say?"

The drummers slowed their beat as the horn section, one saxophone player in particular, began to pay tribute to a Kenny G classic from the late eighties.

We slow grooved for a few minutes. Elisabeth watched us admiringly from her position in the vestibule as she stood between her parents to say goodnight to some of the early leavers.

341

"I'm glad you and Elisabeth bonded so fast. I thank God you found her . . . before anyone else did."

She looked into my eyes gravely as I placed my hands on her hips and led her slowly around to the melody of the music.

"She's bulimic, Bobby. In everything you've told me about her, you omitted that very important detail."

"She's not bulimic. . . . she was treated for anorexia a few years ago, once her sister booked up, never to return over religious disputes with the old man. It devastated her mother so bad, that she did a half-assed job raising Elisabeth."

As usual, Sheila listened carefully to every word I uttered without interrupting me. A deep pensive expression crossed her face as she stretched her neck to seek out Elisabeth's whereabouts to ensure she would not overhear our conversation.

"But, Bobby . . . how can you be sure her treatment was successful? I've read about eating disorders . . . aren't they classified as a disease? I mean, once sick, always sick."

" You dare speak that way to me, of all people? I treat sick people for a living. You know that. Don't you believe in God's saving power? Look what he's done for Brother Khalid, and, not only for him, but for Rhonda Hightower, Austin Jackson, Fred Moore, Charles Stevens, LaQuisha Abernathy and Grace Santiago," I pointed out enumerating at least a half – dozen or so former heroine and crack addicts/new converts who had faithfully graduated from our program at the Interfaith facility.

"I know you've helped clean those people's lives up, Bobby. But, you know they still struggle every single day of their lives. They are always paging you, and ringing your cell phone, it seems like every few minutes or so, which is another case and point. I'm not just looking out for your best interest here. I happen to like the girl. I just don't want to see her illness go further untreated, so many miles apart from her father who seems to dote on her. Let's face facts, Bobby, you are a busy, busy man."

I couldn't deny that. I chewed on my bottom lip, more out of habit then frustration. She pulled away from me slightly and squeezed my biceps in attempt to express the seriousness of her sentiments. "Have you told her about the new alcohol and drug treatment program the interfaith council has asked you to head up and oversee?"

I shook my head.

"Bobby!"

" I know. I know. The right time hasn't presented itself."

"Well, when do you plan on sharing this news with her? I'm sure this will upset her. You only have twenty-four hours in a day...and I know you are only getting a good five hours if that, of sleep each night."

"I've handled it all well, up until this point. I'm thinking about giving Brother Khalid a raise so he can help me adjust . . ."

"Yes, you know I love Yusef, almost as much as I love you . . . but, that brother can't help you adjust to such a high maintenance woman as Elisabeth. He can barely keep his own marriage together."

I nodded my agreement. She and Eddie pissed me off making such judgmental remarks about the state of other folks' marriage. I bet if she had any inclination of the remote possibility of my brother's infidelity, she'd be in divorce court faster than you can say Judge Maybeline.

"One reason Elisabeth fell for me, She, is because of what I do. It's who I am. Besides, they are going to pay a brotha quite handsomely, even a few G's less than what the church is paying me now, just for a measly few hours of counseling, two or three days a week. She likes money. She'll just have to deal."

"Need I remind you, you do about fifteen to twenty hours of marriage and family counseling at the church, as well

343

as . . . the attention she's going to get because she is not exactly the brownest mixed person in the world?"

"Come on, sis. Get off my back. You're starting to sound like Brother Khalid and Pops."

"Well, maybe you ought to stop being so darn stubborn and listen to us. You can't be there for that girl fully, not like she wants you to be. You have other commitments. She won't understand like the rest of us."

"O, ye of little faith," I replied, confidently quoting the words, of our Lord and Savior to his disciples. "Wherefore didst thou doubt? To quote the apostle Paul's words, which were just on your lips, back in the restroom, I can do all things through Christ who strengthens me."

Skeletons

Very early the next morning, Brother Donaldson rushed everyone, with the exception of Brother Khalid and Mark Riley, back to Lambert airport, promising them they would be back in the Motor City in time enough for Pops' eleven o'clock message in my stead. My pockets were starting to feel the pain for footing the costly overnight fee for everyone invited.

Being the self-proclaimed tightwad I am, I accepted the timely offer Emily rendered to the three of us to rest in the two guest rooms of her house so we would be rejuvenated to drive Elisabeth's BMW and the full-sized rented U-Haul back to Detroit.

Tanya willingly gave up her room, located behind the kitchen at the far west end of the estate to Brother Khalid. After the bash they'd disappeared for hours to who knows where doing God knows what. I wasn't mad at the brother.

His marriage had all but officially ended the week after he got home from St. Louis the first time, once Fatima taking their four young sons with her to move back in with her parents, left him a tepid Dear John letter, citing that she'd vowed to Allah back when she'd asked him for a husband to raise all children born to the union in the Islamic faith.

She wrote that his conversion to Christianity ripped their marriage apart and if he'd ever plan to reconcile with her he'd have to set his heart right with Allah, the only true and living God, and separate from that "smooth-talkin'" preacher's charismatic sway.

It was quite definitely the carnal man in me talking, but since he'd lost his former livelihood and his entire family for the cause of Christ, I rationalized, that he'd deserved to be "broken off a piece" from time to time.

At ten a.m. my two partners and I had loaded both the full-sized U-Haul and the mini-attachment to Elisabeth's BMW.

Riley complained under his breath that the good elder/doctor snuck off to Sunday school a half-hour earlier so he wouldn't have to get his hands dirty from lifting and loading the myriad of boxes, most of which, were marked fragile in Elisabeth's own adroit block-style manuscript.

Ms. Maggie, her assistant Dorothy and Tanya carried out Elisabeth's massive wardrobe by the rack. Brother Khalid also did his fair share of murmuring when the Princess from the front entrance, kept barking out orders for him to not pack anything heavy next to her carefully and individually wrapped porcelain doll collection. All of our eyes bulged out of our heads when one by one, all five women including Emily and Elisabeth herself toted out five fur coats.

"Dag, Bob," Riley laughed. " How spoiled is this girl, anyway?"

"I can't call it. But, she's got another thing comin' to her if she thinks she's gon' be prancin' up in front of all those addicts and welfare recipients sporting a new coat every Sunday, when they don't even have decent Sunday gear. I don't wanna have to beat anybody down for callin' her stuck up."

"Well, to quote the words of Brother McNichols and your ole dude," he kidded, sticking his chest out and blustering about as if he were one or the other. " You had better keep all of those lowlifes up in the balcony area, away from our highly respectable middle-class attendants, who pay your salary and throw money away on your brand of hardcore therapy."

"Just a few more suitcases gentlemen and we'll be ready to go," Elisabeth announced cheerfully as she walked over to my tired frame, which was supported by the side of the U-Haul truck. She pressed her entire body up against mine, close enough to send my guilt-ridden thoughts racing back to just hours earlier where'd we gotten a little too intimate on the couch of her parents den once again.

Dancing so close to Elisabeth in the ballroom and later in the den, once Riley finally picked up on my nonverbal cue to get lost, having her whisper in my ear, massage my weary shoulders and swivel her taut behind around in the pelvic region of my lap, as was her custom, sent my repressed urges into overdrive.

I kissed her goodnight before cursing myself underneath my breath for having to take yet another cold shower.

As the situation panned out, I ended up bunking in Lorraine's long since inhabited bedroom.

I 'd kept at least one eye opened tossing and turning in my boxers and white Fruit of the Loom tank, underneath the frilly white down comforter. As accustomed to I was from being away from the comforts of my own queen-sized waterbed, I remained restless, half of my mind reeled from the anticipation of finally taking a wife, while the other half leered through the candle-lit dancing shadows on the wall, half-expecting, though she was very much alive, the oft talked about and mystical spirit of my future sister-in-law to descend upon me to relieve me of my own four-year self-imposed physical torment. After all, it was in her former bed I was lying and it was her illusive, mega-size, framed visage smiling at me from the cameo on the wall just opposite the headboard.

We weren't on East Interstate 70 for a good fifteen minutes before Elisabeth had to go to the bathroom. She'd already wagged her finger at me about my led foot and the fuzz buster I'd placed on her dashboard, reprimanding me for not adhering to the maximum speed limit of 65 miles per hour.

Her opinion that I was breaking the law didn't change much when I explained to her that I wanted to arrive in Detroit by sundown.

She drew in her breath and closed her eyes tightly as I sped up pass the U-Haul Riley and Brother Khalid had been taking turns driving to signal that we were going to make a pit stop.

Brother Khalid, who had been cruising the truck at about eighty miles per hour, honked the horn and threw his hands up in frustration, wondering why I was pulling off the highway so soon.

As I attempted to merge into the far right lane, Elisabeth noticed the blue and white rest area stop and instructed me to keep going until we reached a food area stop, because she "would, like, never, ever, under any circumstances be caught dead in a filthy, urine-reeking, smoke-filled, foul-mouthed hangout for beer-bellied truckers." By the time we reached the food area stop, Elisabeth was doing the funny little can't wait to pee dance women do.

Another hour down the highway, she sat up from her horizontal position in the backseat of her car, leaned forward and wrapped her arms around my shoulder as I was driving.

"Did Sleeping Beauty have a good catnap?" I asked, finding it difficult to concentrate on the road while she was breathing heavily and nibbling on my ear.

"Not really, Bobby . . . I have to use the bathroom. Could you pull over at the next food stop? I promise I won't drink any more water until we get to Detroit."

"Yeah, right," I laughed as I sped ahead once again to signal Brother Khalid to pull over.

Halfway through the journey, she complained of being hungry. My stomach was growling something fierce itself, so I asked her to look inside the two brown paper grocery bags and the miniature beverage cooler to see what Ms. Maggie had packed us. She turned her nose up at the fried tuna fish and ham sandwiches, as well as the fried chicken and sour sream 'n' onion potato chips, all of which I was more than content to eat. She pouted for a few seconds before she suggested we'd stop to eat at a restaurant.

This time, to signal my partners, I used my cell phone. An aggravated Brother Khalid answered on the fourth ring,

"Man, what? Does the Princess have to potty again?" he asked furiously. I heard Riley heehawing away from his position behind the steering wheel. I ignored Brother Khalid's sarcasm and told him that we'd plan to stop to eat somewhere. He didn't take to my suggestion kindly, but after a few more minutes of giving me hell, he conceded. Five miles down the highway, we pulled over to a strip mall right outside of Indianapolis that contained several fast food options, all of which, my lady-love declined.

After stopping at several more restaurants and finally at a Mobile gas station to refill our tanks, Elisabeth sashayed right past Brother Khalid with a six-pack of Dasani bottled-water.

Once the Princess' back was turned, I peeped him holding his hands up, as if to choke the living daylights out of her. Riley and I cracked up laughing.

"Women, " Riley sighed, wrapping a brotherly arm around my shoulder. "She'll have to go again in thirty more minutes. Set your watches by it."

Once we'd settled back into her Beamer and she'd buried her nose into a romance novel, with a picture of a dark-skinned African-American couple embracing and looking lustfully into each other's eyes, I felt that then was as good as any of an opportunity to discuss the sensitive subject that had been weighing unmercifully on my heart since the night before when I walked in on her in the hotel's family bathroom retching her little heart out.

She looked up from her book and stared dreamingly at

———

349

me as my voice blared from the car speaker's on the first cassette in the God's Warriors Bootcamp series:

"First, let me clear some things up. Let me set the record straight. We are not Muslims. We don't recognize Elijah Muhammad as God's prophet, though he was an amazing man who unified our people, instilled racial pride within them, taught them about our history, and rehabilitated more black men than every so-called correctional facility across this land and country has rehabilitated put together!

Though I, along with Yusef Khalid my right hand man, Mark Riley my mentor and left hand man, Darius Smith, my former frat brother and Paul Wilson, my oldest friend in this life . . . though we all profess Christ, and though the first two-hundred inducted members right from our own congregation are all devout Christians, this program, God's Warriors Incorporated is not a religious organization. We welcome brothers from all walks of life, from all faiths. Who we are . . . is an organization of black men who have reclaimed the power, integrity and foresight that was robbed from our ancestors who were strong enough to survive the horrendous Middle Passage and the subsequent inhumanity of slavery forced upon us by white Americans. Who we are . . . is a brotherhood of brothas who have taken oaths to not only serve God to the fullest extent, but to honor ourselves our women, our children, our extended blood and church families and our own communities within the realms of fatherhood, fidelity, fraternity and financial empowerment.

We are not racists. I have been accused of hating white people. Of preachin' hate, preachin' anti-Anglo, anti-Semitic, anti-Arab, anti-Asian. I'm not anti-anything. I'm pro-black!" Raucous applause from an audience of two-thousand potential inductees strong. *"I'm pro-Christian. Pro-health and wealth of my community. Pro-Africa. The gospel, the true and living gospel of Christ that doesn't portray him as some blonde haired, blue-eyed, pale-faced god, but the gospel that portrays him as one who identified, empathized and loved all the people in his creation, that gospel, my brothers, needs to be preached and spread among our brothers in the motherland as well. Talk to me!*

Just because we're teaching our brothers and sisters to love and respect one another . . . to have self-love, to love each other, doesn't mean we hate! Just because we're teaching our brothers to resume their roles as head of the family and chief provider, doesn't mean we hate white folk! Just because we teach our wives, our sisters, our daughters that the feminist movement of the late 60's and early 70's that many sistah's joined in an effort to propel themselves in the workplace and to exert authority of their men . . . just because we teach them that they had no business in that struggle, because that movement, not unlike slavery, was covertly designed by white society to perpetuate mistrust, power-struggles and hostility within the black home . . . does not mean we hate anybody! Just because we're all personally tired of patronizing overpriced Arab owned liquor stores and gas stations in our neighborhoods, and our women are fed up to here doling out hard earned dollars to Chinese and Korean owned nail salons and beauty supply stores . . . doesn't mean we hate anyone.

We're not a people of hate. We, as a people don't even hold hate in our hearts. We are in fact, the most forgiving people who have ever graced the face of this earth! But, it's time for a change my brothers! We want our own stuff! Talk to me! We, as a people, led by our men, need to come together, just like whites, just like Koreans, just like the Arabs and every other group of people for that matter. It's time to pool all of our resources together and to become the self-sufficient people God placed us on earth to become.

"My speaking style, my whole professional aura if you will, has been likened to that of the late, great, phenomenal Malcolm X. I ain't mad. Brother Malcolm was my hero. And, I as a black man, unlike many other black men, don't have a problem with acknowledging my hero. I'm not too proud or too macho to admit that, that brother, God rest his soul, was deep. Must have read everything ever written about him. My five or six copies of his autobiography have all been highlighted and doggy-eared to death. Heh,

351

heh . . . accused Brother Khalid when I first met him, pushing bean pies and Final Calls of being guilty by association for ending Brother Malcolm's life. That was before realizing that Islam, like Christianity, Buddhism, and all major religions of the world are religions of peace and that although some black muslims pulled the trigger in the darkest hour of African-American history, the bulk of the responsibility for his death can be placed upon the bloody hands of a powerful secret society of people who still harbor hate in their hearts for the black man, who dares to call him out to his face!" Another standing ovation.

    *"Oh, my favorite part of the movie, my favorite part of Spike Lee's rendition of Malcolm X is when Malcolm, as portrayed by Denzel Washington tells the young white co-ed after she asks him what could she do to help appease her conscious for all the atrocities her ancestors had committed against his. Ya'll brothers remember that scene? Well, Brother Malcolm's response was, nothing. There is **nothing** you can do for us, **not one thing**! Ha! I wish somebody white would ask me what they could do in order to help our cause. I wish they would. I would tell them flat out that they need to acknowledge that the conspiracy against the black man had it's roots in slavery when he was only considered to be three-fifths of a human being, when he had to watch his own children being taken away from him, and his own wife, who was by law, really not his wife, because black marriages were illegal, how he had to suffer the grave, unspeakable reality of watching her pregnant belly swell with the repercussions of just one of the possible hundreds of times ole' massa crammed his thing where it had no business being!*

    No sir, I'm not a gospel minister tonight. I'm not here to break unto you the good news! God, help me! I'm a truth speaker. I'm here to tonight to break you off a piece on what we as black men need to do to clean up our acts! I'm the voice of black men all over this land and country. God help us all!

    I hope there ain't nobody sensitive in here, or no brotha's listenin' to the sound of my voice gettin' all offended, because if you are, then be warned, you have two options. Option A, buckle yourself up and strap yourself in, because it's about to get rough up in here. Option B, stroll your Amos and Andy behinds up out of here, or pitch this tape altogether, Sambo!"

Since I never enjoyed listening to myself speak on audiotape, I thoughtfully turned down the volume of one of Elisabeth's complete collection of more than thirty of my recent tapes, she'd insisted on toting along with her on our journey in a dainty nauseatingly pink cassette case decorated with the Barbie logo and a can't miss picture on the front of a black doll wearing a headset to a miniature walkman radio.

I found Elisabeth's fascination with doll collecting a bit juvenile, but I didn't dare tease her about it, because at least every doll I'd seen her personally hand wrap and carry out to the car, was black. She thankfully identified with her black side, which would stun the daylights out of Brother Khalid and needless to say, was definitely kosher with me.

"Oh, Bobby. Why'd you turn it down? You were just about to get to the good part," she whined, placing her monogrammed bookmark on the page towards the end of the book where she'd left off.

"Because, baby . . . I really don't feel like listening to my own voice the entire ride back home. Plus, I need to talk to you about last night."

"Lll..ast nn . . . ight," she mumbled nervously, reaching for her favorite strands of hair to twirl around her finger and forgetting that she'd brushed her luxurious locks back into a neat, free-hanging ponytail.

"Yes, baby, last night. We need to talk about what I walked in on. We need to clear the air about it."

"There's nothing to discuss Bobby. I'm perfectly fine."

"I know you've had problems in the past with eating disorders, Princess. I'm going to be your husband. I need to know. . . . ."

"Bobby," she sang impatiently, stroking her hand up and

353

down the right leg of my jeans. "I am, like, so totally over that. Last night, I.... I ... well, I got upset. Haven't been that upset with Mother in a long time, Bobby. Really, I haven't, and, the food. . . . the food was a little too bland for my taste . . . I guess I've just grown accustomed to Ms. Maggie's delicious seasonings, but don't tell her that . . . she'll never let me live that sort of compliment down," she laughed nervously. "I promise you Bobby, it will never happen again. I haven't purged in over a year, baby, I promise."

My professional experience in treating psychosis of any kind would not allow me to swallow the sincerely intended, sugar-coated bait she'd cast down at me from her delusional sinking row boat of a mindset.

I opted rather to swallow the lump of discomfort rising up in my throat, while placing my warm large hand over her frigid ivory fingers. I needed to emotionally detach myself as her soon to be husband and to actively listen, really hear what she had to say about her illness.

"A couple of years after my sister left home, she'd return for one of her rare and last visits. It was Thanksgiving. I had just won a leading role in the Christmas play at my private high school and I had also made it to the top five of one of the last beauty pageants I'd signed up to be in for the senior age divisions. Did you notice all those trophies Brother Kareem packed up?"

"Yes, every one of them," I half-smiled.

"Well, I'd won all those from the age of three on up. Participating in these pageants was the only thing that Mother and I truly enjoyed doing together. She and Ms. Maggie would always doll me up really pretty and buy me all these cute dresses and heels and tons of makeup. Lori was never really interested in that type of thing. Doesn't like a lot of makeup and perfume. She really likes sports, especially stuff like dancing and gymnastics that type of thing. . . . so, you know this pageant thing was really my deal, you know?"

"Yes."

"So anyways, it was Thanksgiving. The pageant directors told me that I could stand to lose a few pounds . . . by Christmas and if I did, I would definitely be a shoe in for the title of Senior Teen Miss Chesterfield right?"

"Senior Miss Teen Chesterfield," I failed in stifling a laugh.

"Don't make fun," she pouted, folding her arms across her chest.

"Sorry, baby. Go on."

"So Lori catches me, like, emptying my whole plate of turkey and stuffing along with macaroni and cheese and ham into my dinner napkin. Then she follows me to the bathroom. I. . . . wasn't . . . doing . . . anything . . . any of the other girls in those pageants don't do. . . . Bobby. I. . . . mean. . . . she totally blew things out of proportion," Elisabeth cried, leering vindictively out of her passenger side window. I stopped minding the road long enough to reach over to smooth my hand over the top of her ponytail and to notice her bottom lip shaking fiercely.

"What happened next, sweetheart?"

"What happened next," she repeated in a shrill, high-pitched shriek. "What happened next, is unimaginable. Mother had me shipped off to this, like, totally weirded out, outrageously, expensive all-white, all girls, exclusive boarding school for *real* anorexics and bulimics out in the hills, near the Ozarks. I had to finish out the rest of my tenth grade year in that ritzy prison of a hospital. I hate her for doing that to me, Bobby! I will never, ever, forgive her."

"The old man briefed me on your having been sent away," I confessed quietly. "That must have been hell for you Princess. I wish to God you would have never experienced that."

"Yeah, well, it's a little too late for that," she snapped. "Now . . . you wanna bail on me too, just because . . . I got a little upset last night . . . I should have known. No one understands me in this world. No one, except, well Daddy, of course."

Resisting the urge to take on the analytical, detached persona of a licensed psychologist, proved to be more difficult of a challenge as I maintained a watchful eye on the road and listened to her frantically rationalize, then angrily misappropriate or project her history of hostile feelings towards her mother onto me.

"I want to understand you, baby. That's why I brought the subject up. We have to keep the lines of communication open. We can't go into this marriage with any secrets."

"I know that, Bobby," she insisted. "But, you're going to have to trust me on this. That eating disorder thing is a moot issue, okay? I just don't want you thinking I'm sick. I'm perfectly fine now that I have you and I'll be almost six-hundred miles away from Mother. Good riddance to her anyways."

She dabbed away at a few more tears with one of her infamous monogrammed hankies and continued to stare out the window, refusing to speak for at least five or six minutes, until she employing her tiny mouse-like baby voice informed me in so many words that she had to pee again.

Ma's Mad

The very next morning, I as usual almost ripped the cord of the nagging alarm clock situated on the nightstand next to my bed right out of its' socket when it went off at five am.

After pumping iron and completing several repetitions of push-ups and jogging on the treadmill, I fed my hungry buds with fur for one of their last mornings with me as a bachelor before devouring my own standard breakfast of three scrambled eggs with cheese, three slices of turkey bacon, wheat toast and grapefruit juice.

Smack dab in the middle of my two hour long Bible study, my phone rang. I started not to answer it, but changed my mind once Ma's tension filled voice sharply demanded me to break away from the Holy Book long enough to come save the life of my soon to be dead fiancée.

"And good morning to you too, Ma," I, too comfortable in my swivel chair at the desk of my second bedroom, make-shift office to search for the receiver dejected the speaker button on the base of the phone.

"Son, I hate to disturb your routine, but I'm just calling to let you know that this little live-in situation with Snow White is not going to fly with me at all," she hissed in a voice barely above a whisper, so as not to probably disturb Pops from the late morning sleep-in routine he'd developed since I had taken on all his previous job responsibilities and then some.

357

"What is it already, Ma? When I left your house at almost midnight last night things were fine . . ."

"Things were not fine, Bobby! That girl came in here, turning her nose up at this house, like it was too small and cluttered for her taste. I know she's used to living in splendor around all those rich white folks and all, but I would think her parents trained her well enough to know that not every one is living high on the hog like they are."

I didn't feel the need to console Ma by mentioning the fact that she and Pops had lived more than modestly, in one of the most distinguished, affluent communities within Detroit ever since I'd been born, nor the fact that she'd kept a relatively clean home. She knew these things already. The sisters at the church had stroked her ego enough in that area. I shuffled some papers around on my desk a few seconds while listening to her ongoing slew of complaints against my woman.

"She's been in the darn bathroom washing and blow drying that stringy hair of hers for over an hour. She has so much makeup on my counter and so many unopened bottles of perfume that I had to bring all my cosmetics back here to our room. You would think she's getting ready to go to another one of those engagement shin digs I'm sure you paid an arm and a leg for instead of to the clinic and to marriage counseling with you."

"Would that be all, Ma? I really have to get going here."

"Son?"

"Yes, Ma?"

"Do you have to marry *her*? Have you really looked at all those beautiful black career oriented sisters at the church?"

"Elisabeth is black, or at least half-black anyway. We've had this discussion before and besides, you've never worked outside of the home or church a day in your married life, Ma, so, why should I want my wife to be any different?"

Ma drew in her breath as a sign of her reluctant defeat.

"Just hurry up and get here son, and bring her something green to eat. She claims everything in our refrigerator will clog up her precious little arteries."

Mickey

The Princess attempted every excuse in the world to avoid visiting the Interfaith clinic with me. An infuriated Ma was standing in the kitchen with her hands on her hips scowling at Elisabeth scraping burnt crumbs from her crust-less wheat toast into the garbage disposal. I knew Pops, who had not awakened to welcome his retired dream world of amateur golf and free McDonald's senior citizen coffee refills, had no clue regarding the definitive lines of battle between his wife and my intended, Ma had amazingly enough managed to superbly draw ousting the records of embittered mother-in-laws everywhere.

Elisabeth played right into Ma's literally outstretched hands when she'd circumvented our usual mother-son greeting hug and pounced merrily into my arms instead. She planted a few scattered kisses on my face, before sliding her warm delectable tongue in between my grinning teeth. Wrapping my hands around the waist of her stylishly inch above knee-length, plaid gray wool skirt, I could hardly contain my fingers that roamed freely through her freshly shampooed strawberry scented hair, as she moaned her pleasure of my wild, reciprocating tongue.

"Hmmm, mmmm," Ma cleared her throat. "Excuse me, you two."

Elisabeth held onto my face as I slowly unloosened the suction I had on her tiny bottom lip.

"Sorry Ma," I replied sheepishly holding my free arm out to her.

Mumbling something about our behavior being highly inappropriate, she walked over to the table belonging to their three-piece kitchenette ensemble, grabbed her dirty cereal bowl and half-emptied juice glass and practically slammed them down onto the metal surface at the bottom of the sink.

"You ready to go, sweetheart?"

"Well, I was wondering if you could swing back by to get me if you have time on the way back from the clinic. I want to put the finishing touches on my pedicure before we go to marriage counseling."

"Brother Forbes is not interested in talking to your feet, dear," Ma replied sharply, now using a Brillo pad to scrape the layer of consolidated lard from the skillet she used to fry bacon.

"Well . . . it's just that . . . Daddy promised to call me at ten-thirty and I'm a little home sick already. . . . if you could just pick me up after you're done," Elisabeth suggested sweetly, batting those incredibly long, soft brown eyelashes up at me, while her arms were still securely wrapped around my neck. She knew how to work me all right, because I was just about to concede to her blatant diversionary tactic before Ma's sharp wit and keen observation lulled me back to my senses.

"That's why they created answering machines, young lady. Besides, I'll be home for at least until noon. Go on with Bobby," Ma ordered. "Let him show you off to some of the staff at the clinic. He works with a bunch of decent people over there. Be sure to introduce yourself to Doctor Giles, and say hello to her for me. I'm sure she would love to finally lay eyes on the source of his distraction."

That was a low blow Ma even for you, I thought, remembering Michelle Giles, the thirty-two year old, ebony complex-ioned, intensely cerebral and sexy all at the same time newly certified full-time psychiatrist the council headed by yours truly, hired the previous January, after she'd completed an impressive three year residency at the Johns Hopkins reha-bilitation treatment facility.

Michelle Giles, the last woman I almost broke my then, three and half year voluntary vow of torture one night at her eastside condo, after she'd cooked me dinner for hooking up her entertainment center. Michelle Giles, the last woman out of only about a handful of hundreds, I 'd thought about highly enough to bring home to meet the folks and to parade in front of dozens of wounded sisters at the church. Michelle Giles, my esteemed colleague and personal friend, the woman I'd forgotten completely about since I'd laid eyes on Elisabeth.

"But, I promised you, Mother McGallister that I would help you polish the furniture in the living and dining areas. My allergies are really, really horrible around tons of dust . . ."

Ma's back stiffened at Elisabeth's hopefully, unintended, innocent insult. "I said, go on with Bobby," she muttered through a tightened lip and gritted teeth.

" Uh . . . I'll get your coat, Princess," I replied.

She pouted and complained of an upset stomach the en-tire fifteen-minute car ride to the five story fairly modern building located off of Greenfield and Joy Road.

"Maybe, I'll just stay in your office and lie down or some-thing. I'm not feeling so hot, Bobby. I think, maybe your mother may have laced my morning tea with arsenic."

At the traffic light of the last intersection before approach-ing the front parking lot, Mickey, the aging vagabond, who'd for longer than I'd been employed at the center made a liv-ing on that corner, scraping off and wiping away insect car-casses from the windshields of vehicles of urban commuters, hurried over and tapped convivially on the passenger win-dow, much to the sheer horror of my shocked fiancée.

"Hey, Reb'n," he shouted through her rolled up window, his cold, most-likely, cheap whiskey breath, thankfully leaving a cloud of fog to camouflage Elisabeth's widened eyes and dropped jaw. She instinctively gathered the fur collar of her ivory leather coat in closer to her neck and darted frantic eyes over at me, awaiting an explanation.

"What's happenin', Mick?" I smiled, reaching over Elisabeth to my glove compartment to retrieve a five dollar bill from a stash I kept handy just for him.

"Who's the pretty lady, Reb'n?" he reciprocated a near toothless grin with his face pressed up right against the glass.

I rolled down the window slowly. Elisabeth leaned in closer to me and latched onto my arm, as if Mickey was about to eat her alive.

"This pretty lady is my soon to be wife, brother," I replied, trying my best to ignore her squeamishness. "Here baby. Hand this bill to my man, Mick."

She looked up at me with pensive, reluctant eyes that accused me of being crazy for thinking that she, though wearing stylish leather gloves, would even consider touching the calloused, ashy hand of a homeless drunken beggar.

"Give him the five, Princess," I whispered, out of the side of my mouth. "He doesn't bite."

Elisabeth snatched the five out of my hand, allowed it to dangle from her fingertips to minimize personal contact and slid it out the window as quickly as possible.

"Thank you, pretty lady. We heard you was tyin' the knot, Reb'n Preacha. Sho' nuff a pretty lady. Is you a model or sumptin', ma'am?"

Apparently flattered, some of the attractive rosy coloring returned to her blanched from fright cheeks as she shook her head quickly and looked once again to me to do all the talking.

"She's being modest, Mick. Elisabeth here has won many, many beauty contests. Ain't she somethin'?"

"Yeah, Reb'n. Most certain is. Most certain is. Can I scrub down the truck today? Ain't got the dogs wit you for me to hose or warsh off, I don't suppose?"

" No sir," I chuckled at the thought of Cherie and Deuce howling protests over their much hated showers on the back lawn premises of the clinic. "I'll bring them by tomorrow morning, Lord willing, that is if your prices haven't gone up any, chief."

"Aw naw. They ain't gone up any for you, Reb'n Preacha. Neva for you. You got a brotha's back, strong," he winked his goodbye to Elisabeth, before limping over to the car besides us with his scraper and bucket in tow.

Elisabeth tightened her grip on my hand as she entered into the same main entrance revolving door compartment with me. It didn't take long for us to be noticed upon signing in with Charisma, the gum-popping, wise-cracking, buxom, divorced mother of three, who all the Muslim and Baptist married preachers affiliated with the council swore had a mad crush on me the size of Mount Everest. She, Ernest, one of the drivers and Triana the first floor appointment secretary, looked up from their serious game of spades at the receptionists area with startled eyes when the wind blew their long lost "Doc" in with a younger, if I do say so myself, more appealing cross between Jennifer Lopez and Cindy Crawford

My usually boisterous, rambunctious staff fell quiet as I escorted the Princess by placing my hand on the small of her back over to the receptionist desk, where she used her well French-manicured hand to fluff out the back of her goldish-brown locks from underneath her fur hood, spraying everyone within a twenty foot radius with the familiar encompassing scent I'd grown to adore.

"Dammmmn, Doc!" Ernest sang, his colossal beer belly rolling rampantly over the worn out leather belt of the too tight blue uniform pants all patient care drivers were required to wear on the six to eight hour shifts. "Who you got there, man, Miss America?"

Elisabeth blushed her greeting at Ernest as he tripped over Triana's big feet to give me some dap and to cop a closer view in order to drool more profusely.

"This is Elisabeth Powell, Ernest, the soon to be Mrs. McGallister," I boasted, winking my encouragement to Elisabeth to at least speak to the doting old cat. "Ernest Wilson here is one of our best drivers. This is Triana Jackson, one of the receptionists and Charisma Banks one of the security guards."

"Hi," Elisabeth said shyly, surprisingly removing one of her gloves so Ernest could kiss the back of her hand.

"Well, well, well," Charisma rolled her eyes three times worse than Kelly ever could on a good day. "This is the chick you've been dissin' me for Doc, huh?"

"I beg your pardon?" Elisabeth asked indignantly in that crisp southern, white girl inflection. "I'm nobody's chick." She shot me a I-know-you-weren't-desperate-enough-in-your-celibacy-to-take-up-time-with-this-cheap-ghetto-floosy-before sweeping-me-off-my –feet look.

It was about to go down in the worse possible way if I didn't hurry up to come in for the save.

"Well ex. . . . cuse the shit outta me," she snarled, slamming her tired hand of hearts and diamonds down, next to a half-empty box of greasy Church's Chicken on the lopsided card table. "Sho gotta lot of attitude for a white girl."

"I'm not white; I'm mixed," Elisabeth snapped back. "And it would behoove you to mind your manners when you are in the presence of a minister and his wife, Ms. Whatever your name is."

"Oh, snap!" Triana instigated, stifling a laugh into her hand of five remaining cards. "I guess she told yo' ig'nant ass girl!"

"Ok . . . ay," I clucked my tongue and clasped my hands

together. "Now that we've all had to the opportunity to exchange niceties, I think I'm going to take Elisabeth on my rounds to meet a few of the other staff members and a couple patients."

"I'll get the elevator for you, Mrs. McGallister," Ernest grinned, obviously smitten not only by the Princess stunning looks but also by her fiery personality. He extended his elbow out to her. Much to my delight, she smiled and took hold of it.

"Well, thank you kindly, sir," Scarlet O'Hara replied contentedly. "Mrs. McGallister," she proclaimed just loud enough for the envying Charisma to choke on the chicken bone upon which she'd released her fury. "Now, a real lady can get used to the sound of that." With that, she did that little sexy whipping of the hair thing and pranced off with the all too compliant Ernest.

Crackhead

Michelle was attempting to wheel a recalcitrant Marcus, the twelve year crack-addict who'd cussed me out more than a number of times for getting on his case about wanting to go AWOL for a quick fix, down the long hallway of the third floor back to his room from group therapy.

By the scraggly, ashen, dried up slob on the corner of his mouth and the full force spastic shakes and twitches that kept threatening to tip his lightweight body over in the chair, I surmised that he'd used his two day furlough to binge around in his old stomping grounds, the Jefferson Projects. He was starting to tap dance on the last shred of patience and compassion for his plight I had left for him.

Elisabeth, wearing an exact replica of the horrified expression she'd sported out on the street corner with Mickey, recoiled three or four steps back towards the elevator, the closer the small-framed, smooth dark-skinned Michelle pushed Marcus our way. Instead of honing in on Michelle's straight beyond shoulder length jet-black wrap hairstyle, that she on the right side highlighted with a silver butterfly shaped barrette and her pearly white straightened teeth, Elisabeth's eyes widened then squinted in disgustedly on the eons of lint and God knows what else in that cat's wildly clumped together doo-doo dreads.

"Let me up out of this mu'fucka you black ass bitch, fo I

tip this chair over and you wit' it, you stank ho!" a delirious Marcus, in the throes of withdrawal reached his fist backwards and belted a hearty blow to Michelle's stomach. Michelle staggered forward a bit more so from the unsuspected delivery of his punch than from pain, leaning over just enough for him to grab a hand full of her straight hair into his balled up fist, before he started chewing and slobbering all on it, probably tasting the coconut oil she reeked of due to her almost nightly scalp greasing ritual.

"Omigod," Elisabeth mumbled more to herself than to me.

Instinctively, I rushed over to Marcus and pried his tight fingers from around Michelle's ever increasing salivated locks before yelling "code red" for the recently hired third floor security guard to get up off his tired, flat behind to help us with a patient. He was nowhere to be found. Angrily, I lifted Marcus up by his fists and ordered him to take his mouth off of Dr. Giles' head.

"Now, you ugly bastard!" I hollered, "before I break yo' little buck o' five junkie body in half."

His clamped jaws loosened enough to allow Michelle to break free, but not before he hurled the nastiest lugie onto the left lens of her small wire rimmed glasses.

Appalled, she backed away from him, stiffening her neck with her palms outstretched as if she couldn't believe he'd disrespected her like that. I tugged on his fist harder until he'd completely freed himself from the grips of the wheel chair, dragging him, kicking and screaming like a punk down the hall to the padded room, stopping behind the trifling new hire who was fumbling through his overcrowded key chain to unlock the door.

"Omigod," Elisabeth cried real tears now. She ran up behind me, afraid to touch me in my frenzied state of anger.

"It's under control, Doctor McGallister," Michelle pleaded quietly through frightened eyes, although I couldn't decipher who she was more afraid of. She reached inside her pocket for the single metallic object on a Las Vegas key ring and asked the guard to step aside. "Don't hurt him, Robert." Ignoring her instantaneous act of forgiveness for the man who'd just spit in her face, I slammed Marcus down in the corner of the empty room and held his wild body down until the security guard with the help of nurse Jamilah, Brother Khalid's wife's twin sister, forced him into a straight jacket.

Elisabeth stood in the doorway sniffing back tears, mumbling at least a dozen more "Omigod's" before Jamilah asked her if there was anything she could get for her.

"Ya'll s'pose to be doctas. Cain't keep me from my medicine. Hear me? I want my medicine, nigga. You hear me? I need my medicine. I'mo be sick," he cried real tears in an effort to con me enough to raise up off of him.

"Hold on Brother Marcus, it's coming," I reasoned, still straddled on top of him, while the out of shape security guard breathed heavily in trying to secure the last snap on the side of the jacket.

"You's a lyin, mu'fucka revran, you's a lyin black nigga. Tole' me that shit last time. I need my medicine. Please mista pimp preacher, I'll suck . . ."

I placed my hand over his mouth, glaring at him, daring at him to bite me. "Jamilah, get my wife out of here. Take her to my office, now!" The words just flowed out, much easier than fiancée' ever would. *My wife*, I liked the sound of that.

"Yes, Doctor," Jamilah answered submissively, taking the daunted childlike Elisabeth by the hand.

The teen-aged volunteer nurse's assistant Candace from one of the local AME churches, followed by the twenty-something white bleeding-heart Methodist Dave, Michelle's first year resident, pushed in a cart complete with syringes, needles and enough morphine to subdue this completely out of it brother for weeks.

"Okay, Mr. Abernathy," Dave announced calmly in a na-

369

sal professional voice. "We hear you're having a rough time coming back from your two day furlough, huh?"

"Yeah, I'mo kill that sonofmabitch Ernest for pickin'me up from the joint. If ya'll let me outta here, I'm gon' fuck all of ya'll up, 'specially Mr. Pimp wannabe hard Preacha' Man here! Here me, man? Yo' ass is dead!"

Dave nervously fumbled with the syringe and needle, glancing up at the clueless Candace as if she could spare him from perhaps doping up his first hardcore addict.

" Come on Doogie Howser!" I yelled. " What's the hold up? One-hundred milligrams sub-Q, stat!"

"Negative," Michelle countered flatly, giving me eye contact for the first time since I'd informed all within earshot who Elisabeth was to me.

"Say what?" I asked, getting tired of Marcus' efforts to kick me in the balls. "He's out of control!"

"Fifty milligrams, Dr. Brewington," she reiterated calmly. "Patient needs to be alert enough later on tonight to be interrogated by the police. Patient was accused of armed robbery of a liquor store last evening."

A bewildered Dave looked to me then to her, then to me again, not knowing whose orders to follow.

"She's the MD," I conceded, throwing my hands up. "Give the lady what she wants."

I stormed out of the room, leaving her and her blasted medical expertise to tranquilize our soon to be incarcerated longtime patient.

Dr. Giles

"You okay, baby?" I asked Elisabeth, unloosening the throat clenching necktie I'd worn for the idiotic purpose of impressing my old CMLA classmate, Daniel Forbes with whom we were scheduled for counseling that afternoon. Jamilah had prepared Elisabeth a cup of hot tea and honey to sip on as they awaited my return on the couch of the office I'd shared with Michelle. Jamilah smoothed Elisabeth's hair back behind her ears as if her own life had been threatened by one of my stoned patients.

They watched me calmly remove my coat and hat as well as walk over to join them on the couch, next to my desk, opposite Michelle's against the east wall of our cramped office. Although the old building which was once the home-base of a major HMO, had been in the process of undergoing major renovations to accommodate the needs of our ever-growing clientele, Michelle and I, in the midst of our eight month, rather sporadic dating period opted to share an office, seeing that I was only there twelve hours a week and that the funds for including another office could be appropriated for patient care.

"Omigod, Bobby. I thought that man was going to kill that nurse. That was like the scariest thing I've ever seen in my life. I want to get out of here. This place gives me the creeps. I hate hospitals. I never wanted to come here," she

371

blurted out in one breath, crying hysterically on my shoulder, her salty tears staining my sharp smoky gray suit coat.

"I'll leave you two alone, Doctor McGallister," Jamilah whispered, patting an oblivious Elisabeth on the back one last time before closing the door behind her.

"I mean, is that what things are really like around here?"

"Sometimes, Princess. What you've just witnessed is a patient experiencing some heavy withdrawal symptoms from crack mixed in with God knows what else. Michelle is not a nurse. She's the psychiatrist. She's in with him now administering a tranquilizer of morphine to calm him down."

"That young looking woman is a doctor?" she questioned, amazed and jealous at the same time.

"Yes. You see that nameplate on the desk across from mine?"

"*She's* Dr. Giles?"

"Yes, she's been here a little over a year."

"I see," she hissed, dragging out the "s" sound to convey her skepticism over the nature of our relationship. She slowly withdrew from my embrace and placed a hand on my shoulder, looking at me with sharp, furtive eyes. "She's the Dr. Giles Mother McGallister wanted to make sure I'd meet today, isn't she?"

Uh-oh. Here it comes. Just let me have it now, Princess, before she enters the room and you cause a big scene.

"Well, is she Bobby?"

"Yes."

"Who is she to you?"

"What do you mean?"

"Now you're playing dumb," she persisted putting her hands on her tiny hips. "Why are the two of you sharing space in this little hole in the wall office? It's so dusty in here, I'm going to have one of my attacks."

"You don't have asthma, Elisabeth," I pointed out, standing up to stretch my legs so I could proceed with rounds I'd intended to complete before noon.

"Where are you going, Bobby? We're so, like, in the middle of a conversation about a woman you obviously care about . . ."

"Cared, Princess. Past tense. Michelle and I are over."

"Over? How serious was this thing with your colleague, Bobby? She's awfully pretty. Who broke it off, you or her?"

"What difference does it make?"

"Bobby," she whined, standing up on her three-inch gray pumps that matched the color of her plaid skirt and my suit. "This is important to me."

"She did."

"Why, because you met me?"

"No, I haven't been with Michelle since the summer."

"Like what do you mean, been with? I thought you have been celi.."

"I have been. I didn't make that up, you know. Trust me." I had never been as close to forsaking my vow, with any woman out of the entire four years than I had been with Michelle.

"How long were you involved with this woman?"

"A few months I guess, baby. Who knows. . . . it's not important."

"She met Mother McGallister and Pops obviously."

"A couple times. Yes."

"You're being vague. You told me you weren't big on opening up and communicating . . . but I'm going to be your wife. If it's not important, why are you being so funny and secretive about it?"

"What else do you wanna know, baby?"

"She's been to your church?"

"Yes."

" A lot?"

"Not a whole lot."

"Did people know you two were sort of an item?"

"Just the few closest to me."

"So she knows Brother Khalid, Mark and Nikki, Paul and Jasmine and all those guys?"

"Yes."

"You all have been out together."

"A few times."

"You kiss her?"

"What?"

"Have you ever shoved your tongue down her throat the way you shove it down mine?"

"Conversation over."

"I'll take that as a yes."

"Haven't thought about her since I laid eyes on you, Princess and that's the God's honest truth."

Maybe it was because all of the late hours we'd spent cramped together in that office reviewing cases, picking each other's brains on the best possible treatment for various patients. Debating our completely different religious philosophies. Eating barbecue rib dinners from Papa Ramano's, the best rib joint in Detroit. Wrapping for hours about everything in general and nothing specifically until I would escort her out, holding her pretty creamy chocolate hand to the empty parking lot so she wouldn't be jacked or even raped in the bad area where Interfaith was located.

We just clicked. But, there was no chemistry. She didn't fit the profile. Too set in her ways. Too independent. Too brainy. Too argumentative. Too self-sufficient. Too educated to a fault. Too Methodist. Too persistent to tear my resistance down. Too willing to give it to me, without my having to pursue it. A fine woman, but I wasn't feeling her. She was no Elisabeth.

"Well, I don't want you working in such close quarters with such a gorgeous woman. You would be like setting yourself up for temptation. So, if you need me to help you box up your things, I'm sure you can find another, bigger space to work, one that's more conducive to a man of your status. I read that showcase in the lobby, you know the one that lists all the board of directors. Your name is like way, way at the bottom, as if you are not like practically responsible for this whole place."

"I'm not."

"Of course you are. You're so sexy when you're being humble. Anyways, whenever you would like for me to help move your things out of here I'm all yours."

I wrapped my arms around her waist and pulled her into me. "You're all mine anyway, baby." I placed my index finger on her chin and lifted her mouth to mine, while allowing my massive hands to circle her backside and tight buttocks, and then back up again and underneath the soft fabric of her light gray mock turtleneck sweater. My expert hands searched her scarce bare backside to unsnap the single hook that held her satin bra together.

I situated her between my legs as I leaned my buttocks onto Michelle's desk

"You're being a bad boy," she whispered, not resisting my touch, but pressing her scant bosom forward into my chest. "We have to wait until our wedding night, remember?" She lifted her heavy hair from over her neck, to allow me to taste her delectable nectar up and down and all round, losing control of my sense of time, place and mission, running my fingers over her hardened nipples, about to flatten her across my perfectly neat desk, until, the door swung open and in walked Michelle glaring at me with eyes that could have melted the iceberg that caused the destruction of the infamous Titanic.

"Oops, so sorry," Elisabeth giggled her embarrassment, all too satisfied that Michelle caught a glimpse of her pink nipple headed in the direction of my mouth. While I helped

Elisabeth refasten her pink lacy Victoria's Secret Miracle Bra, Michelle sauntered briskly past us to get to her desk. She'd obviously rinsed Markus' spit out of her hair, as it was now pulled back into a wet wavy ponytail. Pretending she hadn't busted us about to get our groove on, I suppose was much easier than looking me in the face, and having to be formally introduced to Elisabeth for the first time. She'd replaced her wire-rimmed spectacles with the clear contact lenses she wore whenever her allergies weren't giving her the flux. Seeing clearly, she scrawled a prescription on an RX pad for an anonymous patient.

"Doctor Giles, I would like to formally introduce you to Elisabeth Po . . ."

"How do you do?" Michelle looking up briefly from her work, cut me off at the end pass, before swerving around in her chair to unlock her two-drawer file cabinet.

"Very well, thank you," Elisabeth gloated, with her backside against my frontal area, grabbing my arms and wrapping them around her waist. "Bobby tells me you two used to see each other."

"Bobby?"

"Heh, heh . . . that's what everyone in my family calls me . . ."

"Oh . . . well, we just had a few dates and I attended his church a few times. It was nothing serious," Michelle replied dryly, still creating menial busy work so she wouldn't have to look up at me.

Nothing serious? Dig that. Check Ms.-I-wanna-jump-your-bones, out.

"I liked how you handled that patient. That poor man. Will he be all right? What's going to happen to him?"

Michelle shot me a look that questioned my professional oath of confidentiality. I shook my head coolly to inform her that in calming the Princess, I'd failed to mention that Marcus was headed for the joint.

"We usually don't make it a practice to discuss our patients with anyone not assigned to their case," she snapped eyeballing Elisabeth from the top of her gorgeous head to her long, slim legs to her sexy gray pumps.

"I can respect that," Elisabeth shrugged, stroking my clasped hands around her waist.

"Baby, Dr. Giles and I have to have our usual morning meeting," I announced reluctantly releasing her from my grip. "We'll be in the conference room down the hall."

Michelle with her funky attitude, snatched up the files on her desk and the three hundred fifty dollar hand-held organizer I'd purchased for her on her July 4th thirtieth birthday and headed towards the door without so much as looking back at Elisabeth until Elisabeth in typical fashion further exacerbated the foul situation.

"You're invited to the wedding, Dr. Giles. The Saturday before Valentine's Day," she called out behind us. "It was nice to have met you."

Michelle grunted her response.

———

377

Giving A Damn

She was the consummate professional sitting directly across from me in the newly renovated conference room where I conducted most of the board meetings of the Interfaith Drug and Alcohol Rehabilitation Council, succinctly briefing me on her decision to discharge three of my clients during my absence to out-patient care.

I studied the notes she'd in a meticulous fashion foreign to doctors printed neatly in the file of each of my patients she'd counseled and prescribed or gradually weaned off of certain "step-down" drugs, while she attempted to patronize me and explain to me why she overrode my order to prescribe such a high dosage of morphine to Marcus.

"Your decision to go with fifty milligrams is fine with me, Doctor. I trust your judgment," I replied in earnest, relaxing in my chair and folding my arms across my chest. I watched her fidget around restlessly in her own comfortable chair for a few minutes; even caught her shaking her head and rolling those incensed, frustrated eyes at me, when a habitually thirsty Elisabeth rapped on the door, apologized for interrupting our meeting and asked if we had a vending machine that sold her favorite bottled water.

"No, baby, but the cafeteria is on the second floor. They sell water in there. I'll take you down there in a few minutes."

"Okay, Bobby," she answered sweetly, planting one on, full on the mouth to piss Michelle off further. "We can pick you up something too if you'd like, Dr. Giles."

"No, thank you," Michelle replied, all snotty like. " *I* can go get water *for myself*, on my own."

"Suit yourself," Elisabeth shrugged. "But Bobby, how much longer is it going to be, I'm really, like, so parched . . ."

"Just give me five minutes to wrap things up, baby," I insisted, gently hurrying her exit and closing the door behind her.

Without missing a beat, Michelle picked right up in her dry discourse in filling me in on my patients, in the most smoke-screen, detached manner she could muster, twiddling her thumbs impatiently, her sharp responses attempting to make me feel as if I hadn't spent six years of my life preparing to become a head doctor. I knew what she was doing. Sour grapes didn't become her. I'd had enough when she'd set in to criticizing some of the harsh verbal intervention tactics I'd used with Marcus in the past and how they'd proven to be ineffective, because if it weren't for his going to jail, he would end up dead anyway.

"Sounds pretty cynical for a woman only a few years out of med school," I chewed down on my bottom lip. "Doesn't sound like the kind-hearted, compassionate doctor that wanted me to ease up on an addict who'd just spit in her face. You really look angry about something."

"I'm fine," she hissed. "I just have a lot on my mind."

"You're a heavy thinker. What else is new?"

"You're. . . . getting married," her cracking voice betrayed her stubborn intention to conceal her true feelings.

"Yes, I am."

"Congratulations. I hope she makes you happy. How old is she anyway, all of eighteen?"

"She'll be twenty on Valentine's Day. We're getting married two days before."

"Valentine's Day. How sweet," she grinned wryly, having the same reaction I'd soon rather have forgotten as Brother Khalid.

She tried to blink back tears, but it was too late, a few had already rolled rapidly down her face. Instead of wiping them away, she cupped both her hands to her face and began to bawl like someone had died. I had no idea that she even gave a damn about me after she'd dumped me for rejecting her many tempting offers to make love to her at her over-priced condo, claiming only the partial truth, that I didn't want to nullify my own self-imposed oath.

I'm no masochist. If I wanted her in that way, truly desired her body, like I'd desired Elisabeth's I would have found a loophole, or some sort of distorted justification to do her, and still peddle a load of hypocritical hype to God's Warriors and the thousands of women who'd read *Saving It.*

"What's all this about? You going soft on me?" I asked quietly, confused big-time, over the melting of her tough, I-don't-need-a-man-except-for-getting-laid, outer armor right before my eyes. I walked over to her side of the table and handed her the handkerchief from my own suit jacket.

"Sorry," she sniffed, after blowing her nose into it, balling it up and stuffing it down her white lab coat. Thank God she didn't attempt to hand it back to me. "You could have at least told me. I had to find out from Eddie. He's been hanging around putting in a lot of volunteer time lately."

He'd damned well better be, I wanted to say, *that's the least he could do for getting caught red-handed for ripping off the church.*

"When he'd showed me a picture taken of the two of you together just after you'd met, I couldn't believe my eyes."

Aw man. Here it comes. Another lecture about black pride and my blatant betrayal of the race for choosing a skinny white woman as a wife, after screwing over literally hundreds of willing, available, professional, educated, decent Christian black women. It made me uncomfortable to see her lamenting the loss of something she never really had. I didn't know what to say.

The Q-Dog Robert of old, though he wasn't without complete insensitivity, would have somewhat relished in the fact that he'd broken yet another heart. Made another seemingly well-put together sister cry. Broke her resolve. Would have told her to deal with it. Get over it. Cut your losses.

But that Robert had died along time ago, when he'd stood before his father and a fledgling half-absentee congregation of under five hundred members and became ordained as a full-time minister of the gospel of Christ.

The man I'd become gave a damn. Period.

"It's not what you think," I replied in earnest, rubbing my hand against the taut bicep over her lab jacket.

"The hell it isn't, Robert!" she hissed, snatching her arm away as if I were a leper.

"Tell me what you're thinking."

"I'm thinking *Pastor Jesus Was A Black Man*," she, now fully composed, without a glimmer of a tear remaining in her enlarged sockets, quoted the title of one of the most controversial Wednesday night Bible lesson series I'd ever taught, *"Reverend, Black Women were put on this earth for the express purpose of loving and being loved by the black man. . . ."*

"I still believe that."

"Ha," she laughed sarcastically within three inches of my face. "You could have fooled me."

"Elisabeth's father is a black man, just like me."

"Was she adopted?"

"You've studied genetics in med school, I'm sure. Some bi-racial people look black, others look sorta white, but they're all mixed just the same."

" What's wrong with me Robert? Am I not light enough? I know you like long hair. Used to touch mine an awful lot. But, I guess I look like buckwheat compared to her."

"That's not true. You're a very attractive woman. Bril-

liant. Kind-hearted. Hard-working. I know quite a few brothers, even some of the Warriors who've laid eyes on you, want
you. . . ."

"Yeah, but, why don't you want me?"

"I thought you were over me. I didn't know there were
still some residual feelings left. You told me you couldn't be
in a sexless relationship."

"If you're so pure and holy, then what did I just walk in
on back in the office? You had that girl's eyes rolling back in
her head from feeling her up so good, when I had to practically beg you off of your celibate high horse to finger me a
few times. All that pale skin appeals to you, huh?"

" We didn't mean for you to find us like that. I'm very
so . . ."

"Save your tired apologies," she snapped, standing up
hastily and picking up her patient files. "Here, take this back.
I don't want it anymore."

When I didn't extend my hand to take back the palm-
held organizer I'd bought her for her birthday, she grabbed
me by the wrist and shoved it inside my large opened palm.

"I bought that for your birthday. I don't want it back."

"Well, you don't seem to want anything I have to offer
you."

Not on a personal level, woman. You know that. "Consider
this my two-week notice. I'm going back to Hopkins."

"You're heading back East?" I repeated for the purpose
of clarity.

"Yes. Had you bothered to read your E-mail, you would
have seen my letter of resignation posted. They want me to
oversee their children's psychiatric ward."

Even though Michelle Giles was an incredible rehabilitation therapist, her primary lifelong career objective was to
work towards the emotional and psychological recovery of
children who had been severely abused and traumatized.
She'd made it no secret at her initial one on one interview

with me. Told me she would be willing to work for one third of the salary Hopkins had offered her, for at least one year, just to fulfill a personal mission she'd set for herself, when her own older brother had OD'd on cocaine, while she was in her second rotation of med school. Agreed to put herself to the test, in order to not only understand her only sibling's dependency, but to derive at some sense of closure of sorts concerning his death.

"Are you sure this is what you want?"

"I've never been so sure of anything in my life," she replied pensively looking me squarely in the eyes, something about her own eyes indicating failed hopes and deferred dreams. " There's nothing here for me."

"Let me take you to dinner one night before you leave," I persisted, in hopes of ending our professional relationship and what remained of our strained friendship with an ounce or two of civility. One hand was on her back as I opened the door with the other.

"No, that's okay. I'm sure the little wifey there will be keeping you quite busy in preparation for your Valentine's Day nuptials."

"It's the least I can do. You've been an asset to this program. Why don't a group of us, including Brother Khalid, Jamilah and even Doogie Howser all make it a date, say a week from tomorrow?" I offered before rehearsing my already tight schedule in my mental rolodex. "I'll have Brother Khalid confirm the time and place with everyone."

"Okay," she conceded, "but only if it isn't Yusef's choice. I don't want to go anywhere that doesn't serve ribs."

"I feel you sister," I laughed, sighing a breath of relief that Christ's spirit within me allowed me to break her resolve.

383

Missing You

Another week came and went without anything extraordinary happening around the church. As expected, the holiday season that year brought about its' usual bouts of depression among the young and old adult populations within the congregation. I believe Kelly overbooked my afternoon therapy sessions around the clock to deter me from fully courting Elisabeth. I'd attended the weekly elders' and deacons' meeting Monday night, facilitated the Men's Training Tuesday night class, taught a video and audio taped Wednesday night's ongoing Spiritual Bootcamp class which, since my tenure as minister began, I 'd totally revamped from a traditional, boring, lecturer/audience approach, Bible study to dramatic presentations of real world issues, and had been picked up by one of the local cable stations.

Thursday night and a part of Friday evening I spent at Interfaith getting caught up on paperwork and deciphering the notes one of the other psychologists had left on several of my patients, over the past few weeks. Before I'd agreed to a chess match and a few rounds of spades, the male six-month residential patients on the third floor, along with homeless Mickey, leading the pack had a few choice words for me for dissin' them for almost an entire month.

The rest of Friday night, I plopped down in my office at the church, meditated, prayed, prepared lessons for my Saturday only students at the Christian Men's Leadership Academy and searched the scriptures for appropriate Christmas Eve and Christmas Day messages.

Very early Saturday morning, Brother Khalid and I reviewed my schedule for the upcoming week. He'd also covered the Greek Lexicon class for the first year students as I taped two radio programs in our soundproof audio room.

As I was headed out to my Expedition parked in the lot out back in a spot reserved especially for me, Sheila, who had been there, interviewing a new teacher for the Agape Childhood Development Center, rushed out to the parking lot to ask me to relay the message to the family, Eddie, included that she would be running a little late for dinner.

Much to Sheila's chagrin, I'd failed to inform Elisabeth of my new morning work as the chief therapist at the new east side Hope Springs Rehabilitation Clinic. Since this was a grassroots endeavor on the part of the Interfaith Council, I'd clocked twenty hours, as opposed to the twelve, I'd initially agreed upon, interviewing other counselors, conducting training seminars and overseeing the treasury committee. I didn't want to burden Elisabeth with my complex schedule, nor overwhelm her to the extent that she'd go running back to the old man. Besides, she had enough to get use to, temporarily living with Ma and Pops.

Elisabeth and Pops hit it off like gangbusters, because not only did he quite obviously appreciate a tidy woman with a pretty face, his already balloon sized ego, multiplied a trillion percent, because Elisabeth hung off his every word as gospel.

Now Ma and Elisabeth, on the other hand, were completely another story. I would be in the midst of a session, when one or the other would page me or ring my cell phone, to complain about how unreasonable and selfish the other one had been. When I'd ignore their initial attempts, they would call Sister Calloway's or Kelly's desk directly and insist that I'd come to the phone. Elisabeth offered more than once, to stay at the parsonage and me at my folks house, because Ma hated her.

Their first major blowout occurred when Elisabeth pitched a fit right in front of my family over not having seen me her entire first week in Detroit.

I used my old key to enter through the side door of the two-car garage at my parents' ranch home. Eddie's '68 deuce and a quarter parked partially on the curb and in the three inches of snow on the front lawn, informed me that he and the boys were inside, probably complaining, because Ma had refused to serve dinner without me. I glanced down at my Rolex only to discover that it was seven-thirty.

Earlier, when the men of the CMLA were on lunch recess, I'd called to check on Elisabeth and Ma to make sure they hadn't done each other any bodily harm.

"No son, not as of yet, but, Elisabeth has been out for most of the day, while your mama has been in the kitchen preparing dinner for the family tonight."

"Elisabeth's out?" I asked, finding it hard to believe that someone as sheltered as she had been, would hop into her luxury car to wander aimlessly about the harsh city streets.

"Relax, Bobby," Pops chuckled. "Nikki and Jasmine came by to get her out the house. Took her to get her hair and nails done or something. She and your mama got into it last night when those gals, brought her home with a half dozen or so bags from Lord and Taylor. Your mama claimed she politely asked her, where'd she gotten the money to buy all those things and she allegedly said, you'd given her your Visa to take care of some of her needs. Then, your mama said, she supposedly flipped opened her purse and stuck that little piece of plastic right up in your mama's face just to brag in front of those other gals."

"I'm gon' leave that one alone, man," I replied nonchalantly. "When do we grub?"

"As soon as you get yourself here, son, and you'd better make it fast. I don't know how much longer I can keep that little cute gal satisfied every day watching the soaps with her and playing bridge."

"Pops, you've never played bridge in your ghetto life," I laughed.

"Yeah, son, well, try tellin' that to the Princess."

As soon as I walked into the back of Ma's kitchen through the side door, the scent of Honey Baked ham and homemade freshly baked apple pie hit me. A casserole pan of Ma's special macaroni and cheese, along with candied yams and stuffing, cooled atop the range. I was wondering what special occasion caused for such a mouth-watering meal as I walked over to stick a fork into one of the sweet potatoes.

"Don't you dare," Ma warned, playfully slapping my hand away. Eddie, wearing an earnest expression of contrition, was right on her heels, staring stupidly at me as if we hadn't seen each other in ages. I reached down to kiss Ma on the lips, then I bobbed my head up then down again to greet my brother. He did me one better, by walking up to me and giving me a big bear hug, which made me feel like his real kid brother again. He grabbed my neck, pulled it down to him, and rubbed the back of his knuckles into my ninety-five percent clean-shaven head.

"Congrats, on your engagement, baby bro," he sang, jovially. "What a fine catch, man. A mighty fine catch. Sheila told me how she and Elisabeth hit it off right away."

"They did?" Ma asked dubiously. " You could have fooled me."

"Ma," I sang, shooting her a please-don't-start look.

"Okay, okay, but be warned. She is furious at you. She's been pouting since she's been back from the hair salon and I'm telling you Bobby, if that girl gets up with the Windex bottle and wipes my living room mirrors down or puts on those ridiculous pink gloves, to polish my china cabinet one more time. I'm gon' kill her! Forget preparing for exchanging vows . . . prepare for a eulogy."

Eddie laughed, wrapped his arms around Ma and slowly walked her over to the dinette set for her to cool off.

"Where is she?" I asked quietly, anticipating those little arms enclosing themselves around my neck and the taste of those butter-soft lips on my tongue.

"She's probably locked herself in your old room again, crying her eyes out. Your Pops got tired of all her pointless chatter and went to take a nap on her."

Much to all of our surprise, Elisabeth appeared from nowhere, wearing a long, high-collared, winter-white, wool coat and matching beret over her newly curled ringlets. Although her pink lips protruded outward into an alluring pout, she appeared to be too calm, almost trancelike as if she hadn't heard a word of what Ma said.

"Hey baby," I spoke, rushing over to her to scoop her up in my arms. As I was about to kiss her, she held up her white Isotoner clad hand, and placed it between her mouth and mine, as if to say, "don't even go there."

Eddie pulled out a chair next to Ma who had her arms folded across her chest, glaring at my future wife.

Not one to take a dis' lightly, I stepped back, and eyed her pensively. "What's your problem, woman?"

She shut her eyes tightly and pressed her lips together. A tear formed in the corner of her eyelid.

"If you don't know what the problem is . . . then, we have a big problem already."

"Hmmm, mmm," Eddie cleared his throat as he stood up from the table. He placed his hands gently on Ma's shoulder and whispered to her that they'd ought to give us some privacy.

"Take your hands off of me, Junior!" Ma snapped without removing her harsh glare from Elisabeth. "And go tell the boys to wash up for dinner."

"Where you going, Princess?" I asked, unctuous that she would go to such extremes to prove how much she'd missed me.

"I'm going out."

"Out where?"

"To the mall?"

"After I've cooked all this food?" Ma snapped. "Mercy, girl, I know Emily taught you better manners than that."

"Ma!"

"I'm just saying, Bobby. This is downright dumb! She doesn't even know her way around and I'll be darned if Bobby's going to run up behind you tonight, not after I've cooked some of his favorite foods."

Tears flowed freely down Elisabeth's face. "I can't stand it here! Your mother hates me. I haven't seen you all week, and I want to go home!" She dropped her purse on the floor and bolted away from me towards my old bedroom.

"Ma . . ." I pleaded, shaking my head.

"What?"

"Could you fix me, us a plate? Elisabeth is going home with me tonight."

Knowing I meant business, Ma dropped her head, ashamed over her unwarranted intervention and asked me if I thought Elisabeth would prefer a tossed salad as opposed to her infamous imitation crabmeat pasta concoction.

"That would be nice, Ma."

Of course as the devil would have it, Elisabeth's theatrics intensified once I called to her from the opposite side of the locked bedroom door to let me in. After several pleadings, she'd felt I'd suffered enough and allowed entrance into her own makeshift sanctuary. Her extensive black porcelain doll collection covered the tops of both dressers. She'd also eked out a small space in one of the clutter free corners of the room to erect a vanity table and chair, I'd never seen before. Many of her suits, skirts, dresses and blouses, hung neatly starched and organized by texture, season and color in the long walk-in closet I'd used as a toy storage area during my childhood.

Shoeboxes stack perfectly in rows of ten, formed eight columns on the other side of the closet. More shoeboxes aligned themselves along the foot and both sides of the bed. Many of the suitcases and garment bags she couldn't bare doing without for a few weeks were crammed over to the left of the bed, on which she had replaced Ma's hand-sewn quilt with a fluffy pink comforter and pillow set.

She'd taken her hat and coat off and had neatly laid them across the chair. I watched her climb into the bed, underneath the comforter, fully dressed in an ivory two-piece cashmere sweater long-skirt ensemble and high-heeled leather dress boots.

I plopped down on the foot of the bed and placed my hand on top of the blanket where her leg was.

"Is this how your life really is?" she sniffed through her constant stream of tears. *This girl, can really turn on the waterworks*, I thought, amazed that in all the tears I'd help people wipe away, I'd never seen anyone cry so freely, without reservation in front of almost complete strangers. "Is this how we are going to have to live? Never seeing each other. . . . please tell me the truth, Bobby." How could I answer that question truthfully, without losing her forever? I leaned over and held my head in my hands, wanting to pace the floor.

"I need to hear you say that you don't have time for me."

"You'll never hear me say that," I vowed, looking deeply into her cloudy, reddened eyes.

"But that's how it is, isn't it?"

"No, it isn't. We'll adjust. You'll share in this work with me, won't you?"

She sat up and extended her arms to me. "Of course, I will do what I can. Whenever you want me around."

"I'll always want you around."

"But, you are so secretive about what it is you do all day."

"Not all of it. But, yes I do have to maintain a professional level of confidentiality with church members and with my clients."

"Well, I just, like, don't know how much I can handle not seeing you for nights at a time and . . ."

"You said yes, Elisabeth," I reminded her as I held her securely in my arms.

" I said yes to you, Bobby. Not to your mother. . . . , but Pops is great . . . at least he enjoys my company."

So not to hurt Ma's feelings any further, Elisabeth agreed to sticking around for dinner, although she only ate a small salad and meager portions of green beans and candied yams.

When I'd leaned over to whisper an offer for her to come back to the parsonage with me, her eyes danced with enthusiasm as she bounced up from her seat and in front of my entire family, swiveled her way on to my lap and hugged my neck.

"What's all the excitement about?" Sheila eyed us enviously from across the table.

"Oh nothing, " Elisabeth sang, before practically skipping off to her room to pack her overnight bag.

Less than ten minutes later, when I'd rolled up the sleeves of my gray knit shirt to help Ma bust the suds, Elisabeth re-entered the kitchen, wearing the same off-white coat, carrying garment and vanity bags in one hand and a white mink in the other. Eddie, who had been piling mounds of food onto holiday sectional paper-plates to take home so his family could have leftovers, rushed over to offer her a helping hand. She batted her eyelashes at him coyly and thanked him. He picked up the keys to my truck and headed for the garage via the side door.

"Well, you two," Pops voice boomed, as he and Sheila brought in the last of the dishes from the dining room. " It looks like you and Elisabeth have decided to stay together all night, huh?"

"Yes, sir," I kept right on scrubbing a muffin-pan, Ma had left in the oven too long without paying attention to the sudsy water splashing onto my black slacks.

"Not that you've asked for my opinion or anything son and daughter," Pops reasoned, glancing more at Elisabeth, who was fawning more over his stature and his distinguished aura, by the second. "But, Christmas Eve service is early tomorrow morning and don't you think . . . you two ought to wait until you're back from your honeymoon . . . before sleeping together?"

" For the record, we're not sleeping together, Pops," I replied evenly as I scraped some more food into the garbage disposal.

"But, it just doesn't look right son. You've worked so hard to get to where you are now. Why ruin it?"

I reached for the nearest towel to dry my hands. Elisabeth rushed to roll my sleeves back down and to button my cuffs. Behind her back Ma, childishly stuck her index finger in the middle of her mouth, as if she were going to gag herself. Sheila stifled an involuntary laugh.

"Pops, we understand what you're saying totally, and we highly value your opinion" Elisabeth replied sweetly, much to my disappointment. "I'll have Eddie bring my things back in and Bobby will drop me off back here, later tonight, won't you Bobby?"

I grunted my reluctant consent.

Pops walked over to hug her and pecked her paternally on the cheek. She reciprocated his gesture.

"I just love this baby doll already," Pops beamed.

Now, it was me who wanted to throw up.

Home

"You're really not going to tell me where you've been all week?" she asked, coquettishly running her gloved hand along my thigh as I backed out of my parents' driveway.

This stuff couldn't be starting up already. Hadn't we discussed all this back a couple of weeks ago when we were eating dinner at her bougie, Middle Eastern vegetarian restaurant? Hadn't she readily accepted my spontaneous proposal on the couch of her family's den? Didn't she understand that I had to be a man about mine? I didn't need another mother. Nobody checking up on me, blowing up my pager in the middle of therapy sessions with clients at the church and at both the centers. That's why I'd taken to setting my pager on the vibrate mode. Didn't want to appear to be unprofessional or even worse hen-pecked, before I could even get her down the aisle good.

I'd been a confirmed, unattached bachelor the entire extent of my ministry and well, this keeping tabs thing was just something I knew I would have to nip in the bud right away.

"I've been working, Princess," I punked out, once her wandering hand ran the course of my thigh and up to my groin area.

She leaned over and blew her cool, wintergreen mint flavor breath in my ear, which almost made me run over the Detroiter lamppost in the neighbors yard. "Do you have to

393

keep such long hours?" she whispered. " I've really missed you."

Man, a brother didn't know how much longer he could hold up. I wasn't so sure taking her to the parsonage was a good, wholesome escape from Ma's biting sarcasm anymore.

"Will you take me to your church first?"

"It's not my church, but yeah, we can swing by there first," I complied, securing her hand's position, with my right hand as I started us on our whopping six minute journey.

"Cool," she exclaimed much to my chagrin removing her miracle working hand from my body to clasp them together. "I've been so excited to see it all week. I've seen video footage, but I know I'm just going to fall out when I walk in to the place where you have turned all those people's lives around . . ."

"I haven't turned anyone's life around. I speak as the oracles of God, baby. I, along with the elders and deacons plant and water, but it is He who gives the increase."

"So modest too," she gazed over at me with stars in her eyes. "You know what that does to me."

One thing about our relationship right from the start was that neither one of us had to work hard to turn the other on. In fact, until I'd met her, I'd never subscribed to such wordly, cliché' feelings as physical or animal magnetism, chemistry, love at first sight, poetry in motion or any of those other bogus romanticized notions she read about in those lusty novels, which I by the way, didn't knock completely, because they'd successfully taught her virginal mind a thing a two about how to kick some serious game and how to put all those other smooth-talkin', desperate, more experienced women from the old Robert's life to shame.

At the last traffic light before approaching the woodsy circular drive in front of the Rosedale Park Church of Christ, I held my foot down forcibly enough to afford a smooth lean over to the passenger side of my truck, where my flustered fiancée' passionately accepted the spontaneous kiss that conveyed to her that I indeed knew exactly what I was doing to her.

For a moment, before the light turned green and she'd placed her hand back on my thigh, I thought I'd detected the tiniest flicker of misgiving and mistrust in her glistening hazel eyes. It asked me to make promises to her concerning quality time that at the time, I thought I could keep. It asked me to promise to circumvent the grave repercussions, years of living with an eating disorder brought to the trail of her short life's journey. It challenged me to erase the pain of not ever having her mother's unconditional love and undivided attention. It begged me to fill the void of losing a sister who never died. It implored me to bring her out from behind the ever looming shadow of *Lori the Great*. Most of all, it asked me to never abandon her nor forsake my promises to her.

It was cool that she had yet to tell me she loved me. There was plenty of time for that, I reasoned. Yes, she could be a bit whiny. Yes, she had been spoiled rotten by the old man. Yes, she had a penchant for the finer things in life. Yes, she could be a bit unfriendly and down right cold towards other women. Yes, she was ten years my junior. Yes, she had the tendency to talk white, speak white, think white, and most would argue look white, but I wanted her. She was the one. We fit.

"We're going to *your* church," faintly squeezing my hand, she graced me with one of her rare full-tooth grins. "We're going home. Together. To a new life."

"We most certainly are, baby. We most certainly are."

We had no idea.

The McGallister Fiction Series

Book One

Reading Group/Book Club Discussion Questions for:

Only A Man

General:

- Discuss the appropriateness of the book's title. Which qualities does Robert possess that makes the title suitable?
- What qualities does Robert possess that would classify him as a "good man?"
- Discuss Robert's flaws. Recall several passages from the book to support your opinion.
- Which character(s) do you enjoy the most? Which character(s) bothered/disturbed you? Explain your responses.

- Discuss the scenes that most held your interest, or that sparked a reaction in you.

Robert's sordid past and transformation:

- Robert admits candidly in his autobiographical best-selling book that he'd slept with hundreds of women from the ages of 15-24. What do you think were the contributing factors in his sexual addiction?
- Once Ed McGallister Sr. ordains his younger son to succeed him as minister of the Rosedale Park congregation, Robert takes on a self-imposed vow of celibacy. Why does he think it was important for him to abstain? How did he cope with the stint that lasted four years?
- Discuss Robert's reaction to Dr. Michelle Giles' emotional outburst over what she considers a blatant rejection on his part.

Robert, Elisabeth and "The Color Issue":

- Discuss why Robert is physically attracted to Elisabeth from the moment he sees her. As a man who blatantly takes pride in his African-American heritage, how does he justify being drawn to a woman who looks mostly white? Discuss your reaction to his handling of the situation.
- Robert wastes no time in declaring to Brother Khalid that Elisabeth "fits the profile" of what he was looking for in a wife. Does he get what he wants? Debate.
- Elisabeth is equally mesmerized with Robert. Discuss her possible motivations for accepting his marriage proposal so soon after their first meeting.
- Tension mounts between Robert and many of the female characters in the book, including his own mother Ethel, over his having chosen Elisabeth as his lifetime mate. Why do they have such problems with accepting the Prin-

cess into his close-knit group of family and friends? Are the arguments against his choice valid? Explain.

Robert and his friends and family:

· A special friendship exists between Robert and Yusef Khalid that is rarely depicted among African-American men in fiction or via other media forms. Recall and discuss several passages in which the bond manifests itself.

· Discuss the complicated relationship that exists between Robert and Ed Sr. (Pops), and between Robert and Eddie.

Church Issues:

· The elders of the congregation where Robert serves hold more conservative, fundamentalist beliefs than Robert and his more liberal cohorts. Discuss the benefits and drawbacks of such an arrangement and the implications for future books in this series.

· Angel, not unlike many vulnerable church attendees has a "thing for" the minister. Discuss her proclamation of love for Robert and the consequences she faces because of it.

· Do you believe the God's Warriors program along with its' business initiatives will benefit the Rosedale Park congregation? What setbacks imposed by church leadership may Robert and his fellow Warriors face?

Making Predictions:

· Lorraine Powell's reputation precedes her. Compare and contrast what you have gathered about her in reading Book One with what you know about her younger sister, Elisabeth.

· What do you envision Lorraine's and Robert's first encounters to entail?

If you would like to contact Lisa Drane to sign books, perform a reading and/or participate in a discussion of *Only A Man*, feel free to contact her via her website at www.lisadrane.com.

Her site also features an in-depth conversation with the author about *Only A Man*, her first self-published novel, as well as provides an exclusive outlook for the remaining books in her hot new urban contemporary fiction series.

Now. . . . . turn the page for a sneak peak at *Midnight Warrior*, Book Two of *The McGallister Fiction Series* that will make its debut soon!

The McGallister Fiction Series

Book Two:
Midnight Warrior

59-DRAN

Forgetting

"How many were there, Bobby?" was the intrusive question my bride-to be shot at me on the short ride over from my folk's house to the Rosedale Park Church of Christ.

No need to ask how many what. I knew, already, though I'd tried my damnedest to forget. She wanted to know the sordid details of my past, which triggered me to recall a recent close call I had with breaking my precious vow.

Just a few weeks before I'd laid eyes on the prettiest, softest, sexiest woman I'd ever seen, I'd told Brother Khalid that if I didn't find her soon, I was bound to take advantage of Kelly and let her sleep over at the crib, to give me some quick head, like she used to when I was struggling with avoiding my inevitable calling.

To my seemingly absurd suggestion, Brother Khalid burst into an atypical bout of laughter slapping his knee as if he were watching the comedy stylings of the wise-cracking upstarts featured on Russell Simmon's Def Comedy Jam. When I'd failed to so much as wince at his blatant endeavor to poke fun, he'd stopped dead in his tear laden tracks, wiped the corner of his eyes and said,

"Come on Little Brother, man. You can't be serious."

"I'm dead serious, Yusef. Hell, I'm human. When I think about all the free coochie I used to get before I took that blasted oath, man, I just wanna kick my own ass!."

"Yeah, well . . . you bigger than that bro. You talkin' some crap like what you talkin' now makes me wanna kick yo' blackass too,"

403

he grimaced, without looking up at me from my computer, where
he'd been typing out a list of errands he'd had to run for me as my
personal assistant.

"I was thinking about giving you the rest of the day off so Kelly
and I could go handle ours."

"Yeah right," he chuckled, "and I was thinking about turnin'
back Muslim. Little Brother, man, you startin' to bug me. Go get
your meditation on, read some scriptures. Pray. Pump some iron.
Walk the dogs. Do somethin' to get your mind off of your flesh,
man."

"Easy for you to say. You've had it both ways horizontal and
vertical since the Clinton administration."

"Lord, hurry up and give this man a wife," he pleaded, cast-
ing his light-brown eyes heavenwards. "If not for him, do it for me.
I'm tired of hearing this mess, Father. You know how much I can
bear."

And so there we were, almost married, sitting pulled over
near a curb in my black Ford Expedition less than a block
away from the forest secluded church grounds, wanting to do
something lasciviously productive, like rip each other's clothes
off, instead of play the tired game of cat and mouse over my
past sexual exploits that, I'm of course ashamed to say now,
would have made the late Wilt Chamberlain in his heyday
proud.

Father, give me strength. I can't believe I'm about to
relive the memories of something I'd overcome a long time
ago; doing women for sport.

" Aren't you going to, like, answer my question some-
time tonight? It's dark out here Bobby. I want to go inside
the church."

She was determined as all get out to finally experience
the place where she would, not only by sheer default of being the minister's wife of a church with five thousand members on the books, but by her self-imposed diva like attitude

and fair skin complexion, become the center of much gossip, speculation and downright ridicule. I hurt for her already.

"I was hoping to avoid a discussion of this nature all together, baby. My past is my past," I replied in earnest, placing her ivory leather gloved hand in mine.

She snatched it away and folded her arms across the breast of her fitted winter white leather jacket with the real mink collar. Old Man Powell had spoiled her rotten every one of her meager near twenty years of existence. Hell, considering all I'd done for her, like dropping ten grand on engagement preliminaries, using up all my frequent flier miles until I could arrange for her to move in temporarily with my parents until our Valentine's Day nuptials, giving her two of my major credit cards to keep herself busy and out of Ma's hair, while I had been away at the church or seeing patients at the Interfaith Council Rehabilitation Center all week—considering all the loot that burned a hole right through a brother's pocket, I'd done a pretty bang up job overindulging her myself. Which is exactly why I felt like she had no business questioning my commitment to her.

"On page, I believe eighty-four of *Saving It*, you kinda alluded to the fact that you'd been with like hundreds . . ."

"Yeah, but that was between ages sixteen and twenty-four baby. Not all in one year."

"Oh . . . I feel, like, sooo totally relieved," she said sarcastically, throwing her hands up in disgust.

I laughed. Couldn't help it. With Elisabeth, there was never a dull moment.

"I don't understand what is so funny about a minister, for goodness sake . . ."

"I didn't become a full-fledged minister until I was almost twenty-six, baby. I wasn't serious about it before then. Since your nose is always in my book, you should have known that."

"Were there two hundred? Three? Four?" she persisted. "Do you even, like, remember the names of all those tramps?"

"Princess." Exasperated, I blew warm air into my balled up, frigid fist.

"They were mostly all educated tramps too, huh? Like on page ninety-five, where you talk about the older, married Ph.D. candidate, with two kids, for goodness sake, you were in the same program with at the University of Michigan. How she would let you come right over as soon as her unwitting poor husband would leave out the front door to go to work as a doctor, mind you, saving people's lives and you would come right on in through the back door and have sex, with that, that hussy, while her babies were sleep. I find that sort of thing totally reprehensible, Bobby!"

"Me too, " I nodded guiltily, allowing the dusty tape in my mind to rewind back to Dorothy Collins, one of the longer flings I had, lasting almost two months until she'd started sweating me about all the chicks who'd been blowing up my pager with 9-1-1 messages to come "touch them up," as the cats in my frat used to call it.

"So, then, why'd you write it?"

"To testify to brothers everywhere of the cleansing power of the blood of Jesus."

"Yes, well, you weren't thinking about Jesus when you and your frat brothers were getting drunk and running what'd you call those orgy thingees . . ."

"Trains, with willing participants of course."

"Yes, that's it. What was on your mind then?"

"Come on. I don't think I should have to spell it out for you, Princess."

"You really aren't going to tell me how many are you?"

If I knew the exact number, or even had the slightest, roughest estimate of knots on my bedpost, I would tell her, just to shut her up. Just to get her to stop looking at me like Satan incarnate and to start batting those long pretty eyelashes and running her hand along my thigh, like she had been no sooner than Ma could shove her out of the house for talking and whining too damned much like she was doing now.

"The important thing, baby, is that I've been clean for four years. Four years. Give me some credit."

"Clean? Bobby, I think you've been counseling those drug addicts and alcoholics too long..."

"I was an addict too, baby. That was the whole point of the book. My drug was women and sex. Women and sex. Women and sex. That's partially why I matriculated in psychology and human behavior to understand myself better. I love you. I chose you. So, we shouldn't even be trippin' on the subject," I concluded, placing the gear-shift selector into drive.

"Pops and the elders probably would have never even considered you as the minister of the church if you would have written that book before you took over his job responsibilities."

"You're one-hundred percent right, baby. Nobody's perfect. Nobody. That's what's wrong with the church. It's filled with condescending, self-righteous, pompous hypocrites, not willing to forgive a person for past wrongdoings, when God forgives penitent sinners, completely and immediately."

"Forgiving is one thing, Bobby. Forgetting is, like, so completely another."

"Remind me never to cross you the wrong way," I retorted lightheartedly.

"Bobby?" she had a way with saying my name that made it sound like I was the best thing since Christ himself.

"Yes, Princess," I answered, purposely keeping my eye on the road so as not to make her feel uncomfortable when she'd verbally reciprocated her affections.

"Even though I'm a virgin, I'm a fast learner. I'm going

to make love to you so well and for so long and so many times, that you're going to forget all about all those tramps."

"Bet," I smiled, thinking that her promise was ten times better than the three words I'd been waiting for her to utter since I placed that brilliant rock on her finger.

A First Gift

The immense snow covered pine trees and the winding dirt drive highlighted by lime and cobblestone surrounding the newly renovated, secluded church building cast a rural appearance on the northwestern Detroit subdivision. Elisabeth, mesmerized by the modernized architecture and the grandiose multi-tiered structure of the inner-sanctum, held her mouth agape, as I backed my truck into the short, cemented brick awning, covered walk/make-shift driveway that connected my office to my home.

Jittery over the anticipation of finally viewing her new home and place of worship, she jumped nervously when she'd heard the sound of the car alarm go off, after I'd opened the door for her and had taken her by the hand.

"Bobby, can you please take me inside the church first?" she asked excitedly, pulling on the sleeve of my leather jacket as if she were a child about to be unleashed into Toys "R" Us.

"Aw naw, I can't," I replied with a mock tone of disappointment.

"Oh . . . ," she whined. "Why not?"

I shoved my hands into my jacket pocket and patted my chest down to give her the impression I was searching for a long lost key. "I think Brother Khalid has my set of keys to open the front and back entrances."

She frantically reached inside her purse to retrieve her cute little see-through, pink phone.

"Here," she ordered, her cold breath forming a cloud between us. "You can just call Brother Hareem up . . . and he can meet us here with your keys. Honestly, Bobby, you're the minister and your help keeps your keys?"

I laughed, depressed the car alarm, reached inside my glove compartment and retrieved the keys to the building. I did a little victory dance, by pushing the palms of my hands in the air and bobbing my head up and down.

She beat me playfully in the chest, then picked up a handful of snow.

"Careful now, Libby," I teased, calling her by the moniker she hated, running around the truck. She tried forming a snowball with the meager amount of precipitation in her hands, but the soggy flakes, merely dissipated into her leather gloves. Then she took off chasing me around the truck, slipping and sliding everywhere, over unsalted patches of ice, with those three-inch femme-fatale boots. At one point, I thought she would hurt herself, by falling on her butt and/or by spraining something. I slowed down to allow her to catch me. Turning around, I squeezed her tightly in my arms. Our lips were not even a centimeter apart, before she broke away from my grip and begged me to open the door to my office.

Glad I'd placed my Bible Concordance and book-by-book commentaries, back from their usual spot on the floor next to my computer cubby, to the rich maple-wood book shelves, opposite my desk, I in the darkened room, instinctively found the light switch. Her eyes slowly drank in every nook and cranny of my second home, from the plug-in space heater, left in the middle of the room, away from any flammable materials, to the plush leather love-seat and matching recliner, opposite the wall of my computer center. She accidentally brushed up against one of the faux super-sized potted plants next to a small table for two, that contained my nephews' latest school pictures and a single framed photograph of twenty-five newly inducted men into God's Warriors program, the brainchild that Brother Khalid, Riley, and I created and implemented for brothers who'd vowed to take sincere oaths of fraternity, fidelity, fatherhood and financial empowerment of our community.

She walked over to my book-shelves, performing in vain and much to my satisfaction, a single glove dust check as she read the front of several birthday cards given to me, mostly by female members that past May.

She stooped down to the lowest shelf and read a name engraved plague given to me four years previously, when I had been ordained as a minister of the gospel of Christ. Then, she quietly moved over to the wall space, right next to the book shelves and admired my, then recently renewed twin Ph.D. licenses to practice psychology in the fields of marriage and family therapy and drug and alcohol rehabilitation.

She noticed my larger framed Bachelor's of Arts in Theology and Religious Studies and even got close enough to decipher the fine print that I hadn't bothered to read since I'd received it.

On the wall, just to the left of my private restroom, was an 8x10" photograph of Pops, wearing a black suit and tie and holding an open Bible in his hands, he'd taken in his early thirties, as the new minister of Rosedale Park.

I rested my tired body on the loveseat, unzipped my jacket and admired her appreciation of things I'd begun to take for granted.

She walked over to my desk and reached inside her large, ivory colored Coach, which was more of a bag, than a purse, to retrieve a square-shaped, professionally holiday gift-wrapped box, with a miniature card attached by a decorative string, hanging from the oversized bow.

I stood up smiling and rubbing my hands together to indi-

411

cate how excited I was to be receiving the first of many gifts from her.

"Here, I hope you like it." Her lips curved themselves into their own unique smile.

I took the package, placed it on my desk and eased myself on top it, before gently pulling her into a grateful embrace in between my legs. She placed a round of quick, dulcet kisses on my lips, before our tongues met, and teased each other for a few seconds.

"Open it," she ordered eagerly. "While we're in here, because this is where I want you to put it."

"Well, I don't know," I teased. "Maybe I should wait until the day after tomorrow. You know, a brotha hardly receives anything for Christmas any more."

She rolled her eyes and deflected our attention to all the recent holiday cards and knickknacks, such as expensive fountain pens and paperweights neatly arranged on the desk, bookshelves and tables.

"Hush," she laughed. " It looks like you receive more than your fair share of consolation prizes from the fairer sex."

"Is that right?" I grinned, running my hand alongside the new curly do, I'm sure cost me a small fortune only to have her wash it out the next day.

"Come on, Bobby. I can only imagine how many women have contrived problems, just to come sit on this couch and gaze into your irresistible eyes. Besides, you don't seem like the type of man to buy yourself poinsettias and artsy decorative pictures to hang on your wall."

I couldn't deny that Mercedes Anderson, a cute caramel complexioned seventeen year-old, straight A, high school senior, with a bigger crush on me, than I had on Janet Jackson, back in her sexy, often-watched *Love Will Never Do Without You* video, had donated the luscious green plant hanging from a hook and rope combination in the far right corner of the office.

Kelly, though she was barely speaking to me anymore, purchased the eight-inch poinsettias located on each corner of my massive desk. And Angel Williams on my last birthday, proudly handed me the new gold nameplate, with my name and title engraved in black.

"None of the gifts anyone has ever given me will ever compare to this one," I replied, opening the miniature card, to read the contents inside.

"To my dear and loving future husband, Robert McGallister," it read, the impeccably formed black manuscript letters caught my attention, "on our first Christmas together. Enjoy! Your devoted fiancée, Elisabeth."

"Thank you," I smiled, as she watched me wildly rip open the gift. A few seconds later, she was discarding the wrapping paper, box and Styrofoam encasement belonging to the costly musical snow globe, with the sterling silver engraved base. She turned the wind key on the back of the base. A quiet, piano rendition of *"Amazing Grace"* played as I studied the inside, aesthetic details of the snow-covered trees outside of the colonial designed church.

While sitting it next to my nameplate, I noticed a tiny tag she'd forgotten to remove with the ludicrous price of two hundred ninety-five bucks on it. Relieved that she was too busy opening the door that led out to the back hallway of the building to notice my eyes bulging out of their sockets, I shot the globe one last glance, shook my head and rushed to catch up with her.

The entire tour took thirty minutes. She not only wanted to see every room, including the elders' and deacons' office, the secretary's office, the library, the nursery, the ladies' restrooms located on all three floors, the newly installed, closed-circuit balcony area, she also asked a myriad of questions as she insisted upon trekking down the basement stairs to view the roomy fellowship hall, complete with a private bathroom and kitchen, and the gym, used primarily for playing basket-ball and the ladies' aerobic sessions on the west end, along with the dozen temporarily designated classrooms, four of which joined together by retractable wall partitions, were used for the CMLA, the remainder for the Agape school and the other weekly classes conducted in the building.

In the middle of my elaboration of the classes taught at the CMLA, I stifled several yawns, causing my eyes to tear.

"I know you've had a tiring week, Bobby. But, I really want to see one more place. I know you've saved the best for last."

I took her by the hand and led her back toward the west wing, through the fellowship hall, which had been festively decorated by the social committee for the next day's Christmas Eve dinner, ignored her impressed, gaping stares at the lights, plants and the two twelve or thirteen foot trees and helped her up the dark back staircase to the front of the auditorium.

Having cast her eyes down upon the massive four sectioned, four-aisle auditorium, from the balcony, obviously did not appease her insatiable curiosity.

"Wow!" she screamed, much to my amusement. She ran over to one of the center aisles and swirled herself around with outstretched arms a couple of times until she made herself dizzy enough to have to hold on to the side of one of the front pews.

She dramatically swept her head upward to the light-globes hanging from the ceiling, then, up to the balcony again, before swirling around to behold the pulpit, as if it were Calvary itself.

I helped her in her high-heeled boots up the four steps of the wide platform. She admired the handsomely carved craftsmanship of the podium, that I never used, from which I'd grown up listening to my father's sermons. Then, she sauntered over to sit in one of several plush-velvet chairs, which had been the sole, controversial subject matter of two recent

Monday night leadership meetings. The elders, Pops, as the chief instigator, had accused me, yet again, of excessive dipping and dabbing into the "sinful denominational world" by wanting a special throne to elevate myself above everyone else in the congregation. The deacons, Doug, Paul and Riley, leading the pack defended me fiercely, citing that the four comfortable chairs had been purchased from the building fund, to replace the antiquated, worn-out, traditional hardback benches that had been installed before Pops became the minister.

They doggedly pointed out that, I never sit on the stage, that I'm in fact, only standing on the pulpit for a few minutes, before I descend the steps to be closer to the members.

"This is some building, Bobby!" she cried. I reached for her hand to help her down from the platform. "Although I've seen several of your tapes series and your cable program I had no inkling as to how big this place actually is, I never imagined it being this huge! And, all that land out back belongs to the congregation. I'm excited to finally lay eyes on the place you've talked about on your tapes. I mean, I know there are some impressive sized Church of Christ buildings in the south. We've even visited the really big one out in Oklahoma. But, this Bobby . . . this place is larger than life! It's like it's going to be the church's and the Warrior's own little village," she cried, her voice raised a couple of octaves higher than usual and her arms outstretched in one grandiose gesture to emphasize her point. "How many does this place seat?"

"The balcony seats a thousand. The main floor seats four thousand," I replied dryly. " On any given Sunday, for eleven o'clock worship, almost every seat is filled to capacity."

"Your *mother*," she sighed, as if having to mention her would bring about a headache. "When she was still treating me civilly the first night I got here, showed me video-footage of the building dedication program. On it, were glimpses

of the old building, the way it was before you started preaching . . . it looked to be about the same size as Kingshighway,
only seating about four hundred people on a good Sunday. I
can't believe all of this. . . . has happened since you've become the minister. Can you believe it yourself?"

"Yes," I replied quietly. " I can believe it. . . . because
there are painful memories attached to the two-year process
of having the plans laid, and the actual constructing of it.
The elders, Pops, included were quite furious about wanting
it enlarged to this capacity."

"How could they not be content to worship in a place
like this?"

"That's a long story, baby," I replied closing the double
doors of the front entrance, initiating our hand-holding again.
One I didn't have the energy to delve into now, I thought.
Every time my thoughts led me back to the poignant debates the deacons and I had with the super-conservative dynamic trio of elders, Pops, McNichols and Scott, over ex-
panding to accommodate the needs of the mega-sized membership, since I'd been there, a huge lump of angst and disgust arose in my throat.

I would have never survived those intense deadlocks
without Brother Khalid's help in teaching me the sublime,
mind-clearing tenets of meditation. During that time, I also
had to contend with the possibility of resigning my duties as
minister because of my ever growing population among Bap-
tists, Methodists, Lutherans and Presbyterians, exacerbated
by a stream of steady invitations to speak on special programs once I began forming friendships with other preachers, via my work at Interfaith.

Seemingly content enough with my heavily veiled understatement, Elisabeth shrugged wistfully as she stood underneath the arch and watched me unlock the side-door of
the parsonage.

Lisa Drane, a tenured middle school language arts and history teacher, has written novels and poems since the tender age of eleven. An avid reader who uses her imagination daily to create fresh plots and characters, she has recently completed work on *Midnight Warrior* the second installment of her breakthrough *McGallister Fiction Series*. She lives in Detroit with her husband.

BVG